ISBN 978-0-243-52866-0
PIBN 10803239

This book is a reproduction of an important historical work. Forgotten Books uses state-of-the-art technology to digitally reconstruct the work, preserving the original format whilst repairing imperfections present in the aged copy. In rare cases, an imperfection in the original, such as a blemish or missing page, may be replicated in our edition. We do, however, repair the vast majority of imperfections successfully; any imperfections that remain are intentionally left to preserve the state of such historical works.

1 MONTH OF
FREE
READING

at

www.ForgottenBooks.com

By purchasing this book you are eligible for one month membership to ForgottenBooks.com, giving you unlimited access to our entire collection of over 700,000 titles via our web site and mobile apps.

To claim your free month visit:
www.forgottenbooks.com/free803239

English
Français
Deutsche
Italiano
Español
Português

www.forgottenbooks.com

Mythology Photography **Fiction**
Fishing Christianity **Art** Cooking
Essays Buddhism Freemasonry
Medicine **Biology** Music **Ancient
Egypt** Evolution Carpentry Physics
Dance Geology **Mathematics** Fitness
Shakespeare **Folklore** Yoga Marketing
Confidence Immortality Biographies
Poetry **Psychology** Witchcraft
Electronics Chemistry History **Law**
Accounting **Philosophy** Anthropology
Alchemy Drama Quantum Mechanics
Atheism Sexual Health **Ancient History**
Entrepreneurship Languages Sport
Paleontology Needlework Islam
Metaphysics Investment Archaeology
Parenting Statistics Criminology
Motivational

Technical and Bibliographic Notes / Notes technique et t

he Institute has attempted to obtain the best original
opy available for filming. Features of this copy which
ay be bibliographically unique, which may alter any of
e images in the reproduction, or which may
nificantly change the usual method of filming are
ked below.

Coloured covers /
Couverture de couleur

Covers damaged /
Couverture endommagée

Covers restored and/or laminated /
Couverture restaurée et/ou pelliculée

Cover title missing / Le titre de couverture manque

Coloured maps / Cartes géographiques en couleur

Coloured ink (i.e. other than blue or black) /
Encre de couleur (i.e. autre que bleue ou noire)

Coloured plates and/or illustrations /
Planches et/ou illustrations en couleur

Bound with other material /
Relié avec d'autres documents

Only edition available /
Seule édition disponible

Tight binding may cause shadows or distortion
along interior margin / La reliure serrée peut
causer de l'ombre ou de la distorsion le long de
la marge intérieure.

Blank leaves added during restorations may appear
within the text. Whenever possible, these have
been omitted from filming / Il se peut que certaines
pages blanches ajoutées lors d'une restauration
apparaissent dans le texte, mais, lorsque cela était
possible, ces pages n'ont pas été filmées.

Additional comments /

☐ Coloured pag

☐ Pages

☐ Pages
Pages

☑ Pages
Pages

☐ Pages

☑ Showthrough /

☑ Quality of print
Qualité inégale

☐ Includes
Comprend du

☐ Pages wholly
slips, tissues
ensure the
totalement c
feuillet d'
à nouveau d
image possibl

☐ Opposing pa

best possi
ayant des
orations soni
meilleur ima

roduced thanks

anada

best quality
on and legibility
ng with the

covers are filmed
ending on
trated impres-
propriate. All
jinning on the
impres-
e with a printed

microfiche
eaning "CON-
aning "END").

filmed at
too large to be
are filmed
corner, left to
y frames as
illustrate the

2   3

L'exemplaire filmé fut reproduit grâce à la
générosité de:

Bibliothèque nationale du Canada

Les images suivantes ont été reproduites avec
plus grand soin, compte tenu de la condition
de la netteté de l'exemplaire filmé, et en
conformité avec les conditions du contrat de
filmage.

par le premier
dernière
d'impression
plat, selon

empreinte.

Un des symboles suivants apparaîtra sur la
dernière image de chaque microfiche, selon le
cas: le symbole ⟶ signifie "A SUIVRE", le
symbole ▼ signifie "FIN".

1

2

MICROCOPY RESOLUTION TEST CHART

(ANSI and ISO TEST CHART No. 2)

 1.0

 1.1

1.25 1.4 1.6

APPLIED IMAGE Inc

1653 East Main Street
Rochester, New York   14609   USA
(716) 482 – 0300 – Phone
(716) 288 – 5989 – Fax

1500

Title and Edition

IN SUBJECTION

IN SUBJECTION

BY

ELLEN THORNEYCROFT FOWLER
(MRS. ALFRED LAURENCE FELKIN)

SECOND EDITION

TORONTO
WILLIAM BRIGGS
1906

1906,

Mrs. Felkin,

in the

United States of America

Dedication

TO

THE DAUGHTERS OF SARAH

CONTENTS

IN SUBJECTION

CHAPTER I

ISABEL'S GARDEN

IN the drawing-room of a house on the north side of
Prince's Gardens a man and a woman were seated one
winter's evening after dinner. It was not a large room,
and it was by no means a unique one as far as its
original structure was concerned, for it was of the
orthodox " L " shape which obtains so largely in
London drawing - rooms, excepting in those of extremely recent manufacture; but there was that
indefinable air of comfort and elegance about it,
which certain women have the power to impart to
their dwelling-places. It was furnished entirely with
green—the most satisfactory of all colours for that
purpose, be the furniture that of an ordinary dwelling-
place, or of Nature's great house not made with hands ;
light green paper of the same hue as beech-trees in
spring; dark green carpet and curtains, of the same
tint as mossy glades in summer ; and chairs and
couches of as many and as varying shades of green
as are woods when the evergreens and the larches

9

struggle for a majority. Therefore—although it was only the beginning of February—spring was already at home in this London drawing-room, winter having been kept waiting outside ever since the end of October. There were no outlying districts in this room as there are in so many; the back drawing-room had not been converted, as it usually is, into a sort of Court of the Gentiles, where outsiders congregate on uncomfortable chairs round an unused piano; but was in its own way as much honoured and esteemed as the front drawing-room, and was considered quite as respectable a place of residence.

As for the occupants of this pleasant room, the man—somewhere about forty years of age—was tall and dark, thin and thoughtful-looking: the type of man who takes life and himself seriously, and who finds his sole recreation in hard work. The woman was cast altogether in a different mould. She had the rounded plumpness which is inseparable from a light-hearted and easy-going disposition; and the years—whereof she boasted one or two less than her husband—had dealt more tenderly with her than with him. She was quick and active in all her movements; but it was the activity of boundless energy rather than of feverish unrest. Her dark hair showed no trace of grey, save to her own all-seeing vision; and her eyes were as bright and blue as they had been when she was a girl. They saw further now than they did then, perhaps; but their perceptions, though more acute, were less critical than in the old days. Although she lived in an age when domestic misery was the fashion, and when happy marriages were as completely out-of-date as crinolines or Paisley shawls, she nevertheless loved and admired her husband with all her heart and mind and soul and strength.

Otherwise she was as up-to-date and as modern as it is necessary for any woman to be.

"It seems to me," she suddenly remarked, *à propos* of her own meditations, "that single life is like a road, and married life is like a garden."

"As how?" asked her husband, looking up from his evening paper, which, after the manner of men, he was devoutly studying.

"Well, in this way. Single life is like a road, because it is always leading on to something else. It isn't meant to be a permanent place of residence; and people who make it so are behaving like the children of Israel or the gipsies. They ought to 'fold up their tents,' *à la* Longfellow's cares and the Arabs, and 'silently steal away': it is against the rules not to move on."

Paul Seaton (that was the name of the man in the green drawing-room) smiled with that indulgent kind of smile which husbands are wont to use when they think their wives are talking nonsense and like them all the better for it.

"You seem to consider single life a somewhat chilly and uncomfortable sort of business," he remarked.

"On the contrary, I think there is a good deal to be said for it in its own way. Of course it isn't as cosy and settled and living-on-your-property-ish as marriage; you must see that for yourself. But it is more exciting, because it is always the way to somewhere else, and you are never quite sure where the next turn of the road will take you. It is not only a road; it is a road where all the finger-posts are pure guesswork."

"But the milestones are not."

Mrs. Seaton sighed.

"No; worse luck! The milestones are dreadfully pronounced and staring before you are married, and are always coming to meet you and hitting you in the face. After you are married they seem to get a little moss-grown, and you don't notice them nearly so much. Yes; the portentous flagrancy of the mile-stones is one of the greatest disadvantages of single life; but it has its advantages all the same."

"What else, in addition to the mystery hidden round the next corner?"

"Oh! the delicious stranger-and-sojourner feeling that things are more or less temporary, and so don't matter. You can put up with many little incon-veniences in a wayside inn that you couldn't tolerate for a moment in your own house. It is really the picnic instinct that imbues you as long as you are single—the same instinct that causes water boiled out-of-doors, on a fire of your own lighting, to make so much nicer tea than water boiled in the kitchen kettle, and allowed to cool by the butler till ready for use."

"But that instinct doesn't imbue me."

Isabel shook her head reprovingly.

"That is because you are getting old, and have got married, and the domestic instinct in your character has crowded out the picnic instinct."

Seaton laughed; but he listened. He was one of the rare men (or is it rather the husbands of the rare women?) who find the conversation of their wives more interesting than the newspapers.

"You see," Mrs. Seaton continued, "I married late enough to know what single and married life are like, so I can speak as an expert in both."

"Still, the fact that you knew nothing about either wouldn't have prevented you from doing that," retorted her husband drily.

'Oh, Paul, how rude you are—and just when I am talking so nicely and intelligently to you, too!"

"Intelligently I admit, but hardly nicely. You are now cutting me to the heart with your insinuations that when single life is bliss 'tis folly to be married. You cannot expect your loving husband exactly to relish these panegyrics on single blessedness."

"They aren't panegyrics—they are merely statistics just to teach you the difference between being married and single."

"Good heavens, I don't want teaching that! I know it only too well by experience!" And Paul Seaton laughed the contented laugh of the man who has attained his heart's desire. "But I wish you'd say something now on the other side—something in favour of the holy estate, don't you know? This present attitude of mind is most depressing to me!"

"I'm going to, only you are always in such a hurry to express your own opinions that you never give me time to get a word in edgeways."

"Excuse me, my love; I have never yet expressed my own opinion upon matrimony. I should consider it impolite to do so in present company."

The lady tried not to laugh, but failed. The affection between Paul Seaton and his wife was so great, and the camaraderie so perfect, that they could afford to make fun of each other now and then; but they took care never to do so before a third person. It is a mistake for husbands and wives to chaff each other in the presence of an audience. Brothers and sisters can do so as much as they like; and, as a rule, the more they do it the fonder of each other they are: but with married people it is different. They have the dignity of an office to maintain—the sanctity of a covenant to keep; and it does not do for them to treat such things lightly, when the eye of Europe is upon them. It is only when they are *en tête-à-tête* that they may safely unbend, and may confess to themselves and to each other that there is a great deal that is very funny in both of them. Which undoubtedly there is, whoever they may be.

"After all," admitted Isabel, "although there is a certain amount of very nice excitement in living on a road which leads to nobody knows where, it is the sort of excitement that palls after a time. People get tired of not knowing what is going to happen next. That is why hardly anybody really enjoys a story that comes out in a serial : ordinary human nature likes to be in a position to peep at the end whenever it thinks fit. Hence the popularity of palmists and fortune-tellers and crystal balls."

"I understand. And it is when the road becomes too vague and unsettled that the garden comes in."

"Precisely. And the garden is all that the road is not and never can be—peaceful and guarded and final and secure.'

"And circumscribed," added Paul.

"Yes; but I don't know that it is any the worse for that—especially for women."

Seaton rose from his chair, came across the room to where his wife was sitting, and began to stroke her hair. His face was grave—almost sad. He was wondering whether, after all, Isabel was contented with her part of the bargain; whether his love was sufficient to compensate her for the gaiety and luxury and excitement she had given up when she married him. Though they had enough to live upon even when Paul was out of office, they were by no means rich people: compared with the majority of their world they necessarily led a quiet life. And Isabel Carnaby had been denied no possible luxury nor excitement in the days when she lived with her uncle and aunt, Sir Benjamin and Lady Farley. Her life then—both out in India, when Sir Benjamin held a Governorship, and afterwards in London and at Elton Manor—had been one long round of gaiety and pleasure; and Paul was sometimes afraid that she might find the contrast between the past and the present too great—that she was too modern a woman for marriage completely to satisfy her, as it had satisfied her grandmothers. Wherein he showed that, for all his love, he did not yet entirely understand his wife.

"So the garden is duller than the road," he said; and his voice had a pathetic ring in it.

"Perhaps; that is to say it has fewer possibilities and less adventures."

"And it doesn't lead anywhere."

"Yes, it does," whispered Isabel, nestling up to him; "it leads home."

"It *is* home," he answered, as he stooped and kissed her; "but all the same, I am afraid you find it a little dull at times, my darling."

"That's a man all over! Men never understand how much we say, and how little we mean: they have no atmosphere in their minds which are like those dazzling photographs of foreign places, where the shadows are blacker than the substances. If you remark that you want a bit of fancy-work just to keep your fingers employed, they think that you are miserable in your marriage, and are striving to deaden your anguish by ceaseless toil; and if you say you feel as if you couldn't walk another thirty miles or so after a hard day's exercise, they think you are dying of exhaustion and ought to have an injection of strychnine."

"Well, I can't help being a man; I was born so; consequently, when you talk about marriage being a ho rid sort of walled-in kitchen-garden, I naturally fear tha. you are finding it dull."

"Oh, Paul, you *are* silly—you really are! I don't find it an atom dull—I adore it. But you must see for yourself that a garden is—is—well, a garden is a garden."

Isabel had not intended to finish her sentence thus lamely; but experience had taught her that when people are in a sensitive mood the less one says to them the better. Explanations rarely explain anything, except what had better be left unexplained: therefore wise persons avoid them as much as possible. She held her peace for fear of hurting her husband's feelings; but she succeeded in doing so nevertheless.

"Just so," was all he said; but he said it in rather an injured tone of voice.

"Don't be foolish, darling," she begged, rubbing her cheek against his hand. "Don't you see that when God made man perfectly happy, He planted him in a garden; and when He wanted to punish him, He turned him out on to a thorny and thistly highway? So there's really nothing unkind to you in my comparing marriage to a garden—in fact quite the reverse."

"I see," replied Paul drily.

"No, you don't. Whenever you say 'I see' in that particular tone of voice, it always means that you see something which isn't there."

Paul smiled in spite of himself.

"Well, what is all this leading up to, I should like to know?"

"That's what I'm coming to. A garden, to be a really nice, dressy garden, must have things in it, don't you see—heaps and heaps of things? It wants much more furnishing than a road does. As long as the road has good high hedges on either side to keep travellers from going where they ought not, it needn't have flowers or fountains or shrubs or rockeries, because people merely regard it as a means to an end, and so don't mind if it is rather sketchy. But when you've got a garden of your own, and mean to spend the rest of your life there, you naturally want to fill it with all sorts of beautiful things."

Isabel paused to take breath, but Paul did not speak.

"How nice of you to keep quiet and listen!" she remarked approvingly. "That is where men are so much more restful to live with than women; they let you say what you want to say without eternally trying to poke their own oars in. You see," she continued, "other women have children and careers and parishes and school-boards, and all sorts of things to furnish their gardens and keep them from seeming empty; but I haven't."

Unconsciously her voice quivered as she said the word "children." She did not notice it herself; but Paul did.

"My poor darling!" he said; and again laid a caressing hand upon the neat brown head.

Isabel thrilled at his touch, and in the same breath hoped that he wasn't roughening her hair much. She prided herself upon always being a very spick-and-span person.

"I'm not poor at all," she retorted. "I've got *you*."

s

"But I don't seem to be large enough for the place somehow. That's where the tragedy comes in."

"Yes, you are; you are more than enough, if only I could see enough of you; but I can't. If I could always be with you I should never want anything or anybody else, even for five minutes; you'd furnish any garden as completely as a cedar-tree does, or a large fountain. But you are so busy with Houses of Commons and War Offices and tiresome old things of that sort, that often you haven't time to attend to me. And it is then that the garden seems a little empty."

"My poor darling!" Paul repeated.

Isabel rattled on : "I can't for the life of me see what any woman can want in addition to a husband, if the husband is anything like you, and if he is always with her; but if she is married to an alibi, absentee-landlord sort of a person, who is always somewhere else than where he is at the time, she wants something to fill up the intervals—like those funny little street-scenes in Shakespeare's plays, while the scenery is being changed."

"I am afraid I do leave you alone a good deal," replied her husband, with a sigh; "but I cannot help it. You know that, don't you, my darling?"

"I think you could help it more than you do, if only you hadn't such an elephant of a conscience and such a hippopotamus of a sense of duty. What on earth is the good of a man's being always at his post, when the post happens to be a Government Office? Posts can stand still by themselves, without wanting anybody to help them. It is what they are made for: that and deafness: and when you say 'as deaf as a post,' you mean as deaf as a post in the Government, because they never listen to suggestions nor hear complaints. But that's neither here nor there." And Isabel pursed up her lips and nodded her head with the air of one who could say considerably more if she chose.

"Well, what is the particular new toy that you want just now for the furnishing of your garden?" asked Paul. "I am certain that you have one in your eye at the present moment." He knew his Isabel.

"Right as usual! It's a girl — an Anglo-Indian girl."

Seaton fairly jumped. Isabel rarely succeeded in surprising him or taking him unawares: he was pretty well accustomed to her vagaries by now. But she did this time.

"A girl? Good gracious! What in the name of fortune do you want with a girl?"

"Lots of things. I want to instruct her, and amuse her, and entertain her, and finally marry her."

"To whom do you want to marry her?"

"Several people."

"You'll find it rather dfficult to manage that, the present marriage laws being as narrow and antiquated as they are."

"Paul, don't be silly! What I mean is that I've several people in my eye that I think would do for her; and I shall let her choose which."

"That is very generous of you, my sweet! But won't they have a say in the matter?"

"Oh! that's their look-out. I can't bother about them."

"Who are they?"

"I'm not going to tell you."

"Please do. I'm dying to know."

But Isabel stood firm. "Nothing would induce me to tell you."

" You'd better. It would make you feel much more comfortable in your mind."

" My mind is quite comfortable already, thank you; if anything, too luxurious."

" And it would amuse me immensely."

Now it is always difficult for a woman to refrain from telling her husband anything that she thinks will amuse him; in ninety - nine cases out of a hundred it is impossible. But this happened to be the hundredth.

" I'm not going to tell you," Isabel repeated sternly; "at least not yet."

Paul's eye twinkled. He knew that Time, which reveals all secrets, was particularly rapid in revealing Isabel's. But all he said was;

" Then, if I may not know the name of the happy man, may I know that of the girl ? "

" Oh, yes ! I don't mind telling you that. It is Fabia Vipart."

" And who, in the name of all that's wonderful, is Fabia Vipart ? "

" Her father was a Major Vipart in the Indian Army, and her mother was a Hindoo—at least, her grandmother was ; and they are both dead."

" Both her grandmothers, do you mean ? "

" Of course not ; they must have been dead for ages ; grandmothers nearly always are. I mean her parents."

" How very sad for the girl—at least, presumably so ! But how did you get to know her, Isabel ? "

" I knew her father out in India when I was living there with the Farleys. He wanted to marry me."

" An Oriental custom, I suppose. And did the Hindoo lady object ? "

" Oh, Paul, how silly you are ! He was a widower, of course."

"Why 'of course'? I wasn't aware there was anything especially ephemeral about Hindoo ladies."

"I said 'of course,' because if he hadn't been a widower he wouldn't have wanted to marry me."

"I fail to see the logic of that. *I* wasn't a widower, and I wanted to marry you. I never knew that you set up for being an emporium of only second-hand goods."

"I daresay if you *had* been a widower, you'd have had more wisdom—or perhaps I should say experience—than to want to marry me," suggested Isabel slily.

"Not I, my own! I should always have been a fool where you were concerned. But to return to Miss Fabia. I gather that when you knew Major Vipart, the Hindoo lady—like Wordsworth's *Lucy*—had ceased to be."

"She'd been dead for years. And besides, as I've explained to you, she wasn't a Hindoo at all: her mother was."

"Then is Miss Fabia black?"

"Good gracious, no!" exclaimed Isabel. "Her hair is dark, of course, but not as black as—"

"It is painted; probably not. Many women's isn't."

"When I was out in India she was quite a child; a cream-coloured child with huge brown eyes. She always reminded me of a dress I had of cream satin trimmed with brown velvet. It was a very pretty dress!"

And Isabel's face grew soft with that tender expression which a woman's face always wears when she is recalling bygone garments that became her well.

"It must have been; and the prettiest bit was the lining, as our old nurse Martha used to say. She never said it of my clothes or of Joanna's, by the way; it was generally upon Alice Martin's wardrobe that this criticism was passed, if I remember rightly. Joanna and I were plain children; and it was considered conducive to our eternal salvation to make us believe that we were even plainer than we were. Which really was an act of supererogation."

"You never were plain, Paul!" exclaimed Isabel indignantly. "I won't let anybody say such things of my husband; not even you."

"Nevertheless it is true, sweetheart. I was an ugly little beggar in those days, and a prig at that. But we are wandering from Miss Fabia. Her father wanted to marry you, you say. *He* was evidently a sensible man, whatever her mother might have been."

"Her mother couldn't help being a Hindoo," retorted Isabel, rather huffily. It always annoyed her when English people spoke disrespectfully of foreign races.

"But you have just said that she not only *could* help it, but *did*."

"Oh Paul, I wish you wouldn't quibble in that silly way, when I am trying to talk to you seriously! It was the grandmother that couldn't help being a Hindoo, and Fabia could help it even less; and yet people were very horrid to Fabia about it, and to her father too."

"All right: I understand. Miss Fabia's grandmother could no more help being a Hindoo than her father could help wanting to marry you. Poor beggar! I'm the last man to blame him. But now, where does the girl come in, and what is her connexion with the allegory of the marriage-market—I mean the marriage-market-garden?"

"Well, you see, I have heard through Aunt Farley, who still corresponds with a host of people out in India, that Fabia is extremely anxious to come to England for a time to sample English society. So I thought it would be rather nice if I had her here for a few months, and trotted her about and showed her round."

"And then instructed and entertained and finally married her to that nameless knight whom you have in your eye. Now at last I begin to master the programme."

"You wouldn't mind having her here, would you, darling?" asked Isabel, in a coaxing voice.

"I shouldn't mind anything that gave you pleasure, my dearest—not even a girl, though I own I am not very keen upon them as a rule."

"Well, it would give me a great deal of pleasure to take a young girl about, and watch her go through all the phases that I've been through myself, and to watch her mind working like bees in a glass hive. It would be such fun teaching her all the things that I've learnt by experience."

"She wouldn't learn much that way, my sweet: nobody does. But that needn't interfere with your pleasure in teaching her."

"It wouldn't. She is quite young—not much over twenty, I should think: so I shall be able to do whatever I like with her. It isn't likely that a girl of that age will have many plans and interests of her own as yet. And I shan't knuckle under to her because she is young, as so many women do. I don't kow-tow to the young. I was once young myself, and I know how it's done."

"You must remember, Isabel, that she probably will not look at life through your eyes, as you seem to expect; and you must not be disappointed if she doesn't."

"She will look at life very much as I looked at it when I was her age," replied Isabel, with a characteristic toss of her head. "You may know more about politics than I do, my dear Paul, but you can't possibly know as much about girls."

"Thank heaven for that! But I know a good deal about one woman, and I think you make a mistake in expecting other people to be exactly like yourself: because unfortunately they are not."

"Perhaps I *am* inclined to think too highly of my fellow-creatures," replied Isabel demurely; "but it is a good fault."

"It is an absolutely charming fault, as all yours are, my darling," said Seaton, kissing his wife. "But I must be off to the House. Invite your little Indian girl, by all means; but don't be disappointed if she doesn't turn out to be as absolutely adorable as you are yourself; because neither she nor anybody else possibly could."

Thus it was settled that Fabia Vipart should come to stay with the Paul Seatons for the following Season; and Isabel wrote out by the next mail to make all the necessary arrangements. Would she have written quite so glibly had she known all the trouble that the coming of Fabia would involve? Perhaps not. And yet if we were always prevented from doing anything for fear of possible consequences—if we were always letting "I dare not" wait upon "I would," like the cat i' the adage—then not many a thing would be done when 'twere done, and nothing would be done quickly.

CHAPTER II

FABIA VIPART

A NATIVE gentleman, dressed in European costume, was sitting alone in the drawing-room of an Indian bungalow. He was a man in the prime of life, with the narrow figure and small hands and feet of the true Oriental. His head was small, and his hair absolutely black. No beard or moustache hid his firm yet delicately-moulded mouth and chin; and the upper part of his face showed considerable fineness of form. A handsome man undoubtedly; but with the beauty of the East rather than of the West: a man likewise of considerable fascination; but whose charm had something weird and uncanny about it. He was one of those who strive to lift the veil of the great temple of Nature and to pry into her hidden places; and he had succeeded in wresting from her certain of those secrets, which she, in her wise and tender motherhood, keeps as a rule concealed from the sons and daughters of men. This meddling with the occult had left its mark upon him; had set him apart, as it were, from the common herd, and had loosened those bonds of sympathy which bind ordinary men and women to each other in this workaday world; so that people felt awe for him rather than affection, and found him fascinating rather than lovable.

The house in which he was sitting was not his own, for it was full of signs of feminine habitation; and Ram Chandar Mukharji was a bachelor. It was the house of his distant cousin, Fabia Vipart, whom he had called to see, and for whose appearance he was now patiently waiting. And, like all Orientals, he had mastered the art of patient waiting. He did not fidget about the room as an Englishman in the same circumstances would have done, trying to find some book or news-paper to while away the time, lest one minute of it should be lost—that is to say, should be unoccupied by outside interests; but he sat quite still, absorbed in his own thoughts, with a stillness unknown to the children of Western races.

Presently the swish of silken skirts was heard approaching, and Miss Vipart entered the room. Then for the first time the face of the man showed signs of animation, being illuminated with the light of a great joy that was all the more intense for being silent.

"Good morning, Fabia," he said, as he took her slim brown hand in his own. His voice was as soft and silken in its tone as was the rustle of his cousin's skirts; as sweet, in fact, as a woman's.

"Good morning, Ram Chandar. I am glad you have come, because I want particularly to see you. I have something to tell you."

"Of course I came; I am always coming. I only live in order to come here, and I only go away in order to have the pleasure of coming again."

Fabia smiled, and sank down into a low chair, stretching out her slender form luxuriously. It would have been apparent to the most casual observer that these two belonged not only to the same race but also

to the same family, there was such a strong resemblance
between them. But the infusion of English blood in
the girl's case placed the balance of beauty on her side.
She was some twenty years younger than her cousin,
which is always physically an advantage; but in addition to this she had inherited something of her father's
fibre. Though equally slender, she was taller for a
woman than Mukharji was for a man; as they stood
together their eyes were almost on a level. While his
hair was a dead black, hers was a dusky brown, relieved
by innumerable lights and shadows. Her nose and
mouth were as finely formed as his; but in place of his
thin and colourless lips, hers were a ripe crimson.
They had the same full forehead and flashing eyes; but
the expression of their faces was totally different. There
was no doubt that Ram Chandar was a handsome man;
but Fabia was an exceptionally beautiful woman
Beautiful, indeed, as a dream; but with something
serpentine in the quality of her beauty—something
snake-like in the perfection of her grace.

"I have to tell you," she said, and her voice was like
his in its softness of tone and slowness of movement;
"that I am going away; going away to England."

The man sat still and did not speak. But his
silence was heavy with the weight of suppressed
passion.

Fabia did not trouble to look at him. These two
knew each other so well that words—even looks—were
unnecessary between them.

"I am weary of the life here," the girl went on;
"weary of the routine and the emptiness and the
frivolity; weary most of all of the contempt of the
Anglo-Indians, as they call themselves. So I am going
to England."

Then at last the man spoke. "You will hate it."

"I think not. I am partly English myself, you see, and the English part of me is homesick for England. I can feel my father in me crying out to return to his native land."

"You say the English out here despise you. If they do, what matters it? They are but pariahs and dogs. But still if they do so here, will they not do so also in England; and shall you like it any better there than here?"

"You are wrong, Ram Chandar; there is none of that prejudice in England that there is here against people of mixed races. I have talked to men and women fresh from England, and I know. They will admire me all the more for it—for that and for my beauty. They are so commonplace themselves, those English, that they are ready to fall down and worship whatever is out of the common; so that pure whiteness here and mixed whiteness in England are equally worthy of their adoration."

Mukharji did not speak; but he fixed his wonderful eyes on the girl and willed her to tell him all that was in her thoughts.

She moved her head restlessly under his gaze for half a minute; then she answered him as if he had spoken.

"I do not wish to keep anything from you; I will tell you all that is in my heart. There never have been any secrets between you and me."

"There never can be. I can read your soul, my child, as I read an open book. And I tell you that you will hate those English when you see them in their own land."

"I think not; I think not, Ram Chandar. If I do

not hate them now when they look down on me, why should I hate them when they adore me? For I mean them to adore me: I have made up my mind to that; and what I intend I always accomplish."

Again the man fixed his eyes on the girl without speaking; and again she moved restlessly, yet with infinite grace. She was one of those rare women whose every movement is in itself a thing of beauty.

"I despise them too utterly to hate them," she continued; "but I want to show them my power—to lord it over with them as they now try to lord it over me. And although I despise them they have a certain interest and charm for me; I admire their big bodies and their fair complexions, and it amuses me to trifle with their shallow little souls."

"You had far better stay here, Fabia—among your own people who understand you."

"Among my grandmother's people, you mean; you forget that I am more than half English."

He did not forget; he never forgot that Fabia belonged quite as much to the alien race as to his own; and he was deeply and bitterly jealous of the foreigners in consequence.

For once the impenetrable veil of his reserve was lifted.

"Fabia, do not go," he entreated, and this time there was passion in his voice as well as in his eyes. "Stay here and be my wife. I love you, Fabia; I have always loved you; you are part of my very soul."

Then at last the girl turned lazily in her chair and looked at him; and once more he forced the truth from her by the strength of his will. "I cannot marry you, Ram Chandar: I do not love you; you are too much like myself. If I marry, I should like to marry a big, strong Englishman with a fair complexion and a shallow little soul. If I married you, you would want to be my slave—and I should not like that at all. But the big, strong Englishman would be my master, and would do with me whatsoever he would. He would know none of my thoughts, but I should know all of his; and yet he would be the master, because he would be strong and stupid. In this world strength and stupidity are the great ruling powers; nothing can stand against them. And I should hate him for ruling over me, Ram Chandar —oh! yes, I should hate him; but I should adore him for it all the same."

She paused, but the man made no reply; then—as if impelled by some power stronger than herself—she went on: "And although I despise them, I resent their contempt for me. I want to be one of themselves, and to share their privileges, and to hurt them as they have hurt me and my mother before me. Ram Chandar, I must go, even if only for a short time."

"If you go, you will never come back."

"In that case, you can come to me."

"Perhaps so; perhaps not. That is as Fate wills. But what about all that I have taught you, Fabia? What about all those hidden things to which no woman's mind save yours has ever been opened? Is all this to be wasted, because you choose to live among English dogs who have no thoughts beyond their own vile bodies, and to whom the world of spirits is for ever closed?"

"Not necessarily."

"It will be—and necessarily. But I will waste no more breath in argument. Your mind is made up, and nothing will turn you; you were not even half a Mukharji if it would. I loved your mother, and she preferred an Englishman to me: I love her daughter, and she will prefer an Englishman to me: it is as Fate wills, and nothing can alter it. it is useless to fight against Fate. I submit."

"My plans are all made," said Fabia, in her sweet voice. "I had to make them by myself because y ɹ were away, and Mrs. Seaton wanted an answer by the next mail."

" I wait to hear."

If the man who had been a father to Fabia ever since her own father's death was wounded by her cool Independence of him, he made no sign: he simply listened with an imperturbable face, out of which he had smoothed every trace of his recent emotion.

" I am going to stay for a few months with Mrs. Paul Seaton, who lived here for four years with her uncle, Sir Benjamin Farley. You remember him?"

" Well; and his wife also: a soulless woman with a cultivated mind — cultivated, that is to say, for an Englishwoman. They are generally such crude, such untrained creatures."

"Then do you not remember their niece, Miss Carnaby? She became Mrs. Paul Seaton some years ago. She must be quite old by this time—considerably over thirty; and I shall do whatever I like with her. It isn't likely that a woman of that age will still have many plans and interests of her own."

Fabia little recked that Isabel had made the same remark, almost word for word, about her, merely substituting "young" for "old." Age is, after all, very much a question of perspective.

" I remember her perfectly: a noisy, shallow, sparkling brook of a woman—the sort that Englishmen want to marry, and consider themselves very fortunate if they succeed." And Ram Chandar shuddered slightly.

"Papa did."

"Ah!" A look of ineffable disgust suffused the dark face. "He wanted that woman—that empty, babbling brook—to fill your mother's place? How English!"

"Poor papa! He was often very foolish."

"And you hated her—hated the chattering fool that was asked to step into your mother's shoes?"

Fabia smiled languidly.

"No, my dear Ram Chandar, I did nothing of the kind. To tell the truth, I rather liked her, although I despised her. She was kind-hearted, though too effusive for my taste; and not nearly so offensively clever as she supposed herself."

"A fool, doubtless, like most of her country-women!"

"By no means a fool; a clever woman in a superficial way. Clever enough to know there were some things beyond her comprehension; but not clever enough to try to comprehend them."

"And you can forgive that woman for being asked to fill your mother's place? You are indeed your father's daughter!"

"I can forgive any woman for being asked in marriage by any man. It is her one possible diploma of merit. The only woman I cannot forgive is the woman whom no man has asked in marriage. She is a blot upon my sex."

"You are cold, Fabia—cold as ice; and you are also cruel. Yet I love you."

The girl mocked him.

"And I am also beautiful, and yet you love me. And I am also clever, and yet you love me. And I am also wealthy, and yet you love me. Truly the love of man is a wonderful and a selfless thing!"

Again the handsome face put on its mask of immobility. "And whom did she finally marry — this twenty-first love of your father?"

"A Member of Parliament—what they call a Radical —by name Paul Seaton. He is Under-Secretary for the War Office, whatever that may mean. He was poor, too, and she married for what she called love; by which probably she meant a due sense of the unfitness of things."

"And you can make yourself happy among such people?"

"For a time, yes. I am bored to death here. I am tired of you all, and have seen all there is to see, and have learnt by heart all there is to learn; and I want a change."

"And it never occurs to you to wonder what *I* want?"

"Never."

Wherein Fabia spoke the simplest truth. It never did occur to her to consider what anybody except herself thought or felt about anything. At present she was completely and absolutely selfish. She had schooled herself not to mind the social slights which, in Anglo-Indian society, the fact that she was a half-caste entailed upon her; and she had succeeded in meeting them with the utmost indifference, not to say contempt; but they had had their effect upon her character all the same.

There are few baneful influences more difficult to withstand than that of continual social slights. The iron of them is prone to enter even into the strongest and purest souls; and the iron does not invariably act as a tonic. From sorrow and misfortune men and women often rise ennobled and purified; but it is doubtful if a continuance of petty slights ever has a

c

beneficial effect upon any human being; it almost invariably hardens and embitters, and changes the fairest Elims into Marahs indeed. Perhaps the most cruel part of losing a fortune is not its immediate effect upon ourselves, but its effect upon our neighbours and their consequent treatment of us.

And what right have we, forsooth, in our mean and petty arrogance, to distort and stultify the immortal souls of those men and women who happen to be less wealthy or well-born than ourselves? What right have we, in our smug self-complacency, to deface the Divine Image and Superscription on the current coin of our Father's realm? Our only excuse is that we are ignorant of the harm we are doing, the effect of a social snub being, as a rule, out of all proportion to the cause. Therefore the next time we feel constrained, in our fancied superiority, to teach (as we phrase it) some less fortunate fellow-man his place, let us take care that our innate snobbishness and our cultivated insolence are not endangering the soul of a weaker brother!

Thus it was not altogether poor Fabia's fault that she was cold and selfish and hard; it was rather the fault of those fashionable friends of her father's who felt it incumbent upon them to indicate their own social superiority by displaying a studied exclusiveness towards all those not of their own race or order. But though the fault might be theirs, the onus rested with her; and she, like the rest of us, had to take the consequences of her own failings—to suffer from the results of her own mistakes.

She had loved her mother more than she had ever loved her father; but her admiration and respect were always put down to the latter's score. The fact that he belonged to the dominant race had influenced her every thought of him; and her very bitterness against the attitude of his people towards her, was a proof that she invariably recognized their superiority.

Her mother died when she was still a child; and her father when she was just developing into womanhood. Since his death her mother's kinsman, Ram Chandar Mukharji, had taken charge of herself and her property, providing her with a duenna in the shape of a cast-off though eminently worthy governess whom the family of an English Resident had outgrown.

Underneath the almost Oriental languor of Fabia's manner, her mind was feverishly active. She was never really at rest—never content. Consequently she soon wearied of poor Miss Jones's conscientious supervision, and plumed her radiant wings for wider flight. It was then that Isabel heard of her and her desire to come to England, through one of Lady Farley's Anglo-Indian friends; and Mrs. Seaton sent out her invitation just in the nick of time when Fabia felt that she could endure India and Miss Jones no longer. The girl had inherited a handsome fortune and large estates from her mother; and she had the independence and the intolerance of restraint which are the invariable attributes of moneyed immaturity.

Thus she was as pleased at the idea of coming to the Seatons' as Mrs. Seaton was at the idea of receiving her; and she was just as set upon managing Isabel as Isabel was set upon managing her. And the result of the contest between these two strong and self-willed women still lay in the lap of the gods.

CHAPTER III

THE SCOURGE OF THE RED CORD

FABIA came to England as had been arranged, and was received by Mrs. Paul Seaton with open arms; but Miss Vipart had not been long at Prince's Gardens before Isabel realised that she had opened her arms a little too wide before understanding all the bearings of the case. She at once confided the discovery of this error, and her repentance of the same, to Paul, who, like a good husband (and unlike a good wife), carefully refrained from saying anything which, even by the freest translation, could be construed into "I told you so." He was for sending Fabia back to India by return of post, so to speak, having (again like a good husband) no sense of proportion where his wife and his wife's interests were concerned. The man who is alive to the laws of perspective with regard to the woman that he loves, had better take at once a self-imposed vow of celibacy: for while the world stands he will never make even a passable husband. But Isabel—with that innate sense of justice in which it pleases men to imagine that all women are fundamentally lacking—felt that such a course of conduct would be most unfair to her guest; and put the temptation away from her accordingly.

It was not really the fault of either woman that the two did not, as the phrase runs, get on well together;

they met with the full intention of liking each other
extremely, and of being great friends as the fashionable
world counts friendship; but the fact was that they
were absolutely incapable of understanding one another;
and true friendship without mutual comprehension is a
contradiction in terms.

It was no fault of Isabel's that, in spite of all her
efforts to understand Fabia's character, she signally
failed; on the contrary, this failure was rather to her
credit than otherwise. With all her faults—of which
she had her proper and normal share—there was not
one grain of bitterness or acidity in Isabel's character;
she was constitutionally incapable of feeling either the
one or the other. True, in the old, half-forgotten days,
she had written a book which was noted for its bitter
cynicism; but that was but the expression of a
temporary phase which was altogether foreign to her
natural bent of mind. She had dipped her pen in gall
as she wrote; but the pen-wiper was ever at hand to
remove the foreign substance as soon as she had done
with it; and it had never even temporarily stained her
white fingers. Of acidity she was incapable, even
momentarily; that could never tinge even a passing
thought in her mind. She might have been somewhat
hard and thoughtless and capricious in her young days:
her detractors said that she was; but none of them could
ever accuse her of being soured by the experience of
life. Perhaps there was more invigorating saltness than
cloying sweetness in her nature; but, be it remembered,
salt is further removed from acidity than is even sugar.
And, after all, hardness and thoughtlessness are faults
of youth, which decrease with advancing years; while
bitterness and acidity only eat deeper and deeper as
time rolls on into the lives of those that harbour them,

But because of this very saneness of character, which might make her outwardly hard but never inwardly bitter, Isabel found it impossible to enter into Fabia's feelings; and was consequently perhaps a little severe and unsympathetic with the girl. She had never experienced that social ostracism which had entered as iron into Fabia's soul: therefore she was incapable of appreciating its effect upon the girl's character. She pitied her for it, it is true; but pity is often not akin to sympathy, whatever it may be to love. We must all have the defects of our qualities, and Isabel therefore could not escape the inherent limitations of the healthy - minded, unaffected, humorous, successful woman.

Fabia, on the other hand, could not escape the defects of the passionate, highly - strung, reserved, thoughtful, introspective girl. To her superfine sensibilities, Isabel appeared a little harsh and rough; while to Isabel's common-sense and unfailing humour, Fabia's supersensitiveness of mind and body seemed decidedly unhealthy and morbid.

Although she never mentioned it to anybody, Fabia's visit to England was a far greater disappointment to herself than it was to her hostess. She had had an idea that when once she was in England among her father's people, the feeling of loneliness which had oppressed her all her life would vanish: instead of which she felt more isolated here than she had ever done at home. It is strange, that sense of loneliness and isolation which appears to be the unalterable lot of certain souls! They are set apart from their fellows, why they know not; and nothing that they say or do can break down the wall of partition that stands between themselves and other men. From her earliest infancy

Fabia had been a prey to this terrible feeling of
solitariness. As a child, if other children came to play
with her at her own house, they always played with
each other and left her out in the cold. And as a girl
the same thing happened with regard to other girls.
Even her great beauty and undeniable intellectual
powers did not help her; they seemed rather to place
her still further apart from other people. No one but
herself knew how fiercely she envied those commonplace girls who had their full share of brothers and
sisters, and more than their full share of bosom friends;
nor how passionately she resented those qualities in
herself which prevented her companions from being
comfortably intimate with her. And now that she had
at last attained her heart's desire and come to England,
it was just the same. People admired and fêted her
because of her beauty and accomplishments, but they
never treated her as one of themselves, as they treated
isabel; and Fabia was quick to see this. They
were never rude to her, as they had been in India—
never even impolite; but there was a subtle suggestion
in the atmosphere that she was a visitor rather than a
relation—a stranger to be entertained rather than a
friend to be welcomed. Many women would not have
been conscious of this, but Fabia's perceptions were
abnormally acute; and however much people might
flatter her, she knew in a moment when they did not
like her, and she agonized accordingly. isabel, on the
other hand, possessed to a marked degree the gift of
friendliness and camaraderie. Everyone who knew
her felt that they had known her all her life, she had
such a wonderful knack of finding some common ground
whereon herself and the most unlikely person could
meet and fraternise. And this quality in her hostess

made poor Fabia realize the more poignantly her own
loneliness and desolation.

Humanity is divided into two sets of people: the
people who are inside a red cord and the people who
are outside; there is no other division that really
matters. Those who are inside are cheerful and comfortable and well-liking, at peace with gods and men,
and with everybody except outsiders; while those outside are unhappy and desolate and oppressed, at war with
themselves and with each other, and bitterly vindictive
against those happier beings within the sacred inclosure:
and it is all the fault of the red cord.

There are red cords in all worlds and in all phases of
life—social, personal, religious; and one's happiness
mainly depends upon one's relative position towards
these said red cords.

It is a cruel thing, this red cord—cruel fundamentally
to those on both sides of it. It fills those within with
hardness of heart, pride, vainglory, and hypocrisy; an'
those without with envy, hatred, and malice, and all
uncharitableness. It is old too, this red cord—old as
human nature. Ishmael had felt the scourge of it when
his hand was against every man and every man's hand
against his; and those daughters of Heth, from whom
Esau chose his wife, had learnt how pitiless it could be.
Although inimical to the true spirit of Christianity, it
nevertheless continued to exist after the dawning of the
dayspring from on high; even the great Apostle knew
how to wield it to the confounding of the Gentiles;
and it was not until the vision of the great vessel had
been vouchsafed to him three times, that he was
content to lay it down. It was responsible for the
tortures of the Spanish Inquisition, for the horrors
of the French Revolution; it is still responsible for

most of the evils of social and political and religious
life.

Ever since she could remember, Fabia Vipart had
writhed under the scourge of the red cord; it had
lashed her naturally tender spirit into revolt and
rebellion by its merciless system of exclusiveness; and
Isabel Seaton, who had been born and bred within the
select circle, and who had never known the misery of
those whom Society chooses to consign to outer
darkness, was as ignorant as a babe of all that Fabia
suffered, and as intolerant as a child of the outward
signs of that suffering.

Moreover the two women were somewhat far apart
in years, and so lacked the freemasonry of contemporaries. If we are considerably older than anybody
else, it does not invariably follow that we are wiser;
but it invariably follows that we think we are, and nothing
will convince us to the contrary. Therefore Isabel was
fully prepared to advise and instruct her junior; and
her junior obstinately refused to be advised or instructed: wherein lay the raw materials for the
manufacture of open warfare.

One afternoon, about a month after Fabia's arrival in
England, she and her hostess were sitting chatting in
the drawing-room in Prince's Gardens; and the conversation turned upon Miss Vipart's general discontent
with life.

" You should marry," remarked Isabel. " You'd find it
the only permanently amusing entertainment. And
you can't think how much more cosy and cheerful it
makes everything."

Fabia looked lazily at her hostess through half-closed
eye-lids.

" You didn't always think so, for you were in no

special hurry to get married yourself; you must have been nearly thirty."

"Horrid little thing!" exclaimed Isabel to herself. "I'll tell Paul that the very minute he comes in."

The recital to Paul of Fabia's daily iniquities was one of the chief delights of Isabel's life just now, and a wonderful support to her in the endurance of such an incubus. But all that she said aloud was, "Twenty-nine." And she said it quite good-humouredly.

Fabia smiled. "You have an admirable temper, Isabel."

Isabel had insisted upon Fabia's calling her by her Christian name the moment she arrived. Paul had said privately to his wife that he considered this a mistake, but had been overruled. Now Isabel was never tired of telling Paul how much she wished Fabia would call her *Mrs. Seaton*, as she couldn't bear people who didn't like her to call her *Isabel*.

"I know; it's a regular beauty," she replied. "I'm not sure that I ever met anybody with a better one, taking it all round. I often take it out of its cage and stroke it, to show how tame it is. That is to say, except where Paul is concerned. I used to be perfectly vile to him when we were engaged; a regular little devil!"

"But why?"

"I haven't a notion."

"You were in love with him, weren't you?"

"Of course. That was the reason."

"That is absurd—simply absurd! If ever I were so foolish as to be in love with a man—or so wise—I should be an angel to him all the time."

"Naturally; because you aren't an angel to anybody else. I was."

An expression of languid amusement spread itself over Fabia's face.   Although she was at war with Isabel in her heart, she was usually entertained by the conversation of the latter.   The difference between the two women was this: Fabia sometimes was conscious of Isabel's charm; Isabel never was conscious of Fabia's. Fabia could have loved Isabel had she allowed herself to do so; Isabel had tried to love Fabia and had failed. Yet Isabel was invariably kind to Fabia, and Fabia was often very unkind to Isabel.   Such are the ironies of feminine friendship.

"I fail to see the sequence of thought," she said. " Please explain."

" Haven't you noticed that amiable women are generally cross with the men they love; and cross women are generally amiable with the men they love? I once asked a tremendously wise and clever man the reason of this."

" And what did he say?"

" I forget what he said, but I remember what I said: and that was that we offer the greatest rareties as the greatest luxuries to our guests, on the same principle as we give them strawberries in December and ice in June. So that the good-tempered woman's bad temper, and the bad-tempered woman's good temper are special delicacies."

" All the same I cannot imagine your being bad-tempered and disagreeable.   It would be altogether out of drawing."

Isabel's easy good-humour was a constant source of wonder to Fabia: being made herself on such different lines, she had no idea how easy it was.

Mrs. Seaton nodded sagely.   " Can't you?   You just ask Paul."

"He wouldn't tell me if I did. Don't you know him better than that?"

"Of course he wouldn't. That's where husbands are so splendid. They always stick up for you whether you're right or whether you're wrong; in fact rather more when you're wrong than when you're right. They consider that is playing the game."

"So it is."

"I often wonder," continued Isabel, in a meditative manner, "what Paul really thinks of me. He can't possibly think as highly of me as he seems to do, because nobody could; nobody else even pretends to. And yet he knows me better than anybody else does. It's queer! You can't help admitting that it's queer!"

Fabia laughed softly. "Very queer indeed!"

"And there are plenty of other queer things besides," continued Mrs. Seaton, waxing more communicative. "I used to think, before I was married, that when husbands and wives pretended they didn't see each other's faults it was all humbug. But now I find that it wasn't. Of course it is utterly absurd, I know; but all the same, it's true."

"I don't believe it. If I had a husband I should see his faults fast enough; I couldn't help it even if I tried."

"Yes, you could. You couldn't help not helping it."

"But I should feel such a fool."

"And you would be; that's the beauty of it." And Isabel laughed a rippling little laugh of pure happiness. "That's why married life is so good for one," she continued; "you find yourself doing the very things that you've screamed with laughter at other women for doing; and this teaches you, better than a whole library of lesson-books or a complete course of Oxford Extension lectures, that you are not one whit better or wiser than anybody else."

"But that is a lesson I should hate to learn," objected Fabia, who was one of the women who derive a painful pleasure from the notion that no one ever felt as they feel, or suffered as they suffer.

Although she hated her solitariness, she was in a sense proud of it, human nature having a strange knack of feeling pride in its own deficiencies as well as in its own excellencies. Delicate people are as proud of their delicacy as strong ones are of their strength; and small men are as proud of their light weight as big ones are of their bulk. Life is full of compensations; and our own good conceit of ourselves is by no means the least of these.

"It is no use hating things if you've got to learn them," replied Isabel, with her usual sound sense; "it only makes life more unpleasant than it need be, and does nobody any good. Nowadays we are all wise enough to gild our pills with a silver coating, and never to serve them *au naturel.*"

"But don't you hate to find that you are the same as other people?"

"Not a bit of it; I enjoy the joke; and the fact that it is at my own expense makes me enjoy it all the more, as I can understand better than anybody else can how excessively funny it is." Wherein Mrs. Seaton spoke no less than the truth; for she was one of the happy beings—and their name is by no means Legion—who derive unfeigned and solid pleasure from a joke at their own expense. Such persons are rare; and they are almost always feminine. A man who laughs heartily and naturally at his own absurdity, is a very black swan indeed. Men smile, it is true, at these ill-timed and inappropriate jests; but the smiles are generally of that sickly and watery character which reminds one of a sunset on a rainy day. Nine women out of ten do not even smile at humour whereof they themselves are the unwilling butts: they frown and glower and sulk; but the tenth woman not only smiles but laughs with all her heart, holding her sides in the exuberance of her mirth as no man has ever held his at fun poked at himself. And Isabel Seaton happened to be the tenth. "You didn't really know me before I was married," she continued, with that irresistible candour which had ever been one of her greatest charms; "so you've no idea how egregiously conceited I was, and how much cleverer I thought myself than anybody else—or, in fact, than anybody else thought me either; and therefore you can't understand what a killing joke it is to see me developing into the ordinary, commonplace, domestic, and devoted wife. It makes me laugh every time I think of it. Doubtless it is very romantic when the ugly duckling turns into the snow-white swan; but the real joke comes in when the promising cygnet develops into the humdrum barn-door fowl. And that is my case to a T. I've become very humdrum and excessively barn-door; but I've got the saving grace left to see that it's funny." And Isabel laughed softly to herself. "As long as you are funny and know that you are funny, you aren't—well, you are not quite so funny as you would otherwise have been."

"I do not understand you at all. I could not go on doing a thing that I knew was ridiculous. I might be ridiculous without knowing it; I suppose everybody is sometimes; but I would rather die than be ridiculous consciously. I hate to be laughed at; it is absolute torture to me."

Isabel nestled into her easy-chair with that snug cosiness of hers which formed such a marked contrast to Fabia's lithe grace.

"Then you make a great mistake. Half the fun of life consists in seeing how funny you are yourself, and in watching other people find it out."

But Fabia still looked puzzled. As she had said, it was torture to her to be laughed at, for she was one of those supersensitive souls who are not shielded by a saving sense of humour; therefore Isabel's attitude of mind was incomprehensible to her. Perhaps the fact that one woman had been born inside the red cord and the other outside, accounted for the phenomenon in both cases.

"I used to roar with laughter," remarked Isabel, "at women who couldn't see their husband's faults: it used to seem too utterly idiotic for anything. And yet now, though I see Paul's mistakes and limitations, I cannot discover his faults! I know they must be there, like Mrs. Wilfer's petticoat, because everybody has them and nobody is an exception; but try as I will, i can't find them out!"

"You are candid at all events," remarked Fabia, who was as yet too young to decide whether to despise her friend for being a fool, or to admire her for confessing it. According to the poet Gray, the boys at Eton had learned the truth that sometimes " 'tis folly to be wise"; but the soundness of the inverse platitude that some-times 'tis wisdom to be foolish, is never grasped by those on the so-called sunny side of thirty.

"I always try to be, for there's nothing I hate so much as humbug and affectation. There's too much of that going about nowadays, my dear Fabia, especially ⟨on⟩ the subject of marriage ; and I want you to be on your guard against it, and not to be choked off any really nice match just because of the nonsense preached by silly women and modern novels; which brings me to the point of the conversation from which I started. I generally get round to my starting-point, if you only give me time."

"Like the oft-quoted boomerang," suggested Fabia, thus setting her loquacious hostess upon a fresh tack.

"Oh! my dear, there's no greater delusion than the idea that boomerangs invariably travel with a return-ticket. We've got one, in the corner of this very drawing-room, which was once given me by someone who had been to Australia (if that is where boomerangs grow); I forget who it was; I remember it was someone who was in love with me at the time, but I can't for the life of me recall his name. Anyway, I thought it rather an interesting object to have about—the sort of thing that promotes conversation, don't you know?—so when we came to live here I stuck it up at the back of the cosy-corner, supported by two Venetian glass vases that somebody else, whom I've forgotten, gave us for a wedding-present."

"I have seen it. Happily Captain Gaythorne caught sight of it one day when he was being even duller than usual, and it started him on quite an intelligent description of his travels in India—that being the nearest to Australia that he could manage."

"That is just what it was put there for! Every drawing-room ornament should have in it the germ of a conversation; it is its *raison d'être*. I suppose that is why country-people have on their chimney-pieces bunches of the plant called Honesty. It gives them an opportunity of expatiating upon that overrated virtue, and of so drifting into the universal pleasure of telling unpleasant truths to one's friends and neighbours."

" I remember he discoursed exhaustively upon the time-honoured subject of boomerangs, and told long tales of how they invariably came back, like curses, to roost," continued Fabia.

" Do they? That's all he knows ! If you so much as breathe when you are anywhere near to ours, it at once tumbles behind the cosy-corner, breaking any wedding-presents that it comes across on its way. And then does it come back to where it started from? Not a bit of it ! It remains in retreat, like a devotee, until somebody breaks their own bones and more wedding-presents by creeping under the seat of the cosy-corner to fetch it out. I know its little ways." And Mrs. Seaton shook her head reflectively.

" If you have many friends like Captain Gaythorne I do not wonder that you select drawing - room ornaments that start conversation," said Fabia, with that touch of sarcasm which generally flavoured her remarks. Yet on the whole she liked Captain Gaythorne—liked him better than anyone she had as yet met since she came to England. She was by no means the first woman who has abused men because she liked them, and gone near spoiling her own life and theirs accordingly: nor will she be the last. It is rarely a symptom of a certain sort of shyness; and not the worst sort of shyness, either.

But Isabel was not the woman to appreciate or sympathize with shyness of any kind.

" Now, I won't have you abusing Charlie Gaythorne," she cried. " I won't allow it in my drawing-room under the shadow of my own boomerang ! Charlie

D

is my darling, as you have probably heard before, or words to that effect; and besides, he is one of the men that I want you to marry."

The girl winced. She hated Isabel's easy, half-insolent way of disposing of her as if she were a parcel of foreign imports; and yet there was a sort of attractiveness about the insolence, it was so good-humoured. She was beginning to understand why her father had once wanted to marry this woman. It was the same sort of reason which, in a minor degree, had made him enjoy a sharp wind and a cold bath: a reason which no pure Oriental could ever have comprehended. But Fabia was no pure Oriental: there was a strong strain of Western thought and feeling in her composition, and it was probably her Eastern sense of reserve and mystery underlying her Western inclination towards all that was essentially British and modern, that endowed the girl with so strong a fascination—the fascination of incongruity made congruous. That she possessed fascination there was no doubt; but it was a personal magnetism, not an intellectual one. Those who merely read her history will probably find her without charm; but those who met her face to face felt it in the very marrow of their bones.

"You are always wanting people to get married," she said. "It seems to be your one idea of entertainment."

"I believe it is the only thing that permanently amuses anybody," repeated Isabel.

"And it fails to do even that with some."

"Now, Fabia, as I said before, I won't allow you to get absurd modern notions about matrimony. It is the fashion nowadays to pretend that most marriages are unhappy; but they're not—not a bit of it."

"You think it is all pure affectation?"

"I think it is all pure rot," replied Mrs. Seaton, with more force than elegance. "We are told all sort of nonsense about marriage being increasingly difficult under modern conditions, etc., and all sort of silly ways are suggested of untying the knot. As if modern conditions cancelled Divine laws! Some things alter as times change, and some things don't: and Commandments are among the things that don't. We may need a new Bradshaw every month; but we don't need a new Bible."

"Then do you mean to say that you do not believe that it is far more difficult for us to find happiness in marriage than it was for our grandmothers?" persisted Fabia, who had sufficiently saturated her mind with current literature to have caught the taint of certain phases of modern thought.

"Not an atom!" replied Ism■, with fine scorn. "It is merely the fashion nowadays for women to pretend that they don't fear God or love their husbands; while, as a matter of fact, ninety-nine women out of every hundred do both. We can't help doing it: it's what we were made for. A woman who at the bottom of her heart doesn't fear God and love her husband, is a freak; and the place for freaks is Barnum's."

"Then do you fear God and love your husband?" asked Fabia.

"Yes; with all my heart. And, what's more, I'm not ashamed of it, as so many women are. Ashamed of it, indeed! Why, the sun might just as well be ashamed of shining or the moon of giving light, as a woman of doing the two things for which she was created."

"If I had a husband," Fabia remarked, "I should never let him know how much I loved him."

"Shouldn't you? I know better."

And Isabel whistled softly to herself, in a manner at once inelegant and expressive.

"No. I should just wear his heart upon my sleeve, and peck at it whenever I felt inclined," Fabia persisted; "but I should never let him know what was in mine."

"So I used to think in my single days; but when you're married, you'll find the sleeve is on the other leg, so to speak. He'll wear *your* heart upon his sleeve, and do whatever he likes with it; but he won't peck at it, because men aren't pecking animals. And you'll love to have it so."

Fabia smiled. She was again reminded of her father and his cold baths and windy rides.

"And so you want me to marry that stupid Captain Gaythorne? Surely he is too stupid to want to marry me?"

"Not he! He adores you, and he'd be an excellent husband."

It was characteristic of Isabel that she did not say —or even think—that he would also be an excellent match.

Fabia noticed this omission, and put it down in her own mind to Isabel's credit. There was a strain of fine unworldliness about this finished woman of the world that highly commended itself to a girl brought up as Fabia had been. In the whole of Isabel's complex nature there was not one grain of snobbishness: somewhat rare praise to be given to the sons and daughters of Western nations, and Fabia accorded it ungrudgingly.

"But he has got a face like a cherub's," she objected.

"He has got a much better figure than a cherub's," retorted Isabel.

"I don't know that a cherub has a bad figure—what there is of it."

"But there's plenty of Charlie's figure—such as it is."

At that moment the butler flung open the door announcing, "Mrs. Gaythorne and Captain Gaythorne."

"Talk of the angels and the devil begins wagging his tail," murmured Isabel under her breath, as she rose to receive her visitors.

CHAPTER IV

THE GAYTHORNES

FABIA was right when she said that Charlie Gaythorne had the face of a cherub; and Isabel was still more correct when she asserted that he had not the figure of one. He was one of those huge men, with the form and strength of an athlete and the complexion and heart of a little child, who are essentially a home-product, and flourish nowhere save in British soil. Even more typically than Isabel herself, he represented the denizens of that happy land which lies securely within the precincts of the red cord. For over five centuries the Gaythornes had dwelt at Gaythorne Manor in the county of Mershire, and had done there whatsoever seemed right in their own eyes. In fact in the eyes of all Mershire whatsoever a Gaythorne did became right simply because it was done by a Gaythorne: so that it would have been difficult—not to say impossible—for a Gaythorne to do wrong.

But the Gaythornes were no unworthy race, trailing their honour in the dust and using their liberty as a cloak for lower things. They appreciated the duties and the responsibilities of their local infallibility as seriously as any Pope could have done; and fulfilled and accepted them accordingly. They were one of the families that make us realise the advantages of the

feudal system as it existed in the Middle Ages; and
that it had its advantages there is no doubt. The
Gaythorne men had ever been strong-limbed, light-
complexioned, and clean-living, fearing God and
honouring the King as all true squires should: and
the dames of their choice had ever been fair women,
not without discretion withal, whose husbands and
children had risen up and called them blessed.

Of intellectual gifts to this worthy house Nature
perhaps had been sparing. No Gaythorne had ever
written books, or painted pictures, or intruded his fingers
into the pies of State. There was little originality or
individuality in this blameless family's records: each
Squire Gaythorne had been *the* Squire Gaythorne of his
day—neither more nor less; each had been one of a
set, rather than a unique specimen. An excellent
match to the rest of the set, it is true, but not
interesting as a personality.

Charlie's father had been a perfect instance of the
accepted Gaythorne type; too perfect for there to be
anything else to be said about him. He died just after
an Indian frontier war, in which Charlie had won
distinction and nearly lost an arm; whereupon Charlie
left the service and entered into his kingdom; and was
now reigning at Gaythorne Manor, with his mother as
Grand Visier.

Charlie had a very high opinion of his mother. So
had she. There were few, if indeed any, matters small
or great, upon which Mrs. Gaythorne did not feel
herself competent to give an opinion: and Mrs.
Gaythorne's opinions were of the same nature as Royal
invitations; they were expected to be received as
commands. She had been—and still was—a fine-
looking woman, of the stately and statuesque order ·

and it would be difficult to say whether she most
resembled a highly religious Juno or a somewhat
worldly Madonna. She was not exactly clever; but
had a way of enunciating common-place remarks with
such force and authority that few of her hearers
recognized them as platitudes. She was a very good
woman according to her lights; and though those
lights might be lamps of a somewhat antiquated
pattern, they had proved themselves safe and sure
lanterns to guide more than one pair of wandering feet
into the way of peace.

Mrs. Gaythorne invariably dressed in black, thereby
showing respect for her husband's memory, and for S.
Peter's injunction as to female dress at the same time.
But her broad and ample bosom was as gay as any
flower-garden with various and many-coloured ribbons
testifying to the various virtues she adorned. She wore
a blue ribbon to show she was temperate, and a white
ribbon to show she was chaste; a yellow ribbon to
show she was Conservative, and a green ribbon to show
she was kind; an orange ribbon to show she was
Protestant, and a purple ribbon to show she was
truthful; and so on and so on through the whole prism
of the primary and secondary and even tertiary virtues.
Not that there was any need for the aid of these
coloured illustrations to prove to the most superficial
observer that Mrs. Gaythorne was all—and even more
than all—that she should be; but she wore them, as
she herself explained, for the force of example. She
was a sort of religious decoy-duck, decking herself in
those moral feathers which are popularly supposed to
produce moral birds. If Mrs. Gaythorne wore a ribbon,
all the women in Gaythorne village were expected to
wear it also; and, moreover, to practise that inward

and spiritual grace whereof it was the outward and
visible sign: a practice which did not come quite so
easy to some of them as it did to the lady of the manor.

Now in Charlie Gaythorne's life up to the present
time there had only happened three events of importance—the war in the Indian frontier, his father's death,
and his meeting with Fabia Vipart. It was these three
things that had made a man of him. With the first
two this story has not to deal; but without the last it
could hardly have been written.

The moment that Captain Gaythorne saw Fabia's
face he fell in love with it, and with her in her official
position as its owner. Of the subtlety of her intellect
he knew nothing at all, and cared less; it was enough
for him, and more than enough for his peace of mind,
that she was beautiful; and beautiful without doubt
she was.

There is a theory abroad among women that the love
which is founded upon intellectual gifts is more enduring
than the love which is founded upon personal attractions. Probably it does wear well, as all stiff and rather
wiry materials do; but softer and warmer stuffs wear
well also. The love that wears best of all—in fact the
only love that is really worth having—is not the love
that loves my love with B. because she is beautiful,
nor the love that loves my love with C. because she is
clever; but the love that loves my love with an S.
because She is She, and I am I, and we two are ourselves—and therefore each other—for all time and
eternity. There is no better reason for love than this;
which is still the better for being no reason at all.

Captain Gaythorne had not only fallen in love with
Fabia; he had made up his mind to marry the woman
whom he loved if the woman whom he feared approved.

And it was with the hope of obtaining this approval that he had brought Mrs. Gaythorne to call at Prince's Gardens this very afternoon, to be introduced to the lady of his choice. It was characteristic of Charlie—and therefore of all the Gaythornes—that the woman upon whose probable consent depended his proposal, was not the woman to whom he wished to propose, but his mother. It never even occurred to him that Fabia might object to marrying him; but it occurred to him with uncomfortable persistence that Mrs. Gaythorne might object to his marrying Fabia. And he felt that he could never make his offer of marriage if she did.

Yet Charlie had won a D.S.O. in India, and had been accounted a brave and dangerous enemy by the natives! Thus do our female relations make cowards of us all.

Isabel duly introduced Fabia to Mrs. Gaythorne, and then rang the bell for tea. At least she set out with the intention of ringing the bell, but Charlie, with his accustomed politeness, insisted on forestalling her; and, with unaccustomed haste and nervousness, succeeded in upsetting the boomerang, three vases, two photographs and a bunch of pampas-grass in the attempt. He was eager to repair his crime by picking them up again; but Isabel wisely begged him to forbear, and to upset nothing more; as she said she did not see the use of throwing good ornaments after bad ones—especially when the ornaments happened to belong to her.

"I shall be glad of my tea," remarked Mrs. Gaythorne, when the commotion had subsided; "I am thirsty." She spoke as impressively as if she were announcing some great scientific truth. "I have just been taking the chair at the annual meeting of the Society for the

Propagation of the Church Hymnal among the inhabitants of the Antarctic Circle, and am now on my way to preside at the annual meeting of the Anti-Tomato League, for the suppression of tomatoes as an article of diet; and consequently I require a little refreshment."

Mrs. Gaythorne was guilty of one human frailty, namely, an inordinate affection for presiding over public meetings. On this matter she knew neither temperance nor restraint. As some women take stimulants and others sedatives, so Mrs. Gaythorne took chairs.

"I never partake of this delicious beverage," the good lady remarked when at last her fleshly cravings had been satisfied, "without thinking of the teeming millions in China who still dwell in outer darkness; and without thanking the goodness and the grace which saw fit to plant me in so much more favourable surroundings—favourable alike to my natural and spiritual condition. Charles, the muffins."

Charlie hastened to lift a hot plate of these delicacies from the fireplace, and offer them to his hungry parent. This manoeuvre he carried out successfully, as he was gradually gaining strength and confidence, and was far less nervous than when he entered the room. At present all had gone smoothly between his mother and the young lady she had been brought to inspect; as he phrased it to himself, "They were getting on like a house on fire." True, the conversation had hitherto confined itself to such topics as might have been selected on the occasion of a visit from a thermometer to an aneroid; namely, the present weather and temperature, and the prospects of more weather and temperature in the future; but the interchange of such items of atmospheric information as had been public property for the last twenty-four hours, was carried on in so cordial a spirit that Charlie's spirits rose considerably. His mother, too, was evidently enjoying her tea, which was a good sign. But, alas! her carnal needs having been supplied, she unfortunately turned to higher subjects.

"Isabella, have you seen anything of Gabriel Carr lately?" she suddenly inquired, in her impressive voice.

"Yes, Mrs. Gaythorne. He was having tea with me last Sunday, and was as charming and delightful as ever."

"Having tea—and on a Sunday, too? I should have thought that a clergyman might have been better employed."

Isabel hastened to defend her friend.

"He was better employed, as it happened; he had been preaching in the afternoon at S. Cuthbert's, and was going on to preach at S. Hilda's, so he called and had tea on his way, in order not to waste his time by going back home."

"I cannot approve of Sunday visiting for clergymen; they ought to be preparing their sermons in the intervals between delivering them, and not to be wasting the time in eating and drinking. Charles, another muffin; and you, Isabella, I will trouble for a third cup of tea. I feel quite exhausted after my speech upon Antarctic Hymnology; and I shall never be able to do justice to the Anti-Tomato question unless I am fully fortified."

The dutiful Charles hastened to fortify his mother, assisted by Isabel; and the excellent lady calmly continued:

"I am distressed—deeply distressed—to hear that

Gabriel has introduced flowers upon the Communion
Table at his own Church; real flowers," she added, as
if artificial ones would have been less heinous in her
eyes.

"And why on earth shouldn't he?" demanded Isabel,
who was nothing if not courageous.

"Because it is Popish—and therefore wrong."

"That doesn't follow. In the first place, I don't agree
with you that it is even what you call Popish; but even
if it were, that wouldn't prove that it was wrong. The
two terms are not synonymous. You might just as well
say that because a thing was Protestant, it was therefore
right."

"That is precisely what I should say, Isabella. Moreover, the Romans are so narrow and bigoted, believing
that no man is right except themselves; and we all
know that narrowness and bigotry are most
un-Christian."

"They certainly are, Mrs. Gaythorne. But, all the
same, I cannot agree with you in calling things Roman
which are merely Catholic."

Charlie moved in his chair uneasily. He did not
want to marry Isabel, so it did not much matter what
her religious opinions were; but, all the same, he wished
she wouldn't inflame his mother—and just when things
seemed going so smoothly, too.

"Isabella," exclaimed Mrs. Gaythorne, "I am surprised
at you! You ought to know better!"

"I do know better: that's what I'm just saying,"
retorted the graceless one, with a laugh.

"Miss Vipart," said Mrs. Gaythorne, turning so
suddenly upon Fabia that that young lady fairly
jumped, "I trust that you do not approve of
Ritualism."

"Not at all," replied Fabia, with some truth: and Charlie breathed freely again.

"I am glad to hear that—very glad: it is a terrible snare to the young."

By "the young" Mrs. Gaythorne was referring to Isabel; but naturally Fabia did not grasp this.

"Why to the young especially?" she innocently asked.

"Because the young are foolish and ignorant, being sadly prone to run after any new fad that takes their fancy. Charles, what is the time? I must on no account be late for the Anti-Tomato meeting."

"Half-past five, mother. Shall I call you a cab?"

"Not for another ten minutes. My meeting does not begin until six o'clock; and I consider it just as much a sin against the true spirit of punctuality to be too early as too late. Isabella, I repeat that I do not understand your present attitude of mind."

"Probably not," replied Isabel. "Still, Mrs. Gaythorne, I repeat that if, as you say, Gabriel Carr has flowers upon the Altar, I think he is quite right."

"I did not say so, Isabella; how can you so misinterpret me? I said upon the Communion Table." And Mrs. Gaythorne looked stern.

But Isabel stuck to her guns.

"If it is right for us to beautify our own houses with flowers, why isn't it right to beautify God's House?"

"I consider that even in our own dwellings things of that kind are apt to harbour dust." And Mrs. Gaythorne glanced significantly at Isabel's overturned pampas-grass.

The latter could not help laughing.

"Naturally, when they are strewn upon the floor; but you will do me the justice to admit that this was my misfortune and Charlie's fault. Gabriel's flowers are not strewn upon the floor, you see; and it is Gabriel's flowers that we are discussing."

"Are they not, Isabella? There you make a great mistake. I have heard—and upon very good authority —that upon Palm Sunday Gabriel actually did have his Church strewn with willow-branches, which he chose to call palms. Willow-branches, mark you, actual willow-branches; and that seems to me even worse than having flowers upon the Communion Table. Miss Vipart"—here Fabia jumped again—"you will agree with me, I am sure; I think you said you were not a Ritualist."

"No; but still, Mrs. Gaythorne, you can hardly consider me an authority on such questions, as I am not a Christian."

Mrs. Gaythorne fairly bounced in her chair.

"Not a Christian, Miss Vipart? Surely I cannot have heard you aright."

Here poor Charlie interposed, wondering what evil spirit had prompted Fabia's untimely confession, to lure both her and himself to their destruction.

"Never mind, mother, what she is: she's all right— 'pon my soul, she is! And you'll be awfully late for your meeting if you don't go at once."

His mother brushed him aside as if he had been an irritating midge.

"Silence, Charles, I have yet four minutes." Then turning again to Fabia: "Do I understand you to say that you are a heathen, Miss Vipart?"

"Practically so, I am afraid."

"Then how do you expect to be saved?"

"I don't expect it. I don't expect anybody to be saved—not you nor I nor anybody else."

Here Charlie gasped, and even Isabel held her breath

The mere idea of not expecting Mrs. Gaythorne to be saved seemed almost stupendous in its blasphemy. Poor Charlie felt that all was over between himself and Fabia; and Isabel considered that whatever punishment the affronted lady chose to inflict upon the culprit, would be well deserved. So they both waited in helpless silence to see what form the merited chastisement would take.

But they had reckoned without their host.

Mrs. Gaythorne rose from her chair and walked majestically across the room to where Fabia was sitting, and laid her beautiful hand upon the girl's shoulder.

"My dear," she said, and her voice was no longer stern, but reminded Charlie of what it used to be when he was ill as a little boy; "I should like to see more of you, and to help you. If you will come to my house I will read to you and pray with you and do all that I can—under God—to teach you to be His child." Then, before the other three could recover from their astonishment: "Charles, my cab. It is twenty minutes to six."

Charlie and Isabel were dumbfounded. They thought they knew Mrs. Gaythorne out and out; but they had never calculated upon her behaving in this way. They were altogether out of their reckoning. For they had forgotten that there is a power stronger than prejudice or bigotry or invincible ignorance—a power which constrains men and women to-day, as it constrained the apostles of old—the power of the love of Christ.

CHAPTER V

POLITICAL LIFE

LORD WREXHAM was Prime Minister of England at the time when this story opens. He was a bachelor, for reasons which have been told elsewhere: he was a Premier, for reasons which have not yet been mentioned; the principal one of which was that nobody considered him specially suited—and therefore nobody else considered him specially unsuited—for the office. When half of a political party is crying out to be governed by A., and another half is shrieking equally loudly for the guidance of B., it happens not infrequently that the lot finally falls upon C., for the good reason that he is neither the one nor the other. Nobody is particularly delighted by his elevation to power — consequently nobody else is particularly annoyed by it — and so everybody is pleased all round; or, to speak more correctly, is not displeased, perfection of any kind never being more than approximate in politics.

Of course many men owe their success in life to the fact that they are themselves; but quite as many owe it to the fact that they are not somebody else—which is by no means the same thing, though to the superficial it may appear so.

Lord Wrexham would never have become Prime Minister because he was what he was: he was raised to that dignity and honour simply because he wasn't what he wasn't. Isabel Carnaby once nearly married him because he was not Paul Seaton: she also jilted him for the same sufficient reason; and it was this negative characteristic of his—this power, so to speak, of not being other people—that made it possible for a friendship still to exist between himself and her, and for Isabel and her husband to come and stay at Vernacre. Had she become Lady Wrexham, there would have been no friendship, and no possibility of one, between herself and Paul Seaton.

One might write a treatise upon the men—and their name is Legion—who are neither A. nor B., but simply C. They form a large and influential class of the community. They accomplish much in life; but by negative rather than by positive means. They own more wisdom than charm—more solid sense than strong personality. Theirs is not the magnetic force which sways men and subjugates women—which at first sight either irresistibly attracts or unaccountably repulses; but the staying power which commands respect rather than admiration—the gentle reasonableness which convinces rather than compels. These men of the C. Division of Society make uninteresting lovers, but unexceptionable husbands; they can carry out an accepted policy better than they can lead a forlorn hope. But usually they are honest men and good citizens; and almost invariably they are gentlemen.

Such a man was Lord Wrexham, the Prime Minister.

At the time of this story the then-sitting Parliament had passed its zenith, and there was no doubt that its successor would insist upon a thorough shuffling of the political cards. The party—as is not unusual with Liberal parties—was divided; otherwise Lord Wrexham

would never have been selected as its head. There was
no doubt that if the Liberals remained in power after
the General Election, a place in the Cabinet must be
found for Paul Seaton, the Under-Secretary for War,
and the leader of the more advanced section of the
party; and the inclusion of Seaton in a Cabinet meant
to a great extent the adoption by that Cabinet of the
policy which he advocated; as, in addition to being an
able man himself, he represented a section of the party
too large and influential to be set aside.

Now Mrs. Paul Seaton was an excellent wife, loving
and reverencing her husband with her whole heart as a
good wife should; but she did not agree with him in
politics. She had been brought up in the good old
Whig school by her uncle, Sir Benjamin Farley; and,
being a clever woman, she had not just accepted with
unquestioning simplicity the political tenets in which
she had been trained—she had carefully weighed them
for herself and had not found them wanting. When
mature judgment sets its seal of approval upon the
traditions of youth, those traditions become fixed
principles which it is difficult, if not impossible, to
uproot, as they crown with the sanction of later reason
the sanctity of earlier romance—a combination of
almost impregnable strength. Therefore Seaton's wife
could not see eye to eye with him on these matters;
much as she would have liked to do so. Although in
actual years she was slightly younger than her husband,
in her outlook upon life she was older than he, women
always maturing more quickly than men: consequently
her politics were those of an elderly man, while his were
those of a young one. He had still the hopefulness and
enthusiasm of the knight-errant, who is always setting
forth upon marvellous quests for the righting of the

wrong, or the succour of the helpless, or the seeing of
wonderful and unearthly visions; while she had already
learnt that the patching of old garments with new cloth
often makes the rent worse—that by endeavouring to
right a wrong, men sometimes increase it—and that the
time of visions is overpast. Paul's certainty that he
had discovered a panacea for most political and social
and commercial ills, and his joyous belief in the ultimate
success of the same, awoke no answering chord in
Isabel's breast. She was just as anxious as he was that
the country and the party should alike flourish; she was
considerably more anxious than he was that Paul Seaton
should eventually become Prime Minister; but she
differed from him as to the best means for procuring
these desirable ends. She had unbounded admiration
for her husband's powers—unlimited faith in his
abilities; but she feared that his over-sanguine disposition would lead him to strike before the iron was
quite hot enough, and to attempt to seize the prize
before it was in his grasp.

Paul's chief end in view was the good of his country:
Isabel's chief end in view was the advancement of Paul:
and she was terrified lest in a moment of misdirected
zeal or misguided altruism he should commit himself to
a course of action which should eventually militate
against his personal success. She hated to disappoint
him by refusing to share his enthusiasms; but she hated
still more to see him, as she thought, preparing disappointment for himself by building political air-castles
as unsubstantial as the pageant of Prospero.

From the bottom of her heart Isabel dreaded the
continuance of the Liberals in power after the General
Election. She knew that there must be fundamental
changes in the Government if the country decided on

enjoying six more years of Liberal administration:
Lord Wrexham's sitting-still policy could not last
through another Parliament. The new men with the
new measures would come to the front; and she shrank
from the consequence of what this coming to the front
might mean. Perhaps she was right—perhaps she
was wrong: that is not the business of a mere story-
teller to decide; but she was convinced in her own
mind that the change which her husband and his
friends were contemplating would, if carried out, result
in disappointment to themselves and their party, and
disaster to the country at large; and accordingly she
longed to induce them to stay their hands. Failing
this, she hoped that the Liberals would be beaten at
the next Election, and so be provided with a period of
opposition wherein to learn more about themselves and
their country than they knew at present.

She had lived long enough in the political world to
learn that there—even more than anywhere else—it is a
mistake to do anything in a hurry. But she had likewise lived long enough in the political world to learn
that there—even more than anywhere else—men are in
a hurry to do things; the old men because they are
old, and the young men because they are young; the
young men because there is so much to be done,
and the old men because there is so little time in
which to do it.

But the man who takes his politics from his wife may
be a good husband, but he is not a great politician.
Perhaps he is not altogether the best sort of husband,
either. Modern novelists may know better, but the
Apostle distinctly stated that the husband is the head
of the wife: daily newspapers may take a wider view,
but the Bible gives the wife no option save to be in

subjection to her husband.   The husband has the right
to rule by the most Divine right of kingship; and a
king who is afraid to exercise his royal prerogative is
hardly the highest type of king.

Therefore Paul Seaton believed that in certain things
—politics included—he knew better than his wife; and
he acted up to this belief in all uprightness and simplicity
of heart.

They did not quarrel over the question: they were
far too good comrades for that; but they held respectively their own opinions as to the best way of governing
the country and of improving its outlook; and they
talked it all out fully together.   Although Paul was
too much of a man to take his views from his
wife ready-made, there is no doubt that they were
considerably modified by Isabel's influence.   And no
blame to him for that!   For even the greatest of
the Apostles, who was himself a married man, permitted
that husbands should be won by the conversation of
the wives, so long as that conversation was coupled with
fear.

One evening after dinner Paul and Isabel were sitting
alone, Lady Farley having taken Fabia to the opera;
and were discussing the present political situation and
the prospects for the future.

"You are a faint-hearted fair lady," said Paul; "you
haven't the courage of your convictions."

"I haven't the courage of yours, you mean."

"It comes to the same thing."

Isabel shook her head.   "Not quite."

"Well, just you wait and see!   If we come in again
at the next Election—of which there seems every
possibility; and if they give me a place in the Cabinet—
of which there seems every probability; we shall bring

about such a revolution in domestic policy that the country will flourish as it has not flourished for years. It will be the dawning of a golden age."

But Isabel again shook her head. "You are always so sanguine, Paul. The golden age has never dawned yet; why should it begin now?"

"Dearest, you are growing very Conservative."

"Am I? I don't mean to. But if only you are one thing long enough, you suddenly find that you are another, the difference between one thing and another being merely a difference in time. If you go on being a Liberal long enough, you suddenly find yourself a Conservative; if you go on being a High-Churchman long enough, you suddenly find yourself an Evangelical; if you go on being a young woman long enough, you suddenly find yourself an old one. It isn't yourself that alters; you stand still and the world goes round; so that you inevitably get somewhere else by persistently stopping where you are."

"Silly little child! Just wait and see what the Liberals are going to do, and then you won't be a Conservative any longer. You must march with the times, my Isabel."

"I can't. I'm getting too old for such violent exercise. But, Paul, you always seem to think that any change is of necessity an improvement—that new lamps are invariably better than old."

"Well, aren't they? New brooms always sweep clean."

"And new boots almost always pinch."

Paul laughed. He was so sure of himself—so sure of his convictions—that his wife's warnings rolled off his back like water off a duck's. Underneath his somewhat staid and serious manner was hidden all the confidence

of the self-made man; while Isabel's cheerful and care-
less light-heartedness concealed the half-cynical wisdom
of the woman of the world.

"Darling," he said, with a smile; "your pessimism is
very funny."

"And so is your optimism, when you come to that,"
retorted Isabel.

And then they each laughed at each other like a pair
of happy children.

Suddenly Paul's face grew grave. "There is only
one thing that bothers me," he said.

"And what is that, darling?" Isabel's love was up in
arms for his succour and defence.

"Well, the Governorship of Tasmania will be vacant
shortly; and—"

Isabel interrupted him.

"How is that? The Gravesends' time is not nearly up.
It seems only yesterday that Lord Gravesend was made
Governor of Tasmania to comfort him and Eleanor for
losing the situation of New North Wales, when New
North Wales decided not to keep a pet Governor of its
own any longer."

"That is so; but Gravesend's health is breaking
down, and they are afraid he will have to resign
and come home before his time is up. And if the
Liberals are still in office when that happens, I am
desperately afraid that Wrexham will offer it to
me."

For a minute Isabel's heart stood still. Here was a
way out of all her troubles, and a very pleasant way
too. She would love above all things to be an
Excellency, as her aunt had been before her; and then
—if Paul were busy governing Tasmania—he would
not be hurrying on those measures for the improvement

of England, for which she did not think the times were yet ripe. She considered that the five years of Colonial Government would not only add to her husband's practical experience and increase his administrative ability, but would also enable the English constituencies to become accustomed to the new ideas which the Liberal party—either in office or in opposition—intended shortly to formulate.

"Oh! I should adore it," she exclaimed.

Paul's face grew still longer. "I was afraid you would. It was that which decided me that I couldn't refuse it if it were offered. Moreover, I don't think that a poor man like myself would be justified in refusing such a good thing, from a pecuniary point of view, although I'm afraid it would be the end of my political career."

"Not it! You are still a young man; you can afford to wait. At the end of five years you would be older and—yet not old." She was too wise to say "wiser," though the word was on the tip of her tongue.

"Still Gravesend may be able to hang on—at any rate until the new Parliament," said Paul, with his accustomed hopefulness; "and that would decide the matter for itself. Of course, if I were certain that a Liberal majority would again be returned at the General Election, I should be all right in saying 'No'; but if we are going out of office, and I shall have to drop my official salary, I don't feel it is fair to you to refuse this income and position."

Isabel came up to him and put her arms round his neck. "Darling, promise me that if it is offered to you, you won't refuse."

She was so certain that this would be the wisest course

for him as well as for her, that she did not hesitate to make the request.

"Of course, I promise, my own."

When she asked him in that tone, there was nothing on earth that he would not have promised her.

CHAPTER VI

ISABEL'S VIEWS

THE Secretary of State for War, Lord Kesterton, was dining with the Seatons one evening not very long after Fabia's appearance in their midst. The party consisted of Mr. Greenstreet (a rising author), Miss Vipart, and himself: and the conversation, as is usual in political circles, turned upon politics. There are no such people for talking shop as politicians: there is no shop more fascinating to talk; but in every world — be it the political, or the literary or the artistic or the religious, or any other world that ever was created— there is nothing so well worth talking as shop; and nothing that clever people are more ready, and stupid people more reluctant, to discourse upon.

There is something very weird and strange in the ordinary man's deeply ingrained horror of conversing upon the one subject, upon which he is competent to converse. He appears to consider it a virtue on his part to avoid, as if it were the plague, the one theme upon which he is at home, and to descant at length upon those matters about which he knows absolutely nothing. He is obsessed with a wild notion that he will become a bore to his hearers if he endeavours to interest them in those questions in which he himself is interested: little recking, poor deluded soul! that he is in far more

75

imminent danger of becoming a bugbear if he strives to
instruct them in matters about which they know far more
than he.

People are never really at their best except when they
are talking what is commonly called shop: for it is only
then that they thoroughly forget themselves, and lose
themselves in their subject. Even a plumber, if he talked
pure plumb, would be well worth listening to : he might
enlighten even the most enlightened among us as to why
he always leaves his inevitable white lead at home, and
has to go back again to fetch it before he can do anything ; and why he usually begins his day's work half
an hour before dinner-time : and might explain other
mysterious matters connected with his own peculiar
profession, which the lay mind has long striven in vain
to grasp. But take him off his own subject, and then
probably he will be very poor company indeed. And
what is true of him is more or less true of us all.

It must be admitted, however, that women are less
blameworthy in this respect than men — principally
because, though frequently less selfish, they are as
a rule more egotistic. They rarely shrink from talking
pure and unadulterated shop — especially with each
other. If the shop happens to be in any sense of
the word a work-shop, all well and good : the talker
is usually worth listening to ; but if the emporium
resolves itself into nothing more than a cook-shop
or a baby-linen warehouse — well, then Heaven help
the listener !

All of which brings us back to the starting-point, that
the Seatons and their guests were talking shop.

"How long do you think we shall be able to keep
ourselves in office, Lord Kesterton, with such a mighty
atom of a majority ?" asked Isabel. "It makes life hard

for the women and children of the party when the majority is so small that the men can hardly ever come home to dinner!"

"The men of the party ought to feel flattered, Mrs. Seaton."

Isabel shook her head. "Not if they knew the truth: men would very rarely feel flattered if they knew the truth. That is why really good, kind women try their best to keep it from them."

"A noble effort nobly sustained!" exclaimed Greenstreet.

"What is the unflattering truth in this case?" inquired Lord Kesterton, with the smile which Isabel never failed to evoke from him.

"The truth is that when the men don't come home to dinner, the women don't get enough to eat. Of course when we're dining out, it is all right: as we then not only get enough to eat, but we can tell all our best stories as effectively and untruthfully as we like, without having any tiresome husband at hand to pick the embroidery off. But no woman can order a proper dinner for herself alone: such a course is in direct opposition to her finest and most feminine instincts!"

Paul looked quite anxious. "Isabel, this is very wrong of you," he said. "I thought dinner went on just the same whether I was here or not."

"Ah! that is just what a man would think. To him dinner is the sort of thing that always must happen—like the sunrise, or the opening of Parliament or Christmas Day. But a woman loves to evade it if she can: it is the nature of her to do so—something in her make. Somebody once said that an ordinary woman's favourite dinner is an egg in the drawing-room: and it was quite true. I couldn't enjoy a Lord Mayor's

banquet half as much as the dear little scratch meals I
have on a tray in my boudoir before I go to the theatre
when Paul isn't here."

"I have long noticed," remarked Mr. Greenstreet,
"and marvelled at the universal passion of women
of all classes of society for what they call 'something
on a tray.' To the masculine mind, things on trays
are unsatisfying and repellent; but to the feminine
body they are as the very manna from Heaven. Miss
Vipart," he continued, turning to Fabia, "confess that
you too feel the fascination of something on a
tray."

"I do," replied Fabia; "I confess it unhesitatingly.
I enjoy quite as much as Mrs. Seaton does our little
picnics in the boudoir before we rush off to the
play."

Greenstreet sighed. "I suspected as much. Bread
eaten in secret is the favourite food of the normal woman.
It is merely another proof of her innate distaste for
everything that is straightforward and above-board."

"Not a bit of it," retorted the host; "it is a proof of
her innate unselfishness. If only her menkind are
properly cared for, she doesn't care a rap what happens
to herself."

"Hear, hear!" cried Isabel from the other end of the
table. "I have much pleasure in seconding the amendment of the honourable member. It is our glorious
unselfishness that is at the root of the tray-system; no
woman is capable of the deliberate and cold-blooded
selfishness of ordering a full, true, and particular dinner

Eve couldn't properly enjoy the celebrated apple until
she'd got her husband to share it with her; and we are

"You are, you are!" echoed the devoted husband; "and no one knows it better than my fortunate self."

"It is always elevating," said Lord Kesterton, "to hear the remarks made upon matrimony by Benedick, the married man."

"When his wife happens to be within earshot," added Greenstreet. "At a large dinner-party it is interesting and instructive to note the difference between the conversation of the men whose wives can hear what they are saying, and the conversation of the men whose wives can't."

"There isn't much they can't hear if they want to," said Paul, with a laugh. "The experienced husband doesn't trust too much to any apparent disability on that score."

"For shame, for shame, Mr. Seaton, for letting out the secrets of the prison-house in this way!" exclaimed Fabia.

Greenstreet fairly groaned. "Secrets, good Heavens! She calls them secrets! She thinks that the world cannot see the manacles of the model husband, or else mistakes them for garlands of roses! For an unrivalled power of sprinkling a few grains of sand on the top of her bonnet, and thinking that she thereby successfully hides herself and her foibles from the trained eye of man, give me, not the much-maligned ostrich, but woman, lovely woman!"

"All the same, Mr. Greenstreet," Fabia persisted, "I don't believe that men do see the faults and failings of their wives."

"Don't you, Miss Vipart?" replied Greenstreet. "Well then, all I can say is that Seaton must be a very clever man. You've been staying in this house for several weeks now, haven't you?"

"Yes; five."

Greenstreet looked thoughtful. "A very clever man A marvellously clever man! Seaton, I have always admired your varied gifts, but until this moment I never did you full justice."

Isabel laughed with delight. She had a great liking for Mr. Greenstreet because he always talked nonsense to her, and Isabel was one of the women who revel in the talking of nonsense. Lord Wrexham had never talked nonsense to her; if he had, she would probably by now have been the wife of the Prime Minister, instead of only the wife of the Under-Secretary for War. And even Paul did not talk as much nonsense to her as she would have liked; he would perhaps have been wiser in his dealings with her if he had not always been quite so wise.

"Seaton," Greenstreet continued, "gifts such as yours cannot languish in oblivion; a man with your marvellous slow - sightedness and your unparalleled dulness of perception cannot fail to end your days as either Emperor of China or Prime Minister of England."

Here his hostess interrupted him. "Talking of Prime Ministers reminds me that you've never answered my question, Lord Kesterton. How long is Wrexham going to keep the party in office with such a small majority?"

"Considerably longer than anybody else could do in his place," replied Lord Kesterton; "that is all I can tell you."

"Why will Lord Wrexham keep the party in office longer than other people could?" asked Fabia.

"Because, my dear young lady, he possesses all the qualities requisite for an ideal Prime Minister."

"And pray what are they?" continued Fabia, pursuing the subject, pleased that she should—if only for a moment—have diverted the attention of the Secretary of State for War from Isabel to herself.

"His first and finest gift," Lord Kesterton replied, "is the solid absence of anything approaching brilliancy. The great heart of the English people does not love brilliant men."

"Why not?"

"Because, my dear Miss Vipart, it does not understand, and therefore does not trust them. Human nature rarely trusts what it cannot understand; and how can a nation, whose blood is beer and whose body is roast-beef, place confidence in persiflage or find security in epigram?"

"And what other fine quality has Lord Wrexham besides the absence of brilliancy?" Fabia further inquired.

"He is very practical; and he has an admirable temper."

"And is an admirable temper such an excellent thing in statesmen?" asked Greenstreet.

"Most excellent," was Lord Kesterton's reply; "as indeed in everybody else. The statesman who loses his temper loses his followers; the man who loses his temper loses his friends."

"And what about the woman who loses her temper?" asked Fabia.

Lord Kesterton bowed with mock gallantry. "There is no such person, my dear young lady. A woman never loses her temper."

"Some of them manage to do something singularly like it at times," remarked Greenstreet.

"No," Lord Kesterton repeated; "a woman never

loses her temper; she merely now and again condescends
to give certain persons what she calls a piece of her
mind."

" And what is the difference between doing that and
losing her temper ? "

" The whole difference in the world, my dear Miss
Vipart : the difference between an involuntary loss and
a votive offering ; between the payment of a water-rate
and a libation to the gods."

" Between having one's pocket picked and giving at a
collection," added Isabel ; " and between compulsory
taxation and the revenues of the S.P.C.K."

" Precisely ! " agreed Lord Kesterton.

" And what other qualities entitle Lord Wrexham to
be an ideal Prime Minister ? " Fabia went on.

" He invariably says the obvious thing ; and —
whenever it is possible—does nothing at all. The
great art of popular instruction is to teach people
what they already know ; just as the great secret
of successful leadership is to learn how to stand
absolutely still."

" And what else ? " asked Paul, who was enjoying this
disquisition upon his leader.

" He is very prudent, and he is very Protestant ; and
prudence and Protestantism are the two great corner-
stones of English national life."

" And very good corner-stones, too," added Paul.

" It seems to me," remarked Fabia, " that an ideal
Prime Minister must have all the virtues that begin with
a P. He must be prudent and patient, and practical
and Protestant."

Isabel gave a deep sigh. " I don't think you'll ever be
an ideal Prime Minister, Paul; because you're not very
patient, and you're not at all prudent, and you never say

the obvious thing unless it is the thing that is obviously too good to be true."

Paul endeavoured to clear himself. "Well, anyway, I'm Protestant enough," he said, in self-justification.

Isabel sighed again. "Yes, you are charmingly Protestant; but I'm not sure that that is enough in itself, though of course it is a great deal." Then she put her head on one side, and looked at her husband through her eyelashes as if he were some work of art that she was appraising. "I love my love with a P. because he is Protestant, I hate him because he is progressive; he lives in Prince's Gardens, lives upon platitudes, his name is Paul, and I'll give him the Premiership for a keepsake."

Paul smiled, but he winced a little underneath the smile. Isabel was sometimes so terribly accurate in hitting the nail precisely in the middle of its head.

"My wife is always reproving me for being unpractical and idealistic," he said, turning to Lord Kesterton.

"Is she indeed? Then you will do well to listen to her, Seaton. Men who are married never lack the opportunity of hearing the truth about themselves; and if they are wise men they will sometimes avail themselves of it."

"Hear, hear!" applauded Isabel.

"But—with all due deference to my wife and the other members of the Government—I cannot give up my belief that it is enthusiasm that really makes the world go round; I cannot forswear my creed that it is in what you call idealism that the hope for the future of the race and the nation lies. Surely it is by appealing to the highest in human nature that we evoke the highest; it is by treating men as reasonable beings that we make them reasonable beings; it is by regarding them as heroes that we enable them to attain to heroism."

Lord Kesterton nodded his head two or three times. "Perhaps," was all he said.

Paul went on: "I think all you wise and prudent people make one initial mistake: you confuse cause and effect. You believe that men must be trained to bear responsibility before they can be trusted with responsibility; that they must become good citizens before they can act as good citizens; in short, that they must never be allowed to wet their feet until they have learned to swim."

"It would save a good many lives from drowning if that rule were carried out," murmured Isabel, *sotto voce*. But her husband did not hear her. She did not intend that he should.

"Now I maintain," he continued, his usually grave face alight with enthusiasm, "that you are putting the cart before the horse. I hold that it is only by being entrusted with responsibility, that men learn how to use responsibility; that it is only by reading, that a man learns how to read; that it is only by walking, that a child learns how to walk. I do not believe that men perform heroic deeds because they are heroes; I believe that they finally become heroes because they have got into the habit of performing heroic deeds. Our actions are not the outcome of our characters; it is our characters that are the result of our actions. A king is not a king because he knows how to rule; he knows how to rule because he is a king."

"Then your idea is," said Kesterton, "that we must not withhold power from any section of the people until we believe they are fit to be entrusted with power;

but we must entrust them with it in order to make them
fit?"

"Exactly," replied Paul. "And I further believe
that the more power the people have, the more wisely
they will use it; that the more implicitly we trust them,
the more fit they will show themselves to be implicitly
trusted."

"You believe in human nature more than Isabel
does," said Fabia.

"But he doesn't love it anything like as much,"
retorted the maligned hostess. "He begins believing
that every woman is an angel and every man a hero;
and then when the angel begins to scold, and the hero
flies in terror to his club for refuge, Paul is utterly
disgusted, and washes his hands of the pair for ever.
Now I know that at heart every man is a coward and
every woman a shrew, and I like them all the better
for it. It makes them seem more like relations of ours,
with a strong family likeness."

"It is rather a hard saying on your part to call
every man a coward," objected Lord Kesterton, much
amused.

"No; it isn't. On the contrary, it proves that I am
able fully to appreciate them when they do perform
heroic deeds. If a hero behaves like a hero, there is
nothing in it; he can't help behaving like a hero, any
more than a sewing-machine can help behaving like a
sewing-machine, or an umbrella can help behaving like
an umbrella. But if a coward suddenly behaves like
a hero, it is something very splendid and wonderful indeed; just as it would be if an umbrella
in an emergency ran up a seam, or if a sewing-
machine spread sheltering wings to ward off the
rain."

MICROCOPY RESOLUTION TEST CHART

(ANSI and ISO TEST CHART No 2)

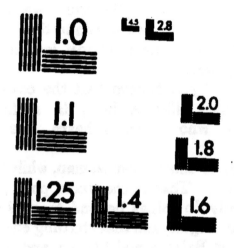

APPLIED IMAGE Inc

1653 East Main Street
Rochester, New York   14609   USA
(716) 482 - 0300 - Phone
(716) 288 - 5989 - Fax

"The soundness of your reasoning is only surpassed by the striking nature of your metaphors," murmured Greenstreet.

Isabel continued: "Naturally, then, I am much fonder of my shrews and my cowards, who on special and great occasions behave like angels and heroes, than Paul is of his heroes and angels, who in everyday life behave like cowards and shrews. I always pity and love, and am sometimes surprised into acute admiration he always exhorts and demands, and is almost invariably disappointed and disgusted."

"Then," cried Fabia, "you believe that the coward who sometimes behaves like a hero, is a finer man than the hero who often behaves like a coward?"

"Of course he is; he is much more human, while his act is much more Divine. That is the whole point; it is when people suddenly do things beyond themselves that the age of miracles begins, and that startling effects are produced. Look at Balaam and his ass, and how awfully upset he was when she did what he believed she was incapable of doing, and reproved him. But do you suppose it would have had any effect upon him if instead of his ass it had been his wife who began scolding and objecting and begging him to stay at home? Not a bit of it. It would have been just what he was used to and what he expected, and would have had no effect upon him at all."

Paul smiled fondly at his wife. "Even if you succeed in convincing us that every man is a coward, nothing will induce me to accept the dogma that every woman is a shrew."

"Now for my part," remarked Greenstreet, "I con-

sidered that by far the more plausible of the two tenets
of Mrs. Seaton's creed."

Isabel laughed gaily.   " Therefore you must see that
when a woman behaves like an angel it is all the more
credit to her."

" Doubtless it would be ; but personally I have never
come across an instance," replied the author.

" I have," said Paul quietly ; " and such a striking
one that it has apparently led me into the not
uncommon error of generalizing from a single
instance ! "

Isabel blew him a kiss. " Thank you," she said.
Then she went on ; " All of which is very nice and
interesting, but it hasn't answered my question as to how
long Lord Wrexham thinks that the Liberals will remain
in office."

" Until the next Dissolution anyway. 1 feel sure
that if we were beaten upon a question in the House
of Commons, he would take the verdict of the country
before he would resign."

" And do you think we shall get a majority at the
next General Election, Lord Kesterton ? "

" That I cannot tell, Mrs. Seaton ; it lies in the lap of
the gods. But one thing I can say : I would rather be
beaten altogether than continue in office with as small
a majority as we have at present. Too small a majority
in the House of Commons is a source of weakness to
any Government."

" I believe that we shall have a tremendous majority
at the next General Election," cried Paul ; " a majority
that will enable us to do great things."

" You do not think your husband is right, Mrs.
Seaton ? " said Lord Kesterton, as Isabel rose from the
table and he moved her chair for her to pass.

"No," she replied slowly, as she looked with half-envious admiration at the enthusiasm shining in Paul's eyes: "I often don't think he is right; but I still oftener wish that I were as wrong as he is!"

CHAPTER VII

GABRIEL CARR

IN a new and hideous vicarage, built in a new and hideous suburb of London, dwelt the Reverend Gabriel Carr. It was not a slum: if it had been, he could have borne it better: it was merely a highly respectable and unbeautiful spot, inhabited by a highly respectable and unbeautiful population. For several years he had worked in the East End, and had fought face to face with Apollyon in that Valley of the Shadow. A hard fight, it is true—a struggle to the very death: but a battle not without a certain dramatic force and reality, which inspired the fighter with courage and strength. Then the Bishop appointed Carr to the forming of a brand-new parish in the centre of a brand-new suburb —one of those staring, yellow-brick suburbs which are increasingly wont to disfigure the face of the earth in the immediate neighbourhood of large cities. Here Gabriel worked as hard as he had ever worked in the Valley of the Shadow, and was as ready to fight; but he was forced to admit to his own soul that the work was less interesting, the battle less exciting. With a criminal class that publicly blasphemed and privately defied the Deity, he knew how to deal; but not with a lower middle-class that outwardly patronized and inwardly ignored Him. Carr's new parishioners seemed far too smug and self-satisfied to need salvation at all; and far too respectable and independent to accept it as a free gift, if they did. He felt that they would resent receiving even the grace of God as a charity, but would expect it to be paid for out of the rates: and, that being so, they had a right to it, without the intervention of any priest or prophet whatsoever.

Nevertheless—so great was Carr's power of success and so strong his personality—he succeeded in doing a good work even in that unpromising locality. When first he was appointed Vicar of S. Etheldreda's, he folded his flock in one of those galvanized iron sanctuaries, which are anything but chapels-of-ease in nature whatever they may be in name: and there he and his people for several years suffered tortures from the frost of winter and the heat of summer by turns. But, with his usual unfailing energy, he gradually collected sufficient money to build a permanent Church, and sufficient worshippers to fill it. He believed that Ritualism and Revivalism were the only two forms of religion which have power to attract the masses; that it is through the seeing eye and the hearing ear that the hearts of the uneducated are reached; so that, while to the wise and learned the visible sign is but the expression of the invisible reality, to the unlearned and ignorant the invisible reality is the explanation of the visible sign. Therefore Carr availed himself of both these handmaids of religion in the services of S. Etheldreda's.

But he also believed that though Revivalism may plant and Ritualism may water, it is not in the power of either of these to give the increase. Results he trusted to higher Hands; and—like all men who do

their best, and then leave the issues entirely in those
Hands—he was not disappointed. He succeeded at
last at S. Etheldreda's as he had succeeded in the
slums; for even crass respectability is not permanently
proof against the power of God.

Gabriel Carr had two distinguishing characteristics:
an intense love for what was healthy and beautiful, and
an equally intense hatred for what was unhealthy and
morbid. And perhaps his upbringing had much to do
with this. An Oxford man, he had drunk deep into the
spirit of that venerable and beautiful city, and had
saturated his mind with its traditions and beliefs. Before
he won his scholarship at Oriel, he was for some years
at the Royal Naval School at Eltham, a school originally
founded by William IV. for the sons of Naval officers,
but long since also thrown open to all sorts and conditions
of boys whose parents are wise enough to avail themselves
of that opening: and a school, moreover, which is not
only a home of sound learning and of admirable physical
and mental training, but is also an emporium of two
other things equally good in their own way, namely, fresh
air and sunshine. In after years, whenever Gabriel
wanted to conjure up before his "inward eye" an
embodied vision of sunshine, he always thought of
Eltham College: of the large and lofty class-rooms,
where the truant sunbeams were always peeping in,
pointing their golden fingers at the masters and winking
at the boys, as if lessons were the greatest joke in the
world from a sunbeam's point of view: of the bright and
airy dormitories, where the summer sun awoke the
sleepers long before it was getting-up time, and yet
"never came a wink too soon, nor brought too long a
day": and, most of all, of the cricket-field—surely one
of the loveliest cricket-fields in England!—which lay in

a shallow cup among the green Kentish uplands, filled
to overflowing with a wealth of the richest sunlight that
Nature ever flung out of her stores of gold. Beautiful
was the cricket-field in the early morning, when the
youthful day had not yet gathered up the showers of
diamonds which had fallen from his hands while he was
yet half asleep: still more beautiful was it in the golden
afternoon, when happy boys played cricket in the sunshine, and still happier parents watched them from the
shade of the fine old elm-trees that stood as sentinels
around: and most beautiful of all when the shadows
began to lengthen, and the old elm-trees stretched out
their arms and wrote strange hieroglyphics upon the
pavement of emerald at their feet.

Thus the sunshine of Eltham and the shades of Oxford
carved their tracery upon the character of Gabriel Carr,
and helped to make him into the manner of man that he
was.

"I am going to have tea with Gabriel Carr this afternoon," said Isabel to her guest, the day after the little
dinner-party in Prince's Gardens; "will you come with
me?"

"Certainly. It will interest me to see Mr. Carr in his
own home and in the midst of his usual surroundings:
it will help me to understand him. I do not think we
ever really know much about other people until we have
seen them in their accustomed environment."

Mrs. Seaton shook her head. "It won't help you
much in understanding Gabriel; as his surroundings are
not an atom like himself."

"I didn't say they were; or even think it."

"And if you expect him to resemble those insects
who look like twigs because they live among twigs, or
those animals who have white coats from dwelling in

Arctic regions, you will be disappointed. He lives in a square house built of dirty yellow bricks—one of those dreary, unornamented houses, that look as if they had no eyebrows or eyelashes, and hadn't the time to wash their faces; and yet his own character is not built of yellow brick at all, but has as many foundations as the New Jerusalem, and is of as rare and costly materials."

"Just so. Unlikeness may be as certain a result as likeness. That is my whole point."

"Oh! my dear, you are too subtle for me."

"Not at all. The whiteness of a diamond is as much the result of its environment as that of a polar bear is the result of his. Sometimes like produces like—sometimes like produces unlike; but both productions are equally results."

"I suppose," suggested Isabel, "that the difference depends upon the strength of the environment: two blacks must be very black indeed before they can make a white."

"No; it depends upon the nature of the thing itself."

Fabia answered rather shortly. Isabel's habit of speaking lightly and half-mockingly about everything, always irritated her. She took life and herself very seriously, and was as yet too young to have learnt how nearly akin are tears and laughter. She did not know that smiles are oftener a surer symptom than tears of a tender and understanding heart.

But Isabel pursued her way unabashed. "I see; no amount of fervent heat would turn a piece of carbon into a polar bear; while the most intense and microbe-destroying frost wouldn't change a polar bear into a diamond tiara; the raw material differing in the two cases. It's like the difference between exports and

imports: one is one and the other is the other, and it is
a mortal sin against political economy to confound the
two; but what is really the difference between them I've
never been able to understand."

Fabia's lips curled slightly. Ignorance of any kind
was contemptible to her.

"I should have thought that you, the wife of a
distinguished politician, would have known a thing
like that. I wonder your husband has never explained it
to you."

"He has, often; that's why I don't understand it.
You will find, my dear Fabia, when you have lived as
long as I have, that all life's mysteries are compre-
hensible, but not its explanations. I have great
sympathy with the old woman who said she 'understood the "Pilgrim's Progress," and she hoped soon,
with the help of the Lord, to be able to understand
the key.' I always understand everything until it is
explained to me; and then I never understand it again
as long as I live."

Fabia did not speak, but silently marvelled. How
could any woman thus positively glory in apparent
ignorance and stupidity — and a woman, too, as
naturally sharp and clever as Isabel? If she had
found herself on any point wanting in knowledge or
intelligence, she would never have given herself away
by openly admitting it; but Isabel took the world at
large into her confidence with regard to her own
deficiencies. But this again—though Fabia did not
know it—was merely a consequence of the red cord.

"For instance," Isabel rattled on, "I used to understand perfectly the difference between exports and
imports. I said to myself: 'The one goes out and the
other comes in;' and that seemed as plain as the nose

on your face—which, by the way, on yours is a
singularly pretty one. But then Paul must take it
into his head to expound to me that what went in at
one ear, so to speak, came out at the other, and was
changed from an import to an export in the process.
And from that moment I was lost. I never again
understood the difference between an export and an
import, and I never shall."

Fabia wondered whether Isabel knew she was a fool
when she talked like this. She did not grasp that it
was because Isabel knew she was no fool—and knew
that her world knew it also—that she amused herself
—and it—by sometimes behaving as one.

" In the same way," the latter continued, " I used to
understand perfectly whether the twentieth century
begins with the year nineteen-hundred or the year
nineteen-hundred-and-one, until the day Paul explained
it to me by taking a hundred apples out of one basket
and putting them into another: and from that day to
this I've never known when the twentieth century
begins—or whether it is like eternity, and has no
beginning at all."

" But we were talking about Mr. Carr," suggested
Fabia.

" So we were. How clever of you to remember! To
know what one is talking about is one of the highest
forms of intelligence. There is only one form higher
—to know what other people are talking about. Well,
will you come and have tea with him this afternoon,
or will you not? It is purely optional; not compulsory; as education is, and as adult vaccination ought
to be."

" I have already told you that I will. I shall be
immensely interested to see Mr. Carr in that home of

his own, which you have assured me is so unfit a casket
for the jewel that it contains."

"Don't be sarcastic, my dear. Men hate a satirical
woman like poison; and a sharp tongue is to them as a
serpent's tooth."

Fabia did not answer, but she inwardly raged. She
always resented Isabel's easy assumption of authority
and superior knowledge; and when, as in the present
case, Fabia knew that her hostess was in the right, she
hated it still more. And there was no doubt that Isabel
frequently was in the right. A woman who has lived
for nearly forty years in the heart of the world, and
has kept her eyes open and unblinded by temper or
prejudice, has generally seen a good deal.

After lunch the two ladies set out for S. Etheldreda's
Vicarage. They soon left what Isabel called the
habitable parts of the earth—that is to say, those
portions of London occupied by its more fashionable
denizens—behind them, and drove through long miles
of mean streets until they reached the dreary suburb
where Gabriel Carr had his abode. And specially
dreary it appeared on this April afternoon when
the rest of the world was alive with the message of
spring. At last they found their way to the yellow
brick Vicarage, and were duly welcomed by its
master.

There was no doubt that the Vicar of S. Etheldreda's
was a singularly handsome man; his beauty, which
was the bequest of an Italian grandmother, being of
that first-class order which impresses the beholders
more with a sense of how fair is the soul that inhabits
such a tenement, than with a consciousness of the
beauty of the body which that soul informs. The
only flaw in the otherwise almost statuesque perfection

of his appearance was to be found in his hands, which
were more like those of an artisan than of a gentleman.
But these also, in their own way, bore testimony to the
beauty of his soul; for he had spoiled them by the
manual labour which he had done as a comrade and
an example to the youths in his parish. He had
worked willingly with his hands in order to teach and
help them to work willingly with theirs; he had opened
a carpenter's shop, and had instructed them himself on
certain evenings every week in all simple and useful
forms of carpentry. For the rest, he was dark and thin,
of a light and graceful build, and with a face expressive
of intelligence and spirituality. So ascetic was his
type, and so refined his style of countenance, that he
looked more like a mediæval monk than a modern
parish priest.

He received his visitors with many expressions of
delight, and conducted them into his bare and bachelor
drawing-room—one of those typical bachelor drawing-
rooms which are, so to speak, full of the absence of a
woman. He might have flowers upon his Altar, but he
had not one upon his mantel-piece; there were none of
those pretty knick-knacks about, whereby women create
a home atmosphere, and at the same time, harbour dust;
but everything looked as cold and clean and unlived-in
as a bedroom that is prepared for the nursing of a fever-
patient. The fire had evidently been lighted just long
enough to awaken into life all the dampness dormant in
the room; and it crackled to itself in that spiteful way
which fires have when they think they ought not to
have been lighted at all. Gabriel had only three
photographs in his room—namely the interior of his
Church, and the exteriors of his mother and his Bishop;
and even these had nothing in the shape of a frame to

soften the severity and squareness of their cardboard
outlines. An unfurnished tea-tray was already upon
the table; but as there seemed little hope of its being
occupied for some considerable period, Gabriel suggested
that they should go and inspect the church to fill up
the interval until such good time as the kettle should
see fit to boil.

So into S. Ethedreda's they went; and were struck
—as were all who entered that Church—with the
difference between its plain and unimposing outside
and its rich and ornate interior. Outwardly it was an
ugly and unassuming structure; but inwardly it was a
perfect instance of how beautiful Divine Service may be
when conducted according to the rites of that branch of
the Holy Catholic Church established in this realm.
Gabriel was strictly Anglican: he allowed nothing in
his Church that was not permitted—nay, enjoined—by
the Ornaments Rubric. He would have scorned to
borrow from Rome any outward form which signified no
corresponding doctrine in the section of the Church to
which he owed his allegiance: he would not even
permit the children in his Sunday-schools to observe
any act of ritual until they had first been taught the
fundamental truth which that act symbolized. He
knew how helpful it oftentimes is to those who see
through a glass darkly, to be reminded by outward
symbolisms of the great truths upon their acceptance of
which depends the salvation of their souls. But he
knew also that while the ceremony which serves
to recall and expound a truth may be a help, the
meaningless form which has no root in reality
must always be a hindrance. Therefore Gabriel was
no mere Ritualist for Ritualism's sake; but he prided
himself upon showing what the services of the Church

of England really are when rightly and rigidly performed. Whatever of symbol and form and ornament this branch of the Catholic Church allows, of that he availed himself to the full; rejecting firmly, however, all mediæval and modern accretions or superstitions, and reverting it as far as possible to the usages of the early and undivided Church.

The beauty of everything within the walls of S. Etheldreda's appealed very strongly to Isabel's artistic temperament. Hers was one of the natures which instinctively recognize the indissoluble connexion between the Beautiful and the True, and which understand that Beauty can never be a rival of Truth, but is rather an exponent of it. Upon Fabia, however, the effect was altogether different. Hers was a more sensuous nature than Isabel's, and she therefore rated the intrinsic excellence of anything in an inverse proportion to its appeal to her senses. She believed that in this she was more purely intellectual than her friend ; but here she was mistaken. It is no proof of intense spirituality when men and women regard as snares of the devil all the beauties of Nature and of art : but rather the reverse. He may be a good man in whom the flesh lusteth against the spirit and the spirit against the flesh ; but he is a still better man in whom the flesh is so subservient to the spirit that the one expresses and typifies the other, turning into a very sacrament every incident in daily life, so that God may be all in all.

When Gabriel and his guests returned to the Vicarage the tea was ready—that strong, rampant tea, stiffened with self-supporting London cream, which many men and few women enjoy. And the Vicar poured it out himself.

"I see you have chairs in your Church instead of pews, Mr. Carr," remarked Fabia; "and I want to know why chairs are always considered more virtuous than pews."

"They are not," he replied, "except in so far as economy is a virtue. They are much cheaper: that is my sole reason for having them."

"They are nothing like as comfortable as pews," said Isabel; "because there's nowhere to put your legs— let alone your umbrella; and my umbrella ought to have a prize for regular attendance at public worship."

"And do you feel you couldn't bring it to S. Etheldreda's, Mrs. Seaton?"

"There would be nowhere for it to sit if I did. That's why I hate chairs; they are so cramped. It may be the right thing to be 'content to fill a little space,' as the hymn-writer was; but I am not content to fill a little space, because I fill it so completely that there are no outlying districts where I can plant my gloves and my boa and my other etceteras; and that is so very uncomfortable both for me and for them."

"Why don't you annex another chair?" suggested Fabia.

"Oh, that would look so horribly greedy and selfish! I don't mind annexing a little bit of extra pew: in fact, I feel that belongs to me by right, on the same principle as a ditch always belongs to the owner of the other side of the hedge—a sort of perquisite. But coolly to annex a whole empty chair, on which an immortal soul might and ought to be sitting—I couldn't do such a thing at any price! I've always been led to believe that it was things like that—with a difference—which brought about the French Revolution."

"Then, Mr. Carr, you don't consider pews sinful?" inquired Fabia.

"Not at all; merely expensive. Sin is always expensive, but expense is not necessarily sinful; and pews are harmless if costly pleasures."

"And you don't object to people paying rents for them, as so many Churchmen do?"

"Oh! but I do object, Miss Vipart—object with all my heart. I consider it contrary to all the principles of Christianity for there to be any difference in the House of God. There the rich and the poor meet together to worship the Maker of them all; and they meet on an equal footing of dependence upon Him. Have pews, by all means, if you can afford them; but let the pews be free."

"You've trodden upon one of Mr. Carr's most carefully cultivated corns," said Isabel, with a laugh.

"That is so," admitted Gabriel. "People—especially English people—love to have something which sets them, as they think, apart from their fellows—something which proves that they are not as other men, or even as this publican. They are never so happy as when they stick up a red cord somewhere, and go themselves on one side of it, leaving everybody else on the other. I feel sure that most British subjects—when they indulge in dreams of Heaven—substitute a red cord for those pearly gates which are never shut. But the cord is fastened across pretty often, and is only let down in favour of themselves and of such of their friends as entirely agree with them."

Fabia was roused from her usual apathy; at last she had found someone who understood.

"I know what you mean by your red cord," she said,

slowly. "It is very common—very cruel—and very English."

"Cruel? I should just think it is cruel," exclaimed the Vicar. "It is positively merciless!"

"I think you exaggerate it altogether," said Isabel; "to me it is more amusing than anything else. After all, if a little bit of red cord at one-and-elevenpence-halfpenny a yard constitutes human happiness, why on earth shouldn't people have as much of it as they want —enough to hang themselves, in fact?"

"For the good reason that they don't hang only themselves; they hang other people, Mrs. Seaton, to whom the operation is less necessary and more painful."

"Well, for my part I like it," replied Isabel coolly; "it may be wicked, but I do. I love to see a red cord fall down before me, like the walls of Jericho, and rise up again the moment I have passed through. Everybody feels like that; it's human nature. And if you try to make out that the Israelites didn't enjoy it when seas and rivers made way for them and not for the Canaanites and Egyptians, I simply shan't believe you: and the Israelites were considered very good people in their way."

Gabriel smiled. "Yes, in their way; but it wasn't the Christian way, you see; and ours is. That makes all the difference."

Isabel sighed. "I forgot that. Yes; I suppose one could hardly call them Christians."

"Hardly, Mrs. Seaton."

Gabriel was still smiling. He knew Isabel; knew that she was far better than she made herself out to be —far better than she herself had any idea of. He knew that her half-childish vanity delighted in passing through

social barriers; but he also knew that more than half
her delight consisted in being able to take other people
with her. She might have enjoyed crossing the Red
Sea on dry land; but she would never have consented
to leave Pharaoh's host behind.

She sighed again. "Oh, dear! Do you remember
the baby in 'Alice in Wonderland' that made a very
ugly baby but a very handsome pig? Well, I seem
to make a very ugly Christian but a very handsome
Jewess: I am referring, of course, to moral beauty. I
am sorry to be so wicked, but I do like red cords, and
it's no use pretending that I don't. I believe the reason
why I always enjoy the preaching at S. Margaret's,
Westminster, is because there is a red cord there,
licensed to hold only members of Parliament and their
wives."

"I'll be bound you always want to take somebody
else in with you," said Carr.

"Yes, I do: partly from good nature and partly
because it is against the rules. Members of Parliament
are only allowed one wife, even on Sundays, poor things!
And it does seem such short commons, especially when
there is a popular preacher turned on!"

"A red cord is just the sort of thing you would like,"
said Fabia, with suppressed scorn. "I should have
expected it of you."

"Then I'm glad you are not disappointed," retorted
Isabel. "I rarely disappoint my friends."

Although Gabriel knew precisely how much Isabel's
liking of this red cord amounted to, he wished she had
not openly praised it in Fabia's presence, as he felt sure
that the girl would misunderstand her; and he was
right: parish priests learn a great deal about human
nature in the course of their ministrations. It is a rule

—and sometimes a very unfortunate rule—that we are apt, in our intercourse with others, to take whatever rôle they may in their own minds have allotted to us, even if that rôle is unlike, even opposed to, our natural one. Instead of endeavouring to prove that certain persons are wrong—when they are so—in thinking us dull or sarcastic or flippant, we become, when in the company of these persons, the very things which they erroneously suppose us to be. Sometimes unconsciously —sometimes even against our will—we are for the time being not our real selves at all, but the creatures of our companions' imaginations. This may be partly due to a sort of false pride that will not allow us to justify ourselves when we have been so misjudged; but probably more to the effect of mind upon mind. By expecting us to have certain qualities, these people temporarily endow us with those qualities; and we actually are dull or sarcastic or flippant when in their society. Therefore it behoves us all to think the best and to expect the highest of each other, until the charity which believeth all things and hopeth all things shall at last see faith and hope lost in full fruition.

"Yes, you have never felt the lash of the red cord, Mrs. Seaton," said Carr gently; "you have always been on the right side of it."

Isabel laughed carelessly. The people who take things for granted never know quite how hard life is to the people who do not. "Well, at any rate, you can't have much of the questionable material in a place like this. That's one comfort for you!"

"Can't I, though? That's all you know about it! Why, it is one of my greatest stumbling-blocks, and is always getting in the way and tripping up my people in their road to Heaven. Don't imagine for a moment

that the sin of exclusiveness is confined to the upper
classes. In fact no sin is. The devil may have his
faults, but he is no snob, I am sorry to say. I only
wish he were! It would make work in the unfashionable
parishes far easier for the clergy."

"But I should have thought that the people here were
all on the same dead level, like their houses," said
Isabel.

"Not a bit of it. They appear so to us, I admit; but
doubtless we appear so to the angels. It is merely a
question of perspective. When I first came here, in
the fulness and innocence of my heart I invited a few of
my leading parishioners to tea: I thought it would bring
them closer together; and so it did—too close. I discovered that there were deep and impassable social gulfs
yawning between apparently co-equal retail tradesmen.
They bitterly complained that not only was it dis-
tasteful to sit at meat with social inferiors, but that—
after thus sitting together—they could hardly 'give
each other the pass-by' in the street, but were compelled to 'move' to one another thenceforward. And
to 'move' to anyone evidently entails serious social
responsibilities which must not wantonly or unadvisedly
be taken in hand."

"Gabriel, ask Miss Vipart to sing to us," said Isabel,
rising from her chair and opening the piano—Gabriel's
one and only luxury; "I'm sure she will, if you ask her
prettily."

It was one of Mrs. Seaton's good points that she
never lost an opportunity of showing off another woman
to the best advantage. She did not know what jealousy
or envy meant.

But Fabia resented even this, regarding it as a form
of patronage; and would probably have refused, had

not Gabriel turned to her at that moment, with a beseeching expression in his eyes, adding his entreaties to Isabel's. Personal attraction had a great effect upon Fabia: it was only beauty in the abstract that failed to command her homage. She would not be as conscious as was Isabel of the beauty of a sermon; but she would be far more conscious of the beauty of the preacher. The one woman admired Gabriel because he was good; the other, because he was good-looking. Therefore, Carr being a handsome man, Fabia did as he asked her: just as she would probably have obeyed Isabel, had Isabel been a beautiful woman. It is an accepted theory that a woman's personal beauty is the surest passport to the love of man; but it is a far surer passport to the love of other women.

So she sat down at the piano and began to sing; and as she sang, the reason of her loneliness and isolation became apparent: for she owned that strange gift which is called genius, the possessors whereof are always set apart from their fellow-men.

As she sang, Gabriel felt as if the heavens had opened, and earth with its sordid cares and petty interests had drifted far away. On the wings of that song his soul was uplifted until he hardly knew where he was or what he was doing. He was only conscious of an indescribable joy and peace which exceeded all description.

It is one of the peculiarities of genius, as distinguished from mere talent, that genius can give what it has never possessed, and can teach what it has never learned. The man of talent can only distribute of his abundance —can only instruct others out of his own stores of knowledge; but the man with a spark of genius pours forth riches which have never entered into his concep-

tion. And that because genius is no mere ownership
of intellectual gifts, but a channel for something which
is outside mere humanity altogether—something which
in its essence partakes of the Divine. A man's talents
are to a certain extent an integral part of himself; but
not so his genius: this is but a pipe—made maybe of
the commonest earthenware—through which rushes the
sound of many waters when deep calleth unto deep.

Of course in the well-known cases of great genius,
talent and capacity are superadded. A man—to do
excellent and lasting work—must cultivate his heaven-
born gift with all the aids of human knowledge and
culture; and, further, he must fit himself to be a vessel
unto honour, sanctified and meet for the use of that
Master Who has entrusted him with the rare and price-
less gift of genius. For even a pipe through which
flows the dew of the mountain and the rain from
heaven, may so foul that stream, by its own unclean-
ness, that the water of life is thereby turned into the
water of death, and the rain of God into a veritable
devil's sewer.

But these matters were as yet hid from Gabriel Carr.
Because Fabia sang like an angel, he believed that she
was in truth an angel—because she lifted his soul up to
Heaven, he believed that she herself was already there
—because she taught him by the beauty of her voice
something of the goodness of God, he believed that she
had already tasted of that goodness, and had proved
how gracious it is. Therefore as soon as he heard her
voice he loved her; as Charles Gaythorne had loved
her as soon as he saw her face. And each man had yet
to learn to his cost that neither voice nor face was
the woman herself, nor in any way representative of
her.

CHAPTER VIII

VERNACRE PARK

LORD WREXHAM invited a small party of his special
friends to spend 'Whitsuntide with him at Vernacre
Park, his country-seat; which party included Lord
Kesterton, Mr. Reginald Greenstreet, Captain Gaythorne and his mother, the Reverend Gabriel Carr, and
the Paul Seatons with their guest, Miss Vipart.

It was the Saturday afternoon, and they were having
tea in the stately drawing-room—a room, for all its
magnificence, as empty of abiding feminine occupation
as was the drawing-room at S. Etheldreda's Vicarage.
Mrs. Seaton would have preferred to have tea out-of-
doors, but she was too wise a woman to suggest it; having
learnt that it is not in human nature patiently to endure
alien interference in domestic arrangements. It may be
very heroic to go forth combating error and redressing
wrong in true knight-errantly fashion; but it is far
wiser to leave the error uncombated, and the wrong
unredressed, if they happen to occur in other people's
houses.

"I am going down to the home-farm after tea to
inspect some model cottages that have been erected
during my absence," said the host; "would anybody
care to come with me?"

"I should be immensely interested, if you'll take me,"

answered Isabel quickly, before anybody else had time
to speak.

She knew that he wanted her to go, and she wanted
to indulge him. It was only since her marriage that
she had learnt to look at things from a man's point of
view as well as from a woman's, and had consequently
realized how badly she had treated Lord Wrexham in
the old days when she was Isabel Carnaby; and now,
woman-like, she tried to make up to him in the things
that did not matter for having failed him in things that
did; because she had once denied him bread, she now
fairly pelted him with precious stones. To tell the
truth, there was nothing that bored her more than
farm buildings and model cottages; but she was
willing—nay ready—to endure any amount of boredom
if she could thereby relieve Wrexham's loneliness and
her own conscience: about the latter part of which
attempt there was not, it must be admitted, much
difficulty. People to whom the world is ready to
forgive much, rarely find it hard to forgive themselves
still more.

Lord Wrexham's face lighted up with pleasure. I
shall be delighted to take you, Mrs. Seaton."

" I want to come too," said Fabia.

Isabel looked annoyed. She was fully aware of the
fact that the lovely Fabia had designs upon the Prime
Minister himself, and she resented it exceedingly. We
none of us really like the people who want to marry our
former lovers; just as we never really like the people
who live in the houses that were once our homes.
Isabel was beginning to feel much as Frankenstein felt
when his monster grew restive.

But Charlie Gaythorne unconsciously came to her
rescue. "Oh! I say, Miss Vipart: that's a bit too bad.

You promised to come for a stroll with me after tea,
don't you know ? "

"So I did. I quite forgot it."

Charlie reddened. It is not pleasant to be forgotten
by the woman you love; and it is still less so to be
informed of the fact before a roomful of your dearest
friends. But this was Fabia's mode of punishing him
for presuming to remember what it had suited her to
forget.

"Perhaps Miss Vipart will let me show her my
cottages to-morrow instead," said the host, with his usual
kindly tact.

Fabia, seeing that the bird in the hand had escaped
from out of her grasp, accepted the substitute from the
bush with the best grace she could muster.

"Thank you, Lord Wrexham : it will afford me the
greatest pleasure to inspect your model farm ; and at
the same time, I may be able to borrow from it some
ideas which may be adapted, on my return home, for
the improvement of my Indian estates."

Lord Wrexham beamed. There are few men who
do not derive gratification from being requested to
instruct a beautiful woman ; and still fewer who can
resist the subtle flattery of being consulted upon the
one matter which they do not understand. In politics
—wherein he really was a proficient—Lord Wrexham
frequently doubted his own wisdom; but with regard
to farming—wherein he was an amateur of the first
water—he spoke with authority and without hesitation.

"I shall only be too pleased to give you any advice or
assistance in my power," he said.

But here Mrs. Gaythorne inserted her usual word in
season. She rarely heard of the formation of any plan,
however simple, without making some attempt to

improve it; and this not from any unkindness of heart, but simply from an insatiable passion for reform in the abstract.

"I cannot think that the Sabbath day is a suitable occasion for perambulating farm-yards and inspecting live-stock."

"But why not, dear lady, why not?" asked Greenstreet. "To my mind there is no more suitable amusement for a Sunday afternoon—no occupation more in keeping with the reposeful atmosphere of the day—than to scratch the back of a pig with the end of one's walking-stick. I always embrace such an opportunity whenever it offers itself: it is so soothing to the nerves that it almost sends one to sleep on the spot."

"There is something better to be done on the Sabbath than to be sent to sleep, Mr. Greenstreet," replied Mrs. Gaythorne, with some sternness.

"Indeed: then why listen to sermons?"

Charlie moved restlessly in his chair. He wished Greenstreet wouldn't rouse his mother, just when she was taking her tea so nicely and quietly, and all was peace.

Gabriel gallantly stepped into the breach. "Surely, Mrs. Gaythorne, the contemplation of God's creatures can never be a desecration of God's day. And besides, we are specially told that if an ox or an ass fall into a pit on the Sabbath day we may pull it out: which surely means that nothing done to alleviate the suffering of the creature can ever be displeasing to the Creator."

"Mr. Greenstreet was not proposing to pull an ox or an ass out of a pit: he was proposing to scratch a pig."

Mrs. Gaythorne was nothing if not literal.

"And in so doing I should be relieving the suffering of another without any inconvenience to myself," added Greenstreet: "the very essence of modern Christianity."

Again Charlie moved restlessly. It was all very well to be brave, he thought; but to wave scarlet bunting in the faces of dangerous cattle is foolhardiness rather than courage.

"Besides," continued Mrs. Gaythorne, as usual plodding steadily along a side issue, "oxen and asses are treated with great respect all through the Scriptures; they were both very useful and important animals in the Holy Land. But no Jew would ever touch bacon or pork."

She had a happy knack of frequently getting the best of an argument by saying something which had nothing whatever to do with the subject under discussion, and yet sounded as if it had; and thereby confounding her opponents.

Isabel was thoroughly enjoying herself. She wished that Paul were here to share her unfailing delight in Mrs. Gaythorne's conversation; but he had gone for a long walk with his Chief, and had not yet returned.

Greenstreet was slightly staggered for a second by the pork-and-bacon thurst; but he quickly recovered himself. "I am always thankful I am not a Jew for that very reason," he retorted. "What would life be without bacon; and what would your morning-tub be without the smell of bacon calling you to breakfast?"

"You are quite right," remarked Isabel; "bacon is one of the things that do not taste at the time half so nice as they smell beforehand: success is another and so is fame."

"And marriage, likewise."

" No, no, Mr. Greenstreet. Marriage turns out to be even nicer than it promises to be."

"Ah! I see; more like cauliflowers than bacon. I think, Mrs. Seaton, you will admit that other people's cauliflowers repel rather than attract when the air is filled with the promise of them: and—as far as I am concerned—other people's marriages have the same effect."

" You are condemning yourself out of your own metaphor," retorted Isabel. " You compare marriage to a cauliflower, and you admit that a cauliflower tastes much better than it smells."

" I admit that it couldn't taste much worse."

" Then in the same way you'll find that marriage will turn out much nicer than you expect."

" I shall not: for I shall never make the experiment."

Here Mrs. Gaythorne again pranced into the conversation. " I am sorry to hear that you are troubled with the odour of cooking in your house, Isabella ; but I am not surprised. Most London houses are the same. It is all owing to that ridiculous custom of building them in the shape of a well with the kitchen at the bottom."

" Like truth," murmured Mr. Greenstreet.

" I beg your pardon, Mr. Greenstreet, I did not catch your remark. My hearing is not what it once was, I regret to say."

" No need for regret, madam, on that score, when I am speaking ; it is rather a subject for self-congratulation on your part."

" Well, as I was saying, if you build your house like a well with the kitchen at the bottom, how can you keep the odour of cabbage-water out of the drawing-room ? "

"Quite easily," replied Isabel. "I always succeed in doing so; and if one can do a thing oneself, it is safe—though humiliating—to conclude that nine-tenths of one's acquaintance can do it equally well."

Mrs. Gaythorne looked sternly reproachful. "Isabella, how can you say there is no odour of cabbage-water in your drawing-room, when you have just been complaining to Mr. Greenstreet that you cannot keep it out—neither it nor bacon? Dear, dear, dear! The young people of to-day are not as truthful as we were when we were young. My dear father never allowed one of us to be guilty of the slightest inaccuracy in our conversation. I remember he once punished my sister Maria severely for saying that Henry the Eighth had a dozen or more wives, when she knew for a fact he had only six."

"But, dear lady, she was right—absolutely right from an artistic point of view," exclaimed Greenstreet; "your sister Maria—pardon me for speaking in such familiar terms of the lady, but I know her by no other name—was a born artist."

"She was not, Mr. Greenstreet. I was the artist of the family, and copied flowers from Nature in water-colours upon hand-screens for bazaars; Maria played the piano, and frequently performed at village concerts —with encores."

"But she was an artist all the same, from a conversational point of view. Every good talker must be more or less of an impressionist. For instance, if you say 'Henry the Eighth had dozens of wives,' you give the correct impression that he was a much-married man: while if you say 'Henry the Eighth had barely six wives,' you give the impression that he erred on the side of celibacy," persisted Greenstreet,

"I do not approve of celibacy" remarked Mrs. Gaythorne; "especially in the clergy."

Once again Greenstreet staggered under the un-expected thrust; and once again recovered himself by clinging manfully to Henry the Eighth and Maria "Therefore, you see, Mrs. Gaythorne, your sister conveyed the correct impression by using the incorrect words. She expressed the idea that King Henry married frequently; which was the idea she intended to express. I am sure that Mrs. Seaton catches my point," he added, turning for support to Isabel.

"Perfectly," she replied: "on the same principle that a touched-up photograph is really a much better likeness than the unmodified negative which cannot lie."

Mrs. Gaythorne as usual ignored the high-road of the conversation, and stalked fearlessly along a by-way. But it ceased to be anything so frivolous as a by-way the moment that the good lady set foot upon it. Had she crossed By-path Meadow itself, it would immediately have been converted into a solid high road.

"I do not at all disapprove of second marriages myself," she said; "not at all." She spoke indulgently, as if she expected everybody present to run out and contract a second marriage at once, now that she had sanctioned the innocent pastime. "And where there are children," she added, "I consider it sometimes a necessity."

"There were children in the case of Henry the Eighth, if I remember rightly," said Isabel, with meekness in her manner and mischief in her eyes: "so the poor man could plead extenuating circumstances."

"There were, Isabella: Bloody Mary was one of them. Think of having Bloody Mary for a step-daughter! I should very much have disliked it."

"I am sure you would," said Lord Wrexham.

"But she would have acted differently," continued Mrs. Gaythorne, "if I had had the early training of her."

"You mean," said Greenstreet, "that in that case the fires of Smithfield would have burned seven times hotter than they did. I admit the theory is not untenable."

"I mean that in that case there would have been no Smithfield," replied Mrs. Gaythorne majestically. "I should have put my foot down upon it at once."

Here Isabel and Gabriel laughed outright, and Lord Wrexham stroked his moustache to hide a smile; but Charlie could not for the life of him see what there was to laugh at. He knew that he dared not have burnt a single Protestant if his mother had, as she called it, "put her foot down "—a favourite form of exercise with her; and he very much doubted if anybody else, Queen Mary included, dared have done so either. But other people did not know the weight of his mother's foot. He did.

And all this time Fabia sat silent, not joining in the conversation at all. She was one of the women who cannot talk except in a *tête-à-tête;* by no means an uncommon type. General conversation invariably sealed her lips. But she looked so beautiful that silence in her was pardonable, if not commendable. Every woman ought either to talk well or to look well, though she cannot reasonably be expected to do both; but if she does neither, she has no place in the scheme of social creation, and is only fit for domestic uses.

In Isabel Seaton the social instinct was very strong. Conversation was to her a game, whereof it behoved everyone to know the rules. Had she lived a century

or two earlier, she could have held a *salon* with the best:
as it was, she was an ideal wife for a diplomatist or a
politician. To ignore your partner's lead in conversation
was in her eyes as bad as to ignore it in whist: to say
the wrong thing, as heinous as to play the wrong card:
to sit silent, as unpardonable as to revoke. In conversation she was a veritable Sarah Battle, insisting
upon "the rigour of the game": so now, according to
her instinct, she endeavoured to restore to animation
the conversation which Mrs. Gaythorne had nearly
trampled to death.

"I am so interested in what you say about all good
talkers being impressionists, Mr. Greenstreet. I know
exactly what you mean, and fully agree with you; but
unfortunately it never occurred to me to put it as neatly
as you have done."

Lord Wrexham looked at her in admiration. How
ready she always was to put people at their ease, and
how successfully she oiled the wheels of life wherever
she happened to find herself. Seaton was indeed a
lucky fellow! It was a pity that a man with such a
career before him as the possession of so brilliant a wife
ensured, should throw it away for the sake of those
political will-o'-the-wisps which have lured men and
their parties to destruction ever since politics were first
invented! So mused the Prime Minister. He made it
a point of honour never to breathe a word to anybody
against Isabel's husband: he made it a matter of
principle not to feel bitter against nor envious of this
man who had taken from him the one thing that he had
really cared for in life; but he found it a great comfort
to say now and then to his own soul that Paul Seaton
was no statesman.

Greenstreet's thin face lighted up with pleasure. The

approval of Mrs. Paul Seaton was a compliment which few men ignored.

"I think I am right," he replied.

"I am sure you are," put in Gabriel Carr; "and that is why very accurate people are always so tiresome. My late Rector was that sort : one of the best men that ever breathed; but so accurate, and so anxious to make other people accurate, that I verily believe he would have liked to correct S. John himself for saying that even the world itself could not contain the books that should be written."

At this point Mrs. Gaythorne was heard to murmur something about belief in the verbal inspiration of the Scriptures being absolutely necessary to salvation; but fortunately she was so much engaged with a large tea-cake—judiciously administered by Charlie—that no one heard exactly what she said ; and she was unable, not from any lack of moral courage but for purely physical reasons, more openly to testify to her acceptance of this saving truth until the occasion had passed by.

"My horror," said Isabel, "is a person who relates an incident exactly as it happened; because then it isn't worth relating at all."

Carr fully agreed with her. "I have an uncle of that kind, who always uses inverted commas instead of the oblique oration ; and, you know how wearying to the flesh that is! Instead of saying, 'My wife's sister told me she had a cold,' he would say, 'My wife's sister said to me, "John;" "Yes, Jane," I answered; "John," said my wife's sister, "I have a cold."'"

By this time the tea-cake had gone the way of all tea-cakes, and Mrs. Gaythorne once more enjoyed freedom of utterance.

"And did he marry her?" she asked cheerfully.

Even the redoubtab'? Gabriel was nonplussed.

"Marry her? Marry whom?" he inquired.

"Why, his deceased wife's sister, of course. Who else were you talking about?"

"I never mentioned anybody's deceased wife's sister, Mrs. Gaythorne."

The Vicar knew better than to introduce so debatable a lady into any conversation of his own free will; he was a lover of peace.

But Mrs. Gaythorne was not easily brushed aside when she had turned a by-way into a war-path and started upon it.

"Yes, Gabriel Carr, you did: you said she had a cold, and that your uncle himself told you so; and what I want to know is whether he eventually married her. Not that I should blame him if he did: far from it! For my part I approve of marriage with a deceased wife's sister. Who, I should like to know, is so fit a guardian of the children as their aunt? I always told Mr. Gaythorne that if anything happened to me I should wish—positively wish—him to marry my sister Maria, I should have had such perfect confidence in her training of Charles. Maria always knew when to put her foot down."

"And did the late Mr. Gaythorne share your opinions upon this vexed question?" asked Carr, with a smile.

"No; he did not approve of marriage with a deceased wife's sister at all."

"I can believe it," murmured Greenstreet; "men are so prejudiced."

"And I cannot think why he of all men should have objected to it," continued Mr. Gaythorne's widow reflectively; "because Maria was the very image of

me. It would have been almost as good as having me
back again."

"It was strange," assented Carr, with a glance at
Isabel's preternaturally solemn face; "very strange
indeed."

"But where I do blame your uncle," continued
Mrs. Gaythorne, once again turning and rending the
unoffending Gabriel, "is for talking about his deceased
wife's sister's cold, and making such a fuss about it;
and you can tell him so from me if you like. It was
enough to make the poor woman nervous, and lead her
to imagine herself far worse than she really was. There
is no greater mistake than to talk about one's ailments."

"Except to talk about other people's," Isabel added.

"Yes, Isabella, you are right. It certainly makes the
other people nervous. But I never knew anything like
the young people of the present day for talking about
their diseases. For my part, I think it positively
improper."

"You consider there is indelicacy in the discussion
of delicacy, do you, Mrs. Gaythorne?" suggested
Greenstreet.

"I do, Mr. Greenstreet. In my young days people
were not always turning themselves inside-out for their
friends' inspection."

"It isn't only the young who are guilty of this folly,"
argued Isabel. "I never meet an old gentleman
nowadays who does not, so to speak, wear his liver
upon his sleeve for daws to peck at."

"Modern complaints always end in *itis*," continued
Mrs. Gaythorne. "I disapprove of diseases that end in
itis."

"Still, you must admit they might end in something
worse," said Carr.

Mrs. Gaythorne majestically ignored such ill-timed levity. "When I was young, the complaints that people suffered from did not end in *itis*, they ended in *ache*; and nobody talked about them."

By this time she had slain the conversation even beyond Isabel's revivifying powers; so—tea being finished—Lord Wrexham suggested a move into the garden.

The company went their various ways; and Fabia soon found herself alone with Captain Gaythorne in a secluded part of the wood. Strange to say, his presence did not irritate her just then. She had seen the expression upon Lord Wrexham's face when he looked at Isabel; and she knew from that instant that her own hopes of ever annexing the Prime Minister were vain. Therefore she was suffering from the combined pangs of envy and disappointment. Also she had felt herself left out in the cold ever since she came to Vernacre—a feeling to which she was accustomed, but which hurt her more cruelly every time she experienced it; and this increased her chagrin and misery. So when Captain Gaythorne followed her across the lawn and into the wood, she felt for the first time a sense of rest and security in the society of this big, silent, devoted man. It was a comfort to find anybody who really adored her, in this easy, pleasant, cruel English society. Love was the thing for which her soul most passionately craved; love given and received; and she had never had her share of it. True, Ram Chandar Mukharji had offered it to her in extravagant excess; but she did not care for the adoration of such as he. She was enough of an Englishwoman to despise her mother's people, and enough of an Oriental for the English to despise her; and love which she did not fully reciprocate could never satisfy her. Poor Fabia! Life was too hard for her just then, as indeed it always had been ever since she could remember. Mukharji wrote constantly to her, and she enjoyed and appreciated his letters. She knew that intellectually he was immeasurably Charlie Gaythorne's superior; yet at the present moment the admiration of the brainless young British soldier was far more acceptable to Fabia's wounded spirit than Ram Chandar's lifelong devotion.

She waited for Charlie to speak, with considerably more kindness and patience than she usually accorded to his conversational efforts; and made up her mind to be what women call "nice to him," whatever he might choose to say.

For some time the two walked on without speaking. They were both naturally silent people—the woman because she thought too much, and the man because he thought too little—so there was nothing unusual in this; and Fabia calmly awaited Charlie's utterance with the pleasing certainty that it would be more soothing to her vanity than stimulating to her mind. Though he was never clever, he was invariably complimentary.

At last he broke the silence. " I can't stand that ass Greenstreet!" he said.

Fabia was surprised. It was not at all what she had expected him to say, and she saw no reason for such violent hostility either, as Mr. Greenstreet had never paid her the slightest attention; but she knew from the sound of Charlie's voice that he was very angry indeed.

"Why not?" she asked.

"He was making fun of my mother all through tea, the confounded bounder! Didn't you hear him?"

Fabia felt as if a douche of cold water had suddenly

been flung in her face. So it was his mother's battles that he was fighting, and not hers! It was the old story over again. They really cared for nothing in the world but themselves and their order, these well-born English people. Even the simple and adoring Charlie was an aristocrat at heart.

"Perhaps he was," she answered coldly.

"Of course he was, confound his impudence! And I won't stand it. If he tries it on again, I'll kick him into the horsepond, Wrexham or no Wrexham! I'm not going to allow anybody's guests to insult my mother; and I'll let Wrexham know it pretty sharp!"

Fabia hardly recognized the usually placid and amiable Charlie in this infuriated young giant.

"And it isn't as if there was anything to make fun of in my mother, either," he went on. "Some fellows' mothers are a rummy sort, I admit; but mine isn't. Of course some women do things that you can't help smiling at; though it's shocking bad form to let their people see you're laughing at them all the same. But my mother isn't that sort: she doesn't do or say things that make a fellow even want to laugh at her, don't you know?"

"I quite agree with you that it would be impossible to caricature Mrs. Gaythorne."

"Of course it would," said Charlie, mollified at once by what he took to be Fabia's assent to his statement; "that's just my point. Now some old ladies are downright funny, there's no denying that; though that's no excuse for a man behaving like a thorough-paced cad."

"I think," remarked Fabia slowly, "that there is only one thing more aggravating than a man when he behaves like a thorough-paced cad; and that is when he behaves like an English gentleman."

But fortunately Charlie was too full of his own grievance even to hear—much less to understand—this cryptic utterance.

"For instance," he went on, "I daresay, if we knew her, we should find Seaton's mother rather a queer sort. His people are nobody particular; so I shouldn't be surprised if the old lady was a bit ignorant and old-fashioned and narrow, and all that sort of thing, don't you know? And no blame to her, either! You can't expect anybody who isn't anybody to know anything; can you? But my mother is quite a different thing!"

"Who was Mrs. Gaythorne before she was married?" asked Fabia, in all innocence.

Charlie opened his eyes wide, in as unbounded amazement as if she had asked who Queen Anne was before she was married. Here was crass ignorance indeed! Then he remembered how Fabia had once said that she did not know that his mother was saved, which was even worse. This was bad enough, but not so bad as that. Not to know whence Mrs. Gaythorne came, showed an indifference to history which was highly culpable; but not to know whither Mrs. Gaythorne was going, proved an ignorance of theology which was positively appalling. Charlie was too polite to testify openly to his astonishment at such a question; so he merely replied:

"She was one of the Latimers of Luske."

"And who are the Latimers of Luske?"

This was worse than ever! But Captain Gaythorne pitied rather than blamed such astounding mental darkness; just as he would have pitied rather than blamed her had Fabia confessed that she did not know how to read and write.

"They are the—the—well the Latimers, don't you

know?—the Latimers of Luske: the Latimers of Leatherby are the younger branch of the family."

"I see; the Latimers of Luske are the Latimers of Luske, and the Latimers of Leatherby a . ; the Latimers of Leatherby."

"Of course. And to think of a little middle-class beggar like Greenstreet daring to make fun of one of the Latimers of Luske. I never heard such confounded cheek!"

"Mr. Greenstreet undoubtedly belongs to the middle-class," remarked Fabia; "he has brains."

"Oh! I don't deny the brute's clever in his way; but I'm glad you agree with me that anybody can see at a glance he is not one of us," replied Charlie, in all good faith.

"Certainly: he has a sense of humour."

"That he has; and it carr' 's him a bit too far at times; a precious sight too far, when he begins to make fun of my mother!" And Charlie returned to his grievance like a giant refreshed.

Fabia moved her shoulders impatiently. She had not come into the wood in order to talk about Captain Gaythorne's mother; but apparently he had: and—as is usual—the slower mind had its own way, at the expense of the quicker one. Miss Vipart felt irritated; and justly so. It is always trying to a woman's temper if a man talks about his own relations, when she wants him to talk about his relations with her.

Now if Charlie had been wise enough to propose to Fabia on that particular afternoon, she would have accepted him then and there, and so would have saved certain further complications. But Charlie talked about his mother instead of proposing, and expatiated upon that good lady's attributes until the time and the

audience were alike exhausted : thereby paving the way
for another to step in and to win the affection which he
longed for. 'If he gives twice who gives quickly, surely
he who asks tardily often receives but half: there are
many Esaus who only obtain the second blessing
because they come and beg for it too late.

CHAPTER IX

GABRIEL THE PRIEST

WHITSUNDAY dawned fair and bright; and the Vernacre party duly to church repaired at the appointed hour. Lord Wrexham was a man who regularly attended Divine worship every Sunday morning; and there was a general impression abroad at Vernacre—though he had never expressed it in words—that he expected his guests to do likewise.

Vernacre Church was a rare and perfect specimen of Norman architecture : and as Isabel Seaton sat in the beautiful and ancient edifice, and watched the sunlight pouring through the old stained windows upon the brows of the stone Crusaders lying asleep upon their tombs, the atmosphere of the prayers of countless generations stole into her soul and filled it with a great peace. For long centuries the incense of prayer had risen up to Heaven from this little western temple ; and now she, too, was adding her humble petition to the unbroken chain of ceaseless supplication—she, too, was saying her Amens to the age-long intercessions of departed saints. For a time the overpowering influence of an historic Church seized her and held her in its grasp. The hymn of praise which she was now singing, had been begun in Jerusalem on this very day nearly nineteen centuries ago : and it would sound on down

the ages yet to come, until it was at last merged in that
new song thundering upon Mount Zion, which no man
could learn save those which were redeemed from the
earth and had the Father's name written in their
foreheads. There had been no break in the continuity
of that song; no pause in the uplifting of those prayers;
no extinguishing of that sacred fire which was first
kindled by the cloven tongues when the Apostles were
all with one accord in one place.

Now, alas! the disciples of the Master are no longer
in one place with one accord: the primitive state of
unity has long gone by. There have been strifes and
persecutions where there should have been love and
peace: yet the chain of prayer and praise remains
unbroken and intact: although even devout men are
apt to forget that though there is but One Church,
there are divers forms of utterance in that Church;
and that it is still given to each of us to hear, every
man in his own tongue wherein he was born, the
wonderful works of God.

When the sermon began, Isabel attuned herself to
listen, for she was ever athirst—like the Athenians of
old—to hear some new thing; but it turned out to be
one of those discourses which George Herbert had in
his mind's eye when he said: "God takes a text and
preacheth patience." So Isabel's thoughts were driven
back upon herself; and her patient meditations took a
personal turn.

She thought of herself and Paul, and of how their
future life was going to shape itself. She dwelt with
a regret half tender and half humorous upon her
husband's wonderful power of seeing only one side of
a question, and that always the brighter side. She did
not as yet understand that it is the men that see only

one side of a question who have the most power in convincing other men—that it is the enthusiast rather than
the wiseacre who storms citadels and removes mountains.
The wise men have their place in the world—the world
could not roll on comfortably without them; but we do
not place them in the forefront of the battle, nor entrust
them with the leadership of forlorn hopes. It is the old
heads that watch and guard and counsel and advise;
but it is the young shoulders that push and jostle and
make their way through the crowd.

Isabel loved her husband with all her heart, and
reverenced him with all her soul; but she had not yet
passed the final and most difficult test of wifely submission, and acquired the conviction that he knew better
than she did: a conviction which—if not always supported
by facts—must invariably count for righteousness to the
woman who is imbued with it.

To Isabel's easy, good-humoured cynicism, Paul's
almost boyish adherence to his ideals appeared
visionary and unpractical. It seemed like believing
in fairies and witches and gnomes. The difference
between their two natures, while it intensified their
love, made it difficult for them to understand each
other; and yet each character had its compensations.
Paul believed in the ideal side of human nature more
than Isabel did; his world was more densely peopled
with heroes and saints than was hers; yet, on the other
hand, his very belief in humanity made him hard upon
it when it failed and fell short; whilst she cherished
an abundant tolerance towards all the faults and
weaknesses of her fellows. The denizens of Isabel's
world were not heroes nor saints, but ordinary men
and women; therefore she was neither angry nor
disappointed when they comported themselves accord-

ing to their kind. But Paul, it must be admitted, was sometimes both.

After indulging in sundry half-humorous, half-pathetic regrets over Paul's singleness of eye and blindness of heart (as she considered them), Isabel's thoughts flew to the possible Governorship of Tasmania as the one safe refuge from the dangers and follies which assailed her husband. There he would be safe for a while, and would have time, to learn that wisdom which only time can teach. And it would not only be a safe city of refuge; it would be a glorious palace of delights. Isabel had been very happy out in India long ago with Sir Benjamin and Lady Farley; and she had ever since looked upon the life of a Colonial Governor as the most perfect form of earthly existence possible, bar one; the one thing more utterly delightful than the life of a Colonial Governor being the life of a Colonial Governor's wife.

To feel that such a lot was practically within her grasp made her almost dizzy with happiness; it would be the realization of her most cherished castles in the air—the fulfilment of her wildest dreams. She could imagine nothing else on earth that she should enjoy so much as thus playing at being a queen; it would suit her artistic nature and her dramatic instincts down to the ground, she thought; and she revelled in the contemplation of the mere possibility of it.

And Isabel was not the only one who saw visions in the old village church on that summer Sunday morning: Fabia also dreamed dreams. She was sitting near to the tomb of one of the ancient lords of Vernacre, who wore upon his helmet the head of a Saracen maid: and Fabia recalled the story of this old Crusader, which his descendant had related to her on

the preceding evening. Sir Godfrey de Rexham had
been taken prisoner by the Saracens, soon after he
joined the first Crusade: and the daughter of his
captor—a Saracen maid of great beauty—saw the
English knight and fell in love with him. Secretly
she visited him in his dungeon, and offered to effect his
escape on condition that he would take her with him
back to England as his wife. The temptation was
great, but Sir Godfrey was a man of honour; and he
therefore confessed to the lady that he was already
betrothed to one of his own country-women, and was
bound—should he ever return to England—to marry
that lady: so that escape, upon the terms now offered,
was impossible. But the Moorish girl boasted that
most precious of all possessions, an absolutely unselfish
love; and she still effected the escape of the knight,
and sent him back to England to marry his lady-love.
Which he accordingly did, and lived happily ever after:
but he henceforth wore as his crest the head of a
Saracen maid, in token of his gratitude.

And as Fabia Vipart looked at the crest upon his
helmet, a great pity for the woman filled her heart. So
this girl had had to learn, as she herself had done, how
cold were the English and how wrapped up in themselves and in each other. She wondered what happened
to the Moorish maiden after the knight had fled. Did
she die of a broken heart because she had loved in
vain? Or did her father slay her, because she had
contrived the escape of his enemy, and had allowed a
Christian to gaze upon the beauty of her face? Upon
this point history was silent; it only busied itself with
the domestic affairs of the Englishman—in chronicling
the ancestry of his highly - respectable wife, and the
number of his commonplace children. So handsome,

however, was his marble effigy that Fabia did not blame the maid for having loved him: and beautiful indeed was the female head upon his crest—beautiful somewhat after Fabia's own fashion. But there was no beauty in the face or figure of the woman lying by his side, mentioned in the fading inscription on the tomb as " Dame Philippa, his wife." Hers was a stiff, prim kind of face, made still stiffer and primmer by the severe and hideous dress of her time. And he had given up the Moorish girl for a woman such as this ! How truly English of him, said Fabia to herself with a little scornful smile. Fabia wondered who this lady had been before her marriage : perhaps one of the Latimers of Luske, or one of the bearers of some equally respectable old name which the English love to conjure with ; for apparently to the typical British mind the glory of a long line of noble Oriental ancestry was as nothing compared with the overpowering honour of being born a Latimer of Luske—or its equivalent.

Then a change came o'er the spirit of Fabia's dream, and she began to envy this Eastern maiden instead of pitying her: envying her because it had been given to her to love another so much that her own happiness became as nothing. After all, there was something in this love which transfigured life and glorified death as nothing else could do; and Fabia had never tasted it— never known for an instant what it was to love another better than herself. She wondered if this had been her own fault, or the fault of her circumstances. She was too clear-sighted not to blame herself when blame was due ; but she was not sure in this case whether she deserved it. She knew that she would gladly have loved if she could—thankfully have merged her own life

and happiness in the life and happiness of another; but
the power to do so seemed to have been denied her
She could always look critically upon her friends,
whoever they might be—always see clearly the faults
of those about her; yet while she plumed herself upon
her own open vision, and despised the blind credulity of
other people, she could not help envying simpler women
their unshaken and unshakable conviction that their
own particular husbands were infallible and omniscient;
and that the judgment of those gifted beings on any
and every subject under (or even above) the sun was
absolute and final. Such perfect confidence in the
other partner to the transaction would certainly very
much simplify the difficulties of married life; but where
was Fabia to find the man who could inspire her with
such confidence?

In vain she ran down the list of possible husbands.
Captain Gaythorne was out of the question, he was
such a consummate fool. Lord Wrexham had rank
and dignity, but he lacked the magnetism of personal
charm, which to Fabia was indispensable. Her cousin,
Mukharji, dominated her intellectually; but he was
wanting in that social prestige, which in her eyes
counted for so much. Gabriel Carr possessed physical
beauty as well as mental power; but—although she
admired him more than any man she had yet seen—
she felt that there was an almost feminine quickness of
perception and subtlety of thought about him, which
would always prevent her from acknowledging him as
the superior power, and cause her to regard him rather
as an equal.

In the depths of her heart she knew that she longed
to find her master—she felt her very soul was crying
out for the touch of a conquering hand. And she knew,

further, that if ever she did find such a one—a man who would rule her absolutely with a rod of iron, and would prove himself once and for all stronger than herself—she could come to his call, whoever and whatever he was, and would submissively acknowledge in the face of all the world the divine right of such a king.

There are two types of women in this world: the woman who is seeking for her master, and the woman who is seeking for her mate. They are equally normal—equally feminine: there is no credit in being of the one sort—no discredit in belonging to the other. Yet it behoves every woman to find out to which classification she belongs, and to marry accordingly; lest haply she should discover too late that she has chosen a prince to take the part of a playfellow, or a comrade to wear the crown of a king.

For the last few weeks the friendship between Fabia and the Vicar of S. Etheldreda's had been growing apace. Carr had seized every available opportunity that he could snatch from his busy life to see Miss Vipart; and Fabia had made such opportunities as easy and as frequent as she could. But the two regarded their friendship for each other from entirely opposite points of view. To Fabia, Gabriel was merely a man who attracted her, and whom woman-like, she meant to subjugate: to Gabriel, Fabia was the only woman in the world.

His life had been so busy and his mind so absorbed in his work, that he had hitherto given but little attention to women and their ways. He had dealt with their souls to the best of his ability, but had not concerned himself much about their hearts: he was intent upon preparing them collectively for

a home in Heaven, but it had never yet occurred
to him to offer one of them individually a home
on earth.

But when Fabia Vipart came and sang to him, then
suddenly the face of the whole world was changed.
Nothing was as it had been before. For him there
were new heavens and a new earth; fresh flowers
bloomed around his feet—unknown stars disclosed
themselves to his view. She seemed to touch his
whole life as with a fairy wand, and to turn the
dreariest pathways into streets of gold.

They had talked much to each other, and upon many
things; that is to say, Gabriel had talked and Fabia
had listened, putting in the necessary word here and
there to show that she understood. And in thus
talking, Carr had revealed his inmost soul to Fabia,
and at the same time to himself—for it is in talking
to other people about ourselves that we, rather than
they, learn what manner of men and women we are.
He believed that Fabia had shown him what she really
was; and he was accordingly grateful to her: he did
not know that he had shown himself what he really
was by endeavouring to show the same to her. "Know
thyself," is advice worthy of being followed; but we
rarely get to know ourselves except by making ourselves known to others; which accounts for the fact
that the most reserved people are, as a rule, the people
who are least cognizant of their own failings and
excellencies.

And Carr had also learnt a great deal about Fabia
as well as about himself. He understood far better
than she did that her faults were the outcome of
circumstances rather than of character; he knew that
she only wanted that master-hand, for which at present

she was vaguely groping, to develop her into as fine a woman inwardly as she now was outwardly—to make her heart and soul as admirable as her mind and body. He recognized the passionate, fiery, loving nature at present hidden underneath the cold and bitter and sarcastic exterior; and he knew that it only needed the kiss of the fairy-prince to awaken the sleeping beauty to life and love.

But there was one thing about her which he did not understand: and that was the absence of any religious element in her nature. The naturally unreligious woman is very rare; but she nevertheless exists. In most women the religious instinct is strongly developed; and it is a good thing for the world in general that this should be so. But there is a minority who are practically without this instinct altogether; and this minority have to be reckoned with, and their deficiency supplied. The unreligious woman need not necessarily develop into an irreligious one: in fact she not infrequently proves herself precisely the contrary: but religion must come to her through the channels of her other attributes, as she has no natural aptitude for it; and these channels are usually found in her love for some good man or woman, who becomes to her a messenger of the gospel of peace.

Milton's Eve was a woman of this kind, or he could never have written the line, " He for God only ; she for God in him." The naturally religious woman loves her husband because she loves God: the naturally unreligious woman loves God because she loves her husband. The modes may be different, but the final results are much the same.

But it is difficult for any man to realize that there may be a woman without this instinct altogether: and

Gabriel made this mistake in his estimate of Fabia's character. He had discovered upon further acquaintance that she was not as absolutely perfect as he had believed her to be when first he heard her sing; and he had also discovered that she was a far finer character than other people—than even she herself —gave her credit for being: but he failed to understand the simple Paganism of her nature—he had no idea how utterly she was lacking in the religious instinct.

For some time he was torn asunder between his love for her and his devotion to his work. Then gradually be came to believe that the two passions were not, as he had at first assumed, opposed to each other—that a wife would help rather than hinder him in following his sacred calling. How Fabia's great gifts, rightly dedicated, would aid in the great work of saving men's souls and bringing them to God, he thought; how the influence of her face and her voice would brighten the lives of many committed to his charge; and how the comfort and happiness of her love and companionship would refresh and strengthen him for the fulfilment of the most strenuous and arduous duties that he could ever be called upon to undertake!

As this idea took possession of him, Gabriel's heart was filled with a great joy; and he made up his mind to ask Fabia to be his wife as soon as he thought she had known himself and his sphere of labour long enough to be able to make a wise decision. He was fully aware that the lot he was about to offer to her was no bed of roses; but he was also aware that it was not in the vapid amusements of a life of pleasure and gaiety to satisfy the cravings of such a soul as hers. He had learnt that she was not as perfect as he had at first believed her to be; but he had also learnt that there were possibilities of perfection in her—as indeed there are in everybody, although some of us are quick to hide them in ourselves, and slow to discover them in others. Nevertheless in every man and every woman there is the germ of perfection, which some day—though neither here nor now—shall develop into absolute fulfilment: for God made man in His own image; and if man could ever finally destroy the image in which he was made, then would he prove himself to be greater than his Maker.

It was an intense joy to Gabriel to find that Fabia and he would spend Whitsuntide at Vernacre together. But keen as the temptation was, he would not have accepted Lord Wrexham's invitation to leave his Church and parish at one of the great Festivals of the Christian year, had not his doctor told him that he had been working too hard of late, and must make up his mind either to take a short holiday, or to have a long—perhaps a permanent—one forced upon him later on. So Carr chose the lesser evil, and went away from London.

When first he left town he went for a week or two to Gaythorne Manor; then he came for Whitsuntide to Vernacre; and after that he was going to stay with his mother for a month or two to complete, as he hoped, his cure. But the fact that he was overdone and out of health, made him turn to Fabia, and to all that she represented, with increased eagerness. He had never before realized how much he missed the feminine element in his life and lot. Until now he had believed his work all-sufficing. In health, Gabriel the priest had ever been stronger than Gabriel the man; but who shall blame him if in sickness the more human part of his nature came to the front—the longing for love and tenderness and domestic bliss?

On that Sunday afternoon he and Fabia were sitting together in a secluded part of the garden; and he was very happy. In his need for human care and sympathy, he gave Fabia credit for qualities which she did not possess. In the nature of most women pity is very closely akin to love: the moment they begin to feel sorry for a man—to realize that it is in their power to help and comfort him—it is all up with them; their hearts have already passed out of their own keeping. Perhaps they never love a man so much as when he has taken some remedy which they have prescribed, and is all the better for it. A husband who swallows his wife's remedies, and recovers in consequence (or in spite) of them, is the kind of husband who is most dearly beloved.

But with the woman whose soul cries out for a master rather than for a mate, this is not so. It is strength that appeals most forcibly to her—not weakness: and the less strong a man is, either physically or mentally, the less powerful is his appeal to her heart and sympathies. She would be his devotee rather than his doctor—his worshipper rather than his nurse.

"Miss Vipart," Gabriel began, "I have something to say to you; something which is of vital importance to me, and which I have been wanting to say for a long time."

"Then why have you been a long time in saying it?" The question certainly was pertinent.

"Because, though I wanted to say it, I was not at all sure that you wanted to hear it."

"Ah?" Fabia's expressed answer was monosyllabic, but her understood one was quite the reverse: there was a complete string of notes-of-interrogation in her beautiful eyes at that moment. She possessed to perfection the charm of looking interested when a man was talking to her; and perhaps that is the greatest charm that any woman can have. It is the women who can listen that are the attractive women—at any rate to the opposite sex. They may talk as well, if they like—just enough at any rate gracefully to fill up the interstices in the conversation while the man is preparing his next remark; but, above all things, they must be adepts in the art of listening, if they wish to belong to that fascinating sisterhood who are colloquially described as "men's women." After all—if we are to be perfectly candid with ourselves—which of us goes into society to listen to what other people have to say, except in so far as it suggests to us what to say next? Who wants to hear about the funny sayings of some other man's child, except as a prologue to the recital of the far apter and wittier remarks uttered by our own more interesting and intelligent offspring? We go into society not to listen but to talk: though we are prepared to play the game and to listen—or at any rate to keep silence—while the other person is having his turn; provided always that his turn does not last too long. But there are some people who allow it always to be our turn; and how popular—how deservedly popular—such people are! Of which deserving community was Miss Fabia Vipart.

Encouraged by the notes of interrogation in his companion's eyes, Gabriel continued:

"During the last few weeks a great change has come into my life. I have learnt for the first time all that a woman can be to a man, both as a help and an inspiration. I have learnt how she can strengthen him when he is weak, and uphold him when he is strong; how she can heal him when he is sick, and comfort him when he is sorrowful. In short, how she can be to him all that God meant her to be when He created her as an helpmeet for man."

"And who has taught you all this, Mr. Carr?" Fabia knew all the moves of the game.

"You; no one but you! When first I heard you sing, I had a faint glimmering of all that you could be to me if you cared; and every time that I have seen you since, this truth has grown brighter and clearer. So now, my beloved, I come to ask you the greatest of all favours that a man can ask a woman—I ask you to be my wife."

Fabia hesitated. She did not love the man; she knew that she did not; but he looked so handsome as he proffered his impassioned appeal that his beauty was almost irresistible to her. And then she wanted to be married to an Englishman; to have an assured position of her own. He was poor, but what of that? She had money enough and to spare for both. And although she did not love him, she was nearer to loving him than she had ever been to loving any man yet—as near, in fact, as she believed it was in her nature to be.

"Fabia, my darling, I am waiting for your answer." And his voice, as he spoke to her, was as beautiful as his face. "I believe that I could make you happy; and I know that you could make me more absolutely blissful than it has ever yet been any man's lot to be."

Still Fabia was silent, and no sound broke the stillness save the hum of summer in the air.

"My beloved, won't you speak to me, and tell me

that at any rate I may hope?" urged the man, after
an interminable pause.

Then Fabia spoke.

"Yes, I will marry you," she said; "but only on one
condition." And she had not the faintest idea that her
condition was in any respect a hard one. In fact she
considered that it would be to Gabriel's advantage as
much as to hers.

"And what is that, my dearest? Though whatever
it is, it is already granted." And he stretched out both
arms to her in passionate longing.

"I will marry you on condition that you will give up
being a clergyman, and come abroad with me. There
is no need for you to work, as I have plenty of money;
and besides, you are not strong enough for it. We will
say farewell to England for a time and travel everywhere,
and see the world together, you and I." She really felt
that she could not endure the lot of a clergyman's wife
in an East-end parish; and she did not see why she
should.

The outstretched arms fell limply to his sides. He
could not believe that he had heard aright.

"What? Give up my Orders? I do not know what
you mean."

But Fabia went on unabashed, thinking that she
was asking but a very little thing.

"I only mean that you must give up your work, and
live to enjoy yourself and to see the world. There is
so much to be seen, and so little time in which to see it;
and most people have either not the time or the money
to see it at all. But you and I will have both the time
and the money; and there is nothing that we will not
see. We will wander about at our own sweet will, and
will pry into all the secret places of the earth: we

will turn our backs upon this provincial English
ignorance, and will be as gods knowing good and
evil."

She spoke with unusual animation, for the picture
she was drawing of their future life together fascinated
her; and the more she thought of it the more certain
she felt that this was the lot which could make her
happy: far happier than anything which Charlie
Gaythorne had to offer. There was a nomadic strain
in her blood—a longing for the wild freedom of desert
places—and the mere thought of the home-staying
existence of the Gaythornes of Gaythorne fairly
suffocated her.

"Yes," she went on, "there is nothing that shall
come between us and the fulfilment of our desires.
Whatever we wish to do, that will we do. We will
have no dreary English estate, with its tenants and its
responsibilities, always dragging at our heels, but—like
Bacon—we will take all Nature for our province.
Truly we will see the world. And then, when we have
seen all that there is to be seen, and are growing old
and weary, we will settle down in some southern place,
as beautiful as a dream, and will drowse away the
remainder of our days in the sunshine."

Thus she spoke, carried away by the vision that her
own words conjured up, and intoxicated by the thought
of her coming happiness; and as he listened, Gabriel's
love for her fell dead at his feet, slain by her own hand.
The intrinsic royalty of his priesthood rose up in his
soul, and spurned the base suggestion that had just
been made to him: Gabriel the man was merged in
Gabriel the priest. His love for the woman was
extinguished in his scorn for the blasphemer who had
thus dared to lay profane hands upon the very Ark of

God. In his eyes they had ceased to be man and
woman : she was but the sacrilegious person who had
defiled the Holy Place, and he was the judge and the
avenger. She had tampered with that which was
dearer to him than life itself, the sanctity of his
priesthood : and in so doing had placed herself
for ever, as far as he was concerned, beyond the
pale.

"Fabia!" he cried, "do you know what you are
saying ? You tempt me to commit the unpardonable
sin as glibly as you would ask me to walk across the
lawn. You have insulted me and defied the God Whom
I serve ; all is over for ever between us." And he turned
on his heel and left her.

Fabia sat still for a minute as one stunned. It was
all so strange, so unexpected. But, with her usual
quickness of perception, she at once realized what she
had done. She knew that she had offended Gabriel
past any possibility of reconciliation—that all was over
indeed between them. And she also knew that when the
priest in him rose up and made him more than man, he
was for the first time stronger than she, and was her
master ; and that at that moment she had learnt to
love him.

Just as she made this all-important and most
disconcerting discovery, who should come sauntering
up but Charlie Gaythorne, with a cigarette in his mouth
and a proposal in his eye. No sooner did he espy the
vacant place at Fabia's side than he flung his cigar and
his caution alike to the winds, and set to work with all
the dogged determination of an Englishman and a
soldier. He succinctly and tersely conveyed to Fabia's
mind the importance of the compliment she was going
to receive, and for which she had every reason to be

truly thankful. Charlie was not much of a talker, as a rule; but when he had anything to say, he said it—and this happened to be one of those rare occasions. With regard to their respective social positions he extenuated nothing nor set down aught in malice: he was too much of a gentleman either to brag about his own advantages or to underrate hers; but he was also far too simple and transparent to hide from Fabia what a magnificent opening he considered it for any woman to be invited to succeed his august parent as mistress of Gaythorne Manor. And, strange to say, it was this very argument—which at another time would only have roused Fabia's wrath and scorn—that on this particular occasion won the day. She could see what a grand thing Charlie thought it was to be Mrs. Gaythorne—she knew that Charlie's world looked at things very much from Charlie's point of view—and she wanted to do something that would win for her the respect of other people and restore to her her own. She was feeling hurt and lonely: and there is no atmosphere so conducive to the acceptance of offers of marriage as the atmosphere of pained desolation. Gabriel's rebuff had left her sore and wounded to the death; and she felt that she could not go on living unless something were done to bring her wounded spirit ease. And this seemed the very thing that was needed.

As Charlie's wife she would have an assured position and a devoted husband — the two finest supporters possible for a female coat of arms. True, she did not love him, and she did love Gabriel: but she was clever enough to know when a thing was beyond her reach, and too clever to waste her time in striving to attain the unattainable. Gabriel would never marry her now: Charlie would: so she decided to accept Charlie.

Charlie, of course, was in the seventh heaven of delight. It never occurred to him that he had anything or anybody but himself to thank for the success of his wooing. He had not yet learned that in many cases it is the hour rather than the man that is responsible for a woman's Yes. If a suitor will only time his opportunity correctly, he can generally ensure the advantage (or disadvantage) of being accepted.

Gabriel, meanwhile, was engaged in a sore struggle with himself. True, his love for Fabia fell dead on the spot, when she trampled on his highest ideals and his most sacred beliefs by asking him to renounce his Orders for her sake; but love, even when dead, is not obliterated, but still requires decent burial and a suitable period of mourning.

Carr's first impulse was to go right away from Vernacre and never to look upon Fabia's face again; but reflection showed him that such a course—though the most comfortable as far as he was concerned—would be most uncomfortable for everybody else, and would therefore partake of the nature of selfishness: and Gabriel had too much of the feminine element in his character ever to be guilty of selfishness in any form. He knew that it would upset things generally—and most especially his host, who was a regular old bachelor with regard to the inviolability of even the smallest plan—if a guest who had arranged to stay until Tuesday fled incontinently upon Sunday afternoon: and Gabriel —always more ready to consider others than himself— decided to spare Lord Wrexham this avoidable agony. Moreover, he felt that by making his speedy escape from the scene of his disappointment and disillusion, he would put both himself and Fabia in a false position: so he decided to bury his own suffering out of sight, and

to behave—as far as in him lay—for the rest of his visit
to Vernacre as if nothing had happened, in order that
other people should not be made uncomfortable by his
distress. Wherein he showed himself a man, a woman,
and a gentleman: a most admirable if rare trilogy.

CHAPTER X

GABRIEL THE PASTOR

On the following day, as soon as lunch was over and the company had variously distributed themselves as they thought fit, Isabel Seaton and Gabriel Carr went for a walk together. They were great friends—had been so ever since they first met, not long after Isabel's marriage—and each enjoyed a talk with the other after the fashion of iron sharpening iron. They passed out of the garden and into the park, and then began the ascent of a grassy hill which culminated in the finest view in the county: and as they went they talked by the way.

It was a glorious afternoon; one of those perfect-days of early summer when the world is ablaze with colour. Every tree of the field had a particular green of its own, unlike the green of any of its fellows; and the banks were carpeted with flowers.

"Has it ever struck you," asked Gabriel, "that summer is the carnival of colour, as winter is the carnival of form? If you love colour, you will prefer the summer woods; but if form appeals to you, you will revel in the leafless trees."

"To tell the truth, it never did; but now you mention it, I feel as if the idea were my own. And this further explains why I like summer so much better than winter, for the same reason that I spend hours among the pictures in the Academy and only minutes among the sculpture: I love colour and don't care for form. Everything has a colour to me—even sounds."

Gabriel's face was filled with interest; he loved new ideas; and, failing them, he liked to find new garments for old ones, as he had learned the cramping effects upon stereotyped forms. "How do you mean?"

"It is rather difficult to explain; but I seem unconsciously to translate sound into colour before I can understand it. For instance, to me, all the vowel sounds are represented by different colours."

"How very interesting! What colour is A?"

"A is green, and E is blue, and I is white, and O is orange, and U is purple."

"And what about W and Y? Haven't they got colours also?"

"Oh! yes; of course they have. W is red, and Y is yellow."

"And why did you choose these particular colours for the vowel sounds?" asked Carr.

"There is no why or wherefore, and ı didn't choose them. To me A is green and E is blue, just as the grass is green and the sky is blue: there is no choice or reason in the matter. It is simply how they appear to me."

"Have other sounds colour to you also?"

"Yes; voices have. Soprano voices are pale blue or green or yellow or white; contraltos are pink or red or violet; and tenors are different shades of brown; and basses are black or dark green or navy blue."

"Anything else?"

"Yes, nearly everything. The days of the week have different colours."

" And what are they ? "

" Monday is green, and Tuesday pink, and Wednesday blue, and Thursday brown, and Friday purple, and Saturday yellow, and Sunday white. Colour is everything to me, and everything to me has colour."

Carr looked at her thoughtfully. " Yes ; you are the type of woman who would be sure to love colour."

" Why ? "

" Because what is vivid appeals to you more than what is suggestive ; because what is expressed touches you more than what is understood."

Isabel tossed her head. " You don't mean that altogether as a compliment."

" Perhaps not ; yet certainly not as the reverse. I was merely stating a fact, and not drawing any deduction from it either one way or the other."

" I see. You were giving me the heads without the application. I think I like that sort of sermon best. Heads or tails—I mean heads or applications ? I say heads, and let the applications take care of themselves."

" It is the application that will do you the most good, Mrs. Seaton."

" Very well, then. Here's for the application, and I'll swallow it whole. 'To be well shaken before taken,' I suppose. I'll shake the head and swallow the application, and so all parties will be satisfied."

Gabriel smiled. " But I have just said that there is no application. You can't swallow what doesn't exist."

" Can't I, though ? I've been swallowing the principles of the extreme Radical party for years."

" I'm afraid you are rather disloyal to that section of the Liberal party to which your husband belongs," remonstrated Gabriel.

Isabel's face grew grave. "I'm not really; I was only joking; but I see the mistakes into which it is rushing, and I want to save it from them. And most especially do I want to save Paul from the making of mistakes and the disappointment which they bring."

"Why?"

Isabel looked at her companion with surprise that he should have wasted time and breath in the asking of so unnecessary a question. "Because I love him, and therefore wish to spare him pain."

"Pardon me, there is no 'therefore' in that sentence. Pain may be good—may be necessary—for a person; and in that case because you loved him, you would *not* wish to spare him pain."

"But i do. I hate Paul to be vexed about any-thing."

"You mustn't spoil him. You are his wife; not his mother. It doesn't do for a wife's affection for her husband to be too maternal: it stunts his spiritual growth."

"But a woman must be maternal to somebody." And there was that pathetic ring in Isabel's voice which always went to Paul's heart. Gabriel heard it, and it touched him also.

"I know," he answered, very gently; "but not to her husband, if she will make a man of him. Besides, it is all the wrong way about. The husband is the head of the wife, and this is in accordance with God's ordinance; but we don't pet our rulers."

Isabel's face grew perplexed. "Then do you mean to say that a woman ought to obey her husband even when she knows better than he does?"

"Certainly; even when she thinks that she knows better than he does." Gabriel amended the sentence.

Isabel was quick to notice the amendment, and to resent it. "But knowing better isn't merely a matter of opinion."

"Pardon me, I think not infrequently it is. People say, 'If I were So-and-So I should do such-and-such a thing.' So they would; but that doesn't prove it would be a better or a wiser thing than what So-and-So is actually doing. It would merely be a different thing; that is all. If I say that I know better than you how to do something, it only means that I know better how to do it in my particular way. It doesn't follow that my way is any better than yours — or even as good."

Isabel was unconvinced: this was not palatable doctrine to a woman who was as sure of herself as she was. But the fact that doctrine is unpalatable, in no way detracts from its salutariness: frequently the reverse.

"Can't you understand," she persisted, "that if a woman loves her husband, she naturally wants to prevent him from making mistakes?"

"She can't do that: everybody must make mistakes. All that she can do is to induce him to make her mistakes instead of his own. She won't make him wise; she will only substitute her particular brand of folly for his: and for the life of me I cannot see any great advantage in that. A man would far rather make his own mistakes than anybody else's—even than his wife's. His own natural mistakes are in drawing with the rest of his character, and assumed ones are not."

"Then you think it is a mistake for wives to interfere too much in their husband's public life?"

Although Isabel might not like Gabriel's advice, she was sufficiently just to weigh it and to give it full consideration. She was always an eminently reasonable woman. At least, nearly always.

"A very great mistake: often a fatal mistake."

Carr spoke strongly. He was sore after yesterday's interview with Fabia, and filled with horror at the mere idea of how she—had she been his wife—would have used her influence to his soul's undoing. Our opinions are always tinged by our experience; and the more recent the experience the deeper the tinge.

"But you wouldn't object half so much to a husband who tried to stop his wife from making mistakes?" said Isabel shrewdly.

"That is a totally different thing. I believe that a woman's place is to look on and cheer and lighten and help, rather than to dictate or do the work herself. I always think that line of Charles Kingsley's, 'Three wives sat up in the lighthouse tower, trimming the lamps as the sun went down,' conveys a very fair idea of woman's place and duty. It is a wife's place to sit up aloft in the lighthouse tower, above the sordid cares and struggles of the business-world, and to trim the lights for her husband so that he may be guided in the right way, even though his sun be gone down; but it is not her place to embark on the high seas of business or politics, and try to steer his boat for him."

Mrs. Seaton tossed her head, as she always did when annoyed or indignant. It was a favourite gesture of hers. "Well, I don't see why it should be all right for a man to dictate to his wife, and all wrong for a woman to dictate to her husband. I don't see why a woman's advice to her husband should be a treasonable document, and a husband's advice to his wife an Act of Parliament."

"Because God ordained it so. There is no other reason."

Isabel was silent: partly because she did not know exactly what to say, and partly because she had not much breath with which to say it, as they had reached the steepest part of the hill just below the summit. The two walked—or rather climbed—on for a few minutes without speaking, and then they reached the top of the hill, and the whole glorious stretch of country at their feet suddenly was revealed to their view. It was one of those typical English landscapes—with green foregrounds and blue distances, with near woodlands and distant hills—which can never be actually described to anyone who has not seen them; and which need no description to us who know and love them, for to us they spell the magic word *home*.

"Isn't it magnificent?" exclaimed Isabel, after they had gazed for a few minutes in awestruck silence. "It fairly takes away one's breath—at least as much of it as the ascent has left."

"It does: it is a wonderful view."

"And so thoroughly English, and therefore so satisfying," Isabel continued. "Have you ever noticed that foreign scenery, however beautiful and magnificent, leaves you with a restless, hungry sort of feeling; but that a perfect English landscape such as this, seems to soak into every little crevice of your soul, and to make you quite peaceful and content?"

"I have. It is a more middle-aged sort of feeling than the other, but much more comfortable."

"Middle-aged sorts of feelings are generally the most comfortable," said Isabel sagely. "When you are quite young you are so anxious to see what is going to happen, that you skip the book of daily life in order to get on with the story; but as you get older you think more of the style and the characters and the dialogue than of the plot; and so you are better able to enjoy and appreciate the work as a whole."

Again the two friends were silent, dwelling on the beauty of the scene before them. Gabriel took off his hat, and let the soft breeze cool his forehead; and as he did so, the misery which Fabia had brought upon him faded away like a mist, and once more he saw plain. But his companion's eyes grew grave, and there was a pathetic droop at the corner of her mouth.

"Isn't it funny," she suddenly remarked, "that there is always something rather sad about the top of a hill? As long as you are climbing, you are full of joy and energy and hope; but when you get to the top everything changes, and you almost wish the hill had been a bit higher so that you might still be on the climb. It is the same with everything. We envy the people who have 'arrived,' and who have attained the summit of their respective ambitions: yet if we were wise in our envying, and directed it judiciously, we should rather envy those who are still swarming up the slopes. Hill-tops, on the whole, are rather sorrowful places." And Isabel sighed.

"A somewhat pessimistic doctrine, Mrs. Seaton, to be enunciated by one of the most popular and successful women in London!" said Gabriel, with a smile.

"Nevertheless a true one."

"I think not."

Isabel raised her eyebrows. She had a great theory that it was the duty of the clergy to offer ample advice to the laity on all questions moral and religious: that a clergyman was a specialist in spiritual matters, just as a doctor was a specialist in physical ones; nevertheless she was always slightly ruffled when the ghostly counsel, which she so freely sought, did not altogether tally with her own preconceived notions on any subject. Wherein she was distinctly feminine, both in her longing for priestly assistance and her rejection of it when found.

"Well, anyhow, S. Paul agreed with me," she retorted; "he particularly mentions that he was always pressing forward and 'had never attained.'" She felt that this was a clinching argument; and that an alliance between the Apostle of the Gentiles and Mrs. Seaton formed an authority which few theologians would dare to dispute. "And surely you'll admit that S. Paul was a past master in the art of contentment?"

"Certainly," replied Gabriel. "And why was he content?"

"Because he hadn't reached the top of the hill."

There was triumph as well as finality in Mrs. Seaton's tone.

"Pardon me: he had reached the top of a good many hills. But he had learnt what you apparently forget, Mrs. Seaton; namely, that when we have gained the summit of one hill, there are always plenty of higher ones still for us to climb."

"Oh!" Isabel had not a good answer ready, so wisely confined herself to the monosyllable.

Carr continued:

"I understand the feeling to which you refer—the sadness of the hill-tops; but, believe me, it is an ignoble sadness. It either means that we are too easily satisfied with our achievements and have neither the strength nor the courage to persevere; or else it means that the hill we have just climbed was not worth the climbing;

in which case, it was a pity that we ever wasted our time and trouble on it at all."

"I see. It hadn't occurred to me to look at it in that light."

Isabel spoke slowly. She was always ready to see when she was in the wrong, although it must be admitted that the sight was not altogether an agreeable one to her.

"S. Paul had not only mastered the art of content," Carr went on, "but he had also mastered the art of discontent. He knew how to be abased as well as how to abound."

"I believe you are right; but somehow that hill-top sadness seemed to me to be rather a beautiful and interesting sort of thing. I quite piqued myself on it."

"You would do," replied Gabriel, with a smile. "Sadness is always beautiful and interesting to us as long as we are young and have never met it face to face."

"It was rather young of me, I confess! You must admit that I was old enough to know better."

"Nevertheless you didn't know better, Mrs. Seaton."

Isabel, as usual, was quite ready to laugh at herself.

"I think you may take it as an axiom," continued Carr, "that when you feel what you call the sadness of the hill-top, the particular hill in question was not worth the climbing. It is a pretty fair test. The hills that are worth climbing always lead us on to other hills that are still more worth climbing: and thus are formed 'the great world's altar - stairs, which slope through darkness up to God.' Therefore there is no time for sadness, and no place for it, either."

"Yes, yes: you are right and I was wrong. And,

after all, I'm rather glad that there is no occasion for
that particular sort of sadness, though I must admit
I've rather enjoyed it at times. But all sadness is
really horrid underneath, however nice and interesting
it may appear on the surface: isn't it?"

Gabriel demurred. He was not going to commit
himself to so sweeping a statement.

"My husband never suffers from the hill-top sadness,"
continued Isabel; "the moment he has topped one hill
he is bounding off to another, like a young hart. The
fact that his hills are not worth climbing has no effect
upon him."

"Your husband is still very young."

"I know he is: much younger than I am, though he
was really born a year and a half earlier."

"That has nothing to do with it."

"Not it! Age is a matter of temperament rather
than of time. Everybody is a certain age by nature:
and the number of years we happen to have dwelt on
this planet, is merely an incident which is nobody's
business but our own. Nothing will make my husband
more than nineteen, however long he lives: while I was
thirty-three and a half before I left my cradle. You
are about five-and-twenty, and always will be: and
Wrexham has never gone below eighty-four since he
was born."

"And what is our good Mrs. Gaythorne?"

"A good fifty-five, with exuberant prejudice keeping
off age on the one hand, and misplaced conviction
staving off youth on the other."

Gabriel could not fail to appreciate this description;
he knew Mrs. Gaythorne so well.

Isabel went on:

"It is Paul's youngness that makes him so ready to

scale heights that are not worth the scaling; and my oldness that makes me want to hold him back."

Gabriel looked at her thoughtfully. This woman always interested him, she was so full of contradictions —so fresh and so *blasé*, so wise and so thoughtless, so gay and so serious, all at the same time. But in spite of her fascination for him he felt it his duty to administer to her ghostly counsel and reproof; and—having seen his duty—he was not the man to postpone it to a more convenient season.

"I think you are wrong in trying to hold him back," he said quietly.

Isabel started. She was not accustomed to being reproved or found fault with, and she did not like it. But she liked it better than not being talked about at all; so she continued the discussion with apparent, if not sincere, humility.

"Why am I wrong? He'd make most awful blunders if I didn't."

"So you have remarked before, and so I still presume to doubt. But even if that is so, you have no right to hamper and hinder him."

"Why not, I should like to know?"

"In the first place, because you are his wife, and so are in subjection to him, and are bound to obey and serve him by your own vow; and, in the second place, because his readiness to attempt the ascent of what you consider unscalable mountains, shows that he has more faith than you have, and so is farther advanced in the spiritual life."

Isabel fairly gasped. She had decided to reverence her husband, and was fully convinced that she did so, according to the dictates of Holy Scripture; but her idea of reverence was a combination of indulgent

tolerance with thinly veiled superiority. It is an idea
which obtains among many otherwise excellent wives.

"I shouldn't call it exactly faith," she objected.

"Why not? That is its name," said Gabriel.

"I see; and so you call it by it, just as you call a
spade a spade, and Branson's Extract of Coffee perfection. But I should not call it faith as long as it was
only applied to political things: I should only call it
faith if it was applied to religious things."

"Oh, dear; oh, dear! You are every bit as bad as a
suburban tradesman! I am always trying in vain to
convince my very respectable and superior parishioners
that there are no such things as religious things. All
things are religious, or else nothing is: there is no
middle course. Religion either permeates every thought
and act and object of a man's life, or else it never really
touches anything in it at all. I hate the cant which sets
a boundary between what is religious and what is secular,
so-called: for unless a man's religion touches everything
about him and around him and within him, that man's
religion is vain."

It was a hard saying; but Gabriel could be hard at
times. He was no rose-water sentimentalist.

"The world has no idea," he went on rapidly, "of the
stupendous power of faith. Men say that the age of
miracles is past; but that is not so—it is the age of
faith which made miracles possible that is past."

"Then do you think that if a man had only faith
enough he could scale every mountain?"

"Scale it? Why he could say to it, 'Be thou removed
and cast into the midst of the sea'; and it would be
done. I believe there is nothing that a man could not
do if only he had enough faith—no miracle that he
could not perform. The present age is not an age of

faith: it is an age of charity. We build infirmaries and we endow hospitals; but we no longer lay hands on the sick that they may recover. Silver and gold we have, and we use it on the whole beneficially; but we no longer bid a man take up his bed and walk.

"Do you think that this lack of faith is felt in all the Churches?" asked Isabel.

"I do. I think that in the present day religion is to the Roman a passion, to the Anglican a principle, and to the Nonconformist an emotion; but I think that to many of them it is not the power of God unto salvation —both of body and soul—that it might be, if there were more faith on the earth. Otherwise we should still have the miracles of the early Church and of the Middle Ages and of the Evangelical Revival."

"You are quite right: the want of faith of the present day is something dreadful. It always sickens me to hear people talk as they do of 'remarkable answers to prayer': yet these people would see nothing remarkable at all in an answer to a telegram! It seems a queer sort of belief that strains at the faithfulness of God, and then swallows without an effort the infallibility of a telegraph-boy!"

"It does indeed: yet it is essentially the belief of the present day and generation."

The two were walking down the hill again by this time, and Carr's face was aglow with the enthusiasms that were stirring within him. It was in matters spiritual that he was always most at home: the secular emotions—such as love, ambition, and the like—though not exactly foreign to his nature, were not quite in perfect harmony with it. But his companion's face was grave. She was made of slighter elements than he; and it was the more human and personal side of life that

L

touched her most closely. Gabriel would have made a splendid monk; but Isabel could never have been anything but fifth-rate as a nun. Therefore she suddenly harked back to that point in the conversation where Carr had turned away from earth and began to soar heavenward.

"You said, firstly because I am his wife, and therefore am in subjection to him," she began: "what did you mean by that?"

With the quick sympathy and ready adaptibility of the man who has been trained for the priesthood, Gabriel fell in with her mood at once.

"I mean exactly what S. Peter meant when he said it," he replied: "neither more nor less. 'Likewise, ye wives, be in subjection to your own husbands.' It seems quite plain speaking."

It is the fashion nowadays, in this very enlightened age, to talk much and not always kindly of the faults and failings of the clergy—of those peculiarities which distinguish them as a body from their lay brethren. But what about the special virtues which are theirs by right of their clerical training, and in which the laity are conspicuously lacking: the intuition, the sympathy, the self-repression, the self-control, which we take as a matter of course in our spiritual pastors, but which we frequently seek in vain in the successful tradesman or the man of affairs? When the enemy has found occasion to blaspheme and is availing himself of the same, it is a favourite gibe of his to discover points of resemblance between clergymen and women. And he is right. As a rule, a clergyman, more than any other man, has the power of discovering other people's joys and sorrows, and throwing himself into them, in a way that is popularly supposed to be the prerogative

of the weaker sex. His very calling trains him to
suppress his own wants and wishes in attending to
the wants and wishes of his flock: just as a woman is
trained to suppress her own wants and wishes in
attending to the wants and wishes of her family.
The ordinary male is not so trained: as a rule
other people do not bother him with their troubles,
nor does he bother them with his: he neither offers
sympathy nor demands it. He is more like a child
than a woman, possessing childlike simplicity and
straightforwardness rather than feminine subtlety and
intuition.

Thanks to Gabriel's clerical training, he understood
pretty well what was passing in his companion's mind
as she walked beside him in silence for a few moments.
He knew that her sound common-sense was at war with
her husband's idealism, and that her womanly wilfulness
was at variance with her wifely submission. But he
meant to tell her the truth when she gave him an
opportunity; and if she did not give him an opportunity,
he meant to make one.

But she did.

"Supposing that a wife knows better than her
husband," she argued, "and that the grey mare is really
a twenty-four-horse-power motor car; do you think even
then she ought to obey and reverence him?"

"Not a doubt of it, my dear Mrs. Seaton. Of course
she should influence him to the utmost of her ability,
and give him as good advice as she can, when he is
taking any; but she must never forget that—by right of
his office—the husband is the head of the wife."

"Even if he is an inferior article?"

"Certainly. As a Churchwoman you believe that the
unworthiness of a priest is no way interferes with the

efficacy of the sacraments: as a British citizen you admit that the personal character of a judge in no way affects the validity of his sentences; and as a wife you must therefore accept the fact that the faults and failings of a man in no way obviate his prerogative as a husband."

Isabel shrugged her shoulders. "You hold the doctrine that the king can do no wrong."

"I do: and I consider it a very sound doctrine, too. Of course as a man he can do wrong, but as a king he cannot; because the king and the priest and the judge and the husband are all—in their own way and for the time being—the ambassadors and representatives of God ; and in reverencing them we reverence the Divine Authority Which is for the moment vested in them ; and submit ourselves to every ordinance of man for the Lord's sake."

Isabel looked up with a glance of warm approbation. "How nicely you put things ! You have such a richly decorative mind, that you make quite common things seem positively gorgeous."

"Do 'quite common things' refer to kings or to husbands ?" asked Carr, with a smile.

"Neither in particular, and roughly speaking, both. But you have a knack of sticking haloes on to everything and everybody, and somehow transfiguring them. I never knew anyone like you at the halo-business, except a few occasional sunsets and certain hymns. There are some hymn-tunes that have precisely the same effect on me that you have ; make me feel good and glorified and treading on air."

"I am glad to hear it."

"Just now I feel as if I couldn't wait another minute without flying to Paul, and implicitly obeying him in something that I know to be utterly absurd. At the present moment I could die for a lost cause, or start a Woman's Liberal Federation without turning a hair. I could indeed. And all because Paul is my husband and you've stuck a halo on to him."

"But I didn't make him your husband; you will admit that. I may have arranged the halo; but it was you who agreed to the wearing of the wedding-ring. There was a certain amount of free-will in the business, after all, Mrs. Seaton. Your king may reign by divine right; I believe he does; but remember, you elected him yourself in the first instance."

"So I did; and I'm very glad I did; and if there was another election to-morrow, he'd still be at the top of the poll. Which reminds me that we are at the bottom of the hill; and I'll run and find him, and obey him this very minute; and tell him how kind you have been in fastening a bit of string to his halo for fear it should get blown off when things are slightly breezy. I must say there is a danger of husbands' haloes blowing off, if they are not properly fastened on. But now Paul's is secured, thanks to you, with an elastic band under his chin, like a little boy's hat; and, unless he deliberately takes it off, nothing can remove it."

"I have known husbands deliberately to take them off," said Gabriel.

"So have I: to some passing lady of their acquaintance: and then the wives can't always put them on again. But thank Heaven! Paul isn't that sort. If ever his halo does tumble off, you can be sure that it is I who have knocked it off: it wouldn't be his fault, poor darling!"

"Certainly it would not. So be careful that you never do such a thing, Mrs. Seaton."

Isabel laughed good-humouredly. "Not I. It is

all very well for the Sergeant-at-Arms to call, ' Hats
off !'; but if he begins calling ' Haloes off !', I shall
protest.   It would never do for my husband to be
without his halo : it would be so cold for him and so dark
for me, and so generally horrid all round !"

CHAPTER XI

JANET FIELD

WHEN the Whitsuntide party at Vernacre broke up, Gabriel went to complete his enforced holiday and regain his enfeebled strength at his mother's home in a small Midland village about four miles from Merchester. It was an ideal house for a widow-lady of limited means. Not more than a cottage in size and design, but stamped all over with the indelible and indescribable signs of refinement and ladyhood. The way in which it draped itself with creepers was modesty personified, and suggested all the sensitiveness and refinement which are associated with flowing veils and lace shawls. Its windows were so shaded with soft greenery, that they could not properly lift their eyelids and face the sunshine; and its chimneys were so clothed with the same, that only the smoke, which now and again emerged from their half-shut mouths, proclaimed them to be anything so commonplace and obvious as chimneys at all. Which things were symbolical of the character of the owner of the cottage, who had never called a spade a spade, nor looked a bare fact in the face, since the day she was born.

Eveline Carr was one of those people who are known in their youth as " lovely young creatures," and in their later life as " sweet women." She was tall and slight,

with fair hair and blue eyes, and a complexion that
retained its apple-blossom tints even until the late
autumn of life. She was elegant rather than stylish,
lovable rather than fascinating. She was amiability
incarnate, and was unselfish to the verge of insipidity:
and, in fact, possessed all the virtues, excepting strength,
courage, and a sense of humour. It really would have
been difficult, even had her friends and acquaintances
been so uncharitably inclined, to find any actual fault
in Mrs. Carr's character: the absence of certain
excellencies was the worst of which anyone could
accuse her. That she had left undone sundry things
which she ought to have done, was sufficiently within
the range of probability to entitle her to take her part
in the General Confession: but that she had ever
done anything that she ought not to have done,
was hardly credible to anyone who enjoyed the
pleasure of Mrs. Carr's acquaintance. Her mind
was cultured and refined: but it was always enveloped
in a soft haze, too indistinct to be called a mist, and too
intangible to be described as a fog. Her distinguishing
characteristic (if such a term could be applied to a
character where everything was indistinguishable) was
vagueness — vagueness in thought, in belief, and in
conversation.

In strong contrast to Mrs. Carr was her adopted
daughter, Janet Field. Janet was no blood-relation of
Mrs. Carr's; if she had been, her claim would have been
too obvious to appeal to that excellent lady. She was
the only child of a fellow-officer of Eveline's husband:
her father was killed in action a few months after her
birth, and her mother did not long survive him; and the
very fact that the infant had no claim whatsoever upon
Mrs. Carr's charity, was the strongest claim that she

could possibly have had. The only thing needed to
clinch this appeal and to make it final and irresistible,
was the fact that the child should be utterly destitute,
and unable to repay Mrs. Carr for any of the care and
expense which that good woman was prepared freely to
lavish upon her; and this recommendation the poor
baby possessed to the full. Therefore Mrs. Carr—being
herself the widow of a young officer in very straitened
circumstances, with a boy of her own to bring up and
educate—saw no reason why she should not at once
apply for the vacant post of little Janet Field's mother:
and the child's relations—being ordinary selfish human
beings—were only too glad to take advantage of the
pretty young widow's inexperience and impracticability,
and to shift the expense and care of the child from their
shoulders on to hers. Which they promptly did ; and
then washed their hands of all further responsibility:
thereby resigning for ever, in favour of Eveline Carr,
their vested interest in all the blessings pertaining to
the great "Inasmuch as ye did it to one of the least
of these."

So it came to pass that Gabriel Carr and Janet Field
were brought up as brother and sister, she being a few
years younger than he.

Janet proved to be a most admirable and healthy
element in the Carr household. Whilst Gabriel was
idealistic and theoretic, and his mother absolutely
indistinct, Janet was the embodiment of definite
clearness. There was no vagueness about her — no
atmosphere even : the lights and shadows in her mind
were as clearly defined as the lights and shadows in an
Egyptian photograph. Even the "grey matter" in her
brain could hardly have been so indefinite a colour as
grey, as it is in the case of the rest of us : it must really

have been actual black and white, or else it never could have formed a part of Janet.

Janet not only knew exactly what she herself thought upon every subject under the sun: she also knew that hers was the only point of view compatible with wisdom and honesty; a most comfortable form of knowledge! She treated Mrs. Carr with unwearying indulgence and maternal solicitude: the latter believed that she had adopted Janet, but in reality Janet had adopted her: and she worshipped Gabriel with that absolute devotion which combines the love of sister and of wife; and which is never felt save by those who fall in love as women with the men who were their playmates as children.

In appearance Janet was by no means as handsome as the Carrs; but she was very pleasant-looking, and not without a charm of her own. She was under rather than over the medium height, and inclined to be plump rather than slight. Her hair was brown, and her eyes were hazel, and she had a bright pink colour in her rounded cheeks.

It had never occurred to Gabriel to fall in love with her, as she had long ago fallen in love with him. Men keep the conjugal and fraternal affections much farther apart than women do. When a man promises to be a brother to a woman, he means to be a brother to her— neither more nor less—with all a brother's reserves and limitations; but when a woman promises to be a sister to a man—well, if she does not mean him to make love to her, she means something singularly like it.

It was to this little household that Gabriel came straight from Vernacre; and highly delighted were both these loving women to welcome him. They showed this delight in their respective ways: his mother by putting vases of flowers on his dressing-table, which upset themselves and baptized him with unclean water every time that he attempted to brush his hair; and Janet by seeing that his bed was aired, and his wardrobe emptied of those overflow garments which are so apt to gather themselves together in the spare-room of every small house.

"I don't think Gabriel is looking at all well," Janet remarked to Mrs. Carr, the first time after his arrival that he left them together.

Gabriel's mother looked up from her knitting with a dreamy smile. "Don't you, love? It hadn't occurred to me, as he never has much colour, his dear father having been pale with such chiselled features, which are characteristic of the Carr family and came over with William the Conqueror and settled there. A very old family, and always such beautifully-shaped hands. My boy is wonderfully like his dear father, only a clergyman, the clerical dress making a certain amount of difference from uniform, and black of course always causing anyone to look paler than in scarlet."

"I know that Gabriel is never rosy; but I am sure that now he looks paler and more tired than usual," Janet persisted.

"No; my boy was never ruddy, though of a fair countenance, like David and Goliath which I always feel is Sin, and his sermons like the stones which he put in his sling, and so fought against the enemy and prevailed, though I cannot help thinking that a country parish would be better for him—especially in the hot weather. It is so difficult sometimes to reconcile one's duty with what is best for one's health, like the pay in the Indian army being so much higher than at home, and yet so hard to choose between leaving one's husband alone in India or one's children alone in England. And I never think that female relations—however kind—are quite the same as one's own mother; though I am sure, dearest, I have always tried to do my duty by you."

To live with Mrs. Carr, and to listen to all she said would have made life impossible Janet never attempted or pretended to do it.

"I am sure that he is working much too hard, Aunt Eveline."

Mrs. Carr was the type of women who always insisted on being called Aunt by all young persons not related to her by the ties of kinship.

"Do you think so, dearest? Still, after all, youth is the time for work, before the night cometh when no man can work, or even take a Canonry or a rural parish. I am always hoping that in the future my Gabriel will be given a Canonry by some of his influential friends, and a sweet house in some secluded close, if not a rural parish with a good stipend and a substantial Easter offering, and one sermon a week with the curate preaching the other, and that not always a new one."

"It worried me his taking that suburban place," continued the imperturbable Janet. "It meant so much struggling and working it up, and he was completely worn out already by his work in the slums. I was always against S. Etheldreda's, as you know."

"Still, darling, when a distinct call comes it seems hardly right to disregard it, since as our day is so shall our strength be, even in a town parish without a curate and no endowment to speak of. We must have faith according to our needs."

"And rich people must have charity according to

their means," retorted Janet, "or else how can the work of the Church be carried on? I always think that the clergy of the Church of England are horribly underpaid. Nonconformists would scorn to be as stingy with their ministers as we are with ours."

"Yes, dearest, I have heard that said by quite clever people as a proof of disestablishment or disendowment, or something of that kind. But to my mind, there is a solidity about a State Church which the world cannot give nor take away, even though the stipend be inadequate and often such large families. An Established Church seems to me like family prayers in a private household: beginning the day with an open acknowledgment that God is the Head of everything, and regarded as such even by the most worldly and ambitious."

"All the same, Aunt Eveline, I think that the living of S. Etheldreda's is too hard work and too little pay for Gabriel."

"Well, love, since you think it, I'll send in to Merchester by the carrier to-morrow, and get him a bottle of that tonic which did me so much good just after dear Gabriel was born. I frequently take it when I am at all run down, and find it of the greatest benefit. A mixture of quinine and iron for exhaustion and lassitude in water exactly half an hour after food."

Mrs. Carr was the type of woman who usually relies upon home-made remedies for ordinary infirmities of the flesh; but who, in more urgent cases, will now and again meet the emergency by a bottle of medicine from the chemist's. To such women the advent of the doctor is on a par with the Commendatory prayers.

But the wise Janet shook her head.

"Prevention is better than cure," she said; "and it

is wiser to avoid being ill at all, than to cure yourself
by taking medicine."

" Of course, dear love, I admit that a stitch in time
saves many a bottle of doctor's stuff, and is less
upsetting to the digestion, many people not being
able to assimilate iron without headache and quinine
in a liquid form. But for such people there are always
pills, and so much more convenient if you are lunching
or dining out."

" All the same, I am wretched about Gabriel. I am
sure he isn't well and he isn't happy. I saw it the
moment he entered the house."

It was not easy to turn Miss Field from any matter
on which her attention had alighted.

" He may not be well, my darling, but I am sure he
is happy, since happiness consists in the fulfilment of
duty unhampered by domestic trials; and I know no
man who so thoroughly fulfils his duty as my Gabriel
does, excepting his dear father, who, if he had lived,
would by now have obtained his colonelcy, given the
ordinary flow of promotion, which is always quicker in
time of war. He is very like him: I see it more and
more : being now so much the same age, though slightly
thinner ; and of course the difference in dress between
a soldier and a clergyman, as I've said before."

At that moment the subject of the ladies' conversation
entered the room, and the discussion as to his physical
condition had perforce to be dropped.

Gabriel stayed on and on at his mother's, living out-
of-doors as much as possible in the bracing Midland
air : but he did not gain strength as quickly as he had
hoped and expected. Mrs. Carr naturally did not
notice this; but no symptom of his weakness and
weariness was lost upon Janet. Her eagle eye pene-

trated the depression that he fain would hide: and she was not far from guessing the cause of that depression, although she had no idea of the name of the woman who had caused it.

"I cannot think what has come to me," said Gabriel to her one day as they were walking in the fields together.

"I can," was the prompt reply; "you have been doing too much for years; and now the bill has come in, and you have nothing to pay it with."

"But I have been doing God's work, not my own," pleaded Gabriel.

"That has nothing to do with it. If you spend more strength than you have got, the fact that you have spent it on God's work won't keep you from breaking down; just as if you spend more money than you have got, the fact that you have spent it on charity won't prevent you from becoming bankrupt."

Gabriel sighed. Janet was as hard upon him as he had been upon Mrs. Paul Seaton: only in Janet's case he called it harsh dealing, and in his own, plain speaking. The pronoun which we place before a verb makes all the difference to the verb we use. For instance, "*I* speak the truth," "*You* are unwarrantably severe," and "*He* makes himself detestably disagreeable," are really in essence the same verb adapted to fit the various pronouns.

"You've got to use commonsense even in religion," Janet went on, as if she were stating a paradox.

"Well, haven't I used commonsense?"

"Never: you've never had an atom of it to use."

Gabriel could not help laughing. It was an old joke between them that Janet had made "a corner" in the commonsense of the little household.

"But I have sometimes borrowed yours," he argued,
"and used that."

"Well, it doesn't seem to have done much for you."

"Perhaps there wasn't enough of it. As you have
just so wisely remarked, my dear Janet, I could not
spend more of an article than I had got to spend; and
in the same way I could not borrow from you more of
an article than you had got to lend."

Then Janet laughed too, for she possessed that most
excellent of all gifts in woman, a perfect temper.
Nothing ever put her out or even ruffled her: and so
she was eminently fitted for that vocation for which it
is commonly and erroneously supposed that all women
are equally fitted by nature—the vocation of matrimony.
The power to become a good wife is as much a gift as
the power to become a good painter or a good writer or
a good musician; and no woman has it who is not
endowed—either by nature or by grace—with a good
temper. There is no quality which so mars and spoils
and destroys the happiness of married life as bad
temper. True, it interferes with the peace of all
domestic relations, and is not a comfort in any department of life; but it is worse in a married woman than
in a single one, because a wife has far more power to
make another person miserable than has a spinster—
and there is no more successful way of doing this than
by a frequent display of temper. Therefore let the
woman who has a bad temper, which she cannot or will
not control, make up her mind to select the cloister
rather than the hearth as her sphere of usefulness—
giving the word "cloister" the broadest and most
modern interpretation possible, inclusive of the college,
the club, the art-school, the hospital, the parish and the
political platform: for she is no more fit to be a wife

than she is fit to be a steam-engine; and she might as well attempt to draw a railway train as to make a man happy. It is not in her to do either.

Janet Field's amiability was established beyond doubt or demur; so much so that every man who did not marry her—given the possibility of doing so—made more or less of a mistake. She had also (another most valuable asset in married life) a sense of humour, though—as is the case with all of us—not as strong a sense as she herself believed it to be. There are two things which every man or woman believes about himself or herself, namely, that he or she has a strong sense of humour and is a small eater! Most people are convinced that they are poor sleepers as well; but this is not quite so universal an article of belief as the other two.

"I can't see the sense," Janet persisted, "of doing twice as much as you can to-day, in order that you won't be able to do a quarter as much as you can to-morrow. It seems to me poor economy."

"I believe in putting one's whole strength into everything that one does, and doing it with all one's might," replied Gabriel.

"That is just what you would believe in: it is exactly what I should have expected of you." And Janet shook her head as if she were reproving him of a fault.

Gabriel was amused, but not penitent. "Then what do you believe in, may I be permitted to ask?"

"In regulating one's expenditure by one's income and not by one's enthusiasms; and in not putting more strength into a thing than a thing actually needs."

"Oh, wise young judge, how I do honour thee!" murmured Gabriel, in mock admiration.

But in spite of his gibes Janet calmly had her say. She was by no means a great talker; but if she meant to say a thing she said it, and it was generally to the point. "Have you ever tried to open a door which you thought was hard to open, and which was really easy; and nearly tumbled backwards in consequence?"

"Often and often."

"That is just what you do with everything, Gabriel. You put your whole heart and strength into the doing of something that anybody' else would do with very little effort at all: and then you fall backwards and hurt yourself: and some day you'll fall backwards so hard and hurt yourself so badly that you'll never get up again."

"Then what do you want me to do to prevent this catastrophe?" Gabriel still spoke mockingly, but his mockery was kind.

"Take things more easily, and consider yourself a little. Oh! Gabriel"—and here the hazel eyes were raised pleadingly—"do take care of yourself: you see, you matter so dreadfully, and it would be so terrible if you became ill or anything."

The expression in the hazel eyes was enough to touch any man—even a man who had never regarded them as anything but sisterly eyes; and it touched Gabriel a good deal.

"You see, dear," he said, "I have my flock to consider as well as myself: you mustn't forget them."

"But I do forget them: I forget them utterly; I don't care what becomes of them compared with you." Though Janet's diction might be involved, her meaning was clear. "I would sacrifice the whole of S. Etheldreda's parish to save you a pain in your little finger, Gabriel: I would indeed. What do the souls of a

thousand costermongers matter in comparison with
your health? Nothing at all!"

"Oh, hush, Janet, hush! You mustn't talk like that.
In the sight of God the soul of a costermonger is worth
as much as mine. Besides," he added whimsically,
"they are not costermongers; they are petty tradesmen
of arrogant respectability; and so their souls are worth
more than a costermonger's because they are so much
rarer."

But Janet was too much in earnest to smile. 'I'm
not looking at it from God's point of view: I'm
looking at it from mine and Aunt Eveline's; and it
breaks both our hearts to see you sacrificing your
splendid, clever, handsome self for a lot of horrid, dirty,
good-for-nothing shopkeepers."

Gabriel shook his head. "Janet, Janet, haven't I told
you that they are not dirty?"

"I don't care: no amount of washing will ever make
a million of them equal to you, and nothing could
ever convince me that it will."

MICROCOPY RESOLUTION TEST CHART

(ANSI and ISC TEST CHART No. 2)

 1.0

 1.1

 1.25 1.4 1.6

APPLIED IMAGE Inc

1653 East Main Street
Rochester, New York 14609 USA
(716) 482 - 0300 - Phone
(716) 288 - 5989 - Fax

CHAPTER XII

FABIA'S MARRIAGE

WHILE Gabriel Carr was endeavouring for the sake of his health to let the grass grow under his feet in Mershire, Mrs. Paul Seaton was doing nothing of the kind in London. She had made up her mind to give Fabia Vipart in marriage to Charlie Gaythorne; and she allowed herself no rest until this mission was safely accomplished. Over the trousseau she was simply indefatigable. She loved clothes, other women's as well as her own: even in Isabel's smallnesses there was nothing really small: and she and Fabia were drawn nearer to each other over this trousseau than they had ever been before. There is a wonderful freemasonry among the women who love clothes, which the women who do not love clothes cannot in the least understand.

Fabia had grown much more amiable since her engagement: success had a beneficial effect upon her, as it has upon so many people: and now that she was about to make what the world calls an excellent match, she received unstintingly that praise of men which is only accorded to those who do well unto themselves.

True, her relations with Charlie Gaythorne were by no means ideal in their nature. She regarded him with mingled feelings of contempt and gratitude—gratitude for what he had, and contempt for what he was; and

there was no modicum of love in the composition. As
for him, he was more infatuated with her than ever;
and the blindness of his adoration and the slavishness
of his worship were just the things most calculated to
strengthen Fabia's present attitude towards him. Had
he shown himself in his dealings with her the man that
he really was, it would have been better for her and
better for him; but he did not: and so had to bear the
consequences of his own want of wisdom. There is
nothing so severely punished in this world as a blunder.
A crime is oftentimes forgiven—still oftener undiscovered: but a blunder has to meet its liabilities even to
the uttermost farthing: and this is usually done in the full
light of day before an audience that neither spares nor
pities.

Naturally Fabia had not forgotten her encounter
with the Vicar of S. Etheldreda's; but her feelings for
him also were mixed. She was to a certain extent
angry with him for his treatment of her; but she was
nothing like as angry as Isabel would have been in
similar circumstance. With all her faults—and doubtless she had many—Fabia was no egotist: she was able
to regard a thing or a person apart from that thing or
that person's relation to herself: and she could not
therefore fail to admire Gabriel's uprightness and
singleness of heart, even though these had combined to
her own undoing. Moreover, she had loved him from
the moment she discovered that he was stronger than
she. His very sternness, which would have repelled a
typically Western woman, was irresistibly attractive to
the Oriental strain in Fabia's nature. She was born of
a race of women who were accustomed to obey; and
the more masterful a man was, the readier was she to
fall down and worship him: therefore nothing could

have been more inimical to their future happiness
than the humble and deferential attitude which Captain
Gaythorne adopted towards his bride-elect.

"What is going to happen to Mrs. Gaythorne?"
Paul asked of his wife in one of the few moments
which she spared to him out of the whirl of nuptial
preparation.

"Happen to her? What on earth do you mean?
Nothing is going to happen to her that I know of.
She isn't going to be married!"

"Heaven forbid! But isn't she going to turn out to
make room for Fabia?"

"Mrs. Gaythorne turn out to make room for
anybody? Oh, Paul, what an idea! You'll be asking
next whether the sun isn't going to turn out to make
room for some acetylene gas-company: or whether
London isn't going to turn out to make room for the
garden-city."

Paul smiled, but he held his ground. "I thought
mothers-in-law always turned out when their sons
married: went to a Dower-House, or something of that
kind."

But Isabel met him with open scorn. "Dower-House
indeed! Think of Mrs. Gaythorne in a Dower-House!
I don't believe the Dower-House is built that would
contain Mrs. Gaythorne."

"Mrs. Gaythorne is an excellent woman," began
Paul; "but—"

His wife interrupted him.

"I know what you are going to say—that her only
failing is infallibility, and I agree with you. But
it is a common fault. Wrexham has it badly, and
so have others. I often wonder what people like
Wrexham and Mrs. Gaythorne do to pass

the time while the rest of the congregation are repeating the General Confession. You are a bit inclined that way yourself."

"Oh, Isabel!" Paul looked really hurt.

His wife patted his shoulder encouragingly. "It is only a tendency in your case—not a really vicious virtue at present. But if you don't take care to make not less than one trifling mistake a week, and to be wrong on some unimportant question at least every other day, you'll most assuredly be infallible by the time you are fifty. But you can't locate infallibility in a Dower-House at any price. Its natural habitations are Vaticans and places of that kind."

"Well, all I can say is, then, that I pity poor Fabia."

Mrs. Seaton shook her head. "I don't. She won't mind. She likes Mrs. Gaythorne better than she likes me."

"Oh, I say, that's impossible! You are talking nonsense, my darling. Nobody could like Mrs. Gaythorne better than they liked you—not even old Gaythorne himself if he were alive!"

"Possibly not: Mr. Gaythorne was a man. But heaps of women would—Fabia included."

"Well—with one notable exception—I haven't a very high opinion of female intellect, as you know; but I must say I don't think so badly of the sex as all that."

And Paul touched the tip of his wife's ear caressingly. He wanted to stroke her hair: but experience had taught him that when a woman's hair is what she calls "done," he is a brave man who, even in the way of kindness, lays his hand upon it.

"You never do Mrs. Gaythorne justice, Paul."

"By Jove, I do, though! I think she is the most

domineering woman that Providence ever made—bar none."

Isabel sighed reproachfully. "That comes of being a Radical! You Radicals don't really appreciate our old national institutions, such as the Divine Right of kings, and the Established Church, and the Penny Postage, and Mrs. Gaythorne. These things are part of the Empire."

"Are they?" Paul laughed and kissed his wife. "Then do respectable old Whigs such as yourself appreciate them?"

"We do. For my part, I feel towards Mrs. Gaythorne exactly as I feel towards the British Constitution, and the Union Jack, and the House of Hanover. They rouse noble and patriotic feelings in me—they make me proud of my country—they induce me to 'thank the goodness and the grace'—and heaps of things like that. Roast - beef on Sunday has exactly the same effect; and so have Handel's music and some of Macaulay's Essays."

Isabel was quite right. Mrs. Gaythorne had not the slightest intention of turning out to make room for anybody; nor would Charlie ever have imagined such a thing possible in his wildest dreams. And, to tell the truth, Fabia did not altogether object to the present arrangement. She did not care enough for her future husband for the prospect of a *solitude à deux* to offer any attractions to her: and she entertained a very strong and real regard for Mrs. Gaythorne. The very masterfulness of the elder woman fascinated her and held her captive, since strength of any kind appealed to Fabia. As has been remarked before, Miss Vipart doubtless had her faults: but she was of a stuff which is not bad raw material for the fashioning of daughters-in-law; good daughters-in-law not being in any way synonymous with good daughters or good wives.

Much is written and said about mothers-in-law: little or nothing about daughters-in-law: yet the one class is as important as the other, and has equally its distinguishing characteristics. Roughly speaking, the better a woman is as a daughter or a wife, the less satisfactory will she prove as a daughter-in-law: and this in the very nature of things. For the more devoted she is to her husband, the more will she resent and be jealous of any influence which in any way whatever comes between her and him: and the more devoted she is to her own people, the less will she be in sympathy with the customs and traditions of another family. It is all a part of the great law of compensation: no woman can be a success in every relation of life—no woman can be a failure in all. Therefore, when all her little world condemns tiresome old Mrs. Jones because she does not properly appreciate that charming young Mrs. Jones, who was so excellent a daughter in the days when she was Miss Smith, let it remember that the very characteristics which make Mrs. Jones, junior, a help meet for young Jones, and a polished corner in the temple of the house of Smith, are the very characteristics which are most aggravating and irritating to young Jones's mother; and that probably in this matter the disagreeable old lady has far more to try her than the amiable young one, and should be judged accordingly.

So it came to pass that when the season was drawing to a close—when women recklessly put on their best clothes and their finest conversation for dinner-parties, and did not take the trouble to go to non-R.S.V.P. parties at all—when Bills which would have travelled through Parliament at the rate of the South Eastern earlier in the session, now rushed through it with the speed of falling stars—when the streets smelt of wood-pavement and cabbage-stalks, and there was neither excitement nor oxygen in the air—then did Charles Gaythorne take to wife Fabia Vipart, with múch show and ceremony, and ringing of bells: and gave her the right, for the first time in her life, to meet her equals with equality, and to be of, as well as in, the fashionable world: in short, he admitted her within the precincts, and endowed her with the freedom of the red cord. For the which she was accordingly thankful.

CHAPTER XIII

GABRIEL THE MAN

THE weeks passed on and still Gabriel did not gain strength. There was nothing definite the matter with him; perhaps it would have been better for him if there had been, since a definite evil demands a definite cure; but he had simply done too much—had overdrawn his account at the bank of vitality—and Nature, that most merciless of creditors, was now summoning him before her county court, and stationing her bailiffs, Weakness and Weariness and Depression, in his house, until he should have paid her back to the uttermost farthing.

At the end of two months spent with his mother in the country, Gabriel returned to town to consult the great doctor who had taken his case in hand; and there he was met with the crushing blow that he must—if he ever wished to regain his shattered health and strength —resign the living of S. Etheldreda's, and take a country parish for a term of several years. That was the only course open to him, the doctor said, unless he were bent upon suicide.

He came back to his mother's well-nigh broken-hearted: it seemed as if Fortune had indeed been outrageous in pelting him with her slings and arrows. First the disappointment about Fabia; and then this still severer blow about S. Etheldreda's: love and life-work taken from him at one fell swoop, just when he thought he was nearing the summit of success in both; and for a time the burden seemed greater than he could bear. He had meant to do such wonderful things with his work before him and Fabia by his side; he had intended to remove mountains and to overthrow principalities and powers—to stand in the forefront of the great battle between good and evil, and to go forth conquering and to conquer. And suddenly he was met by the stern decree, "Thus far shalt thou go and no further"; he was bidden to stand no longer with the Ark in the middle of Jordan, but to court ease and obscurity in the backwater of a country parish.

And the very fact that he was out of health, made it all the harder for him patiently to endure and cheerfully to submit; for a man's faith is often very much affected by his physical condition. Satan understood human nature when he suggested that even the patient Job might curse God to His Face when once his flesh and his bone were touched. As a matter of fact, Satan always does understand human nature: it is Divine Nature That passes his comprehension; so that when —as frequently happens even in this present world— this mortal puts on immortality, Satan's reckonings are upset and his premises falsified.

So poor Gabriel went a day's journey into the wilderness of blighted hope and bitter disappointment, and laid him down under the juniper tree of doubt and despair, with the old cry, "It is enough: now take away my life!" And as he lay in the dark shadow of the juniper tree, behold as aforetime an angel touched him. and the angel came in the form of Janet Field.

Now, had uninspired humanity been writing the

history of Elijah, it would have dealt with this scene
in the story very differently. It was a striking moment:
a moment when spirits were finely touched to fine issues.
Think of it: a scene with only two *dramatis personæ*;
and they the very choicest of their kind. First, the
prophet who had just played the principal part in the
most splendid drama ever written—who had stood upon
the summit of Carmel and called down fire from Heaven
to confound his enemies; and who had then made the
very clouds his chariots and refreshed the parched earth
with abundance of rain. Did ever conqueror return
from a more magnificent victory than this? Did ever
mere man before or since constrain clouds and fire and
stormy winds to the fulfilling of his word. This was
the first person in the drama. The second was no less
wonderful, being one of those mysterious beings who
excel in strength—one of those sons of God who shouted
for joy when the foundations of the earth were laid,
chanting their *Amen* to the *Venite* of the morning stars.

And what did this angelic messenger say to the
mighty conqueror who was for the moment overthrown?
Did he strengthen him with the recital of past triumphs,
or encourage him with a battle-song of still greater
things to be?

Listen! "And behold an angel touched him and
said unto him, Arise, and eat."

No war-songs or battle-cries or heroics. Nothing but
such ordinary, everyday, homely comfort as would be
given to a weeping child.

And there was more than mere comfort: there was
tender sympathy: for "the angel came again the second
time and touched him and said, Arise and eat; because
the journey is too great for thee."

Dear, human, commonplace, comfortable words: such

words as we should all like to hear in our dejected
moments, when the road is too stony for us and we fall
by the way like tired children : such words as are
spoken to one whom his mother comforteth !

Thus Gabriel found consolation in the loving sympathy
and cheerful companionship of Janet. She talked no
heroics to him : she did not attempt to prove by argument that all things are for the best in this best of all
possible worlds : she first looked after his bodily com-
forts, and then shared with him the sorrow of his heart.
Her whole walk and conversation were but an amplifica-
tion of the words, " Arise and eat ; because the journey
is too great for thee."

There are many women in this world who would fain
give consolation in sorrow to the men whom they love ;
but they do not know the way. They argue and
encourage and cheer and exhort, and yet it is all in
vain. Such women would do well to learn a lesson from
the angel of Elijah.

Gradually Janet became more than an angel to Gabriel
—more than one of those heavenly visitants who neither
marry nor are given in marriage : she began to occupy
the niche in his heart which the defalcation of Fabia
had left vacant. It is a true saying that the affections of
many men are caught on the rebound ; and these, as a
rule, are what are commonly known as " marrying men."
The man who is described by his friends as " not a
marrying man," is rarely, if ever, enslaved in this way :
his affections, when once wounded and repulsed, are
even more impregnable than they were before.

There are two kinds of bachelors in this world : the
men in the walls and structure of whose hearts are
empty niches all ready for the image of the unknown
goddess ; just as in some houses there are book-shelves

built into the original fabric : and the men who have
no place prepared when Diana of the Ephesians falls
straight down from Jupiter, and consequently walls
have to be knocked down and furniture removed to
make room for her.

Carr belonged to the former class : from his boyhood
he had worshipped the Ideal Woman. Feminine
sympathy and companionship and approbation were
essential to him : he could not live without them.
Therefore when—as he imagined — Fabia had once
embodied the Ideal, he could not again— even though
Fabia had failed—disembody her. If he had not first
fallen in love with Fabia, he would probably never have
fallen in love with Janet : but the doors of his heart,
having once been thrown open by Fabia, would not
close again ; so Janet found at last an easy entry. She
would never have succeeded in opening that door
herself : she lacked the special power to do so : but,
after another hand had forced the lock, there was no
one so well fitted as she to enter in and sweep and
garnish.

Janet was one of the rare women who are proficient
performers on that useful instrument popularly known
as the "second fiddle." It is a great gift. The women
who are content to play second fiddle and to make the
best of it, give much sweet music to the world : there
are no more essential performers in the orchestra of
life than they. Do we not all know them and the
soothing harmonies which they make—patient spinsters,
kindly stepmothers, comfortable second wives : humbly
and cheerfully taking the part allotted to them by the
Great Conductor, and never struggling nor straining
after the first place ? Are not all our lives the richer
for their music ? And can we doubt that these blessed

musicians shall take one day a leading part in that
chorus which shall stand on the shores of the sea of
glass striking the harps of God?

Janet was aware that she was not Gabriel's first love:
during the sunny afternoons of that long summer
holiday he had confided in her the whole story of his
infatuation for Fabia, and the disappointment that it
had brought him: and she was content that it should
be so. He was so utterly first with her that she never
even asked what place she took with regard to him. It
was enough for her to love: she did not trouble about
any return.

There is always something rather small about the
jealous woman—the woman who refuses to marry a
widower, or who begs her husband to promise that he
will never marry again should anything happen to her.
Something is lacking in the quality of her love: at the
bottom of her heart she loves herself more than she
loves him. Were her love perfect, she would want him
to be happy even at the cost of his memory of her: she
would be content to be forgotten if only he could be
comforted. The maternal element in her love would
help her to this: and the wife who has no maternal
element in her love for her husband, falls considerably
short of the mark of her high calling.

But Fate was not without its irony for poor Gabriel,
even in the compensations of his present lot. It was
hard that he should at last have fallen in love with
Janet just when the fiat had gone forth that he had no
home to offer to her. Had he only learnt her true
value any time during the past half-dozen years, he
could have married her at once: and in all human
probability his health, in that case, would never have
broken down at all, for Janet was just the sort of wife

to look after a man well, and to see that he was
cherished and comforted as well as honoured and
obeyed. But, like many another good man, Gabriel
did the right thing at the wrong time: and was sorely
punished, as are all such innocent offenders, for the
unpunctuality of his well-doing. So while Janet soothed
him in his dual disappointment over his slighted love
and his arrested life-work, she unconsciously drove him
out of the frying-pan of transitory infatuation for Fabia
into the fire of unswerving devotion to herself: and
thus rendered the second state of poor Gabriel worse
than the first.

He could not tell her in so many words of his new-
born love for her; honour forbade it now that he had
neither home nor income to offer; but Janet—though
not a clever woman in the accepted sense of the word—
was quite clever enough to see what had come to pass:
and to be thankful accordingly. It was characteristic
of her that she did not waste her time nor her strength
in regretting that Gabriel had not learnt to love her
sooner: she returned thanks that he had not
postponed this awakening until even later: and
the mere knowledge of it made melody in her
heart.

"I expect I must give up S. Etheldreda's, and give
it up at once," said Gabriel one summer's evening, as he
and his mother and Janet were sitting in the garden of
the little Midland cottage. "I cannot extend my
holiday further: and it is time that my successor was
appointed and given his work to do. But I shall miss
it—oh, I shall miss it!"

His voice broke as he concluded the sentence.
Gabriel had one of those impressionable natures which
rise to great heights and sink to great depths: he was

N

always either upon Mount Carmel or lying down under the juniper tree.

"As you say, dearest," replied Mrs. Carr, "it seems time that something definite should be done, as no *locum tenens* can stay permanently anywhere because of his own work at home, and being a stranger, as it were, and therefore the course of teaching more disjointed than in the case of the real incumbent, besides his not having the threads of all the parishioners in his hands, and so less able to administer advice and counsel."

"It is hard to give it all up," Gabriel groaned; "and just when I was getting some hold upon the hearts of the people!"

"Never mind," said Janet, in soothing tones; "it will all come right."

"But I must mind: I cannot help minding: it is my business to mind."

Janet shook her head. "No, it isn't: it is your business to get strong and well as quickly as you can, and God's business to look after S. Etheldreda's."

"Yes, love, yes; of course it is; how clearly dear Janet always puts things! You must have faith, my Gabriel, more faith. Think of the grain of mustard-seed that the woman hid in three measures of meal till it leavened the whole lump. It is faith of that kind that you need, dear child, and in fact all of us."

Mrs. Carr was apt to confuse her parables: but she held fast to the truths which they set forth.

"It is so easy to have faith for other people, and so hard to have it for oneself," sighed Gabriel.

"But the fact that a duty is difficult does not make it any the less imperative."

"That is so, dearest Janet," assented Mrs. Carr; "if

we have to do things we have to do them, however
impossible they may be, and not even in good health or
up to our usual spirits, which always makes everything
more of a burden than otherwise, and increases the
necessity for a strong tonic and complete rest of mind
and body."

"And even if—as Janet so wisely counsels—I leave
my work in God's Hands, what is to become of me,
deprived suddenly of home and income?"

Janet smiled. "You think that God is equal to the
task of looking after S. Etheldreda's, but not quite to be
trusted with the responsibility of looking after you as
well? Oh, Gabriel, I'm ashamed of you!"

Here his mother flew to Gabriel's rescue.

"Really, Janet love, I cannot allow you to speak of
my one ewe lamb in that way; you seem to insinuate
that Gabriel is guilty of irreverence towards his Maker,
which anything further from his thoughts I cannot
imagine. But one cannot help feeling that the charge
of a parish is more worthy to be left in the Hands of
the Creator than attending to a man's private income,
which is really a layman's duty, or even a mere man of
business."

Depressed as Gabriel was, he could not forbear a
smile at this remark, especially when he saw Janet's
hazel eyes twinkle in sympathy; it was so thoroughly
indicative of Mrs. Carr's attitude towards her Maker,
Whom she regarded as a sort of deified Archbishop,
not to be troubled with affairs unconnected with the
Church.

"If you think that, mother, you ought never to say
grace before meat. Surely it is what you call a mere
layman's duty to preside over a meal and to bless
common food to our use."

" My dear Gabriel, I have always said grace before meat and always shall : it is no use trying to dissuade me from it. It was my custom in my cradle as it will be my custom upon my death-bed, taught me by my dear mother; and a meal upon which no blessing is asked always terrifies me for fear of undigested food or a fish-bone in the throat, if not ptomaine poisoning and typhoid from milk. I never should expect to recover from a meal upon which no blessing had been asked, not even if the fish were boned and there was only semolina pudding. And by what right, I should like to know? Except the Lord build the house, men sow and reap in vain."

Gabriel suppressed a laugh, as he wondered what his mother would do if she were asked to parse one of her own sentences.

" It is all right, mother; you misunderstood me. I am the last person to object to your saying grace before meat."

But Mrs. Carr was a past mistress in the art of mis-understanding people. Nothing was too plain or too simple for her to misunderstand. She even amazed her own son sometimes by her powers of misapprehension.

" Then why did you say so, dear love, and cause me so much pain ? Both you and Janet are so fond of saying things and then saying that you didn't say them, which makes it so confusing for the other person, with the best intentions in the world. If you don't object to my saying grace, why did you say you did ? And if dear Janet doesn't think you irreverent, why does she say you are ?—everybody being judged by their words, or else how could you know them at all ?"

" What I want to know is what will become of me after I have resigned the living of S. Etheldreda's ?"

Gabriel's passing amusement was over, and he was down in the depths again.

"Something is sure to turn up," the cheerful Janet hastened to assure him. "I feel certain that God will look after you, even though it be but secular work to do so."

Janet could not resist making fun of Mrs. Carr sometimes, though to do her justice she struggled manfully against the temptation.

"What you need, my dear boy, is more faith and hope and a country parish, though not too scattered in case of bad weather, and the Squire at your back should the funds run short and no private means."

"But how am I to get a country parish, mother? It is none so easy. And especially as I need one with an income sufficient to keep me from starvation, having— as you point out—no private means."

"True, love, they do not grow on every bush like sand on the seashore, as you say; but there must be plenty somewhere, or else why aren't all the clergy in the workhouse? Though, as Janet is always saying, it is no credit to the Church of England that they are not, being so miserably underpaid and the labourer always worthy of b's hire. Certainly, the Nonconformists set us a good example there, though sometimes not Catholic in doctrine; and of course you would find it a little dull after the constant toil and turmoil of a London parish, which would make it so much more soothing and restful. I often wish that my small means were sufficient to do more than just keep Janet and myself: but it is often difficult for us as it is to make both ends meet, even pinching ourselves at every turn, and only one joint of meat a week."

"It is supper-time," said Janet, rising and folding up

her work; "and I propose that we go in and enjoy it, and don't take thought for the morrow any more to-night. There's steak-and-kidney pie and a junket, both of which I made myself because I knew that they were two of Gabriel's favourite dishes; and it is no good making them disagree with us all before we eat them, through worrying over what can't be helped."

"Thank you, Janet."

Gabriel was touched. He was one of the men—and their name is Legion—who love to be petted.

"And for my part," added Janet, as they strolled towards the house, "I have perfect confidence that God will find a way for us out of this difficulty, and prove Himself a very present help in the present trouble. Why, you always preach so beautifully about faith, Gabriel!"

"I know I do; but it is so much easier to preach than to practise."

"It isn't easy to do either on an empty stomach," said the practical Janet; "so let us have supper at once!"

CHAPTER XIV

THE LIVING OF GAYTHORNE

THERE was woe and lamentation in the parish of Gaythorne over the death of the Rector, who had held the incumbency for the last five-and-thirty years. As he had agreed with and echoed all her own opinions, Mrs. Gaythorne had no anxiety as to his condition in the future state; but she missed a friendship which had lasted through the whole of her life as matron and widow, and she shrank from the idea of a new incumbent who would not obey her as implicitly as Mr. Cattley had done. True, the latter had suffered from occasional lapses in obedience. There was one never-to-be-forgotten occasion when he introduced the custom of carrying out the Psalmist's original intention and singing the songs of degrees, instead of reading them aloud alternately with the congregation: which daring innovation so upset Mrs. Gaythorne that for some time she absented herself from her Parish Church and attended a Wesleyan Chapel in the neighbourhood. But even here the poor lady could not long find rest for her soul; for, when the season for it came round, the Wesleyans thought it meet and right to offer a public thanksgiving to God for the joy of harvest, and they decorated their Chapel on this occasion with corn and flowers. This was too much for Mrs. Gaythorne.

199

She scented Ritualism in every dahlia, Popery in every
ear of corn; and when she espied upon the front of the
pulpit the Sign of her salvation wrought in white
chrysanthemums, to bring before the faithful the
Symbol of their faith, she shook the dust of the place
off her feet for ever, and left the Chapel to re-enter it
no more.   But she did not go so far as to withdraw her
subscription to the Wesleyan Missionary Society in
consequence: in which, perhaps, she was somewhat
inconsistent; since the object of all missionary societies
is to take their part in fulfilling the Divine Command
to preach to every creature that Cross which was to the
Jew a stumbling-block, and to the Greek foolishness,
and to Mrs. Gaythorne the sign-manual of Rome.   But
her practices were ever superior to her precepts; and
she always atoned, by the kindliness of her conduct, for
the sternness of her creed.

So she returned into the fold of her own parish, and
gradually forgave Mr. Cattley for his unseemly attempt
to carry out the intentions of the original authors in his
presentment of the Psalms; but she continued to read
these same spiritual songs in a loud voice while the rest
of the congregation were singing them.

Once again was Mr. Cattley convicted of backsliding
by the introduction of the intoning of those responses
which fall to the people and not to the priest.   Mrs.
Gaythorne did not leave the Church again; but she
entered her protest by still repeating the responses in
as conversational a tone as she could command, and
beginning them full two seconds before anybody
else.

The living of Gaythorne was a very good one, as
livings go nowadays; five hundred a year and an
excellent rectory; and the income was regular and

secure, not being dependent upon either glebe or tithes: so there was much speculation as to who would be Mr. Cattley's successor.

· "Who has the presentation to this living?" asked Fabia of her husband, a few days after the old Rector's death.

"It belongs to me," replied Charlie; by which he meant to his mother.

"I thought so: and I want you to give it to Gabriel Carr."

"Oh, Fabia!" And poor Charlie's distress was poignant.

He adored his wife and would do anything in reason that she asked him; but he did wish she would not ask him such unreasonable things.

Mrs. Charles Gaythorne shrugged her shoulders impatiently. "It is no use saying 'Oh, Fabia!' in that timorous and ineffective tone. I have told you what my wishes are, and I expect you to carry them out."

"But, Fabia—"

"But me no buts, if you please. Surely you can make anybody Rector here that you like, seeing that even if you cannot call your soul your own, you can so call the living of Gaythorne."

Charlie winced: his wife's gibes never failed to touch him on the raw.

"But, Fabia darling, you must see that mother would never consent to a High Churchman being made Rector here."

"I thought you said the living was in your gift."

"I did, but—"

"Then I fail to see where your mother comes in."

Poor Charlie fairly groaned,

"Oh! Fabia, I really couldn't go against my mother in a thing like this. She minds so awfully about Churches and services and things of that kind, that I should feel a regular brute if I didn't pan it all out to suit her."

Fabia's lip curled: her husband's fear of his mother never failed to rouse her contempt.

"Then you do not mind going against your wife's wishes?"

"Yes, I do, darling; I mind most awfully. But can't you understand that religion is the mater's particular hobby, while it isn't yours? I mean you don't really care about High Church or Low Church and all that sort of business, while it is just meat and drink to mother. I believe it would kill her to have a regular High Churchman planted down under her very nose: she couldn't stand it at her age."

"That is simply absurd. She would soon get used to it."

"Not she! I know my mother. You can't remember what an awful shindy she made when old Cattley took to bawling out the Psalms all together, instead of making them into a sort of ride-and-tie business, turn and turn about, as they used to be. But I can; and I shall never forget it. By Jove, it regularly knocked her to pieces!"

Fabia still occupied the seat of the scornful. "I thought the Psalms were meant to be sung: songs usually are."

"Not a bit of it! Why, nobody ever thought of singing them at Gaythorne Church till old Cattley got a ridiculous idea into his head that it would be an improvement, or some idiotic notion of that kind. And it upset the mater most dreadfully. She forgave

the old fool after a bit, because she is so awfully
Christian and charitable and all that, don't you know?
But the Church has never been the same to her since.
I was quite a little boy at the time, but I remember the
fuss."

"And what did your father say?"

"Oh! father did his best to smooth her down; said
that a Psalm was a Psalm, don't you know? and comforting things of that sort. But it drove her to the
Wesleyan Chapel for all that, for weeks and weeks.
She used to take me with her, while father stuck to the
Parish Church, and I used to enjoy it; it was a bit of a
change for a little chap whose nose was generally glued
to the Prayer-book in his family pew."

Fabia smiled. Her husband's ideas and traditions
never failed to rouse her mirth.

"Then did Mr. Cattley ever go so far as to sing the
hymns; or were they also performed on what you call
the ride-and-tie principle in those primeval days?" she
asked.

Charlie looked at her in innocent amazement. "Of
course they sang the hymns. What are hymns made
for but to be sung?"

"The same argument applies, then, to singing the
Psalms, since Psalms are hymns."

"They can't be, because they are in the Prayer-book;
and the Prayer-book and the Hymn-book are quite
different books, don't you know? You might as well
say that the Army-list and the Racing-calendar are
the same as say that the Prayer-book and the
Hymn-book are."

"Well, then, you hold that the Bible and the
Prayer-book are very much the same thing, don't
you?" retorted Fabia, who never could resist the

temptation to wave a red rag when she saw one lying
about.

"Good gracious, no; what an idea! I'm glad the
mater didn't hear you say that. Why, nothing would
induce her to read what she calls her daily-portion out
of the Prayer-book Psalms; she wouldn't do it for
anything. She always reads them out of the regular
Bible."

"That is enough about the Psalms," said Fabia, in a
bored tone of voice. "What I want to know is, are you
going to oblige me about the living of Gaythorne, or are
you not? In short, are you going to offend me or your
mother?"

Charlie looked — as indeed he felt — absolutely
wretched. He hated to deny his beautiful wife anything that she desired; but the alternative was by no
means an alluring one. He could have faced a charge
of cavalry without turning a hair; but when it came to
facing his mother it was a different thing, and the flesh
was weak. So he feebly temporized.

"I don't believe mother would ever stand Carr's
goings-on—his flowers and vestments and early services
and things of that kind."

"But she is very fond of him," said Fabia, stooping
to argue with her trembling lord and master.

"Oh! that's quite a different thing. She can't help
liking him as a man; nobody could; he is such a
pleasant chap that nobody would ever take him for a
clergyman," replied Charlie, with unconscious humour;
"but it's as a parson that he roughs her up."

"Of course you are master in your own house and so
must do as you think fit," said Fabia, with a satirical
smile. "I have told you my wishes and there is no
more to be said. But I should have imagined that you

might have done it for Mr. Carr's sake if not for mine; you must see how hard it is for him to have to give up one living with no prospect of another."

"Oh! I'm sorry enough for Carr; there's no doubt on that score," Charlie ruefully replied: " he's a rattling good fellow, and it's deuced hard on him to have to chuck everything like this—deuced hard! But all the same, I can't have my mother's peace of mind sacrificed to him, and there's an end of it."

Fabia rose from her seat and left the room, her clinging robes trailing gracefully behind her. She did not deign to vouchsafe another word to her recalcitrant husband, whose misery was very real indeed. Poor Charlie! He was highly inexperienced in his management of Fabia. If he had put his foot down and said that he would not give the living to Carr because he did not choose to do so, she would have submitted to his decision with a good grace, and would have respected him for knowing his own mind, even if it did not coincide with hers: but when he refused to do so on the ground that his mother did not wish it, he threw over his prestige as a husband, and lowered himself in his wife's eyes   A wise man never backs up his marital authority by quotations from any woman—not even from his own mother: for wives despise a constitutional government, and at heart love the despot who rules them by divine right; provided, of course, that he is not too despotic, and does not take undue advantage of his kingship. And they invariably support the Salic law, and will have no woman—not even a mother-in-law—to reign over them.

Now, if the truth must be told, Fabia understood Mrs. Gaythorne a great deal better than Charlie did. She knew that the lady's sympathies were considerably

broader than her views; so she retailed to Mrs. Gaythorne
the exhaustive account of Gabriel's afflictions, which she
had received by letter from Isabel Seaton; and left the
seed thus sown to bear fruit accordingly.

Charlie's mother, though an excellent woman and a
consistent Christian, was most delightfully human: and
consequently she was so much pleased with Gabriel for
having ruined his health (as she believed) by his High-
Church practices, thereby proving that she was righteous
in her judgments and justified in her sayings, that she
completely forgave the sinner in contemplating the
satisfactory results of the sin. So after hearing several
times the full account of poor Gabriel's overthrow, as
written by isabel and illustrated by Fabia, she went to
spend a day with her old friend, Eveline Carr, in order
so see for herself how the land lay.

Mrs. Carr and Mrs. Gaythorne were friends of long
standing, and were warmly attached to each other—all
the more warmly because they did not understand one
another in the very least. Many sincere and constant
friendships are thus founded on a basis of profound and
mutual misunderstanding. We are all of us prone to
esteem certain people for qualities which they do not—
and never have pretended to—possess; but we, in the
vain imagination of our hearts, have endowed them with
these qualities, and feel affection for them accordingly.
Mrs. Gaythorne loved Mrs. Carr for being a mystic of
deep and clear spiritual perceptions, with an intuitive
conception of the mysteries of Evangelical dogma:
while Mrs. Carr reverenced Mrs. Gaythorne as a broad-
minded and experienced woman of the world, equally
conversant with the wisdom of God and the foolishness
of man.

"This is an unfortunate business, Gabriel, that I

hear from Isabella Seaton about your health," began Mrs. Gaythorne, when the preliminary greetings were over and the party had seated themselves at what was Mrs. Gaythorne's lunch and the Carrs' dinner. "A very unfortunate business!"

Some people would have left the discussion of unpleasant subjects until the meal was over; but that was not Mrs. Gaythorne's way. What she had to say, she said, regardless of any other consideration whatsoever. She was a woman distinguished by singleness of purpose and freedom of utterance.

Gabriel sighed. "It is a great trouble and a bitter disappointment to me to have to give up S. Etheldreda's: I can assure you of that, Mrs. Gaythorne."

"Then why talk about it?" interrupted Janet. "I never see the use of talking about disagreeable things, especially at meal-times."

Mrs. Gaythorne turned upon her a look of reproach. "I have come here for the sole purpose of talking about it, Janet Field, so it must be talked about, mealtime or no meal-time. I cannot consider the meat that perisheth when I have Gabriel's soul under my consideration."

But Janet had her retort ready. "It was Gabriel's body that I was thinking about, Mrs. Gaythorne; and as his soul just now is in a far better condition than his body, I think it is the latter that should claim our attention."

"Still, dearest Janet," said Mrs. Carr, feeling electricity in the air and being intent on peace; "a body without a soul is not of much avail even in a country parish with no daily service and the Litany on Wednesdays and Fridays, which is what I crave for my boy just now, complete rest and absence from all worry being the thing prescribed : though I admit that when one scents the sound of danger one should profit by the warning, and husband the lost strength until it has regained its accustomed tone and vigour."

"I am not surprised," replied Mrs. Gaythorne, saying what she had come to say. "What could any man expect from daily services and all the other performances at S. Etheldreda's but a complete breakdown in his health ? I knew it would come to this from the very beginning : and it has."

The good lady conveyed the impression that, if it had not, she would have been as much dis- apppointed as was the Prophet Jonah at the sparing of Nineveh.

Gabriel was distinctly amused : Mrs. Gaythorne never made him angry. "I did the little I could, and am thankful that my health allowed me to do as much as I did ; but I grieve sorely that it prevents me from doing more."

"There is nothing to grieve over in that, Gabriel Carr : be thankful that you are prevented from doing any more mischief in that benighted parish, instead of fretting that you are prevented from doing any more good."

"I will gladly raise that *Te Deum*, Mrs. Gaythorne," replied the persecuted Vicar, stifling a laugh ; "but all the same, I did my best."

"According to your lights," added Mrs. Gaythorne, amending his sentence.

"Certainly : I accept the emendation. But no one can act save according to his lights : you cannot yourself, Mrs. Gaythorne."

"But I take care to see that my lights are the right lights : that makes all the difference."

"How do you know that they are the right lights?" asked Janet.

The lady looked at her more in sorrow than in anger. "What an absurd question, Janet Field! How do I know that the sun is shining above our heads?"

"You don't," retorted Janet; "because, as a matter of fact, it isn't. There is no above or below in space."

Mrs. Gaythorne shook her head reproachfully. "Janet Field, I perceive you are becoming a free-thinker, if not an atheist: and that is quite as bad, if not worse, than being High Church. I do not approve of young people filling their heads with all these modern speculations."

But Janet held her ground. "It is not modern at all: it is a notion that dates from the days of De Quincey, not to say from the foundation of the world. Don't you remember that magnificent passage of his where he says that among the constellations 'above was below, below was above: depth was swallowed up in height insurmountable, height was swallowed up in depth unfathomable'? It is one of the finest paragraphs ever written."

"I do not approve of De Quincey: he took too much of something. I forget what it was: but I know he would have been a great deal better without it."

"Still," argued Janet, "he proved that there are really no such things as height and depth in space."

"Nothing of the kind," replied the Indomitable. "He proved that he himself did not know the difference between above and below: but there was nothing remarkable in that; persons who take too much of anything frequently confuse the two."

"Hear, hear!" cried Gabriel, in applause: "in this respect the meeting is entirely with you."

Q

"And besides," Mrs. Gaythorne continued triumph-
antly, "if there is not an above or a below, there
cannot be a Heaven or Hell : and if that is so, what
is to become of us all, I should like to know?"

Gabriel laughed outright. Mrs. Gaythorne's theology
never failed to afford him the keenest pleasure.

Here the hostess thought it time to interfere, as she
was afraid that the young people were not showing
proper respect to their guest.

"Of course, dear Mrs. Gaythorne, as you say, we
couldn't possibly do without Heaven and Hell, both
as a punishment and an inducement, modern theology
being so lax in matters, of doctrine, although very
charitable in all good works ; and though we are
expressly told that the spirit matters quite as much
as the letter, yet we must pay attention to the articles
of our faith, or else where should we be?"

"I would rather not express an opinion," answered
Mrs. Gaythorne. "All I can say is that I feel sure De
Quincey knows the difference well enough by now, and
wishes that he had not taken quite so much of that
stuff that made him confuse the two."

Gabriel and Janet were rocking themselves to
and fro in a silent ecstasy of mirth ; but their levity
fortunately was hid from Mrs. Gaythorne, who calmly
continued :

"And now that my prognostications have been fulfilled,
and you have ruined your health by your forms and
ceremonies, I want to know what you are going to do
for a living, Gabriel Carr ?"

"That is just what I want to know myself, Mrs.
Gaythorne. I have no private means at all, and my
mother has only just enough to keep herself and Janet :
so that now I have been compelled to resign the living

of S. Etheldreda's, there seems nothing before me but the workhouse."

"I never approved of the name of that Church," said Mrs. Gaythorne. "I never approve of any saints that do not come out of the Bible: they seem to me Popish."

"Gabriel didn't christen the church," suggested Janet in extenuation.

"I have nothing to do with that. All I say is that I do not approve of fancy saints."

"Yet the lives of some of them were very beautiful," said Mrs. Carr: "think of S. Francis of Assisi preaching to the birds as he sat on a gridiron heated seven times hotter, if it wasn't S. Laurence, which I almost think it was: and then S. Catherine whirling round on fireworks till she was burnt up: and S. Sebastian pierced all over with arrows, which had poisoned heads and barbed points. Surely all these set us a beautiful example, though of course to be adapted to modern needs, manners and customs being so different now to what they were then, and arrows and gridirons being used for such different purposes or not at all."

"I should like a few words alone with Gabriel," said Mrs. Gaythorne, when lunch was over.

It was not her custom to beat about the bush and intrigue for *tête-à-têtes*, as it is the custom of some women. So Mrs. Carr and Janet retired, and left the two others together.

"Now, Gabriel," the lady began, "you have brought this illness upon yoursel. by your own foolishness: there is no doubt on that score; but what is done is done, and it is no good harping on it any further. The thing we have to consider is what is to be done now."

"Precisely, Mrs. Gaythorne: that is what I have

been considering for several weeks, and I am as far
from any conclusion as I was when I began."

"Then I am not. I have decided to order my son
Charles to confer upon you the living of Gaythorne."

Gabriel was dumbfoundered. He understood perhaps
better than anyone what it must have cost Mrs.
Gaythorne to make this decision; and he felt almost
overpowered by the magnitude of her sacrifice.

"But, dear Mrs. Gaythorne, consider what you are
doing."

"I have considered. I am not one to act without
due consideration."

"I am not of your way of thinking upon many
subjects."

"No one knows that better than I do."

"And though I would do anything in my power to
please you, dear Mrs. Gaythorne, I could not put aside
my own convictions for you or for anybody. I mean
that if I were appointed to the living of Gaythorne, I
should feel it my duty to conduct the worship of God
as I believe He has ordained, and not as I think my
parishioners desire. In some things a minister of religion
is the servant of all; but in others he owes no allegiance
to any but the Master Himself, and to Him alone he is
responsible; and I believe that the form in which he
worships the Master is one of these latter things. I
want you fully to understand this before you urge
your son to appoint me Rector of Gaythorne."

"I do fully understand it. I know you well enough
to be aware that you are as obstinate as possible where
your conscience is concerned; as obstinate as I am
myself: and I respect you for it."

Gabriel could hardly forbear smiling. "And yet you
wish me to become Rector of Gaythorne?"

"I do, although I know that you will do many things of which I heartily disapprove, and that you will count them to yourself for righteousness. But as I grow older I am beginning to see that the spirit is of vastly more importance than the letter; and that it is possible to serve God in various ways, though I never shall believe that one way is quite as acceptable to Him as another. But I have learnt to say from my heart ' Grace be to all them that love our Lord Jesus Christ in sincerity,' even though they show their love in peculiar ways: and I do believe that you love our Lord Jesus Christ in sincerity, although I admit that you are prone to display your devotion in a very remarkable fashion. Therefore I shall command my son to offer you the living of Gaythorne, since I believe it will be better for the parish to be ruled by a misguided man who truly loves God, than by one of my own way of thinking who does not."

Gabriel's eyes filled with tears of gratitude as he took his old friend's hand and kissed it.

"I can never express in words what I feel about this matter, Mrs. Gaythorne. I am not only profoundly grateful to you for thus coming to my help in a time of sore need; but I am even more grateful for the testimony you bear to my efforts in the past to do what is right, by offering the charge of your own parish to a man who does not see by any means eye to eye with you on many religious questions. And I swear to you that I will do all in my power to prevent you from ever regretting the choice into which you have been led by the kindness of your warm and loving heart: so help me God."

Thus Gabriel went on his way, and the angels of God met him in the form of Janet Field and Mrs. Gaythorne

and the Lord sent him bread and meat, as well as the
spiritual comfort of the still small Voice. So he went
forward rejoicing, little dreaming of the darkness of
desolation which awaited him a little further on the
road.

CHAPTER XV

THE LOST RECTOR

GABRIEL had not long been appointed Rector of
Gaythorne before he became engaged to Janet Field;
and he had not long been engaged to Janet Field before
he married her. It was a quiet wedding in the little
village in the Midlands where his mother lived: and as
it was now November, the newly-wedded pair went
south for their honeymoon, in order to catch the last
flutter of autumn's skirts before she faded into winter
altogether.

Janet was in the seventh heaven of delight. To be
Gabriel's wife was to her the summit of earthly bliss—
the one supreme happiness which she had dreamed of
ever since her girlhood as too absolutely ideal ever to
be realized. Gabriel also was content, in that peaceful
fashion, which, to a highly-strung temperament, is far
more satisfying than any fiercer emotion.

But Fabia was greatly annoyed at the marriage of
the new Rector. Had she known he would bring a
helpmeet with him to the Rectory, she would not have
moved heaven and earth to compass his appointment.
She still loved him—loved him all the more for his
rejection of herself: but she hated his wife with the
intense hatred of the woman scorned for her successful
rival. It is a noteworthy fact that a woman can

forgive a rival who is better-looking than herself far
sooner than one who is not so well-favoured. Beauty is
the one thing in which women acknowledge each other's
superiority: the woman who is more attractive and yet
not so handsome as another is beyond the pale of
pardon. Therefore the beautiful and distinguished
Fabia could not forgive the ordinary-looking girl who
had won the love of Gabriel Carr after she herself had
forfeited it.

Moreover, Fabia had found her own husband utterly
incapable of supplying her intellectual needs; and she
had imagined that Gabriel, as a spiritual adviser, might
help to fill the vacuum thus created. But to the
woman who regards the confessional as a luxury rather
than a discipline, a married confessor is not nearly so
satisfactory as a single one: a strong argument in
favour of (or, perhaps, against) the celibacy of the
clergy. Finding her hopes of Gabriel's supporting
friendship fruitless, Fabia took to writing long letters
to her cousin, Ram Chandar, confiding to him her
unsatisfied longings for suitable intellectual companionship, and begging him to come to England to console
and help her. At first he refused, being offended by
her marriage: but it was not long before she thought
she saw unmistakable signs of his relenting.

Mrs. Gaythorne was delighted about Gabriel's
marriage. She was one of the women who heartily
approve of matrimony, and highly disapprove of the
reverse: an old maid was always visited with her
severest censure: and she meted out as unqualified a
condemnation to the woman who did not marry, as to
the woman who ate or drank anything between meals.

Gabriel and Janet went for their honeymoon to a
little inn on the borders of Dartmoor; and revelled in

the exquisite and yet awe-inspiring scenery of that part
of England's most beautiful county to their heart's
content; discussing at the same time every subject
under the sun and above it, in the delightful intimacy
and comradeship of married life. It is only when the
twain are one mind as well as one flesh that the true
happiness of marriage is realized: and this was the case
with Gabriel and his wife.

"The only thing I don't like about Dartmoor is the
prison," remarked Janet one day, as they were sitting
together in the twilight which now seemed to come
almost in the middle of the afternoon. "I hate to
think of all those wicked people being so near
to us."

"Poor souls! I'm sorry for them, whoever they may
be," said the sympathetic Gabriel, "and whatever they
may have done."

But Janet was not made of such slight elements.
"I'm not: and I daresay you wouldn't be if you knew
more about them."

"Yes, I should, my love; I should be all the sorrier."

Janet shook her small brown head severely.

"I'm never very sorry for people who bring things
on themselves. If they do wrong they ought to be
punished," she replied.

"And they generally are, my child. God may forgive,
but Nature and the world never do."

"And quite right too!" Janet could be very hard
upon occasion.

"You can never judge any man's sins until you know
what his temptations have been, Janet: and as only God
knows that, only God can judge. The newspapers can
tell us what some poor wretch has done, who is now
being punished for his sins in that gloomy prison; but

only God could tell us how sorely he has been tempted,
and how often he resisted temptation before he finally
fell. And God will remember it to his credit when the
day of reckoning comes."

"But some of the prisoners have been very wicked
people."

"So they may have been ; but we do not know that
we should have turned out any better had we been
exposed to their temptations and put in their place."

Janet looked horrified at the bare suggestion. "I
don't think it is likely that we should take to flat
burglary."

"No ; that would not be any temptation to people
brought up as we have been, my dearest. But we may
be beset by other temptations which will prove too
strong for us. I think there is no text which is more
necessary to be constantly borne in mind by (so-called)
good people than, 'Let him that thinketh he standeth
take heed lest he fall': for it is when we are most
certain of our firm footing on the narrow way, that
the danger of falling is at its zenith."

"Well, anyhow, I'm sure that no temptation would
ever be strong enough to make you do anything wrong,
Gabriel."

"My darling, my darling, how little you know me !
Do you remember the story of holy John Bradford who,
on seeing a murderer being led to the gallows, exclaimed :
'There but for the grace of God goes John Bradford'?
When I was in the East End I never saw any poor
wretch being taken up by the police without saying
to myself: 'There but for the grace of God goes
Gabriel Carr'!"

"Dearest, I hate to hear you say such things."

"I cannot help that, Janet. You must know me as

what I am, and not as what you think I ought to be."

"I know that you are one of the best men that ever lived."

Gabriel smiled and stroked the brown head that was leaning against his knee; for Janet—unlike Isabel Seaton—had hair that was never the worse for any amount of stroking. But even though a man may smile at the extravagance of his wife's admiration for himself, it has an extremely soothing effect upon him: the doctrine of the infallibility of the husband is a very comfortable one, both to worshipper and worshipped—so much so that it is a pity it has gone, to a great extent, out of fashion.

"I am far from being one of the best men that ever lived, my dear," he said: "but all the same, it is rather nice to know that you think I am.'

' I shall always think so."

"I believe you will, my Janet: and, as far as I am concerned, it is a most comforting heresy. But all the same, you must learn not to judge other people so harshly. I think it is very difficult for a really good woman not to be rather hard: nevertheless, she ought not to be."

"Do you think I am hard, Gabriel?"

"Just a little, my dearest; because you are so good." And he bent down and kissed the little round face raised in such profound adoration to his. "You see," he continued, "it is never safe to feel oneself safe from any particular temptation. The question, 'Is thy servant a dog that he should do this thing?' is frequently answered by the servant doing the very thing that he condemned as so dog-like. I have seen this happen over and over again in my experience as a pariah priest. Whenever I hear a man say, 'Oh! such and such a thing may be dangerous for certain persons, but I can do it with impunity,' I know that the devil has made everything ready for the overthrow of that particular man."

"But surely, Gabriel, no man is tempted above that which he is able to bear. We are expressly told that a way of escape is always provided."

"So it is; but it does not follow that we shall always be willing to avail ourselves of that way. Therefore I hold that it is necessary for the best of men, as for the worst, to raise to Heaven the daily petition, 'Lead us not into temptation': for we have to be in the thick of temptation before we realize how irresistible it is."

Thus Gabriel and Janet passed the long evening in holding sweet converse about all the deeper interests of life; they " reasoned high of providence, foreknowledge, will, and fate," and everything else that concerned their truest welfare.

The next day was wet and inclined to be misty. There was not much good or much pleasure to be derived from going out in such raw, damp weather; but the holiday was so near its conclusion that the newly-wedded pair felt they could not squander any of the few remaining hours of their honeymoon by spending them in the house: so they were out on the moor all morning, in spite of driving rain and mist. But it requires more than feminine fortitude to be wet through twice in one day; so after lunch Janet decided that she really could not brave the inclement elements again, especially as there was no special object to be gained by so doing. Gabriel therefore went out for a good spin across the moor by himself, leaving Janet to amuse herself with an interesting book until his return, and faithfully promising to be back in time for tea. He loved to be in solitude upon that wild stretch of country: there was something in the atmosphere of the moor that appealed to one side of his nature—the side which Janet could not understand.

Different phases of natural scenery call forth various emotions of the human heart. When we wander upon the seashore, we feel a restless sadness and an unsatisfied longing quivering within us: when we tread the leafy glades of a forest, thoughts of romance and heroism stir our blood: dreams of simple joys and domestic happiness delight us, as we look down upon a rural landscape of cornfields and meadows and red-roofed homesteads: whilst we seem to come within reach of the great secrets of eternity, when we stand under the shadow of the everlasting hills. And in the same way wild stretches of moorland call up an answering spirit within us; but it is not a spirit which makes for righteousness or peace. The spirit of the moorland is a fierce, untutored spirit, with the restlessness of the sea without its sanctifying sadness, and with the mystery of the mountains without their soul-restoring peace. Demons that would shrivel into nothingness before the awful mystery of sea or mountain, fly shrieking over the moorland to their evil hearts' content: witches that would be powerless to withstand the spell of homestead or forest, ride recklessly upon the swirling blasts that sweep across the heath. True, the moorlands have their fascination for those who understand them; but it is the fascination of evil rather than of good; for evil is strong in those desert places, and the powers of darkness hold high carnival there. One can imagine the scapegoat, with his necklet of scarlet dashing to and fro across the dreary scene: or th

child, whose hand was doomed to be against every
man, wandering with his outcast mother across the
barren waste.   And surely He, Who knew what was
in man, knew this also—knew that the spirit of the
waste places of the earth was at war with the Spirit of
God, and that evil had more power in the desert than
on the shores of Gennesaret and in the groves of Olivet
—when He went apart into the wilderness, there to be
tempted of the devil.

After Gabriel had gone out Janet was so much
absorbed in her book that for an hour or so she never
even looked out of the window; but when at last she
did so, she was somewhat disturbed to see that the mist
had turned into a thick fog. This did not however
unduly distress her, partly because she was not a woman
with a genius for worry, and partly because her husband
knew the moor so well that she believed he would have
been able to find his way across it blindfold. But when
tea-time came, and no Gabriel, she began to feel anxious;
and when dinner-time came, and still no Gabriel, she
felt more anxious still; and when at last bed-time came,
and he had not returned, her distress of mind was very
great indeed. The innkeeper and his wife were deeply
concerned and extremely sympathetic; but they pointed
out to Janet that it would be useless, and worse than
useless, to send men out to seek for her lost husband in
such a fog as this, as it was now so thick that even a
lantern could not be seen for more than a yard in front.
They assured the half-distraught little bride that her
husband—finding it hopeless to make his way back
through the fog—had doubtless taken refuge in some
shepherd's hut or sheltered spot, and would remain there
until the fog lifted; and with this poor Janet had to be
content, although no sleep visited her eyes that night.

The poor girl never even attempted to go to bed; but sat up all night long alternately crying and praying for Gabriel.

Next morning the fog had cleared, and search parties were immediately organized to go in quest of the lost bridegroom. All day long they scoured the moor, but alas! with no result; not a trace of the missing man could they find. The assistance of the police was soon called in, but was likewise of no avail: Gabriel Carr seemed to have been swept off the face of the earth.

Janet's agony was almost more than she could bear. It seemed too cruel to have attained, after years of hope deferred, her heart's desire, only to have the cup dashed from her lips at the very moment of fruition. Of course she telegraphed to her husband's friends: and Captain Gaythorne and his mother came to her at once. Poor Mrs. Carr was so prostrated by the news of her son's disappearance that she was confined to her bed and unable to travel; but Mrs. Gaythorne was a rock in times of trouble, and Janet was more thankful to her than she could express.

Yet even Mrs. Gaythorne was unable to find the missing Rector.

All the searchers comforted Janet with the assurance that if—as she feared—her husband had lost his life upon the moor, some trace of his body must have been found. There are no glaciers upon Dartmoor, as there are in Switzerland, down which a man may fall head-long, leaving no trace behind; and as no one could have walked fast in such a fog, he really would not have had time to go so very far afield before the fog lifted, and he could see about again. But if he were still alive, what had become of him? What was he doing whilst his newly-made wife was eating her very heart out for the want of him? That was the question which no one could answer; at least no one who was ignorant of what powers of darkness had been let loose that night upon Dartmoor to work their wicked will; no one who knew not how Good and Evil had met and fought together in that wilderness, and how Evil had won the day and had prevailed.

Mrs. Gaythorne was as loving as any mother to poor Janet: nothing could exceed her care of and tenderness for the unhappy little bride, who seemed to be neither wife nor widow. It was at times such as this that Charlie's mother showed her best—and therefore her real—self.

As for Janet, she was well-nigh broken-hearted. Could anyone imagine a more tragic ending to a honeymoon than this? She wandered out all day and every day upon the moor, in the vain hope of finding her lost husband, with Mrs. Gaythorne in close attendance, that good woman knowing neither hunger nor fatigue where the fulfilment of what she considered her duty was concerned. Like many of her particular school of thought, Mrs. Gaythorne made up for the sternness of her principles by the wisdom and tenderness of her practices. Her written epistle might be a hard saying; but as a living epistle, known and read of all men, she set forth in unmistakable terms the gospel of love.

One evening Captain Gaythorne came into the inn-parlour when his mother happened to be sitting alone, Janet having retired to her own desolate chamber to weep undisturbed.

"It's all up," he said hopelessly, as he sank into a chair: "we had better pack up and go home to-morrow."

"Charles, do you mean to tell me that poor young man's corpse has been found at last?"

Charlie groaned. "Worse than that, mother."

"There is nothing worse than death," replied Mrs. Gaythorne. "I mean of course for the survivors," she added hastily.

"Yes, mother, there is; disgrace is worse than death."

Mrs. Gaythorne drew herself up. "Charles, never let me hear you use such a word as disgrace in connection with that man of God, Gabriel Carr."

"It sticks in my throat, I can tell you, mother; but I'm afraid you'll use it yourself when you hear what I've heard."

"And what is that, Charles? Where did they find the corpse of that excellent young man?"

"They haven't found it at all. Don't you see, mother, there's no corpse in the question. That's the whole point of the thing."

"Charles, explain yourself."

Captain Gaythorne endeavoured—as he had always endeavoured from his youth up—to obey his mother, but lucidity of expression had never been one of his most distinguishing characteristics.

"Well, don't you see, the police have at last traced Carr to Newton Abbot?"

"Newton Abbot! What on earth did he want at Newton Abbot—and on his honeymoon too?" exclaimed Mrs. Gaythorne.

"That's just the whole point."

"Then I don't believe he ever went there. Gabriel was the last man to do anything foolish, especially in a thick fog—except of course in matters of ritual, with regard to which he always seemed to have

P

a bee in his bonnet, to say the least of it. But he was not a fool all through: and it is one thing to have early services and flowers upon the Communion Table, and quite another thing to go to Newton Abbot in a dense fog on your honeymoon with no object."

"All the same he went there, mother. An old fossil of a farmer has turned up who gave him a lift in his cart as far as Newton Abbot."

Mrs. Gaythorne still bristled all over with doubts.

"And what did he do when he got to Newton Abbot, I should like to know?" she asked.

"He went straight to the station, and off to London by the next train. The railway fellows can tell us all about that, as they sold him his ticket and saw him get into the train."

"I do not believe a word of it. It is a trumped-up story invented to injure Gabriel and to annoy me."

"But, mother, you must believe it. A countryman drove a parson in a grey Norfolk suit, exactly answering to the description of Carr, into Newton Abbot on the morning after the fog."

"That is not proof. There may have been hundreds of clergymen in grey Norfolk suits wandering upon Dartmoor in the fog, for all I know. Besides, I never believe the word of agricultural labourers without some proof."

"Well, mother, if you doubt the evidence of the farmer and the railway people and the whole of Scotland Yard put together, you can't doubt the evidence of your own senses. Look here! Carr left this behind in the cart when he got out at Newton Abbot." And Charlie spread out before his mother's eyes one of Gabriel's pocket-handkerchiefs, neatly and clearly marked with his name by the careful and efficient Janet.

Then at last Mrs. Gaythorne was convinced. For some minutes she sat quite still, great tears rolling silently down her weather-beaten cheeks. " Oh ! Charles, what does it mean ? " she said, after a time. "What does it mean ? " And it was pitiful to hear the quiver in the usually steady voice.

" I'm afraid it means that Carr has behaved like a blackguard, mother."

" But he was such a good man," Mrs. Gaythorne pleaded ; " such a sincere and God-fearing man, though in some matters so misguided."

" I know that, mother ; but even the best of men come a cropper sometimes, don't you know ? Look at the great Lord Nelson."

" Charles, never again let me hear you refer in my presence to the lover of Lady Hamilton."

Charlie was contrite at once. " I beg your pardon, mother : I didn't mean to rough you up. All I meant was that it's sometimes too difficult even for the best of men to keep straight. Women haven't the ghost of a idea how deuced difficult it is ! "

" But women have a very good idea indeed of how distressing it is when they do not," replied Mrs. Gaythorne, with some truth.

" My notion is," said Charlie, who had inherited a goodly portion of his mother's sound sense, " that Carr made a mistake in marrying a quiet, dowdy girl like Janet Field : she wasn't the sort to hold a brilliant, good-looking fellow like him, don't you know ? Showy men want showy girls to hold them : or else there's soon the devil to pay."

" There are other attractions than those of the flesh, Charles. I was never a particularly handsome woman, but I had no difficulty in holding your father. He always did exactly as I told him, from the day of our marriage till the hour of his death."

Charlie fully believed this.

"Of course, of course, mother: and you are very good-looking, all the same. But I mean I never much believe in those boy-and-girl sort of attachments. You see, Janet was always like a sister to Carr, and she had no more influence over him than a sister would have. A man wants something stronger than a milk-and-water, brother-and-sister 'feeling to satisfy him in married life. Why, it even says in the Prayer-book that a man may not marry his sister any more than his grandmother, and that's the same principle, don't you know?"

"Charles, I admit there is something in what you say. But that does not seem to me to excuse a man from running away from his wife on his honeymoon."

"Of course not: but in a way it explains it. I believe that poor Carr married Janet out of a sense of duty or honour, or something of that kind, because she'd been in love with him from a kid; and then, when he'd done it, he found it was more than he could stand; so he just cut and run. You see, clever people find it awfully slow to be married to people who aren't clever," Charlie added ruefully, remembering how obviously he himself always bored his wife.

"We must keep this from Janet at all costs," said Mrs. Gaythorne, after a short pause. "It is better for her to think her husband dead than false."

"We can't keep it from her, mother. The papers to-morrow will be full of it, and you know how she reads every word."

"Then we cannot keep it from her, Charles: she

must know the worst. And perhaps it is better that she should. We cannot spare people more than God intends to spare them, and it is no use our trying to do so: and surely the Lord knows best."

CHAPTER XVI

FORSAKEN

ON her return from her ill-starred honeymoon, Janet insisted upon taking up her abode at Gaythorne Rectory, as if nothing had happened. She had read in the papers the account of Gabriel's departure to London from Newton Abbot, and had been wonderfully comforted by this proof that her husband was still alive. But she absolutely refused to believe any ill of him. She persisted that he must have had some good reason for rushing off to London in that strange fashion, or else he never would have done so; and she was convinced that before long he would return to Gaythorne and take up his duties there, with a full and satisfactory explanation of his apparently unjustifiable conduct. Her absolute faith in him remained unshaken.

But this attitude of mind on Janet's part made things very awkward for other people. The parish of Gaythorne was practically without a Rector; and as Carr had not resigned the living, and there was no proof of his death but rather the contrary, he still held the incumbency; and therefore a new Rector could not as yet be instituted in his place. So it was arranged between the Bishop and Mrs. Gaythorne, who were great friends, that—for the present at any rate—Janet

and her mother-in-law should draw the stipend and
stay on at the Rectory; while a curate should be paid
by Mrs. Gaythorne to take charge of the parish, which
was a very small one, and to do duty in the Church.

Weeks rolled on, and nothing further was heard of
the missing Gabriel. It seemed as if the Devonshire
farmer had indeed seen the last of him; and as if when
he left the station of Newton Abbot he had disappeared
for ever. But his wife's faith in him remained un-
touched. She still clung as closely as ever to her
conviction that one day he would come back and
explain everything, and stand justified in the eyes of
the world; though how he would do it she had not the
ghost of an idea.

Mrs. Gaythorne, however, had her own explanation
of his apparently inexplicable conduct. She was bound
to arrive at a conclusion of some sort, as it was agony
to her to feel that there was anything in heaven or
earth undreamed of in her own peculiar philosophy.

"I have made up my mind what has become of
Gabriel Carr," she announced one morning at breakfast,
a couple of months after the Rector's disappearance.

Her son and daughter-in-law were sitting with her at
table, as well as Isabel Seaton, who was spending a few
days at Gaythorne Manor while Paul delivered a course
of political speeches in the north of England. Isabel
had been very much attached to Gabriel, and very
much surprised and disturbed at first by his disappearance. But she had soon got over it. It is astonishing
how little power events outside the circle of her own
household and family have in destroying the peace of
the happily-married woman. Things which would have
agonized her in her single days hardly disturb her at
all. Mrs. Paul Seaton had much in common with the

old woman who said that "as long as her husband's
dinner didn't disagree with him, she didn't mind how
soon there was a European war." It is by no means
an uncommon type : for matrimony, when reverently,
discreetly, and advisedly taken in hand, becomes an
absorbing profession.

"How clever of you, Mrs. Gaythorne!" exclaimed
Isabel. "Do let us hear what it is."

"I believe that Ritualism—and nothing else but
Ritualism—is responsible for all this trouble," replied
Mrs. Gaythorne, as ever true to her colours.

"But there is nothing in the Ornaments Rubric in
favour of deserting your wife on her honeymoon,"
argued the irrepressible Isabel.

"But there's something in the Bible about people
with wives being as though they hadn't any," hastily
added Charlie, wishing to agree with his mother, and
believing that he was doing so.

But Mrs. Gaythorne was not so easily agreed with.

"No, Charles; I think you have misinterpreted that
particular text; but you shall look it up in the
Commentary as soon as you have finished your
breakfast, and see exactly what it means. My impression, however, is that it was not intended to inculcate
the regular practice of such behaviour as Gabriel's."

Charlie at once subsided. He felt that, with the best
of intentions, he had somehow made a mistake.

Here Fabia broke into the conversation :

"He who weds and runs away, may live to wed
another day, and another young woman."

Mrs. Gaythorne pursed up her lips in stern
disapproval:

"No, my dear; Gabriel Carr was never one of that
sort. I have known him from a child and his mother

before him, and that is the last thing that either of
them would ever think of doing."

"Still I must say there is something in Fabia's idea,"
said Charlie.

He was always ready, whenever it was possible, to
show up his wife to his mother in a favourable light.
This was one of the poor fellow's many conjugal mistakes. There is nothing that a wife resents more than
being screened by her husband from her husband's
relations: just as there is nothing that makes a husband
more indignant than being translated, with emendations
by his wife, in order to earn the approval of his wife's
people. Yet the intention on both sides arises from the
best of motives, although it generally brings about the
very result that it was originated to avoid. Unsancti-
fied human nature cannot endure to be revised and
Bowdlerized for the benefit of its in-laws.

"We don't want to hear what you say: we want
to hear what Mrs. Gaythorne thinks," was Fabia's
unwifely retort.

Poor Charlie again subsided.

"What is your idea about Gabriel Carr, Mrs.
Gaythorne?" Fabia continued.

"It is not an idea, Fabia, it is a conviction. It has
been borne in upon me that Gabriel had so saturated
his mind with Popish notions about monks and nuns
and celibates, and all sorts of nonsense of that
kind, that they turned his brain—never very strong at
the best of times, or else he would not have gone in for
the mummeries he did. By the way, what do they call
a nunnery for monks?"

Mrs. Gaythorne always shammed ignorance upon
subjects such as this, in the same way as His Majesty's
Judges frequently feign an ignorance, to which they

really have no claim, with regard to matters unconnected with their high profession. Just as a judge
would feel it incumbent upon him in his official capacity
to assume innocence regarding race-meetings and the
like, so Mrs. Gaythorne felt it incumbent upon her high
calling as a militant Protestant to know nothing whatsoever about the ceremonies and institutions sanctioned
by Catholicism in any form.

" I suppose you mean a monastery," replied Fabia.

" Monastery, indeed ! I should rather call it a
monkey-house," retorted Mrs. Gaythorne, with grim
humour. " Well, I am convinced that Gabriel was
suddenly seized with a ridiculous and papistical notion
that all clergymen ought to be bachelors ; and so he
fled away from Janet into a monastery. What are those
horrible places called where no women are admitted and
nobody is allowed to speak, Fabia ? "

" Trappist monasteries, do you mean ? "

" Yes, that is the name and a very suitable name too,
for they are indeed traps set by the devil to catch the
souls of men ! Not long ago I read a novel about a
man who, after he was married, remembered that he was
a Trappist monk ; so he at once gave up being married
and returned to his monastery. I thought it a most
improper proceeding on his part : but I feel convinced
in my own mind that poor Gabriel has gone and done
likewise."

" But Carr wasn't a Trappist before his marriage,"
objected Captain Gaythorne.

His mother shook her head ominously. " You
never can tell what those High-Church parsons may
not be in disguise. I dare say he was a Trappist and
a Jesuit as well, if we only knew. Lots of them are,
and believe that they are thereby doing God service."

"But Carr would never have justified a married man
going into a monastery unless there'd have been some
rattling good reason for it," persisted Charlie: "you can
bet your boots upon that."

"Anybody who will justify a man, in any
circumstances, in hiding himself in one of those
dreadful, horrible nunneries, will justify anything,"
replied Mrs. Gaythorne, unwittingly speaking the truth,
as a man in a nunnery would indeed be as dreadful a
thing as a lion among ladies. "And, Charles, never
again let me hear you use such an objectionable word
as 'bet'; for betting is one of the things that I have
never allowed either you or your father to indulge in
and never shall.

"I don't agree with Mrs. Gaythorne that Gabriel has
followed Hamlet's advice and got him to a nunnery,"
said Isabel; "but I shouldn't be surprised if she were
correct in the spirit if not in the letter; and that some
impractical and quixotic notion were accountable for
his disappearance. I feel certain that he thought he
was doing right, or he wouldn't have done it."

Charlie looked doubtful.

"It's all very well to be romantic and quixotic and
all that sort of thing; but deserting your wife on your
honeymoon is rather a large order," he remarked.

"I agree with Charlie's notion," said Fabia; "that
Janet bored him so intensely that he literally could not
stand another day of her."

Charlie beamed with pleasure at the great compliment Fabia paid him in endorsing his opinion on any
matter. "He is a clever sort of chap, and he wanted a
clever sort of wife to keep him company, don't you
know?"

"I dare say Mrs. Gabriel Carr isn't a dazzling genius,

remarked Isabel, "but I shouldn't have called her by
any means a fool. She seemed to me the pleasant,
easy-going sort of a girl that one asks in at the last
moment to make the fourteenth at table, and things of
that kind. I saw her once or twice before her marriage,
and that is how she struck me: not too clever to get
married, and yet too stupid to remain single—the sort
of woman that makes a man really happy."

Isabel was always ready and more than ready to do
justice to another woman.

"But she's so short." Captain Gaythorne, like Lord
Byron, hated a dumpy woman.

"Still he knew that when he proposed to her,"
retorted Mrs. Seaton. "It is absurd to marry a woman
of five foot three, and then to run away because she
doesn't grow to five foot six before the end of the
honeymoon! If you want 'outside ladies' size,' you
must order it in the first instance."

"I did," replied Charlie, looking at his tall wife with
adoration in his honest eyes.

"We are all as God made us," said Mrs. Gaythorne,
her voice heavy with reproof.

"But you can't deny you are glad that there was no
skimping in your case, Mrs. Gaythorne, and that you
were cut out a good five foot seven, with ample material
for bodice."

"Isabella Carnaby, do not be flippant."

It was a habit of Mrs. Gaythorne's frequently to
address married ladies by their maiden names. It was
also her habit never to use a diminutive; diminutives
being among the numerous things of which she
disapproved.

"I'll try not; but it is difficult to change the habits
of a lifetime at my age," replied Mrs. Seaton meekly.

" Nevertheless," added Mrs. Gaythorne, who was nothing if not accurate, " I confess that it is a cause of thankfulness on my part that it was ordained by Providence that I should not be a small or insignificant person. Presence is a thing which I have always considered most important, my dear Isabella."

Isabella was not Isabel's name; but Mrs. Gaythorne thought it ought to to have been, and so invariably addressed her by it. She regarded the name Isabel in the light of a diminutive, and disapproved of it accordingly.

" It's always a mistake for a fellow to marry a dowdy little woman," said Charlie sententiously : " frumps have no staying power."

"And it is an equally grave mistake for a girl to marry a fool," replied Fabia.

Charlie winced, but Isabel came to his rescue.

"Lots have to, or they'd never get married at all. Nobody but a fool would propose to them," she said.

Thus Gabriel Carr's friends discussed his mysterious disappearance; and none of them could come to any satisfactory conclusion, since none of them knew of the tragedy which had occurred upon Dartmoor on the night of the fog. That was known to only two living people : and of those the instinct of self-preservation forbade the one to tell, and nobody would accept the testimony of the other. So the testimony was in safe keeping.

Janet was very brave, but her sorrow told upon her: her face grew older and her figure less plump, and the merry look died out of her hazel eyes. But she carried a bold front before the world, and she abundantly fulfilled her duty to her husband's parish. She was an ideal wife for any clergyman; and even the overwhelming blow which had well-nigh crushed her, in no wise

interfered with her adequacy in adorning the lot to
which she had been called. The parish of Gaythorne
was but a small parish, it is true ; but it was better looked
after than any other parish in the county, every cottage
being constantly visited and every sick person carefully
ministered to by Janet herself. Thus her desolate days
were filled with deeds of charity and acts of mercy, and
so were kept from being quite as desolate as they would
otherwise have been : for work—and especially work for
others—is the best panacea for the pain of the human
heat.

Another source of comfort to Janet was the possession
of a gift which is usually reserved for the stronger sex
and is rarely bestowed upon women, namely, the gift of
not seeing anything that she did not wish to see.
Women, as a rule, are too keen-sighted and too quick in
their perceptions to be able to close their eyes at will,
and a stone wall is generally to them as plate-glass : but
men—happy creatures !—have a marvellous power of
not seeing the unpleasant truth at all, unless they desire
to do so. Even though you may illuminate it with
Chinese lanterns and dangle it under their very noses,
they will remain as blind as if it were an undiscovered
planet. They do not choose to see it : therefore for
them it does not exist. Most men are mute, inglorious
Nelsons, putting the telescope to their blind eye when
they think the signals will be against their wishes. It
is a most comfortable and convenient custom, and shows
the superior wisdom of the sex which is proficient
in it. Janet Carr, however, had less subtlety than the
majority of women, and less quickness of perception :
she was almost as easily deceived (when she
wished to be) as a man. She had none of that
marvellous power of intuition which distinguishes some

—and not always the cleverest—women: and she had intensely strong and deeply-rooted prejudices—things which are always useful as blinkers. Therefore the stream of gossip about Gabriel flowed by her unheeded: she was as little affected by it as a man would have been.

But Janet's chief stronghold lay in the fact that she never for a moment doubted her husband, or questioned the purity of his motives and the soundness of his wisdom in leaving her. What wise reason had prompted his apparently unaccountable action, she of course could not tell: but that there was a reason—and an all-sufficient one—she had not the faintest shadow of a doubt. Thus she not only fulfilled her duty to her husband's parish, but she also fulfilled her duty to her husband, the parish-priest. She regarded the husband as the head of the wife; and therefore held that it was not in the wife's province to criticize his actions or to question his motives. She was accountable to him: but he was not accountable to her. It was a counsel of perfection, perhaps: but perfection does not spell impossibility: otherwise " Be ye perfect," would never have been a command issued to the sons of men. Janet Carr implicitly obeyed the apostolic injunction, that wives must be in subjection to their own husbands: she had no new-fangled notions as to the equality of the sexes and the independence of the wife. She was content to accept the holy estate of matrimony as what God and the Church ordained it to be: and she did not trouble her mind with problems as to the permanence of home-life or the sanctity of marriage. To her, marriage was a sacrament, and was therefore not open to observation: and she held as most unseemly the modern habit of setting aside, by means of problem-

novels and scientific treatises and open discussions in
the daily papers, the very oracles of God. She would
as soon have thought of wondering whether the grass
were red or the sky green, as of wondering whether the
bond of holy wedlock were dissoluble.

She believed in her husband's integrity with all her
heart—believed that what he had done had been done
with the best of motives and would end in the most
satisfactory of results. But if she had not believed this,
it would have made no difference at all in her attitude
towards him. If she could have been convinced that he
had purposely forsaken her and had been wholly un-
faithful, she would not have regarded herself as one
whit the less his wife, or considered her duty to him as
in any way cancelled.

Such was the simple faith of Janet Carr: an out-worn
creed, according to modern notions, and one which
contained in its vocabulary no words such as "incom-
patibility of temper," "temperamental differences," and
the like

CHAPTER XVII

THE BEGINNING OF TROUBLE

As time went on, the relations between Captain Gaythorne and his beautiful wife grew more and more strained: her contempt for him was more openly showed, and his unhappiness at her indifference more fully displayed, every day they spent together. Of course no wife is justified in behaving to her husband as Fabia was behaving then: but still it cannot be denied that poor Charlie managed her very badly. Fabia was the type of woman who wanted to find her master; and Charlie persisted in fawning at her feet as if he were her slave or her spaniel. And yet he was a manly enough man where his own sex was concerned: his men had always obeyed and his fellow-officers respected him, from the time that he first entered the service. But as a boy he had been trained to be afraid of his mother, and consequently as a man he was afraid of his wife. He would do anything compatible with reason and honour to avoid the storms of feminine temper; and yet—or, perhaps, therefore—the lightnings of female wrath were for ever hurtling round his devoted head. It never answers to kowtow to a subject race: it always renders that race exacting and overbearing. It is Man's place to rule: and the minute that he lays down his sceptre, Woman snatches it up

and hits him over the head with it—as he richly
deserves. Women invariably bully the men who are
afraid of them, be they husbands or brothers or sons;
and the more a man cringes before them, the less consideration they show him. The true man will always
regard his wife as a queen, and treat her with all
homage and reverence as such; but he will know in his
heart that she is really only a queen-consort, though on
that score entitled to all the more chivalry and consideration. In the smaller things of life he will render
to her every courtesy—it will be his to fetch and carry,
hers to order and command. Because he rules in the
greater things, he will always submit to her wishes in
the lesser: because the crown is really his, he will
always allow her the full prerogatives of the coronet.
The man who domineers over his wife in trifles, is as
unworthy of his kingship as is the man who trembles
before her with regard to the weightier matters of the
law: for the very fact that he is by right her lord and
master, should make him all the more eager never
publicly to display himself as such, or to lower his
royal dignity by dragging it in the dust of petty
domestic affairs. A crown is not the fitting headgear
for the daily walk abroad or the peaceful evening at
home: a sceptre is not the suitable implement for the
stirring of tea-cups or the making of puddings.

There is nothing which so cheapens and vulgarizes
an article as over-advertisement: there are some things
so delicately made that to talk about them destroys
them. There is truth as well as beauty in the legend
of the bride who lost her fairy-lover as soon as she
asked him his name: as he told it to her, he vanished.
The man who tells us that he is great, thereby proves
his own littleness; the woman who announces that she

is a lady, thereby forfeits her right to the title. Have
we not all in our time come across some of those
members of the great army of snobs who show their
lack of social position by their constant insistence on
the same; and who prove the ordinary and commonplace tint of their blood by their incessant testimony
to its azure hue? In the same way, the man who
tyrannizes over his wife in trifles and is always eager to
prove himself the master of the house, shows that in
reality he is nothing but a pretender, and is no ruler by
divine right. For such divinity doth hedge a king,
who is in any sense a real king, that he cannot stoop to
haggle and squabble and nag. His patent of royalty is
too obvious to need any announcement: his rank too
inherent to require any herald to proclaim his style.
And this rule obtains in every other department of life.
Good wine of any kind needs no bush. The really well-
bred person does not boast of his good-breeding: the
really beautiful woman does not trouble to explain her
charms. The moment that a thing requires bolstering
up by advertisement and explanation, that thing begins
to be a sham and a humbug, and had better be thrown
overboard altogether; for in its very nature it is doomed
to perish.

It was a great pity, for her sake as well as for his
own, that Captain Gaythorne did not better understand
how to manage his young wife: for her present attitude
towards her husband was the worst thing possible for a
woman of Fabia's temperament. She was bound sooner
or later to get into mischief of some sort or another:
since matrimony, if not an absorbing profession, is a
very unsatisfactory pastime. Fabia was a woman who
needed occupation and interest in her life; and if she
could not get them from one source, she would get them

from another. After Gabriel so signally failed her all along the line, she fell back upon her old friend, Ram Chandar Mukharji. And Ram Chandar was a clever man, who knew how to make the most of his opportunities. He answered her letters in full, giving her in unstinted measure all the intellectual stimulus and sympathy in which her husband was so conspicuously lacking; and he scrupulously refrained from writing a word which could by the freest translation be construed into anything approaching love-making. He knew that Fabia was as yet unprepared for the actual existence of a lover, although she was quite ready to amuse herself with the shadow and spirit of the thing; and he also knew that when once a married woman begins thus to amuse herself, the appearance upon the scene of the actual lover is but a matter of time. Some Commandments are broken suddenly or not at all; but others demand a more gradual process of disintegration, lest the breaker should be so shocked at the idea of the catastrophe that the Commandment would never get broken at all. Whatever defects the devil may have otherwise, he always shows himself an adept in his own particular line of business; and he is unrivalled in his powers of manipulating that effective instrument known as the thin end of the wedge.

It unfortunately happened that Fabia was left very much to herself and her husband just then. Christmas was over, and Mrs. Gaythorne was plunged in a vortex of godly dissipation and holy mirth; and was submerged in a whirlpool of public meetings, which would gain in force and number all through the spring, until they reached their very maelstrom at Exeter Hall in May. Therefore, she spent a considerable portion of her time in London; and when at home was far too much

occupied by the stress of rampant philanthropy to have
any leisure or attention to bestow upon her son's
conjugal difficulties.

Isabel Seaton, however, saw pretty clearly how things
were going; but she was one of the rare women who
have mastered the fine art of minding their own
business; and, having possessed herself of so valuable
and uncommon an accomplishment, she was naturally
prone to practise the same. Nine times out of ten—
nay, rather ninety-nine times out of a hundred—harm
instead of good is wrought by the intermeddling of well-
intentioned persons in affairs not their own. Probably
far less evil is brought about in the world by really bad
and unprincipled people, than by conscientious and
well-meaning ones who interfere with matters that do
not concern them. And women far more than men are
offenders in this respect. When a really good woman
is seized with a strong outpouring of the missionary
spirit, the amount of mischief that she will effect in a
short time is almost incredible. She will come between
sister and brother, parent and child, husband and wife:
she will estrange devoted lovers and separate very
friends; and all the time she will purr contentedly to
herself with satisfaction over her successful efforts, and
will thank God on her knees every night for what she
will euphoniously term "opportunities of usefulness."
She will never have the ghost of an idea that she is one
of Satan's most approved emissaries for introducing
discord and stirring up strife. Let the first of us
who has never suffered from the well-meant interference of a conscientious woman, say a word in her
defence! I trow her advocates will be few and far
between.

Therefore it was to be counted to Isabel for righteousness that she never attempted to set matters straight between Charlie and Fabia. She was a married woman herself, so she knew the danger of meddling between husband and wife. She was perhaps overbold as a matchmaker; but she shrank from the awful responsibility of putting asunder—by word or hint or innuendo —those whom God had joined together. A single woman would doubtless have rushed in where Mrs. Paul Seaton feared to tread. But she had learnt wisdom in the only school where it is properly taught—the school of experience: so she held her peace.

There is a delightful story told (and a true one, too) of a lady with a very naughty little boy, who consulted a friend—one with seven children of her own—as to how she was to train this rebellious olive-branch. " I'll tell you what to do," replied the mother of seven; "go straight to the first old maid you meet, and she will teach you exactly how to deal successfully with the matter. But it's no good coming to me, because I know no more about it than you do."

Now childless women are not more omniscient in the training of the young, than are old maids in the management of husbands. And by the term "old maid" I mean the typical "old maid": not the broad-minded, large-hearted spinster, whose singleness is her own fault and every man's misfortune; but the petty, provincial, narrow-minded woman, sneering at her more fortunate sister and poking her crooked fingers into everybody's pies, who would be just as much an old maid had she been married and had a large family—who would, in truth, have been just as much an old maid had she been a man. In fact, many old maids have been men, and it has not made them any the less old-maidish: indeed rather more so. And it is this typical, old-maid nature which is generally most strongly imbued with the missionary spirit.

Perhaps there is no type of woman more utterly fascinating and delightful than the really charming single woman—the woman who retains the fascination and freshness of girlhood after she has attained to the culture and wisdom of maturer life. The dew of the morning is still in her eyes, even though she has watched the lengthening of the shadows: the scent of the spring is still in her hair, even though it be crowned with the garlands of autumn. She has never been awakened, by the cares and realities of marriage, from the dreams of her girlhood: her place is in the glades of the forest rather than in the market-place—in the garden of spices rather than in the store-closet. Consequently she has more sympathy with and understanding of the young than has the busy matron: for she still stands upon the mountain-top, and sees the promised land through the magic haze of distance, as the young are standing and seeing! This type of woman will never be obsessed by the missionary spirit; for she will be too shy to rebuke, too sensitive to interfere. She will do good and not evil all the days of her life, by the tenderness of her heart and the purity of her soul: and the children of countless of her contemporaries will rise up and call her blessed. Because she does not belong exclusively to one man, she will have leisure to sympathize with many: because no child calls her mother, she will have a wealth of universal mother-love to lavish upon all.

But unfortunately the interfering style of old maid is by far the more common species; and Isabel Seaton had known so much harm done in this fashion by persons not really evil-minded, that she herself was perhaps inclined rather to err upon the other side, and to keep silence even from good words, when such words would have been helpful and salutary. There is a distinct difference between unjustifiable interference and the necessary word of warning: but it requires a very astute mathematician to know exactly where to draw the line between the two! Anyhow, it came about that Isabel refrained from saying a word to Charlie as to the danger of his wife's obvious indifference to him, and of her determination—if he failed to afford her sufficient amusement—to seek the same elsewhere, and she likewise refrained for the present from saying anything to Fabia upon the subject either, as she did not wish to be the confidante of Mrs. Charles Gaythorne's feelings towards her husband.

Isabel was a woman of the world; and she knew that there are no people so much disliked as the people who are made—even though it be against their own wishes—the recipients of confidences to which they are not entitled. We hate for ever afterwards the persons to whom, according to common parlance, we have "given ourselves away"; even although the libation may have been purely voluntary at the time, and quite undesired upon their part. Therefore wise men—and women—do not receive confidences the giving of which they know will afterwards be regretted by the donors.

Of course Isabel might have spoken to Charlie's mother upon the subject; but she shrank from doing this; partly because such a course savoured of the most unjustifiable kind of interference; and partly because she loved popularity, and there is nothing that renders anyone so unpopular as the imparting of disagreeable information.

The Lady Constance hit upon a great truth when she exclaimed to the bearer of evil tidings—"This news hath made thee a most ugly man!" Hideous indeed in the eyes of us all are the faces of those who come to us as prophets of evil: and likewise lovely are the messengers who bring us the gospel of peace! Yet there are men and women who wish to be attractive and desire to gain the affection of their fellow-men, who nevertheless do not hesitate—indeed rather hasten—to carry the ill news and the evil report to those whose good opinions they most covet; every word they utter is either a reflection or a complaint; every criticism they make is an unfavourable one. It never occurs to them that the ugliness of the message which they bear is reflected in their own countenances: otherwise they would surely hold their peace.

So Charlie and Fabia drifted further and further apart; and Fabia clung more and more to the support and sympathy of Ram Chandar Mukharji.

"This new agent that I've got is a fool—an utter fool!" exclaimed Charlie, as his wife and he were sitting at luncheon one day, Mrs. Gaythorne being busily engaged in London in carrying on bloodless revolutions for the benefit of the whole human race.

"Then why did you engage him? I thought an agent's duty was to supply the deficiencies of his employer—not to emulate them."

"Of course, darling, I didn't know he was a fool when I engaged him: otherwise I should have been a fool myself for doing so."

"Precisely: still you might have done it nevertheless. I have known you and wisdom part company before now."

"I often wonder what fools were made for," the irate Squire grumbled on.

"So do I: but I should have imagined that you would have found that out before now."

Charlie was hurt, but he tried not to show it; and Fabia despised him all the more for being so thick-skinned, so she imagined, as not to feel the cut of her lash. In the interests of peace he changed the subject: another mistake on his part, as then Fabia despised him for being frightened and running away.

"I wonder if poor old Carr will ever turn up again," he said.

"A good many people are wondering that: you are not by any means solitary in your speculations."

"It is desperately rough on Janet! She looks wretchedly ill, poor little thing!"

"You would hardly expect her to laugh and grow fat upon such a catastrophe, would you?"

It was certainly uphill work talking to Fabia; but Charlie bravely went on his patient, dogged way, trying his hardest to make himself pleasant, which was the very last thing he should have endeavoured to do.

"Of course not, old girl; by Jove, no! I should think it would knock any woman to pieces for her husband to chuck it all up, and cut and run on his honeymoon."

"Not necessarily: it would depend upon the husband," answered Fabia, in a tone which implied that if only Captain Gaythorne had seen fit to cut and run on his honeymoon, it would have been the most advantageous arrangement possible for all parties concerned.

"But I really think the poor little thing was awfully gone on Carr, don't you know?" persisted Charlie, still intent upon his cowardly desire for peace at any price.

"Naturally. Those plain, dowdy little women are

always off their heads with gratitude to any man who will marry them: and it is extremely bad for the man."

"Well, no one would say you were the sort of woman to be grateful to any lucky beggar who was so fortunate as to marry you," said Charlie, with a brave attempt to be jocular.

"I am not."

The reply was sufficient to crush a bolder man than Charles. Again he changed the subject.

"I say, Fabia, don't you think we ought to do something for that poor little woman, to make things a bit easier for her? Especially now the mater is so busy, and can't see after her."

Charlie had inherited much of his mother's kindness of heart.

Fabia looked up languidly.

"What sort of a thing? Find her another husband, do you mean?" she asked.

"Oh, Fabia!" Charlie was really shocked. "By Jove, no! She isn't that sort. You talk as if husbands were like footmen; so that if one doesn't suit the situation, you can dismiss him and get another."

"That is how I regard them."

Charlie was positively helpless.

"But what about marriage-vows, and 'till death us do part,' and things of that kind?" he argued.

"I do not believe in them."

"I say, old girl, you should just have heard my father's views about marriage, and all that sort of thing! He'd got most tremendous notions about the sanctity of it, and everything in that line, don't you know?"

"I cannot help that. I never married your father."

Charlie looked puzzled.

"Of course not; you couldn't have done, as he was married long before either you were born."

"Which was his misfortune," added Fabia.

"I say, darling, I wish you wouldn't say flippant things. I don't like it."

"Not like me to commiserate your father's ill-luck? How very peculiar of you! Men generally like their family misfortunes to be deplored."

Fabia's smile was distinctly impertinent; but all the same, she felt a faint glimmering of respect for a husband who had the courage to admit that there was anything about his wife that he did not like.

But the ill-starred Charlie rapidly extinguished that faint glimmer.

"Not in that way, my pet: I'm sure the mater wouldn't approve of it; so don't do it, there's a good girl!"

Fabia shrugged her shoulders. How could she respect a husband who was always bolstering up his marital authority by quotations from his female parent?

"My point is," continued the well-meaning blunderer, "that my father was a married man himself, don't you know?"

"Well?" There was a volume of scorn in the monosyllable.

"Fabia, don't be stupid, there's a good child! What I mean is, that being a married man himself, he knew what he was talking about."

"And the fact that he was married—and married as he was—makes his opinion upon the indissolubility of marriage all the more valuable—and remarkable. There I agree with you."

Although, in her way, Fabia had a sincere respect

for her mother-in-law, she could imagine that an eternity spent in that lady's society would not appear short.

"He had most awfully fine notions about marriage, about its being 'for better for worse' and 'for richer for poorer,' and all that, don't you know?" continued Charlie.

"He didn't know much about 'for poorer,' did he?"

"Of course not. How could he? He and my mother both had very tidy fortunes, as well as the Gaythorne estates?" In vain poor Charlie endeavoured to follow the intricate workings of his wife's mind.

"Then his opinions did not count for much after all. It is when you come to 'for worse' and 'for poorer' that the shoe begins to pinch. Many married people can stand the strain of 'for better' and 'for richer'—though that is no slight one at times, I admit."

"Oh! Fabia, I don't know about that. Look at love in a cottage and all that kind of thing. Heaps of people are most awfully keen on it."

"I never was in love and I never was in a cottage; so I cannot form an opinion upon the advantages and disadvantages of either."

Charlie's face went very red, but he was too much wounded to lose his temper. "I wish you *were* in love, Fabia," he said pleadingly.

His wife laughed lightly.

"It might be rather unpleasant for you if I were! But it is really very unselfish of you to put my pleasure before yours in this way," she said.

"I mean in love with me."

Fabia laughed again. "What an idea! It is quite gone out of fashion for a woman to be in love with her own husband. Of course, a person like Janet Carr is; it is just part and parcel of her general dowdiness. I thought you hated dowdy women."

"So I do; I detest the sight of them."

"Then there is nothing dowdier than to be in love with one's own husband. It is on a par with a shawl and ringlets, and a white camellia fastened by the brooch."

Charlie looked—as he felt—very miserable. He knew that his own views were right and his wife's wrong: and he also knew that he was not clever enough to demonstrate either of these propositions. So he took refuge in an illustration: the safest resource for all those not gifted in argument.

"Isabel Seaton is not dowdy, and she is in love with her own husband," he said.

"That is so: but Isabel is an exception—to that as to every rule."

Since her marriage, Fabia had learnt to appreciate Mrs. Seaton as she had never appreciated her before. A friendship between a married woman and a single one is rarely successful, unless it dates from pre-matrimonial days. The husband and the confidential friend are not often compatible ingredients.

"Yet she always fancies herself as being so commonplace and normal and natural, and all that sort of thing, don't you know?" Charlie persisted.

"Of course she does: that is where she shows herself so exceptional. It is the commonplace people who think that no one ever felt as they feel, or suffered as they suffer, or loved as they love. I used to be like that myself at one time, till I learnt from Isabel how very commonplace it was."

"When did you think that no one ever loved as you did?" asked Charlie eagerly.

Men are very like children in one respect: they always get hold of the least important part of a toy or a conversation, and fix all their attention upon that, to the exclusion of the really characteristic and interesting portion of the business in hand.

Fabia told her husband the truth. She saw no reason for not doing so on the present occasion.

"I never actually thought that nobody ever loved as i did: but I used to think that nobody ever could love as I could, till Isabel and experience taught me what a fool I was."

"Isabel would be pretty mad if she heard you say that she was an exception."

Fabia smiled.

"Would she? She is very fond of calling herself normal and commonplace; but I doubt if she would be equally pleased if her friends endorsed her statements," she replied.

"Well, anyhow, you can't deny that she is jolly smart, taking her all round, and that she is in love with her own husband," repeated Charlie, sticking to his point.

"I cannot: and yet I wonder at it. Mr. Seaton always appears to me an extremely dull person."

"He is the sort of chap that wouldn't care a rap how he appeared to you or to anybody, as long as his own wife liked him," said Charlie, speaking truth.

"I know: that is one reason why I dislike him. Men who are very much in love with their wives always bore me to extinction."

"Well, I am very much in love with mine, heaven knows!"

"And—unlike Isabel—you are not an exception to the rule."

The arrow went home. Charlie got up from his chair and walked towards the door.

"I say, Fabia, you are a bit too hard upon a poor devil who worships the very ground you walk on. Heaven knows I do all in my power to please you and make you happy: and yet the more he does for you the more you seem to despise and hate a fellow! What else can I do to make you care for me and treat me as a wife should?"

And poor Charlie went out of the room, banging the door after him in his futile misery: while his wife decided within herself that unless some new interest or occupation were brought into her life—and at once—she should die of ennui. So she made haste to write to her cousin, Ram Chandar.

CHAPTER XVIII

DR. MUKHARJI

EARLY in the spring a considerable sensation was created in the fashionable world by an Oriental occultist who set up a sort of séance in a small flat in Mount Street—a Dr. Mukharji. He told fortunes, consulted crystals, cured nervous disorders, and generally comported himself after the manner of his kind. With that passion for anything absolutely new —and especially for anything new concerning the eternal verities—which characterizes the denizens of London to-day as it characterized the denizens of Athens long ago, it became the mode to run after Dr. Mukharji, and to accept with faith and humility his additions to accepted dogma and his emendations of revealed truth. In short, Dr. Mukharji became so much the fashion that he would have found no difficulty, had he been that way inclined, in starting a brand-new religion and securing countless converts to the same; but it happened that he was not that way inclined, so he contented himself with teaching a sort of neo-Buddhism and Pseudo-Theosophy, and embellishing it with certain embroideries from the occult.

Of course it was women who ran after him, not men. Men—let it be admitted to their credit—are more diffident in exchanging old lamps for new than women

are; they hesitate before giving up the Word which
has been a lantern unto their feet, in favour of some
new fad in electric lighting. Therefore women crowded
to the little flat in Mount Street, and confided their
respective pasts to Dr. Mukharji; on condition that
he would in return confide to them their respective
futures.

Many silly women were led captive by the strange
devices of the occultist; but none attended his rooms
in Mount Street with such frequency and regularity as
Fabia; so much so that ere long scandal began to busy
itself with the names of Dr. Mukharji and Mrs. Charles
Gaythorne, and to hint very unpleasant things concerning that lady's repeated visits to the Oriental
fortune-teller.

Then at last Isabel Seaton broke through her rule
and interfered.

"I've got something rather horrid to say to you,
Fabia," she began: "I hate saying it, and you'll hate
hearing it, but it has got to be said, so here goes."

"Then why say it at all?" Fabia interrupted her.
"If neither you nor I will derive any pleasure from
the communication, why impart it?"

"Because my conscience insists upon it: and my
conscience so rarely mentions anything or makes itself
in any way troublesome, that I hardly like to refuse it
on the rare occasions when it does."

"Yours certainly is not an importunate conscience,"
Fabia admitted, with her languid smile.

"No, it isn't. Its worst enemy couldn't call it a
chatty sort of conscience, for it hardly ever speaks.
From week's end to week's end I don't hear its voice.
Therefore when it does begin to whisper I feel bound
to listen to it, as I certainly shouldn't do if it were one

of those tiresome, garrulous consciences which never give their owners a moment's peace. You should just hear Paul's! The thing can't hold its tongue for five minutes together, but is always poking its nose into matters that don't concern it."

"I could imagine that Mr. Seaton's conscience is the sort that might give trouble to its owner."

Paul's wife sighed deeply. "I believe you, and not to its owner only! It is a typical specimen of the Nonconformist conscience in full working order, with all the latest improvements laid on. The moment he gives it its head, it begins grumbling and spluttering like an infuriated motor-car, till his life and mine become burdens to us. And the more we suffer, the more that terrible conscience sets all its hideous machinery in motion. Unfortunately Paul is such an unselfish husband that he shares everything with me, even down to his conscientious scruples : and they, alas! are so numerous and so active!" And Isabel sighed again.

"Poor Isabel!'

But there was envy rather than pity in Fabia's tone. She could not help feeling the contrast between Isabel's half-laughing and wholly devoted attitude towards her husband, and the dreary dulness of her own relations with Charlie. She despised him far too much to laugh at him.

"When first I was married," Isabel continued, "I used to picture myself as a bold young Perseus about to deliver my Andromeda of a husband from his monster of a conscience : but as the enlightening time of early married life went on, I realized that Paul was rather like those Indian people who allow white bulls and white elephants to trample them to death because they worship the animals. So now I hang garlands round the neck of the creature on its gala days, and lie down alongside of my husband while it plays the giddy Juggernaut over our prostrate bodies. Believe me, my dear, a husband with a conscience is no joke!"

"Yet I can imagine that a husband without a conscience would be still less of one."

"Far less: that's the difficulty! But we have wandered to my beloved husband's conscience, while the conversation began about mine."

"I think you said that yours was not of the white bull and white elephant species?"

Fabia endeavoured once more to stave off what she guessed was coming, although she knew that this procrastination would have no effect in the long run. Isabel might not be as direct in her methods as was old Mrs. Gaythorne; but she invariably arrived finally at the point from which she had started.

"Not it: it is more like the War Office, or the Local Government Board: never interferes until it is too late to mend anything, and never locks a stable-door until all the horses have died of typhoid."

"A convenient sort of conscience to keep!"

"Very: and very little expense. But just now it is so noisy in clamouring for a new lock on the empty stable-door that I've no option but to listen to it. Fabia, you are going too often to see that horrid cousin of yours, Ram Chandar Mukharji. People are talking about it—and about you!"

Fabia smiled scornfully. "Let them talk!"

"But, my dear, that's just what I don't want to let them do: talking is a most hurtful and dangerous practice."

"I do not care what they say about me and Ram Chandar."

"But you ought to care, my dear Fabia: you really ought! Already their talking is beginning to do you harm: and as for Charlie, he will go mad when he hears of it—as he is bound to do sooner or later. Even the people whom it most concerns, hear of a thing eventually—though of course not till long after everybody else."

"I do not care," Fabia repeated.

"You ought never to have let that tiresome cousin of yours come over from India at all! I met him when I was out there years ago, and thought him a most weird and uncanny person. I'm sure Charlie wouldn't approve of him, as men always hate what is weird and uncanny and different from what they learned at their mothers' knees. Paul disapproves most frightfully of anything to do with occultism and spiritualism, and things of that kind, so I never let him know how intensely they interest me."

"I do not care whether Charlie approves of my visits to Mount Street or not. It is no business of his."

Stern disapproval looked out of Mrs. Seaton's blue eyes.

"Oh, Fabia, how horrid of you to speak of your husband like that! Why, if Paul disapproves of anybody, it always turns me against them, even if I've adored them up till then: and if he disapproves of my doing things, I never really enjoy doing them, even though I have revelled in it before. In fact I often refrain from asking him his opinion of things and people, for fear he should spoil my pleasure in them for the future."

Again the scornful smile curled Fabia's lip:

"If you really loved him as much as you think you do, you would obey him in the spirit as well as in the letter."

"Now, Fabia, don't begin teaching your grandmother how to love her husband, because I know a precious sight more about that than you do! I may not know much: but I do know how a woman feels who is absolutely devoted to her husband, and I know that she doesn't feel by any means a fool. If you've lost your heart, it doesn't follow that you've lost your brain as well."

"Still if you lose your heart, it frequently follows that you will also lose your head," persisted Fabia.

"My head isn't of the losing sort, thank you! I rarely mislay it, but generally carry it about with me under my arm, à la St. Winifred, so that I can lay my hands on it whenever I think fit."

"Well, Isabel, you must admit that *your* husband's opinions would carry more weight with anybody than *my* husband's would: therefore you cannot wonder at my thinking less of Charlie's disapproval than you do of Mr. Seaton's."

Isabel's eye twinkled in a manner which in a less mature and distinguished matron would have been called a wink.

"But I am affected by Paul's opinions even when I am aware that he doesn't know what he is talking about, and that they aren't worth the breath in which they are uttered. That is where the rich joke of being married comes in!"

"And yet you say you are not a fool?"

"Certainly: because I know that I am: and to be wise enough to know that you are a fool, is proof positive that you are not one."

Suddenly Fabia's conversation took a desperate turn.

"Oh, Isabel, you have no idea how awfully dull it is

to be married to a man like Charlie! I've borne it as long as I can, and I don't feel as if I could bear it any longer! It is all very well for you, who are married to a clever man, to preach about the due subjection of a wife: but you would sing a different tune if you were married to a well-meaning goose."

Isabel shook her head. "I don't think so. I should never find out that he was a goose if I were in love with him. For all I know, Paul may be one of the dullest men on the face of the earth; in fact I know certain people consider him so; but to me he is the one supremely interesting fact in the universe—the one sufficient and satisfactory entertainment of creation. It is far more interesting to me to hear Paul say that there is a button off his shirt, than to hear the greatest men of the day hold forth upon the most burning questions. But that isn't cleverness, bless you!—it's love."

"But am not in love with Charlie, you see. I never pretended to be. That is where the tragedy of my life comes in. If only I loved him, then everything would be different!"

It was on the tip of Isabel's tongue to say, "Then you ought not to have married him;" but once more her usually somnolent conscience showed signs of vigour. Had she not done all in her power to bring about a marriage between Fabia and Charlie Gaythorne; and was not a portion of the responsibility of their unhappy union hers?

Fabia went on somewhat pathetically:

"You cannot imagine how horribly dull it is to be married to a man with whom you are not in love; you get so deadly tired of his anecdotes. I believe that if a woman isn't in love with her husband, she could bear anything—even his neglect or his downright cruelty—better than his anecdotes."

"You didn't object to Charlie's anecdotes so much before you married him; and I'm sure you heard them all then, so you knew exactly what they were about. You married with your ears open."

"I know I did; but things sound so different before and after marriage. A man may be an admirable pastime but an extremely poor profession. He may excel as a recreation but become wearisome as a duty. He may prove delightful as an *hors d'œuvre*, but deadly as a *pièce de résistance*."

"Fabia, you really ought not to discuss your husband with another woman in this fashion," said Isabel reprovingly; then—having satisfied her awakening conscience—she added: "What anecdote of Charlie's is it that bores you most?"

"There are several of them that almost kill me with exhaustion. No harm in them, you know, but as long and pointless as a darning-needle. And nearly always about his parents; so dutiful and yet so dull! I think, however, the story that wearies me most is about Mrs. Gaythorne and a harvest-thanksgiving. It lasts for ages, and always requires a book-marker."

"I know it," replied Isabel sympathetically.

"You must, if you know Charlie! Well, I am now twenty-three years old and Charlie twenty-six, so we shall in all probability have about another half century of each other's society; and just think how often during that time I shall hear the story of Mrs. Gaythorne and the harvest-thanksgiving! It is appalling to contemplate!"

"It is like thinking of eternity or climbing up a winding staircase—no end and no beginning!"

"I suppose, however," Fabia continued, "that in the most favourable circumstances marriage, like politics, is the science of the second-best, and it is absurd to expect the ideal in it."

"Not a bit of it," retorted Isabel, with some heat; "it is either the height of bliss or else the depth of boredom. It is the very opposite of the second-best, as it must be the very best or the very worst. A husband is either the one man in the world, or else the one man that you wish wasn't in the world; there is no 'happy mean' in matrimony."

"Well, Isabel, I should have been abundantly satisfied with the second-best, if only I could have secured it." And there was a wistful sound in the sweet voice.

"Second-best indeed!" retorted Mrs. Seaton, tossing her head. "And yet I must admit," she added, with a humorous twinkle, "that a good many men like their second best."

Fabia agreed with her. "That is so; I fancy that my late respected papa-in-law would have been among that number if only he had had the chance."

"Paul won't," remarked Paul's first, with much decision in her tone.

"You would hate to think that he could ever have a second, wouldn't you?"

"Not I," replied Isabel airily. "I'm not that selfish, dog-in-the-manger sort of a woman! I've told Paul over and over again that if anything happens to me he is at liberty to marry again as soon as he likes. Of course he'll find any other woman awfully dull after me, but I can't help that: he must take the rough with the smooth, and the dull with the lively, as other much married men have had to do, from Henry the Eighth

downwards. It is unreasonable of any man to expect
to get all his wives cast in the same mould!"

And thus—having shot her arrow and given her hint
—Isabel wandered off into indifferent subjects. She
had learnt the great social art of punctuation—she
knew when to stop; and was far too clever a woman
to indulge in the unpardonable practice known as
"rubbing it in."

But in spite of Mrs. Seaton's well-timed word of
warning, Fabia continued to visit the small flat in
Mount Street far oftener than was wise or desirable.
She was constantly seen going in and out, and people
talked more than ever in consequence. In time this
gossip reached the ears of Captain Gaythorne; but he
made no sign. He was the sort of man who would find
it impossible to speak to his wife upon such a subject as
this: his innate chivalry revolted at the mere idea.
But although he was slow to speak and slow to
wrath in his dealings with women, he was neither
the one nor the other in his dealings with his
own sex; and he made up his mind that if things
continued to go on like this, it would not be long
before Dr. Mukharji had a very bad quarter of an hour
indeed.

Charlie Gaythorne might be afraid to scold his wife;
but he was not at all afraid to give his wife's cousin a
sound horse-whipping; and he intended to do so at the
earliest opportunity.

Isabel, finding that her hint to Fabia had been of no
avail, decided, with characteristic courage, to tackle the
occultist himself upon the subject. She was still firmly
set against speaking to Charlie. Although she knew
too much about men to suppose for an instant that they
are as blind as they frequently, in their mysterious

wisdom, pretend to be, she nevertheless recognized the
bare possibility of Captain Gaythorne's being as ignorant
of Fabia's goings-on as he appeared; and in that case
she felt she would rather die than be the instrument
employed to open his mercifully-closed eyelids. Therefore—having taken the wise and wifely precaution of
not mentioning to her husband beforehand what she
intended to do, lest he should see fit to forbid the same
—Mrs. Paul Seaton joined herself to the multitude of
silly women who were being led astray by the false
doctrines of Dr. Mukharji, and presented herself at the
door of the flat in Mount Street.

She was shown into a waiting-room tastily though
scantily furnished, and already half full of fashionably-
dressed women. To her profound relief there were
none of them who were known to her personally,
though she knew one or two quite well by sight; and
as she had added to her toilet a thick motor-veil,
she cherished vain hopes that no one would recognise
her.

"It's a good thing that I put on a motor-veil like
the ostrich, and so am invisible," she said to herself;
"though I'm convinced that some of these horrid old
cats will know who I am all the same, and talk about it
till it gets round to Paul. But that won't matter, as I
shall tell him myself at the proper time, when it is too
late for him to prevent my coming. Fortunately it is
often too late to forbid and never too late to forgive;
and that is the psychological moment for making
confessions to a husband!"

Mrs. Seaton had plenty of time for meditation as she
watched her predecessors being summoned one by one
by Dr. Mukharji's messenger: but at last her turn come;
and she then was ushered, by a closely-veiled female

attendant in gorgeous native dress, into the presence of the popular charlatan.

Isabel thought him looking much older than when last she saw him, in those far-off, pre-nuptial days when she was living with the Farleys: but that was hardly to be wondered at; as she herself had then been in the early dawn of the twenties, and now she was fast coming within sight of her fortieth milestone. There was no doubt that she did not look as young now as she had looked then; but she took the flattering unction to her soul, which we all take when we meet friends and acquaintances whom we have not seen for several years; namely, that though we may have aged a little, they have aged much more. And there was more ground for Isabel's assumption than there frequently is in such circumstances: Ram Chandar had certainly altered more than she in the long years since they had met. In the first place he was no longer clean-shaven, but a long black beard protected his chest from the inclemencies of the English climate; and a beard always ages a man. But his dark eyes retained their youthful brilliancy; and his hands, as small and delicate as a woman's, testified as of yore to the highly-strung, nervous temperament concealed under his manner of apparently immutable calm. He had not adopted the good old English custom of measuring the flight of time by the weights of avoirdupois: on the contrary, he looked if possible slimmer and slighter than he used to do, and had lost none of his Eastern, panther-like grace.

"So you also are among my disciples, Mrs. Seaton, as I also am among the prophets?" he said, as he advanced to meet his visitor, whom he recognised at once in spite of her attempted disguise.

He was amused at her coming to consult him, and he showed it; he was fully aware of Paul Seaton's uncompromising hostility towards everything connected with occultism; and anything in the form of wifely insubordination tickled his sense of humour.

Finding her incognito thus ruthlessly thrust aside, the ostrich threw back her inadequate disguise somewhat haughtily.

"I have hardly come to ask advice, Dr. Mukharji, but rather to administer it."

"Pray be seated," he said, in his soft, Oriental voice, placing a chair for Mrs. Seaton.

"I shall not detain you long," Isabel began; and her manner was that of the *grande dame*, which she could assume when she thought it necessary and worth the trouble. "But I have just one thing to say to you."

"Regarding your future?"

"No; regarding yours."

The occultist bowed politely.

"I await your instructions, Mrs. Seaton. It is an agreeable change for me to take the rôle of learner instead of that of teacher." How like his voice was to Fabia's!

"I have come to speak to you, Dr. Mukharji, about my friend and your cousin, Mrs. Charles Gaythorne."

Again Mukharji bowed. "An ever-interesting subject to me."

"You are doubtless unaware," continued Isabel, more stately than ever, "that unpleasant remarks are being made about your cousin's too frequent visits to your house. I gave her a hint upon the subject, but with no avail: she is still so young that she hardly realizes how dangerous it is to bring down scandal even upon the most undeserving head. But you and I are older than she, Dr. Mukharji, and we understand how much harm can be done to a woman by ill-natured gossip, however unfounded it may be; and I therefore come to you to ask you to make some excuse for lessening Fabia's visits to you, both as regards length and number."

A mocking smile lit up the dark eyes that were fixed upon Isabel.

"I see: you make an appeal to me to give up the one pleasure of my life at your bidding; the one thing that has brought me all the way from India here? Certainly you have great confidence in your powers of persuasion, Mrs. Seaton! I congratulate you upon so valuable a possession as unlimited confidence in yourself."

Isabel threw back her head haughtily.

"You mistake me, Dr. Mukharji: I use no persuasion and I make no appeal. I merely point out to you what is required of you as a gentleman, and I take it for granted that you cannot disappoint me."

The mocking eyes still smiled. "And you do not call that an appeal, Mrs. Seaton?"

"Certainly not: it would be an insult to you to do so. One can hardly appeal to a gentleman to act as a gentleman, since it would be impossible for him to do otherwise."

The charlatan was far too clever not to recognise and admire cleverness when he saw it; and just now his admiration for his visitor was marked. The girl whom Ram Chander had once condemned as shallow and noisy, had developed into an extremely accomplished woman of the world.

"Then may I ask precisely what you did come to say to me, Mrs. Seaton?"

"Merely to inform you that malicious gossip is

beginning to couple your name with that of your cousin."

"And did you suppose I did not know that already?"

"Your conduct in allowing her to continue her visits, proved conclusively that you did not."

"So you took the trouble to come here in the midst of your busy life to enlighten an ignorance which had no existence save in your own mind?"

"Your supposed ignorance did not originate in my mind, but in your manner, Dr. Mukharji. I had no alternative but to believe that you were unconscious that Fabia's visits here were doing her harm, as otherwise you would have declined to receive her."

"You flatter me, Mrs. Seaton."

"If you consider it flattery to take you for a gentleman, I do," replied the undaunted Isabel, rising from her seat. "And now, having said what I came to say, there is nothing left to say but good morning."

But the fortune-teller was not going to let her escape so easily.

"Stop a minute, Mrs. Seaton; not so fast. Now that we have disposed of my cousin Fabia's affairs, would it not interest you to hear something about your own?"

"Not at all, thank you," conscientiously lied Isabel.

If there was one thing she would have loved more than another it was to have her future foretold by the Eastern seer; but she knew that her husband profoundly disapproved of all such dabblings in the unseen; so she forebore.

"You would not care to know what office Mr. Seaton will hold in the next Cabinet, or whether he will hold any office at all? You are indeed curiously lacking in curiosity!"

Isabel was sorely tempted, yet she still withstood.

"I will not trespass on your time so far, Dr. Mukharji."

"Because your husband has forbidden it, I see. You are indeed a wifely wife, Mrs. Seaton!"

Isabel did not deign to make any reply to this; but she could not fail to feel there was something rather uncanny in the occultist's knowledge of her inmost thoughts and reasons.

"But do you not think it a pity," continued the fortune-teller, "to allow your husband's narrow views and unfounded prejudices to limit your own mind and intelligence? Do you not think that in a matter such as this—wherein, if you will permit me to say so, you are far more competent to judge than he is—it would be better both for you and for him that you should disobey Mr. Seaton's somewhat unreasonable and arbitary dictum?"

"I neither disobey nor discuss my husband, Dr. Mukharji: so I can only bid you good morning." And Isabel swept out of the room with the air of an offended queen.

As soon as she had gone the occultist laughed aloud. "To think of a brilliant woman like that subjecting herself and submitting her judgment to a narrow-minded fool such as Paul Seaton! A woman in love is a wonderful and remarkable creature!"

Isabel at once confessed to her husband where she had been—and why—and why she had not told him of her visit beforehand. She was always candour itself, unless there was any very special reason to the contrary —as in this case there undoubtedly was, for Paul would have vetoed her visit to the charlatan at once had he heard it mooted. It was not that she was afraid of her husband, but that she was afraid of herself: not that she

felt Paul's fiats must not be disobeyed, but that she knew
she was incapable of disobeying them. It was she,
not Paul, who would be really vexed if her obedience
to her husband did not come up to her own somewhat
elastic standard. So she adapted herself to what she
considered her own weakness, by preventing the
commandment from being made until it was already
broken.

Paul, for his part, was immensely amused at the
opportunism of his wife, though he did not always
consider it politic to let that lady know how much
amused he was. Matrimony—like experience—is a
certificated teacher.

But Isabel had reckoned without her host when she
treated Dr. Mukharji as an English gentleman. He
was not an English gentleman, and he did not behave
as such: in spite of Isabel's appeal to him, Fabia's
visits to Mount Street continued with undiminished
frequency.

Then at last Isabel saw no option but to have
recourse to her *dernier ressort* and to speak to Charlie.
Gossip was making free with the names of Fabia and
her cousin: and the snowball of scandal increased in
size with every rotation, as is the way of snowballs and
scandals. It had proved useless, and worse than useless, to tackle the principal performers themselves: so
there was nothing left but to appeal to Charlie to save
Fabia from herself.

But Isabel knew better than to deal with him as
she had dealt with the others. Charlie might not be a
genius, but he was a gentleman—quite as good a thing
in its way, and better for the persons with whom he
had to do. There is a wonderful freemasonry among
really well-bred people: they know the rules of the

MICROCOPY RESOLUTION TEST CHART[1]

(ANSI and ISO TEST CHART No. 2)

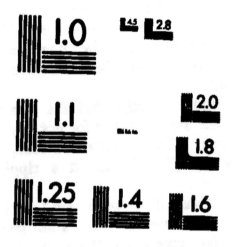

APPLIED IMAGE Inc

1653 East Main Street
Rochester, New York   14609   USA
(716) 482 - 0300 - Phone
(716) 288 - 5989 - Fax

game: and are as slow to give or take offence as they are quick to give or take a hint. The art of taking a hint is a fine art: the art of taking offence a debased one. Therefore all that Isabel did was to remark airily one day in the middle of a conversation with Captain Gaythorne·

"By the way, Charlie, don't you think that Fabia is looking rather pale and overdone? Why don't you take her for a run over to Paris at Whitsuntide? The London season is a trying time for unseasoned Londoners; and Fabia is new to the inhalation of wood-pavements as yet."

Charlie knew in a minute exactly what she meant: and was grateful to her for saying it and for not saying it. But all he replied was: "That's not a bad idea, by Jove! not a bad idea at all! I call it a ripping good one."

"I should adopt it, then, if I were you," Isabel continued. "I'm sure it would do Fabia good. And you wouldn't miss much, as there is never anything going on in town at Whitsuntide. I think this is a trying sort of season, the hot weather began so soon and so suddenly: March came in like an Arctic sea-lion, and went out like a hot roast lamb. A cold in the head tied me by the leg, so to speak, at Easter, and we couldn't get away then at all; so I've persuaded Paul to take me for a good long holiday at Whitsuntide, and I should advise you and Fabia to do the same."

"But I thought
to keep their noses
retorted Charlie, as
will Seaton be able

"Well, you see,
during the Whitsuntide

required: and after that I shall make him find some Conservative nose which—like 'Charlie's aunt'—is 'still running,' and pair with it for another week or so."

"I'll bet you five to one that the Whips won't let him off with the present Government in such a hole."

"Oh! they will. I know them."

"They won't; especially now that the present Ministry is in such a bad way that it may smash up at any moment."

Isabel shook her head with her wisest air as she replied:

"Not it: it is feeble and effete, I admit, but it is a chronic case—not a dangerous one. Nurses always neglect chronic cases because they are so boring and tiresome; and Members of Parliament do the same."

Thus Isabel conveyed to Charlie that it was his duty to take his wife out of danger as soon as he could, the only possible refuge being in flight: and Captain Gaythorne thanked her for her solution of the difficulty, and decided to adopt it: and yet neither of them had mentioned either the nature of the difficulty or the detested name of Ram Chandar Mukharji.

CHAPTER XIX

WHAT HAPPENED IN PARIS

THE Gaythornes were abroad for the best part of a month, and did not come back until the leafy month of June was decidedly *passé*. Charlie would have liked to stay away still longer, but Fabia was so tired of the *solitude à deux* that she insisted on bringing their stay in Paris to a close, as they had seen but few people whom she knew and none who amused her.

It was a noteworthy fact, and one which set the tongues of gossip wagging faster than ever, that Dr. Mukharji left town when the Gaythornes did, and did not come back to his flat until after their return; thus proving conclusively to all the scandal - mongers interested in the matter, that his object in coming to London was not to tell the fortunes of ladies in general, but to have the spending of Fabia's in particular—not to divulge the futures of his numerous *clientèle*, but to destroy that of Mrs. Charles Gaythorne.

On the evening of their return, Charlie and his wife were dining in their own house in town, old Mrs. Gaythorne having foregone a meeting in order to have dinner with her son and daughter-in-law, and welcome them back to their native shores. When dessert was on the table, and the servants had left the room, Fabia suddenly interrupted the stream of unmemorable conversation by saying:

"Whom do you think we saw in Paris, Mrs. Gaythorne?"

"Somebody who had better have stayed at home I have no doubt."

Mrs. Gaythorne highly disapproved of foreign travel.

"We saw Gabriel Carr," said Fabia quietly.

The bomb-shell took full effect. The elder lady fairly bounced in her chair.

"I cannot believe it!" she exclaimed. "Surely you are trifling with me."

"No, I am not; I only wish, for Janet's sake, that I were."

"Charles, is this true?" asked Mrs. Gaythorne, turning for confirmation to that son whom she had never known from his childhood to tell a lie.

"Yes, mother; as true as gospel. As Fabia says, I wish to goodness that it w n't, for poor little Janet's sake; but it is, worse luck!"

"Describe the circumstances," was Mrs. Gaythorne's next command.

"Tell the mater all about it," said Charlie to his wife; "you're a much better hand at reeling off a yarn than I am."

Fabia, thus adjured, began:

"When we were in Paris we often went to the theatre, as we found it so very dull in our own sitting-room at the hotel."

"Which you ought not to have done," her mother-in-law interrupted her. "Mr. Gaythorne and I never found it dull wherever we were. I had my Committees as perennial sources of interest, and he had Me."

Mrs. Gaythorne, when referring to herself, always emphasised the personal pronoun as if the other cases, as well as the nominative, began with a capital letter.

" Of course ; but Charlie and I are different," replied Fabia sweetly : as indeed they were. " Mr. Gaythorne wisely allowed his wife to enjoy herself in her own way ; but unfortunately his son does not follow his example."

" We will leave Mr. Gaythorne for the present and return to Gabriel Carr. Where did you see him, and what did he say, and what excuse did he give for his extraordinary behaviour ? "

Mrs. Gaythorne practised to full perfection the art of keeping to the point.

" Well," continued Fabia, " one night when we were in a theatre, whom should we see in a box opposite to us but Gabriel Carr ? "

" At a theatre—and a French theatre too—and he a clergyman ! I cannot believe it ! You must have been mistaken."

" But unfortunately we were not," said Charlie. " I saw him as plain as I see you now. But he was aged a bit, as the sort of life he is leading leaves its mark on a man, don't you know ? "

" I know nothing of the kind, Charles ! Proceed with your narrative, Fabia."

" As Charlie says, he was aged, and he had a worn and dissipated look ; but we both recognized him in an instant. And although he looked older, he was just as handsome as ever," Fabia continued.

" Handsome is as handsome does ; and therefore I cannot call any man handsome who deserts his wife on her honeymoon, and then hides himself in the city of Babylon," remarked Mrs. Gaythorne, not without some reason on her side.

" He didn't behave handsomely, I admit ; but he is a jolly good-looking fellow, all the same, and always will

be," said Charlie, echoing both his wife and his mother
as usual. "But never mind his looks. Fire away with
the story, there's a good girl!"

"The moment we saw and recognized him, I told
Charlie to go round at once and speak to him, and find
out what had happened."

"Which I did in pretty quick time," supplemented
Captain Gaythorne; "as I was afraid he would cut and
run as soon as he caught sight of us, and I wanted to
collar him before he'd got the chance."

"Was he alone?" inquired Mrs. Gaythorne.

Charlie looked confused:

"Well—not alone exactly; I mean, I can't precisely
say that he was alone, don't you know?"

"Then who was accompanying him?"

Still Charlie stammered, and Fabia looked on in
silent amusement and in mute protest against the
unsuccessful old custom of Bowdlerising for the benefit
of in-laws. She was sick of her husband's attempts to
re-edit her for the perusal of Mrs. Gaythorne; and she
enjoyed his difficult and futile endeavour to perform a
like office on behalf of Gabriel Carr.

"Well, mother, don't you see?—I can't exactly—it
wasn't anybody you'd know, don't you know?—and it
hasn't anything to do with the point of the story."

"Charles, do not prevaricate. It is a pernicious
habit, only one step removed from actual falsehood.
Tell me at once who was with Gabriel Carr."

"It was—I don't exactly know—and I couldn't
exactly say, don't you see?"

"I conclude it was a brother-clergyman who had
been also led away by Ritualism into Papistry, and you
are trying to screen him from me."

"Good heavens, no! It wasn't anybody of that kind,

I' can swear," Charlie hastened to asseverate, while Fabia stifled a laugh.

A new idea replete with horror seized Mrs. Gaythorne. "Was Gabriel dressed as a monk, I should like to know?"

'Great Scott, no, mother! What questions you do ask! He was not even dressed as a parson."

Mrs. Gaythorne looked mollified:

"I am relieved to hear it. I was afraid the poor, misguided young man might have been trapped into a monastery. But that is enough subterfuge: it is no use trying to screen him from me. If it was not a Romish priest or a monk, who was it?"

Fabia was enjoying herself immensely, and she would have died sooner than respond to the constant appealing glances which her husband threw to her for help: so she held her peace and let him flounder on.

"Well, you see, mother—I don't like to tell you such things—and it really isn't any business of ours—but it was—it was—well, it was a woman."

"A nun? You don't mean to say he was with a nun?" almost shrieked Mrs. Gaythorne.

"Great Scott, no! Far from it!" Charlie ejaculated, while Fabia, who could not stifle her mirth any longer, laughed outright.

Again Mrs. Gaythorne looked mollified: things after all were not as bad as they might have been.

"Then if it was not a nun—for which I am devoutly thankful—what sort of a woman was it?"

"Well, mother, it was—it was — well, not quite a proper sort of a woman, don't you see?"

Then at last Mrs Gaythorne understood.

"Oh dear, dear, dear!" she exclaimed: "How very, very shocking!"

But it must be admitted that the anguish in her voice was less poignant than when she had asked whether it was a monk or a nun.

"Gabriel did not see us as soon as we saw him," said Fabia, taking up the thread of her narrative again; "so Charlie went round to his box and knocked at the door."

"It was a pity that I was not there, as I should have gone too! Of course you could not go in the circumstances, my dear, considering the sort of person that Gabriel had with him: but a woman of my age can go anywhere and do anything. Proceed with the narrative."

"Charlie must tell now, as this is his part of the story."

Charlie, as was his wont, meekly obeyed.

"Well, when I knocked at the door Carr opened it, and didn't recognize me for a second as I'd got my back to the light. So I said, 'Hallo, Carr! I've found you at last! I think it's time you gave some account of yourself.' I didn't speak as strongly as I felt by a long shot, as I didn't want a row in the theatre. If I'd done as I wanted, I should have knocked the fellow down then and there!"

"Then, Charles, I am thankful that for once you controlled your inclinations. It would have distressed me for my son to be involved in a vulgar brawl—especially in such a wicked place as Paris."

"Well, mother, anyhow I did control myself, and that is what makes what happened next all the more rummy. The moment I had spoken—though I tell you I was as mealy-mouthed as I could induce myself to be when speaking to a cad—Carr turned as white as a sheet, with such a look of sheer fright in his eyes as I've never seen except on the faces of recruits in their first engagement before the poor beggars had got seasoned to being under fire. And then—before you could have said 'Knife'—he dashed past me, and ran for his life down the corridor, and was out of the building before I knew what he was up to. By Jove, I never saw a fellow in such a blue funk in my life before! It was a rummy go altogether!"

Mrs. Gaythorne gasped, and then shook her head reprovingly.

"Charles, you should have stopped him! You should not have allowed him to escape before he had given some explanation of his extraordinary conduct, and sent some sort of a message to Janet."

"I tell you, mother, I couldn't help myself. The brute was out of sight before I knew what he was doing."

"If I had been there, I should have stopped him."

"You couldn't, mother, I swear! Besides, who'd have expected an English gentleman, whatever he'd done, to turn tail and run away like a frightened skunk?"

"There is nothing that I do not expect from misguided persons who are in secret league with the Jesuits."

"Well, anyhow I couldn't stop the beggar, and I didn't."

"It was a great pity that I was not with you! I should have stopped him, and should have insisted upon an explanation then and there."

"I did ask the woman who was with him where I could find him," continued Charlie; "but she refused to tell me anything about him. He'd evidently given her his orders that the word was 'Mum,' as far as he was concerned; but I could see that she knew a precious sight more than she chose to tell."

"If I had been there I should have insisted upon her telling," persisted Mrs. Gaythorne, who for ever afterwards was rooted in the belief that had she been present on that memorable occasion, much further sorrow and suffering would have been avoided. The extreme unlikelihood of her presence in such circumstances—considering that nothing would induce her ever to enter either a theatre or a Roman Catholic country—did not seem to occur to her; and in some feminine and recondite manner she contrived to lay all the blame of her absence upon her son's devoted shoulders.

"The whole affair upset me most tremendously, I can tell you," continued Charlie. 'I always thought Carr such a ripping fine fellow—a really good chap with no humbug about him but as straight as they make 'em—and then to find him turn out like this—well, it seems to shake a fellow's belief in everything."

Tears came into Mrs. Gaythorne's eyes, and began to course slowly down her weather-beaten cheeks.

"That is what makes any sort of wrong-doing on the part of the clergy so very terrible," she said sorrowfully. "It brings their high calling into disrepute, and appears to give the lie to the truths which they have preached. But it ought not to do so. However sadly His servants may fall away from the holiness of their first estate and may do despite to their sacred profession, the Master is still the same, yesterday, to-day, and for ever. With Him there is no variableness, neither shadow of turning Never forget that, my son."

Charlie was touched, and therefore shy and uncomfortable.

"Of course not, mother, of course not. I shouldn't think of doing such a thing. Besides," he added

boyishly, " those of us who have good mothers don't
want any parson to teach us about things. The
parsons may fail us, but our mothers won't : and we
shan't go far wrong if we take our mother's love as
a sort of sample of what God's love is like, and depend
on it just the same, don't you know ? "

Fabia was interested and puzzled. What a strange
and wonderful thing this Christian religion was ! Mrs.
Gaythorne, as a rule, was a Martha rather than a Mary,
and busied herself with the practical side more than the
spiritual side of religion ; but just now there was a look
in her face whic. must compel awe and reverence in
all who beheld it. Fabia had seen the same look in
Gabriel's face in London and at Vernacre, though not
a trace of it in the Parisian theatre. She called it
Illumination and Inspiration, for want of a better
name : had she been brought up in the same school
as Mrs. Gaythorne, she would have called it the
Indwelling of the Spirit.

The three Gaythornes talked over with one another
the problem of Gabriel ; and on the following day went
and talked it all over again with the Seatons. But
they could none of them arrive at any satisfactory
conclusion, or see that anything more could be done.
After the encounter at the theatre, Captain Gaythorne
had explored Paris for further traces of Gabriel, but in
vain : the latter had evidently taken fright at Charlie's
recognition of him, and had once again disappeared.
Searching for him in Paris was like looking for a needle
in a bundle of hay. So, as there was nothing further
to be done, they all agreed to do it.

Then Fabia did about the worst thing that she had
ever done in her life. It might not be as foolish as
were her repeated visits to the flat in Mount Street, but

it was more evil in its essence, since it was intended to do harm, while the visits to Mount Street were only organized *pour passer le temps :* and—like the worst things that are done by the majority of us—it had its origin in jealousy. She went down for the day to Gaythorne, and told the full and complete history of the scene in Paris to Janet Carr.

Fabia was not only jealous because Gabriel had rejected her and chosen Janet, although—in spite of all that had happened—she still hated her on that score. The cause of the hatred might be over, but the hatred itself remained, since hate, like love, has a wonderful power of surviving its instigators. Her own love for Gabriel had died a sudden death on that night in Paris. Just at first, when she saw him in the opposite box, the sight of the man's physical beauty stirred the embers of her love into flames again : she was always particularly sensitive to the influence of beauty ; but when she beheld, across the theatre, the pitiable exhibition of craven fear which the appearance of her husband produced, her love was turned into loathing and contempt. If there was one thing that she adored more than beauty it was strength—strength as shown by physical courage, for Fabia was too elemental a woman to feel the fascination of moral excellencies : and as she had first loved Gabriel when he showed himself her master, so she ceased to love him as soon as she believed him to be in terror of her husband.

But Fabia had still further cause of jealousy of Janet ; for—in spite of all her sorrow and misery—the supreme joy of womanhood was about to crown poor Janet's life. And again Fabia's nature was too elemental for her not to be jealous of every woman to whom had been granted the happiness which she had hitherto been denied—the culminating happiness of motherhood.

We shall all do well to remember that the unclean spirit which seeketh rest and findeth none, and so returneth to the house whence he came, taking with him seven other spirits more wicked than himself, is nearly always the spirit of jealousy. Among all the evil demons, there is none so clever as he in paving the way for his comrades, and in opening the doors for their ingress which, but for him, would have remained closed to them for ever.

So Fabia went down to Gaythorne on purpose to retail the miserable Parisian episode to Gabriel's wife.

Janet heard her to the end, with no sign of emotion save a somewhat heightened colour: then, when the wretched story was finished, she quietly asked:

"And why have you told me this, Mrs. Gaythorne?"

"Because I thought you ought to know it," Fabia replied.

She had indeed managed to persuade herself that it was wrong to keep a person so deeply concerned in the matter as was Janet in the dark with regard to the kind of life which her husband was apparently leading: and that therefore it was the duty of Janet's friends to enlighten her upon the point. So specious are the arguments of the spirit of jealousy!

"Why?" Janet never wasted words.

Fabia was somewhat nonplussed.

"Oh! because you are Mr. Carr's wife, and therefore his conduct affects you more than anybody," she lamely explained.

"That was rather a reason for not telling me," was the quiet reply.

Fabia was silent for a moment. She found the calm

scorn in the hazel eyes decidedly uncomfortable.   Then
she said:

"I should imagine now that you know what manner
of man your husband is, you will leave off hoping or
even wishing for his return."

The hazel eyes flashed at last.   "And you expect me
to believe this tale you have come to tell me?"

"I fail to see how you can help believing it.   My
husband is quite prepared to corroborate my statement
that we both saw Mr. Carr with our own eyes: and
although you may not think much of my accuracy,
everybody knows that Captain Gaythorne is a painfully
truthful person."

"And given that it is true, what difference will it
make?"

"What difference?   I do not know what you mean?"

Fabia gasped with astonishment: it would have made
all the difference in the world to her had she been in
Janet's place.

Then the pent-up storm of Janet's wrath broke:

"I don't believe that what you tell me is true—I
can't believe it.   But even supposing that it were, what
is that to me?   Does it make Gabriel any the less my
husband?   Whatever he is, and whatever he had done,
I am still his wife, and he is my lord and master.
Nothing can alter that.   I belong to him, body and
soul, to do with as he pleases.   Whenever he comes
back he will find me waiting to welcome him home as
if nothing had happened."

Fabia was aghast.   "I am at a loss to understand
you," she murmured.

Janet laughed in her scorn.

"*You* understand *me*—of course you can't!   You who
never loved anybody in the world but yourself, how

can you understand the mysterious unity of marriage?
Gabriel and I are indissolubly one, whatever happens:
nothing can put us asunder: and even if it is true that
he has sinned and suffered, then he will need me even
more than he did when he was one of the saints of God:
and he will find me all the more ready to comfort and
cherish him when he comes to himself. Do you
remember the story of S. Anne, who—after her husband
had been stoned out of the synagogue—received him
with more love and reverence than she had ever shown
him before? And do you think that there are no S.
Annes to-day? Not perhaps of your world or in your
circle, but they exist all the same. Doubtless you will
find plenty of people ready to help you in casting
stones at my husband when he does come back; but
from me, whom he has most wronged if he has wronged
anybody, he shall never hear a word of reproach, but
only words of love and welcome."

And Janet, in the dignity of her outraged love, flung
back her head with such a queenly gesture that Fabia
stood before her cowed, as she had once stood before
Janet's husband. She said good-bye and got herself
out of the room as best she could, feeling for the second
time in her life like a beaten cur. And from that
moment she liked and respected Janet Carr: and felt
that she would give the half of all that she possessed if
only she could love anyone as Janet loved Gabriel.

It is loving—not being loved—that makes a woman
as a king's daughter all glorious within, and clothes
her spirit as with wrought gold.

CHAPTER XX

ISABEL'S TEMPTATION

ONE afternoon, not long after the return of the Seatons from their Whitsuntide holiday, the Prime Minister called upon Isabel at her house in Prince's Gardens. She was glad to see him, with the gladness which the sight of a man who has once loved her almost always produces in a woman's mind. There are few people towards whom women feel so kindly as towards the men whom they might have married, but did not : just as there are none whom they regard with such scorn and loathing as the men who might have married them, but did not. Men dislike those to whom they have behaved badly, even more than they dislike those who have behaved badly to them : women, on the contrary, prefer those whom they have treated badly, even to those who have treated them well. "He never pardons who hath done the wrong," is a true saying as long as we stick to the pronoun "he"; but substitute "she" for "he," and the line becomes utter nonsense. For she who hath done the wrong not only pardons— she commends, she praises, she rewards. There is no kindness too extreme to be showered upon the injured one—no favour too great to be shown to him. If a man wishes a woman to become really attached to him, he must not be kind to her—he must allow her to be unkind to him. It is part of the divinely feminine law of compensation.

Therefore Mrs. Seaton—who had behaved abominably to the Prime Minister before he was ever a Prime Minister or she a Mrs. Seaton—cherished a sincere and lasting affection for Lord Wrexham; and was always pleased to see—and to be seen by—him: especially when, as on the present occasion, she was conscious that she had on a becoming gown. She was too true a woman to flirt after she was married; and she was much too true a woman not to want to do so. The consuming passion to attract, which is so incomprehensible to the women who do not feel it and so irresistible to the women who do, was bred in the very bones of Isabel: when she ceased to feel it she would cease to breathe.

As for Lord Wrexham, to him Isabel was the only woman in the world, and always would be: but he had loved her far too well to make love to her now that she was another man's wife. The bitterest day of his life had been the day when she wrote *Tekel* across his name: nothing had ever made up to him for that. Fate had thrown into his lot certain ingredients which are supposed to compensate for a good deal in the lives of men—notably the Premiership: but nothing had ever compensated him for the loss of Isabel, and nothing ever would. He felt towards Fate as we all feel towards that mysterious entity in shops, called "Sign," who comes forward, after we have finally discovered that the article we want is not in stock, and endeavours to persuade us that we did not really want that article at all, but something absolutely different, of which the shop is full. Fate had treated poor Lord Wrexham very much the same as the being called "Sign" treats

us all in our season: he had asked for Isabel Carnaby
and Fate had given him the Prime-Ministership—not
by any means the same thing: and he felt, as we all
feel in like circumstances, both impatient and un-
grateful.

"I am very glad you are at home," he began, "as I
have something particular to say to you. I came late in
the hope that I should find you in and alone."

"In that case you should have come early," retorted
Isabel; "as a rule the later the hour the larger the meet.
You remind me of a very worthy girl I once knew, who
was apologizing to me for being married in Lent, and
she said that as so many people seemed shocked at her
being married in Lent, she had put off her wedding
until the very last week!"

Wrexham smiled. It always charmed him to hear
Isabel rattle on in her old inconsequent way.

"Nevertheless events have proved the wisdom of my
course: I have found you in and alone."

"Because nothing happens except the impossible:
and you should never expect anything but the unexpected, or foresee anything except the unforeseen.
That is the wisdom of life."

"Then I will follow wisdom," said Lord Wrexham:
"and certainly her ways are ways of pleasantness when
they lead me here."

"You don't want to follow her, Wrexham: she dwells
with you. It is not often that she avails herself of
official residences; but for the time being she has
certainly taken up her abode in Downing Street."

Lord Wrexham fell in with Isabel's mood.

"I hope she will take up her abode their again when
it is Mr. Seaton's turn to occupy one of the official
residences."

He never spoke of Paul without the prefix " Mr." It was the only sign he made of not having forgiven Isabel's husband for having married Isabel. Also he rarely addressed her by any name whatsoever: the natural man kicked at having to say " Mrs. Seaton," and the spiritual man hesitated at calling another man's wife by her Christian name. In many ways Lord Wrexham was very old-fashioned.

Isabel shrugged her shoulders. " Not she : wisdom won't be *dans cette galère.* But *I* shall ; and I shan't make a bad understudy, in the enforced absence of the real article."

" Certainly you will not. You are by far the wisest woman that I ever meet, as well as being the most brilliant."

Isabel shook her head. " No, I'm not—not the wisest, I mean; I'll give in to you about the most brilliant. But I'm not really wise, Wrexham : that is why I admire it so much in you. You'll find as a rule that the people we all admire most are the people who really are what we ourselves pretend to be."

" I do not agree with you : I consider you extremely wise : and I think you should use your wisdom for the benefit of your husband and his followers. I know that you and I are one in thinking that they are going too fast, and that in grasping too much they will lose everything; and I feel that it is for you to influence the advanced section of the party through your influence over your husband. You know as well as I do that there is nothing that Mr. Seaton would not do for you : and I want you to use that power in order to save the party from being first disintegrated and then destroyed."

Lord Wrexham was far too just a man not to admit

to the full his rival's excellence as a husband and power as a politician.

Again Isabel shook her head. " But that's just what I don't want to do. I would give anything to convince Paul that I am right and that he is wrong with regard to the present political crisis, which, according to you and me, isn't a crisis at all and shouldn't be treated as such : but I couldn't bear him to do what he thought wrong and I thought right, just to please me. Which is what he is quite capable of doing."

Wrexham looked puzzled. As long as a drag was put on the Radical wheel, he did not see that the inner machinery of the drag used was a matter of much moment.

" You see," Isabel went on confidentially, " it is like this: a man will do anything that a woman asks as a favour, and nothing that she advises as the wisest course. If she begs her husband to stand on his head just to please her, he'll be found for hours togethe wrong end uppermost, waving his feet aloft as if he were a pigeon in a pie : but if she tries to prove to him that the head is a safer mode of locomotion than the feet, and that he will be acting more wisely if he adopts it as such, that man will stick to his own feet as long as the world stands, and won't even go to the Antipodes for fear he should thereby seem to be following his wife's superior advice, and walking upside-down. Oh ! I know them." And Isabel sighed over the weaknesses of the stronger sex.

" Well, that makes everything all the more easy for you," said the Prime Minister, endeavouring to follow the thread of her argument.

" No, no, no; it doesn't: just the very opposite ! That way of managing a husband is quite the best way

in domestic politics; no home is complete without it.
But it doesn't do in really big things: it is too great a
responsibility for the woman. Don't you understand;
it is the knowledge that Paul will do anything that I
ask, which often keeps me from asking anything? Of
course, it is excellent to have a woman's strength, but it
is tyrannous to use it like a woman."

"I think I begin to see what you mean," replied
Wrexham slowly.

Isabel babbled on:

"I do hate a bossy kind of wife—the sort that makes
up her husband's mind' for him, and then sees that he
doesn't change it. That isn't playing the game. Now
I always pride myself on never doing anything that I
can't do really well: that is why I never play the violin
or talk to young girls."

"I am sure you could do both extremely well."

There was not much that Wrexham did not believe
could be done excellently by Mrs. Paul Seaton.

"No, I couldn't: therefore I don't do them at all. But
you'd be surprised at the things I've done well in my
time," Isabel added naïvely.

"I should not! That I can swear!"

"Yes, you would: I've been surprised myself, and you
can't think better of me than I do! I remember once
Mrs. Gaythorne made me go to a village Dorcas-meeting
with her, and you should just have seen the flannel
petticoat that I made! It was a perfect dream!"

"I can well believe it!"

"Well then, you see, having laid down a rule that I
would never do anything unless I could do it well, I
did not marry without making up my mind to be one
of the best wives that ever hopped through a wedding
ring. And the best sort are not the bossy sort, and it's

no good pretending that they are!" The moment
Isabel had delivered herself of this statement it
occurred to her that it was not quite the happiest thing
imaginable to have said to her present company; but
—being a woman of tact—having said the wrong
thing, she stuck to it. The crowning mistake of conversation is to show that one knows one has made a
mistake: just as nine times out of ten the greatest
insult one can offer is to offer an apology. So she went
gaily on: "Therefore, having become a past master in
the fine art of being a good wife, I cannot debase my
art by using it for a worthy purpose. 'Art for art's
sake,' is ever the motto of true artists, be they artists in
words or in colours—paperers or painters, so to speak;
and art ceases to be art when it becomes a means and
not an end."

Isabel had succeeded in covering her retreat neatly.

"Yes, yes, doubtless you are right: at any rate I am
sure you know best as to how far you are justified in
influencing your husband's political life. But that is
not really what I came to say to you this afternoon:
there is something else."

"And what is that? Something very interesting, I
hope."

"It is something which concerns yourself, and
therefore is of supreme interest to me."

"Thank you, Wrexham: you always put things so
nicely that one is apt to forget you are a Prime
Minister."

"The long and short of the matter is this," continued
Lord Wrexham in his slightly ponderous manner: "on
account of his health, Gravesend has had to resign the
Governorship of Tasmania; and I want to know if you
would like me to offer the post to your husband?"

Isabel gasped. It is always a little overpowering suddenly to find one's heart's desire within one's grasp.

"That is what I really came to say to you," added Wrexham.

" But why say it to me and not to my husband ? "

Isabel was herself again—that impertinent self which could ask such pertinent questions.

Wrexham began to explain in his usual somewhat laborious fashion :

"Because we hear from our agents all over the country that—owing to certain measures which the present Government have brought forward—there is every probability that we shall be returned to power at the next General Election with a considerably larger majority than we have at present; and, you must understand that it is not customary to offer a Colonial Governorship to a man who is sure of a seat in the Cabinet before long : it looks too much like shelving him."

"Then why shelve Paul ? " was the quick rejoinder of Paul's wife.

" That is just what I am endeavouring to explain to you : because I happen to know that you would very much like this appointment : and because it is you who are my friend—not Mr. Seaton. I only feel an interest in him because he is your husband ! " (He meant that he only felt a hatred for Paul because Isabel was Paul's wife : but that was neither here nor there.) " It is your pleasure and happiness that concern me," he went on : " not Mr. Seaton's."

" My happiness is bound up in my husband's," said Isabel haughtily.

The woman was suddenly merged in the wife, and for a moment she hated Wrexham.

"Then so far as it is, Mr. Seaton's wishes are of supreme importance to me," replied Wrexham, with unfailing courtesy; "and, if you wish it, I will offer him this appointment at once."

"No, no, no; wait a bit: don't be in such a hurry. I want to think."

Isabel spoke impatiently. She had noted the "Mr.," and knew the social exclusiveness which it implied; and the moment of hatred was prolonged into two.

"Believe me, I would not hurry you for anything. I will leave you to think the matter over, and you can send me a line in a day or so. Just Yes or No will be sufficient: I shall understand," said the Prime Minister, rising from his seat.

"No, no; don't go: stay here. I can think it over just as well in a few minutes as in a few days—better. I never make a mistake except through caution."

"Just as you like: my time is at your disposal," replied Wrexham, with his usual old-fashioned politeness: and straightway buried himself, after the manner of the Babes in the Wood, in the "sweet green leaves" of the *Westminster Gazette.*

Isabel got up from her chair and went to the window at the far end of the back drawing-room, where she stood looking out upon the gardens in the rear of the house. It was a tremendous temptation, and she recognized it as such. Not only would she herself have the sort of life she liked best, but—if she accepted Wrexham's offer—Paul would be saved from making those mistakes which she felt convinced he would make as soon as he became a Cabinet Minister. The country was not ripe for the reforms proposed by Paul and his section of the party—would not be ripe for some years to come; and the increased Liberal majority which, owing

to the turn that affairs had taken, now seemed probable
after the General Election, would be speedily turned
into defeat by the oft-repeated Radical error of plucking
the apple before it was ripe. And then where would
Paul and his followers be? Deeply buried under the
onus of having broken up the Liberal party, and restored
to power the present Opposition. Just now the Government majority was so small that nothing vigorous
in the shape of reform could be contemplated; but
when the hands of the Radicals were strengthened, as
there seemed every likelihood that they would be after
the forthcoming Dissolution, there was no revolution
too immense—no mistake too egregious—for them to
attempt to affect. Thus Mrs. Seaton reasoned: and
felt that it was her duty as well as her pleasure to accept
the Prime Minister's offer, and to save her husband from
himself.

Of course there was the bare possibility that Paul
might be right and she wrong with regard to what was
best for the country: but that possibility seemed so very
remote, that she speedily dismissed it from the line of
argument.

But, on the other hand, there was Paul himself, with
his own hopes and desires and wishes. What right had
she to frustrate these hopes, even if she believed them
to be delusive: what right to disappoint those wishes,
even though they might be opposed to hers? There
was no doubt that his political position was strengtening
every day. A year or two ago the possibility of his
having a place in the Cabinet was frequently hinted at:
now the possibility of a Liberal Cabinet being recon-
structed without him, never occurred to anybody. And
even if her forebodings came true, and his reign was
doomed to a swift and suicidal ending, he would still

have been a Cabinet Minister—and that is something
in a man's life: in fact the only thing, except herself,
that Paul had ever set his whole heart upon. And had
she any right to stand between him and the realisation
of his life's ambition—any right to stand between him
and the fulfilment of his heart's desire?

She knew that he would at once accept the Colonial
appointment if it were offered to him: she had no doubts
upon that score. Had she not once said that she wished
for it—and were not her wishes always paramount with
him? She was well aware that unselfishness was one of
the strongest elements in her husband's character; and
that he carried it to such a pitch where she was concerned that her happiness was really and truly his—
that his could not exist apart from hers. But how
far was she justified in taking advantage of this
passionate and selfless affection, even if she believed
that she was acting for his good as well as for her own?
The very plenitude of her power made her pause before
exercising it.

All these thoughts raced through her mind as she
stood looking out upon the trees in the garden, and
Lord Wrexham studied the pages of the *Westminster
Gazette*.

Then suddenly there came into her head a conversation
she had once had with poor Gabriel Carr about the
sanctity of marriage; and stray phrases from the
marriage-service rang in her ears. "Wilt thou obey
and serve him?"—did that mean, Wilt thou so order
his life that he shall have no voice in the matter?
"That this woman may be loving and amiable, faithful
and obedient;"—did this mean, May she have such a
strong will of her own that her husband for the sake of
peace will always give in to her? "For the husband is

the head of the wife;"—did that convey the idea that it
was hers to command and his to submit; hers to express
a wish and his to carry it out? "Ye wives, be in subjection to your own husbands;"—was this an apostolic
rendering of the modern notion that it is a woman's
right to take her own way independently of the man
she has married, and to live her own life utterly
regardless of him?

And as these thoughts rapidly chased each other
through her active brain, Isabel knew for a certainty
that she would reject Wrexham's offer. It was the
only course open to her, as long as she regarded her
marriage as a sacrament, and her husband as her lord
and master divinely appointed: there was no alternative.
"Subjection" might mean all sorts of things; but it
could not possibly mean having one's own way at all
costs and in defiance of all authority: if she attempted
to prove that it did, not a dictionary in England would
support her. As she herself had said, she could make
up her mind as well in a few minutes as in a few days;
and she had made it up.

"It's no good, Wrexham," she said, as she came back
into the front drawing-room; "I can't accept. It was
nice of you to think of me, but the thing is impossible!"

"Just as you please."

Lord Wrexham's manner was as ponderously polite
as ever; it was impossible to tell from the expression
of his face whether he approved or disapproved of Mrs.
Seaton's decision.

"I can't put my interests before Paul's in that way:
it would be too horrid of me!"

"I thought you said they were identical."

Lord Wrexham always experienced an indulgent
pleasure when he convicted Isabel of inaccuracy.

Isabel drew herself up:

" I said that our happiness was identical. If you do quote, you should always be careful to verify your quotations—especially if you use them to point morals or to adorn tales."

Wrexham took his snubbing quite meekly: he thought that he had deserved it. But he did not think that Paul Seaton had deserved the happiness which was identical with Isabel's.

A few nights after this, when Paul and Isabel were sitting together after dinner preparatory to Paul's going back to the House, Isabel said:

"What is wrong, Paul? You've been so quiet all through dinner, that I feel sure something must be the matter with you; but I didn't like to ask before the servants if it was an ill-digested foreign policy or merely an ill-digested meal. Has anything vexed you really?"

"Well, darling, it has and it hasn't."

What a statesmanlike answer! Go on."

" Well, my sweet, if you want to know the truth, it is this. You remember once saying to me that you should like me to be appointed Governor of Tasmania in Gravesend's place if he resigned, don't you?"

Isabel remembered only too well, and intimated as much, as she came and sat on the arm of her husband's chair while he enjoyed his post-prandial cigar.

"Well, then," continued Paul, "I was wrong in imagining that Wrexham might offer it to me: that's all. Gravesend has resigned, and Wrexham has given the place to Lord Bobby Thistletown."

"And you are disappointed? Oh, Paul!"

There was positive anguish in Isabel's voice: surely her great renunciation had not been in vain after all!

"Only on your account, my sweet. I ^bought you wanted it." And Paul's arm stole lovingly round his wife's waist.

"And didn't you want it yourself?" There was still anxiety in Isabel's blue eyes.

"I ?—for myself? Good gracious, no! But I want everything that you want, sweetheart, as I can only find my happiness in yours. You know that well enough."

"But you wouldn't have wanted it if you hadn't thought I did? You are quite sure of that?" Isabel persisted.

"Good heavens, no! How could I? It would have been the final shelving of me and the end of my political career. But all the same I should have taken it if Wrexham had given me the chance, because I thought it would please you."

Isabel laid her cheek tenderly against the top of Paul's head. "Then that would have been very wrong, dearest; very wrong indeed! *Your* wishes ought to regulate our lives—not *mine.*"

"Yours will, however, as long as I am master in my own house. I can tell you that."

"Well, they oughtn't to."

"Well, they will."

"I don't think that that is the proper way of bringing a wife into subjection to her own husband."

Paul laughed. "Subjection be hanged! Your happiness is my first object, and always will be. It makes me far happier to see you happy than to be happy myself, if you will excuse the bull. I can only be happy through you: so that it is really the height of selfishness on my part to do the things that give you pleasure.'

Isabel nestled up to him.

"You are quite the nicest husband that was ever invented," she whispered. "It was a happy find of mine when I chanced upon you!"

"Not so lucky as mine by a long way," answered Paul, kissing her. "But about this Tasmanian business? Are you disappointed, my darling? Because if you are, I shall never forgive Wrexham as long as I live for not shelving me."

"No; I'm not a bit disappointed, Paul. I've changed my mind since that time I talked to you about Lord Gravesend. I'd much rather see you a Cabinet Minister than a Colonial Governor."

"I'd much rather see myself one, I can tell you that," replied Paul, with a huge sigh of relief. It was such a comfort to find that Isabel had not cared about that Tasmanian appointment after all! "But what about yourself, my sweet? I thought you had set your heart upon being an Excellency."

"So I had, but I've changed my heart—I mean my mind: and now I'd far rather be a Cabinet Ministering-angel than a Colonial Governess, if these are the proper terms for the wives of those offices."

"Well, I'm very glad to hear it," said Paul, kissing her again: "exceedingly glad, I can tell you! For much as I should like to be in the next Cabinet, it would be no pleasure to me if it didn't please you as well."

"But you really would enjoy it for yourself, wouldn't you?"

"Rather! My only fear is that I am not a big enough man for the place."

"Oh! you are big enough for that," replied Isabel coolly: "you are what I should call 'ordinary Cabinet size.'"

"But it would please you too, wouldn't it, my darling?" Paul persisted.

"It would; it would please me most tremendously," answered Isabel. And as she thrilled at the touch of her husband's arm round her, she knew that she was speaking the truth.

After Paul had gone back to the House, she went up into the drawing-room and stood with her elbows on the mantel-piece, looking thoughtfully down upon the mass of flowers which filled the unused fireplace. " I have done the right thing," she said to herself : " there's no shadow of doubt whatever upon that score. The poor darling would simply have jumped at that silly Governorship, if Wrexham had offered it to him, just to please me : and it would have spoilt the rest of his life for him, poor dear ! It was my turn to give way this time—and never to let him know that I had done so : it would be all spoilt if he were to find out that I had given it up for his sake, so he never must. I really think that I am on all fours with S. Peter as to the meaning of the word ' subjection ' : this was the sort of thing he had in his mind at the time. But nevertheless," she added, with a sigh, as she glanced at herself in the mirror of the overmantel, " I should dearly have loved to be an Excellency ! It is, after all, the only really graceful way of growing old."

CHAPTER XXI

CAPTAIN GAYTHORNE'S HORSEWHIP

CAPTAIN GAYTHORNE was intensely unhappy: there could be no two opinions as to that: and his misery was beginning to show itself in his countenance and bearing. His ruddy complexion was fast losing its claim to that epithet; and his round face was growing pinched and haggard.

His mother did not notice his depressed spirits and changed appearance. She was just then so fully occupied with a fresh scheme for the further enlightenment of the inhabitants of the South Sea Islands that she had no time nor attention to spare for domestic and family matters. Moreover, Mrs. Gaythorne had a great deal of the masculine element in her cast of mind—notably that power, usually the prerogative of the stronger sex, of steadily refusing to see a thing at all for a long time, and then as persistently declining to see anything else. The natural and normal man either believes that his nearest and dearest are as Behemoth in their strength; or else he beholds the very jaws of Death gaping to receive them: he knows no middle course for the treading of the feet he loves, between the path of the young hart upon the mountains and the *Via Dolorosa* that leads direct to the grave. And in this

U

respect Mrs. Gaythorne was one with the normal man.

Fabia saw what was wrong with her husband; but she hardened her heart and did not care. She was in a chronic state of irritation against him; and there is nothing so hardening to the heart as irritability. To use a horrible and popular expression of the present day, Charlie "got on her nerves"; and a woman who is capable of allowing things to "get on her nerves" is capable of anything.

Our grandmothers—bless their memory!—did not allow things to get on their nerves—either their husbands or things of less importance. They knew the devil when they met him; and therefore did not confuse ill-temper with ill-health, nor call by the euphonious name of "nerves" the ungoverned passions of their own sinful hearts. It is one of the devil's latest and most successful disguises, that of the irresponsible and neurotic invalid: the pose termed "neurasthenia" has completely thrown into the shade his old make-up of the angel of light: as it not only deceives the victims of the performance, but takes in equally the performers themselves.

And perhaps there was something—if not much—to be said on Fabia's side. Charlie simply adored his wife; but he did not take the trouble to understand her. A not uncommon mistake among married men! Charlie had cut and dried rules as to what women liked and what women did not like: and he regulated his behaviour towards each and every member of the sex accordingly. He had a deeply rooted conviction—implanted by his father and cultivated by his mother's fostering care—that the more a man permitted a woman to trample upon him, the better that woman was

pleased: and therefore he persistently made himself
into a door-mat under Fabia's feet, without pausing to
consider whether this was the conjugal attitude most
likely to suit her particular requirements. Charlie's
rule of conduct was to do and to say everything that
he thought would please his wife: so far so good: but
he made the initial mistake of omitting to discover in
the first place exactly what would please her. In which
error again he did not stand alone. If he had worshipped Fabia less and understood her more, things
would have been better for both of them, and much
misery might have been averted. But a firm conviction
is hard to uproot—especially if it be implanted in the
mind of a man, and most especially if it happen to be
an incorrect one. There is an innate loyalty in the
masculine nature which makes it cling to wrong im-
pressions as it would cling to lost causes: it seems
somehow rather shabby to throw them over simply
because they happen to be unfounded. This trait—
which is not without its excellencies—is a survival of
mediæval chivalry, and accounts for much that is
otherwise difficult to understand in the sons of
men.

Therefore if Charlie were miserable, Fabia was
miserable also: and—let conventional moralists say what
they will — there are few things more selfish than
misery. It is the happy people who are the kind and
unselfish people; and it is quite right that they should
be so. It is not when our own pockets are empty that
we see to the replenishing of our neighbour's; it is not
when our own teeth are aching that we accompany a friend
to the dentist's. With regard to suffering—although not
with regard to sin—we have neither the time nor the
inclination to remove the mote from our brother's eye,

until the operation for beam has been successfully performèd upon our own.

Fabia Gaythorne was bored to extinction : the dulness of her life was well-nigh killing her : and the truth that having chosen her own lot she was in duty bound to make the best of it, in no way affected the fact that she neither made the best of it nor even attempted to do so. Life without love is far too dull for the majority of women ; so, as a rule — with their usual power of adaptation — failing the real article, they invent a substitute ; which is often as difficult to distinguish from the real thing as is Elkington's Best - Electro from solid silver: the hall-mark being in cypher and known only to the gods. Mortals are only able to differentiate between the two when the electro begins to wear off; and that rarely happens until it is too late to change the plated goods.

Of course *ennui* is no excuse for wrong-doing; but it is often a reason for it. It is the idle hearts, as well as the idle hands, that are supplied with occupation by Satan.

The one person who saw Charlie Gaythorne's misery and was made wretched by it, was isabel Seaton. How she wished that she had never invited Fabia to England at all! And how she wished that she had left a few stones unturned in her efforts to bring about a match between Fabia and Captain Gaythorne! If wishes were horses, isabel would have had a fine stud; but as it was, they were absolutely useless. Charlie had married Fabia, and Fabia was breaking his heart; and — unless isabel were much mistaken — Fabia would soon break up his home also. Isabel was not the sort of woman to believe in platonic friendships, unless she happened to have any special

reason for professing that article of faith: she was far
too fond of admiration: but she knew that if such
friendships did exist, the contracting parties were
rarely—if ever—newly and unhappily married women
and their recently rejected lovers. Of course there was
the case of herself and Wrexham to prove the contrary;
but she was nearly forty and Wrexham fifty-nine; while
Ram Chander was in the prime of life, and Fabia only
twenty-three. Time not only heals many sorrows; it
also obviates many dangers. Then, again, Lord
Wrexham was an Englishman and a gentleman;
and Dr. Mukharji was neither the one nor the other,
as his treatment of Isabel's appeal to him had proved.
Moreover, Isabel was passionately in love with her own
husband, while Fabia utterly despised hers: therefore,
the intimacy between Fabia and her cousin was not to
be classed in the same category as the friendship between
Isabel and Lord Wrexham; and as Mrs. Seaton contemplated what the end of this mad folly on the part of
Fabia would probably be, her heart was very heavy
indeed.

The visit to Paris had done no permanent good.
The relief it afforded had only been temporary. As
soon as Fabia returned to London, her visits to the
rooms in Mount Street became as frequent and as
prolonged as ever. In vain her husband besought her
to go back with him to Gaythorne; in vain he
suggested another trip abroad. Fabia was as
immovable in her decision to remain in London as
she had been in her decision to return to it from Paris.

Charlie felt that he could not speak to her about
what was filling his thoughts; nothing would induce
him to do such a thing. His chivalrous nature revolted
at the bare idea of suggesting to his wife that her

relations with another man were too intimate: all that
he could do was to have it out with the other man
himself. Therefore the only course open to him was to
go direct to Dr. Mukharji's rooms, and tell the popular
charlatan what he thought of him. And the instrument
which appeared best to lend itself to the appropriate
and adequate expression of this opinion, was a good
old English horsewhip.

There were many reasons why the horsewhipping of
Dr. Mukharji appealed strongly to the taste of Captain
Gaythorne. In the first place Charlie hated the Hindoo
because the latter had once wanted to marry Fabia:
and no man really likes the other men who have wished
to marry his wife. In the second place Charlie was far
too normal and healthy-minded an Englishman to
entertain anything but disgust and contempt for any
juggling with the supernatural: he disapproved of
everything of the nature of occultism, spiritualism, or
prying into the future, classing them all together in his
own pellucid mind under the generic term of "rot."
And thirdly Charlie loathed Dr. Mukharji, because he
held the latter entirely responsible for the present state
of affairs. Fabia was young and inexperienced: but—
as he argued, and argued with some reason—Mukharji
(or, as he called him, "that confounded nigger") was
old enough to understand the irreparable mischief he
was causing by allowing scandal to associate his name
with that of his beautiful kinswoman. Thus Charlie
hated Ram Chandar with a threefold cord of hate, and
decided to deal with his enemy as it pleased him.

Fabia and her husband were sitting together at
breakfast one morning, close upon the end of the
season. It was always Fabia's habit to rise early: she
had learnt it in India: and the English custom of

getting up late never appealed to her. Neither did she enjoy having her breakfast in her own room, with nobody to talk save her old ayah, Saidie, who now fulfilled the part of maid to her. She liked life and society; she hated solitude and dulness; and although she found Charlie dull enough, still even he was better than the ayah, who never did anything but echo all that her mistress chose to say. Charlie did not do very much more, it must be confessed: but Mrs. Gaythorne did—that dear woman never erred on the side of being too subservient to anybody. On this particular day, however, the cries of the South Sea islanders for disused *Sunday at Homes* had apparently become so importunate that Mrs. Gaythorne had risen while it was yet night to attend a breakfast-meeting which had been organized in order to satisfy the spiritual hunger of the heathen abroad, and the more physical necessities of their Committee at home.

"How are you going to amuse yourself to-day, my pet?" Charlie asked.

He felt a horrible suspicion that his wife was going to see her cousin, but hoped against hope that she was not.

Fabia sighed wearily.

"How am I going to amuse myself? Not at all. I may try various means for the securing of that end, but it is a foregone conclusion that they will none of them prove successful," she replied.

Charlie's kindly face at once assumed an expression of sympathy. He pitied Fabia profoundly for having married a fool, but he did not see how the evil was to be cured.

"Poor old girl! I wish to goodness that I could hit upon something to amuse you!"

"I wish to goodness—or even to badness—that you could!"

"You don't seem to feel any interest in the sort of things that I talk about." Poor Charlie's voice was very wistful.

Fabia raised her delicately-pencilled eyebrows. "Does anybody?"

It was extremely rude of her, but Charlie was very patient: too patient for the type of woman with whom he had to deal.

"I wish I could talk about things that you are interested in, Fabia dear."

"I wish that you could: it would make a considerable difference to me."

"But other people can. I'm not the only person in the world!"

"Fortunately not."

Even then the worm did not turn.

"Now, there's Isabel Seaton, don't you know? A rattling good sort of woman! Surely she is interesting enough for anybody! I never knew such a woman in my life for talking about thoughts and feelings and rot of that kind, and all the sorts of things that women spin yarns about for hours together. You ought to like talking to her, old girl."

"When she talks rot? Thank you."

The gentle Charles hastened to eat his words.

"By Jove! I didn't mean that. When I say 'rot' I don't mean 'rot': I only mean that women like talking about a lot of high-falutin and sentiment, that men—poor brutes!—are much too great asses to understand. And if you're on the high-falutin, sentimental war-path, Mrs. Paul Seaton is your man."

"Still it is possible that an undiluted and age-long

tête-à-tête with Isabel might pall in time—especially upon another woman."

" Perhaps it might: though hardly upon another man, if that man happened to be Seaton. I never saw a beggar so cracked on his wife in my life; and after being married all this time, too! He isn't like a husband; he's more like a fellow that only meets his best girl once in a way, and has to make the most of it. He never looks at anybody else when she's in the room, and he is always straining his ears to hear what she is saying."

And Charlie laughed aloud at the memory of Paul's infatuation. There is always so much more humour in a thing done by someone else than in the very same thing done by ourselves. A joke, like an oil-painting, is best appreciated when seen from a little distance. Our mere performance of an act at once robs that act of humour and clothes it with dignity—in our own eyes.

" I thought you approved of that sort of thing," said Fabia coldly. " You once told me that your father laid great stress upon the sanctity of marriage."

" By Jove, so he did! He was a tremendous stickler for it. I should think he did lay stress on it! Just a few—rather!"

" Then why laugh at Mr. Seaton for practising what the late Mr. Gaythorne preached?"

" I'm not laughing at him! I admire the fellow for it most tremendously, I can tell you! But somehow it seems a bit rummy for an old fellow of that age to be so deuced spoony. Why if he's a day, he must be forty: and though the fair Isabel is a duck, she's no chicken!" And Charlie laughed again, in the insolence of youth, at his own wit and the Seatons' folly.

Fabia smiled too. It struck her as so distinctly comic for her husband to be laughing at the Seatons and good-humouredly tolerating them.

"Then I gather that your late father would have commended the admirable Seaton."

"Great Scott, yes: just a little! I commend him myself. He's not a bad sort, good old Paul! But as for my father, you should just have heard him on the subject of how husbands ought to obey and reverence their wives. And so they ought. They're told to in the Bible, or something on the same lines, don't you know? I'm a poor hand at quotations, but I fancy that's the idea."

"It is a good thing that Mrs. Gaythorne is not present, or she would make you look it up in the Commentary after breakfast."

"By Jove, so she would! The dear old mater never can bear me to be shaky about the hang of a text: she likes it all cut and dried, and committed to memory. I remember once when I was a little chap there was a harvest-thanksgiving at a Methodist Chapel—the place where she went to when old Cattley made such an ass of himself over the Psalm-business — and what should catch her eye the minute she got up from that face-in-the-hat affair at the beginning, but a cross worked on the beam-end of the pulpit in white chrysanthemums, or Michaelmas - daisies, or some other flower of that persuasion, don't you know?"

Fabia knew only too well—so well that she felt it would asphyxiate her to know it any better; so she rose from the finished meal and the unfinished story, and left the room, saying as she went: "You'd better put 'To be continued,' and finish the tale some other time. Seria· publication is the only form possible for stories of such a length as that one."

Charlie sat quite still after she had gone: for a few minutes he was too completely crushed to move. Then other thoughts roused him. "I wonder if she's off to that d—d scoundrel," he said to himself. "I expect he's come round her with his devilish hypnotism or some vile humbug of that sort, and the poor girl can't resist him. By Jove, if I was sure of that, I'd blow his brains out!" Then a sudden idea struck him. "Great Scott! I'll go straight to the brute's place now, and see what the skunk is up to; and if I find Fabia there—!" Anyone who had seen Charlie's face then, would hardly have recognized the usually good-tempered Captain Gaythorne.

It was not long before Charlie put his threat into execution, and jumped into a hansom, taking with him a brand-new riding-whip which he had only bought a few days ago. But quick as he had been, somebody else had been quicker: he dismissed his cab at the end of Mount Street and walked the rest of the way. Another hansom overtook him; but as it was going the same way as he was, he did not see the occupant until it pulled up a few paces in front of him at the door of the house in which were Dr. Mukharji's rooms: and out of that hansom stepped Fabia.

This was enough, but it was not all.

She did not stop to ring the bell: she was too much at home for that: she opened the door by means of a latchkey and went straight in, shutting the front-door behind her, and leaving her husband—whom she had not seen—standing stupified on the pavement.

Then Charlie saw red.

His wife to possess the latchkey of another man's house

so that she could go in and out undetected ! The mere
idea of such a thing was insufferable, and drove him to
absolute frenzy. It proved an intimacy between Fabia
and the occupant of that house far greater than Charlie
had ever insulted his wife by supposing possible. If
she had a latchkey to her cousin's rooms—? Well, the
scandal-mongers were not so far out after all !

Charlie was obliged to walk a little way up the street
and back again in order to steady himself. He knew
that if he rushed straight into Dr. Mukharji's presence,
he should kill the man then and there ; and for Fabia's
sake he did not wish that murder should be done. But
after a turn or two in the open air his frenzy of rage
subsided sufficiently to allow him to present himself, as
any ordinary English gentleman, at the fortune-teller's
door, and to ask in a fairly natural voice if he could see
Dr. Mukharji. He duly sent in his card, so that there
might be no mistake ; but he took care to follow closely
upon it, to prevent the possibility of being denied
admittance : he also kept his whip in his hand, so that
there might be no mistake about that either.

His first impression on seeing his enemy was surprise
at the strong family likeness between the occultist and
Fabia ; Mukharji looked more like her father or her
elder brother than her distant cousin : and his second
was still greater surprise that a man as old as Ram
Chandar should obtain so great an influence over a
handsome young woman such as Fabia. Youth is
always sceptical as to middle-age's power to charm. It
struck Charlie as rather a joke that a man of forty,
like Paul Seaton, should be able to fascinate his own
wife ; but that a man apparently of about forty-five
should be able to fascinate Charlie's wife, was considerably more than a joke—was altogether an inexplicable

mystery, and a thing to be neither understood nor endured.

While these thoughts raced through Charlie's brain, the Oriental came slowly forward with outstretched hand and a scornful smile which was the very counterpart of Fabia's.

" How do you do, Captain Gaythorne?" he said, in his low, Eastern voice, which was as soft as a woman's; " allow me to welcome my cousin's husband to my humble lodging."

But Charlie put his right hand behind his back to where the left one was gently fingering the horse-whip.

" I haven't come here for any infernal palaver," he replied, and his face looked as nobody had seen it look except his comrades in action. " I've come to tell you that I won't stand any more of your d—d nonsense. There's been about enough of it as it is."

The Oriental paused a moment in admiration before he answered. How splendid these English people were when they were angry! When he saw the look on Charlie's face he understood why the English wherever they go are the dominant race. Then he began suavely :

" Surely Fabia—"

But he was promptly cut short by the infuriated young giant before him :

" Mrs. Gaythorne's name does not enter into the present conversation : please remember that."

" Then may i inquire to what I owe the honour of this visit ? "

The fortune-teller tried to keep up his scornful smile, but he was trembling all over. He had never in all his life seen a man look at him as Charlie was looking. He understood now why the native tribes were in awe of Captain Gaythorne : he was in awe of the man himself.

" I can soon tell you that. I've come to pay my little account of what I owe you for your infernal hypnotism and treachery and general damnableness. That's what I've come for ; and if you please I'll settle my little bill at once." And with that Charlie showed him the horse-whip and looked like business : his rage was breaking through its leash again.

The other shook from head to foot with sheer fear. Charlie saw his enemy's terror and it infuriated him still further. What a coward the hound was !

" Surely you are not going to beat me with that thing," pleaded the trembling occultist.

Charlie laughed a grim laugh that was not altogether pleasant to hear :

" But I am, though. I'm going to thrash you within an inch of your life for bringing your confounded fortune-telling and hypnotism and all the rest of your infernal rot into decent English houses, and among decent Englishmen's wives : and then I'm going to pitch your miserable little body out of the window. That's what I'm going to do, and the sooner it's done the better ! I've no pity for d—d scoundrels such as you !"

And as the memory of how this man had come between himself and Fabia rushed on Charlie, it maddened him so that he lost all self-control, and seized his enemy by the throat, meaning to shake him as a dog might have shaken a rat. But before he had time to fulfil his intention, or to bring down the raised horse-whip upon the trembling form that was struggling in his iron grasp, the slender figure collapsed altogether and fell in a heap upon the floor, leaving in Charlie's hands a tangled mass of false black hair and beard: and Charlie saw lying at his feet no grovelling Indian juggler, but the unconscious form of his wife, Fabia Gaythorne!

CHAPTER XXII

THE EFFECT OF THE HORSEWHIP

DUMFOUNDERED with amazement and hardly knowing what he did, Charlie shouted for help; and the veiled attendant came rushing into the room with her veil thrown back, thereby disclosing herself to be none other than Fabia's old ayah, Saidie.

"See to your mistress at once," commanded Charlie. "I believe I've killed her." And the big man trembled now as his wife had trembled a few minutes before.

"The Memsahib is not dead: she is only fainting," replied the ayah, unfastening her mistress's robe and pouring something between the white lips.

"Are you sure?" groaned the distracted man, kneeling at her side.

"Quite sure, Sahib. See! even now the colour returns to the Memsahib's lips, and she begins to recover."

"Then I must go," said Charlie, rising to his feet. "After what I've done I am not fit that she should ever look at me again. But first tell me, where is the real Dr. Mukharji?"

"There is no real Dr. Mukharji, Sahib. It has always been a play of the Memsahib's."

"No real Dr. Mukharji?" Charlie could not believe his ears.

"No, Sahib. There is Ram Chandar Mukharji out in

India, but he has never been to England at all. It has been a play of the Memsahib's because she found tue English life so dull."

Charlie put his hand to his head as if he were dazed: "And I've knocked her down for nothing. It has all been my own infernal folly. What a confounded fool of an ass I've been!"

The ayah tried to comfort him. Like the rest of his servants she adored Captain Gaythorne.

"See! the Memsahib is not really hurt. She is opening her eyes."

"Then I must be off." And before the dark eyes had time to unclose themselves, he was out of the room and out of the house.

At first he did not know where to go. He fairly reeled with misery. He had assaulted his own wife—had ill-treated her so that he had reduced her to unconscious-ness; and he felt that the shame of this would kill him. He was a branded man—he had disgraced himself and his manhood—and he felt he would never lift up his head again. That he had attacked Fabia in ignorance was not of much comfort to him, for it was his own unfounded suspicion of her that had brought him to this pass. If he had never doubted her, this terrible thing would not have happened. The hideous fact remained; he had knocked down a woman, and that woman his own wife—the woman whom he had sworn to love and to cherish: and nothing else mattered. He had done the one thing which he could never forgive any man for doing, and he could never forgive himself. He was a blackguard and a coward, and he deserved to be drummed out of his regiment: there was no palliation of such an offence as his—no excuse for such dastardly conduct.

Such were poor Charlie's meditations.

He never attempted to make any excuse for himself; excuses were not in Charlie's way. He had done a shameful thing and he must abide by the consequences: that was the beginning and the end of it.

Of course he should never see Fabia again: she would not— nor would any woman in like circumstances —be able to endure the sight of such a brute as he had proved himself to be. No; she and his mother must continue to reign at Gaythorne, and he must go away and hide himself as best he could. There was no place in decent society for such as he!

He did not know where to go—what to do: and half-unconsciously his steps led him across to Prince's Gardens. People in trouble instinctively turned to Isabel: her common-sense and cheerful disposition made her a veritable tower of strength to storm-tossed souls: and Charlie felt that if anyone could help him in this terrible strait, it was Isabel Seaton. Naturally he clung to his mother for comfort: but even the filial Charlie could not but see that Isabel was far more of a woman of the world than was Mrs. Gaythorne, and therefore more competent to advise him what to do in a matter of this kind.

So he went straight to Isabel, and fortunately found her at home; and he told her the whole story, extenu-ating nothing with regard to his own conduct, nor setting down aught in malice with regard to Fabia's. Isabel was one of the rare women who can not only talk cleverly but can also listen cleverly; and therefore she heard Charlie's tale to the end in silence, her expressive face alive with sympathy. One of her many gifts was that she could always put herself in another's place and see a thing from another's point of view: it is an attribute never lacking in dramatic temperaments, and an attribute which perhaps more than any other enables its possessor to attain to that universal comprehension which involves universal pardon. Therefore she understood both Charlie and Fabia's position in the present crisis, and sympathized with both accordingly.

When Charlie had finished his recital, Isabel did not say much: she knew he had come to talk and not to listen: and he then confided to her his intention to banish himself from his beloved home for ever, and to leave his insulted and outraged wife to reign there undisturbed in his stead. It was his old mistake: he set himself to do the thing that would best please his wife, without first setting about to discover what that thing was.

But Isabel did not fall into this error: she was considerably older than Charlie, and moreover a woman; and she made up her mind that Fabia herself should have a voice in pronouncing sentence upon her own husband.

"The only bright spot in the whole ghastly concern is that it is I who have come a cropper, and not Fabia. I'd a million times sooner know myself for the confounded cad I am, than that there should be the shadow of a reproach against her. She is all right, bless her! as I might have known from the beginning, if I hadn't let my infernal jealousy make such a besotted ass of me. But I was a suspicious fool, not fit to black her boots, and I deserve all the misery that I shall get."

And poor Charlie looked out of the window so that— as he imagined—Isabel should not see the tears that stood in his honest blue eyes.

Isabel remembered Browning's lines—

"Would it were I had been false—not you;
I that am nothing, not you that are all."

And she felt that the man in the poem would agree with Captain Gaythorne that in this case the worst had not happened.

Her voice was very gentle as she said: "Poor boy! Things have gone crooked, haven't they? Now what can I do to set then straight again?"

She knew perfectly well what she was going to do; but she thought it much better that the suggestion should come from Charlie himself. Wise women rarely make valuable suggestions: they guide men into making them, and then they carry them out. It is the surest—in fact the only—way of avoiding masculine opposition. If they are very wise women indeed, they begin with a slight demur: this not only ensures the carrying out of the suggestion on the part of the man concerned—it ensures its being carried out with enthusiasm.

"That's just what I'm coming to," replied Charlie.

But he did not come at once: it took him all his time just then to avoid what Wolsey would have called "playing the woman," but what Charlie himself would have described as "making a blooming ass of himself."

The wily Isabel thought aloud. "I wonder how Fabia is now."

"That's what I'm coming to," repeated Charlie: and this time he came. "I want you to be so awfully good as to take a hansom at once and run round and just see how she is, and how badly the poor darling is knocked about. I should be so tremendously grateful if you would! And then you can just tell her that she need never see me again, for I'm not fit for it."

And once again the big tears hung on Charlie's golden eyelashes.

"Of course, my dear Charlie, she'll be very angry at first: you can't wonder at that; but I don't believe she will prove as implacable as you seem to imagine. She'll get over it. You see, you didn't mean to knock her down."

"But I did it. I can't get over that, and she won't either.

Simple natures look always at results; complex natures at motives: therefore Charlie's point of view was diametrically opposed to Isabel's.

"Well, all I know is, that if Paul knocked me down, imagining all the time that I was someone else who wanted knocking down, badly, I should get over it."

"Because you're fond of Seaton; and Fabia has never been fond of me. It makes all the difference, don't you see, whether you are fond of a fellow or not? There's nothing that a woman won't forgive if she is: and precious little that she will if she isn't."

Isabel's heart overflowed with pity for the big man looking out of the window. He seemed such a boy, after all, and such an unhappy boy.

"Well, Charlie," she said cheerfully, getting up from her chair, "ring the bell and tell Perkins to whistle me a hansom, while I go and put on my hat; and i'll run round to Fabia at once and see how she is. And mind—if I do this for you—you must promise me in return to stay here till I come back."

There was a despairing look on the boyish face that made Isabel afraid the poor fellow might do something desperate.

"I promise," he said simply. And she knew that he was incapable of breaking his word. "But tell her," he continued, "that if after what has happened she'd rather I was dead, I'll go abroad and shoot myself where it would never be spotted or found out. She's but to give the word. See?"

"I see; and I'll give you her message."

As soon as Isabel had gone, and there was no need to keep up any longer, Charlie sat down on the sofa and sobbed like a child. He cried as he had not cried since his father's death: for there seemed the same upheaval of all known laws—the same awful transition of the ordinary and familiar things of life into some dread and horrible nightmare—now as then. And now as then poor Charlie felt that he should never be happy again.

Fabia meanwhile was undergoing a new and strange experience.

She was not long in recovering from the shock of Charlie's assault upon her, as he had not had time really to hurt her before she fell unconscious at his feet, and in so doing revealed her identity: but although she was physically none the worse for this unparalleled incident, she was mentally completely changed thereby.

As she gradually grasped what had happened, and re-enacted the scene in her own mind again and again, her feelings for her husband underwent a total revolution. When she saw him towering above her in his righteous indignation, and literally trembled at his wrath, she realized for the first time that this man was her master: she understood at last that what she had mistaken for the cowardice of a weak man was in reality the patience of a strong one—that what she had despised as a sign of vacillating feebleness, was really the outcome of infinite self-control. Her husband had not endured and condoned her insolence and ill-temper because he had not the power to control her: but because he had the power to control himself.

As with her usual quickness Fabia comprehended how totally she had misunderstood and misinterpreted

Charlie's dealings with her, her emotional as well as her mental attitude towards him changed. She had scorned the man whom she believed to be her slave; but her spirit humbled itself in the dust before him whom she recognized as her master. As she had fallen in love with Gabriel when he showed himself morally stronger than she, so now she fell in love with Charlie because he had shown himself physically stronger than she : and she fell in love all the more deeply this time, because she was one of those to whom the material world is ever more present than the spiritual. And Charlie had not only showed himself her superior as regards mere brute force: there had been a look in his eye when he imagined that he was dealing direct with Dr. Mukharji, before which a braver man than Ram Chandar would have quailed: much less a highly-strung woman such as Fabia.

Herein she showed her Oriental blood and training. An English woman would have resented the outrage to her feminine dignity, even if she did homage to the virile strength which prompted it : but Fabia belonged to a race whose women had long lived in slavery, hugging their chains: and when she recognized her lord and master, she fell at his feet and owned his authority, loving him all the more in that he had used her roughly and treated her with contempt. As long as her husband placed the sceptre in her hands, she merely belaboured him with it ; but as soon as he took his rightful place and invested himself with the insignia of his own sovereignty, there was no more humble and devoted subject to be found in the whole realm of matrimony than she.

Her soul had long ago been crying out for its master, and had only so far found its mate: now that at last it

had discovered its rightful lord, it was ready to fold its
tired wings in the shelter of his strong arms, and there
to make its permanent resting-place.

When Isabel arrived at the rooms in Mount Street,
the ayah ushered her at once into Fabia's presence.
The latter was lying on a sofa looking rather pale and
shaken, but otherwise none the worse for what had
happened. For a second or two Isabel stood looking
at her; and then simultaneously the two women burst
out laughing.

"It was a magnificent hoax, Fabia!" cried Isabel, as
soon as she could speak; "simply magnificent! I
wouldn't have believed that any woman could have
taken in half London so completely!"

"I think it was cleverly done."

"Clever? It was marvellous! And do you mean to
say that Ram Chandar never came to England at all?"

"Never. I wanted him to do so, but he refused.
And then I thought what fun it would be to personate
him and perform some of the tricks which he had
taught me. And it was fun! Glorious fun!"

"I can believe it! It must have been simply killing
to hear all those women's secrets and give them advice.
I should have adored doing it!"

"I did."

"But what made you begin in the first instance?"
Isabel asked.

"Dulness—dulness, pure and simple. I was so bored
that I felt I must do something to amuse myself or else
I should go mad: and this seemed a fairly harmless and
yet absorbing pastime."

"It was brilliantly contrived and carried out."

"It was quite simple. Saidie took the rooms for me,
and I dressed up in native dress and a false black wig

and beard. You see I have the sole control of all my own fortune: Charlie always refuses to touch a penny of it, or to know how I spend it: and with plenty of money at one's command, everything is easy."

The mention of Charlie recalled to Isabel the purport of her errand.

"That reminds me I have come to you with a message from Charlie. He is simply wild with anxiety to know how much you are hurt."

"He need not be. There are some bruises on my throat, but that is all. I am quite right again now; the faintness soon passed off."

"Fabia, I have come to plead with you for him. He is so mad with horror at having knocked you down that he proposes never to see you again: he thinks he isn't fit; and he is full of a wild scheme of disappearing altogether, and leaving Gaythorne to you and his mother. He even says he will go quietly away and shoot himself if you'd rather he was dead. But, oh, Fabia! won't you forgive him? He did not know what he was doing, and he is so broken-hearted about it." And there were tears in Isabel's eyes.

Fabia looked puzzled: "Forgive him? What have I to forgive?"

"Forgive him for having knocked you down and hurt you," Isabel explained. "And after all, as I said to him, he didn't know it was you."

"What if he had known? I am his wife."

It was now Isabel's turn to look puzzled. "I don't see what that has to do with it."

"Don't you? To me it seems to have everything to do with it. Surely a man has the right to do what he will with his own."

Isabel gasped. To her Western ideas this was heresy

indeed; but Fabia, the daughter of a long line of Eastern women, saw the matter in a different light. It was one of her inherited instincts—instincts which had come down to her through the purdah and the harem—that a husband is a lord and master, and a wife a chattel and a slave; and instinct is ever stronger than reason, especially in elemental natures.

"Then do you mean to say that you don't resent his having treated you like that? Oh, Fabia!"

"Resent it? No; a thousand times no! And more than that," added Fabia, sitting up in her eagerness, a soft light coming into her beautiful eyes, "it has changed my whole life; for it has made me fall in love with Charlie — fall in love with my own husband!"

"What do you mean?" Isabel was so interested that she could hardly speak.

"I mean that at last I see what a fool I have been, and that there isn't—and never was—any other man in the world but Charlie! Isabel, don't you understand? I used to despise him because he was so meek and gentle, and always let me have my own way and be as rude to him as I liked: and I believed it was because he was weak and feeble and not a real man. But I was a blind fool!" The usually deliberate Fabia was now so excited that she could not get out her words fast enough: they tumbled one over the other. "But when he thought I was a man, and a man that he hated, he treated me as he treats other men, and I recognized him for the man he is. Oh, you should have seen him when he said he was going to thrash me: he looked simply splendid!"

"I never heard of such a thing in my life!"

Isabel was still well-nigh speechless. This Oriental

attitude of mind was a thing as yet undreamed of in her philosophy.

Fabia went on:

"When I saw him look like that, I loved him—loved him with all my heart and soul and strength. And when he took hold of me, and I felt like a reed in his grasp, I simply worshipped him. I thought he was going to kill me, and that made me adore him all the more. I shouldn't have cared if he had: it would have been a splendid death to be killed by his hand!"

Isabel continued to gasp from sheer amazement: this new Fabia was a revelation to her. Mrs. Seaton was Occidental to her finger tips; and the idea of being slain by Paul's hand did not appeal to her in the very least.

"Now I know what he looks like in a battle," continued Fabia; "now I know why his men are afraid of him! He is a splendid hero, and I have been treating him as if he were a stupid child. What a fool—what an arrant fool—I have been!"

By this time it occurred to Isabel that it might be well for the hero to learn the surprising results of his prowess. She judged—and judged rightly—that he would be, if possible, more astonished and certainly more delighted than she herself.

"Fabia, I'm going to fetch him," she cried, springing to her feet.

Fabia caught her dress:

"No, no: he will never forgive me. I'm not fit that he should ever speak to me again after the way I have treated him. Why, I used to jeer at him and flout him, and all the while I was not fit to black his boots!"

Isabel burst out laughing. It was very funny to hear Fabia speaking of Charlie in so much the same terms as he had spoken of her,

"Well, as you say you aren't fit to black his boots, and as he has just told me that he isn't fit to black yours, I should advise you both to go in for brown boots in the future, if you want them well cleaned!" And then she hurried back to the waiting Charlie.

He started up as she came into the room.

"How is she? What did she say? Can she ever forgive me?" His questions followed each other in rapid succession, never waiting for an answer.

"It's all right," replied Isabel, as if she were speaking to an unhappy child. "There's nothing to worry about."

"She isn't badly hurt?"

"She isn't hurt at all. And, oh! Charlie, the most killing thing has happened. She has fallen in love with you!"

Charlie looked dazed.

"Fallen in love with me after I've been such a brute to her? What in heaven's name do you mean?"

"I mean exactly what I say."

And then Isabel told him, as briefly as she could, of the unexpected turn that things had taken.

As she had anticipated, he was as much astonished as she had been; in fact this good news—following so closely on his recent despair—was almost too much for him. But he quickly pulled himself together like the man he was.

"By Jove, this beats cock-fighting!" was all that he could say at first; and he said it several times. Then, as the effects of the shock gradually subsided, he announced his intention of going with all possible speed to his newly-reconciled wife.

"Go at once," replied Isabel, who was nothing if not practical. "I kept my hansom, as I knew you'd want one in a hurry."

"Mrs. Seaton, you're a brick!" cried Charlie, grasping her hand till the rings cut into her fingers, and almost made her scream.

"But look here, Charlie," she added, laying her uninjured hand upon his arm, "don't go and make the old mistake over again. You have won Fabia's love by showing her that you are her master; now don't go and throw it away again by behaving like her slave."

"But I can't behave like a brute to the poor darling!"

"Yes, you can: like a nice brute. The long and the short of it is, Charlie, that you've been much too meek: women don't like meekness—especially Eastern women; they spell it 'with a 'w,' and despise it. Remember the husband is the head of the wife, and must behave himself accordingly."

"Is he?" Charlie looked doubtful.

"So the Bible tells us."

Does it, by Jove? Well, there's no getting round the Bible, is there?"

"Certainly not."

"I've always had a sort of notion that it was the other way on—that the wife was the head of the husband. But I suppose I was up a wrong street."

"You were: an absolutely wrong one," replied Isabel firmly. But considering that his own mother had been the living epistle known and read of Charlie, she felt that she could not altogether blame him for this misinterpretation of revealed truth.

"Well, I'll try and get the right hang of the thing this time," cried Charlie, as he escaped from Isabel and sprang into the cab.

Both he and Fabia were solely exercised as to what they should first say to each other: they composed

reams of pretty confessions which never saw the light.
But when the moment came they said nothing at all,
but just flew into each other's arms, and blotted out
all their past misunderstanding and misery with kisses.
As a patent past-eraser there is nothing equal to a kiss:
it will remove every stain, and make things generally as
good as new. Some people endeavour to erase things
by means of explanations; but these are not a success:
they nearly always leave a larger mark than the
orginal one, as benzene often does. But kisses rarely
if ever fail: they clear away everything: provided, of
course, that the genuine article is used, and not a
counterfeit. And the genuine article comes straight
from the heart.

CHAPTER XXIII

A SECOND GABRIEL

JUST at first Charlie was sorely tempted to fall into his old mistake of making himself into a door-mat for Fabia to walk upon, and thus once more upsetting the apple-cart which had so recently regained its equilibrium; but, supported by Isabel's constant encouragement, he nobly struggled against the old man that was in him, and bravely endeavoured to put on the new man of whom he himself so heartily disapproved. And his efforts were amply rewarded by his wife's increasing devotion to him. As she said one day to Isabel: "When he looks particularly adoring, with that old dog-like expression of abject devotion, I just shut my eyes, and see his face as it appeared that day in Mount Street: and then I worship him more than ever."

She kept the riding-whip as a sacred treasure, and fondled it at intervals: the humour of which arrangement strongly appealed to Mrs. Seaton.

" I think it is perfectly fascinating of you to cherish a horsewhip as a relic," she remarked : " it is so much more original than flowers and letters and ordinary rubbishy things of that kind. I've got hidden away somewhere—goodness knows where !—a spray of roses and maiden-hair that Paul once gave me before we were engaged : and now the roses look like scraps of worn-out boot-leather, and the fern like dried essence of mint-sauce. But a horsewhip never grows old! It will be as fresh a hundred years hence as it is to-day —and as full of meaning."

Fabia laughed. "Yes; the meaning is fairly obvious."

"That's one of the beauties of it. Flowers want such a lot of letter-press to explain there special fragrance. Ben Jonson had to write a whole song to expound to the uninitiated that his rosy wreath smelt 'not of itself but thee': and my aforesaid rosy wreath smells neither of myself nor of Paul, but of decayed vegetation. But a horsewhip requires no explanation: it smells of leather and speaks for itself: and he who runs may read, as may also he who runs away."

"You would not have liked a whip as a relic, Isabel: you know you would not. It would be to you a symbol of all that you most disliked in a husband."

Isabel sighed:

"Perhaps not; but I wish I'd something more interesting to treasure up than dried herbage: and I don't even know where that is! It is so fearfully commonplace to express love by means of roses, and so original to express it by means of a horsewhip!"

"Not so original among the lower classes, I fancy."

"Perhaps not. But the whole heart of the great middle-class offers itself to its respective young women by the token of roses and maiden-hair: and it is the love of the great middle-class that is so respectable and so dull!"

"But, my dear Isabel, I thought that you prided yourself upon belonging to the great middle-class; and upon being absolutely normal and commonplace."

There was a mischievous gleam in Fabia's eyes as she spoke.

"Oh! I forgot: so I do. I'm glad you reminded me of it. To tell the truth it is one of my favourite poses." It was one of Isabel's many virtues that she was always ready to laugh at herself. "Now I come to think of it, I'm very pleased that the romance of my life is enbalmed in the absolutely ordinary and normal form of a spray of roses and maiden-hair: and I shall set about finding it at once, and treasuring it accordingly; though I can't for the life of me remember where I've put it."

Fabia was right: the submission which was delightful to her was difficult to Isabel. The Eastern nature loved to submit: the Western nature found it hard to do so. Yet both did it in the spirit, if Isabel sometimes failed in the letter: and each in her own way fulfilled the apostolic injunction.

And now Fabia no longer grumbled at the length of Charlie's anecdotes: on the contrary, she listened from beginning to end, laughing and applauding at the right moments, as a good wife should. Even in the story of Mrs. Gaythorne and the harvest-thanksgiving, she murmured responses of the correct sort at the correct places, never omitting one. It is always amusing, as well as profitable, to see a wifely wife listening to her husband's stock anecdotes: the recital becomes a sort of litany, wherein he takes the part of the parson and she that of the parish clerk. He pauses for her responses, and she utters them almost before he has time to pause, and thus gives the lead to the rest of the congregation. She is not too enthusiastic — not too much surprised or too much amused: that she leaves for those of the audience (if there be any such) who

have never heard the tale before. She does not laugh
herself: she merely shows others when to laugh. In
short, she uses a mental tuning-fork, and starts the
tune for the others to sing: and she generally affords
the same official support to the reciter of the anecdote
as the clerk affords to his parish priest.

At the end of July the Gaythornes duly migrated to
their country house; and there found Mrs. Carr and her
daughter-in-law pursuing the even tenor of their way
uncheered by any news of Gabriel. It seemed, indeed,
as if the lost Rector were blotted out of existence: and
as if that passing glimpse in the Parisian theatre were
the last that would ever be seen of him by those who
had known him in his former state of existence.

Janet was very calm, very resigned; and her love
for her husband stood the test of time and of absence,
remaining as firm and devoted as ever. She carried
the art of perfect wifehood to a point not attained by
Fabia or by Isabel. They loved and honoured and
obeyed men who would only be obeyed in spite of
themselves; men who freely and chivalrously offered
the submission and devotion which they had the right
to demand: men who in spite of (or, rather, perhaps on
account of) their divine right of kingship, always
rendered to the consort the special honour and the
higher place. The theory of wifely submission might
be naturally acceptable to Fabia and naturally
unacceptable to Isabel: they approached the question
from the opposite sides of two hemispheres: but the
practice of the thing was simply child's play where such
men as Paul Seaton and Charlie Gaythorne were
concerned.

But with poor Janet it was different. She had sworn
allegiance to a monarch who had vacated his throne as

soon as he had the right to occupy it: she owed her submission to a king who had flung away his crown the moment after it was placed upon his brow. Yet her fealty remained unaltered, her loyalty unchanged. She was married to a husband who had apparently repudiated her without the slightest reason for so doing; and yet her wifely devotion was as deep and absorbing as it had been on her marriage day. She was prepared, should Gabriel return to her, to welcome him back as if nothing had happened, and to love and to cherish him as tenderly as ever, asking no questions and uttering no reproaches: and, should he never return to her, to mourn for him all the days of her life, and to go down to the grave, honouring and respecting his memory.

And then it came to pass that a great change came o'er the spirit of Janet's dream. For her there was a new heaven and a new earth, so new and so wonderful that for a time sorrow and sighing fled away, and her former miseries were forgotten. In the middle of August her baby was born, and she touched the high-water mark of human happiness, and entered into the earthly paradise: that paradise which was opened to Woman after her banishment from Eden, and the gates whereof have never yet been closed. True, those gates are still guarded by the twin cherubim, Sorrow and Suffering, whose fiery swords pierce to the very bones and marrow: but they are not impregnable: and those blessed among women who win through those fiery barriers and reach the other side, find themselves resting at the foot of the tree of life which grows in the very midst of the paradise of God.

To Janet's delight, the baby was a boy: and her mother-in-law shared her joy; for Mrs. Carr was one

of the people who consider that the world was made
for men only, and that girls and women are merely
padding. To bear a son, was in Mrs. Carr's mind, the
height of feminine honour and glory : to bear a daughter,
only one degree more creditable than being an old maid.
It is not an uncommon type ; and it came to perfection
in the early Victorian age.

Mrs. Gaythorne was as early-Victorian as Mrs. Carr ;
but in this respect the two ladies fundamentally differed.
It was the grief of Mrs. Gaythorne's life that she had
never had a daughter to train up in the way that she
herself had so ably and so firmly trod : and she had
abundant sympathy with the regret which the immortal
aunt of David Copperfield summed up in the expression,
"Your sister, Betsy Trotwood." Even now Mrs. Gaythorne's maternal mind bristled with devices whereby
Charlie's sister—if he had ever had one—might have
benefited the human race. A son was all very well,
she admitted : he could fight for his country, and he
could follow in his father's footsteps and step into his
father's shoes : but he could neither conduct a Mother's
Meeting nor regulate a Ladies' Needlework Guild, and
it was no use pretending that he could. Yet duties
such as these might—and probably would—have been
ably fulfilled by his sister, if only he had had one :
therefore Mrs. Gaythorne never ceased to regret the
absence of that amiable and efficient young lady.

Thus it followed that Mrs. Gaythorne seriously
objected to the sex of Janet's baby ; and was the more
deeply rooted in this objection—which she experienced
more or less towards every mother's son whose advent
was chronicled in the first column of the *Times*—by
the peculiar circumstances of the case. In the first
place, she argued in her own mind, it was far more

difficult for a woman to bring up a son than a daughter without her husband's help; and in the second, another Gabriel Carr did not seem likely to make for the comfort of those concerned in him, judging from his father's recent example.

But Janet's happiness was complete. God had given to her the desire of her heart—a son to fill Gabriel's place and to take Gabriel's name—and so she was content. Of course she could not fail now and again to be overpowered with longing for her husband to share this new bliss with her: but she was one of those rare people who really and truly have faith in God.

The majority of us believe in Him more or less: so do the devils who believe and tremble: but how many of us believe in Him as the great Controller of all things —without Whom not even a sparrow can fall to the ground, and yet Who calleth the stars by their names that not one faileth? How many of us actually hold fast the truth that our times are in His Hands, and that nothing can happen to us save what is ordained and permitted by Him? If we really believed this, what would become of all that worry and anxiety which burden our hearts and line our faces? Where would be our despair for the present or our doubt for the future? If we believed with our hearts what we profess with our lips, that all things work together for good to them that love Him, according to His promise, we should mount up with wings as eagles and should walk and not faint. But we do not really believe it. Every foreboding for the future, every doubt, every fear, are so many contradictions of His Word, so many slurs upon His faithfulness. And thus by our own limitations we limit the power of God; and He cannot do many mighty works among us because of our unbelief.

But Janet Carr was so rooted and grounded in the faith that all things are made by Him, and without Him was not anything made that was made, that she accepted all the orderings of her life as direct from Him, and therefore never chafed nor rebelled. She was as certain that the cloud which had darkened her life had been sent by God, as she was certain that the birds and the flowers were the works of His Hands: and she knew that all things were working together for her good, however hard it might be just now to understand their why and their wherefore.

There was much consultation and discussion over the baby's name, the fact that his mother had already settled it in no way interfering with the full expression of Mrs. Gaythorne's views upon the subject.

"If only it had been a girl," she remarked, as she and Mrs. Carr were sitting by Janet's sofa, "it might have been called after Me." As usual she used the capital letter in speaking of herself. "I approve of children being named after their god-parents."

Janet had already asked Mrs. Gaythorne to act as god-mother: that lady seemed so admirably fitted to renounce the devil and all his works on behalf of anybody or everybody.

"So it might," agreed Janet: "but being a boy there are difficulties in the way. I never heard of a boy's being christened Eliza."

"Neither did I, my dear; nor should I approve of such a thing. I do not like boys to be christened by girls' names; it savours of Popery. There is nothing that shocks me more than to hear of Roman Catholic kings being called ' Joseph Mary,' and mixed names like that."

"No," replied Janet demurely · "I agree with you that Eliza is not a suitable name for a boy. I don't remember ever hearing of even a Roman Catholic king's being christened Eliza."

"I do not recall one myself at the present moment: but I daresay there are plenty if we only knew. Romanists are capable of anything."

Here Mrs. Carr joined in:

"Still, dear Mrs. Gaythorne, I always considered Eliza quite a Protestant name—so suggestive of good Queen Bess and the Electress Sophia of Hanover and people of that kind; and I almost think that Martin Luther's wife was called Elisabeth if it wasn't Catherine, and there is nothing at all Romanizing in the poetry of Eliza Cooke."

Mrs. Gaythorne was pleased at this complimentary reference to the name given to her by her godfather and godmothers in her baptism.

"Yes; I think there is a good Protestant sound about Eliza, and I thank Heaven for it! I should not have liked to bear a Popish-sounding name. That is my only objection to Mary; to my mind it savours somewhat of Roman Catholicism, even when applied to a woman."

"Oh! no, no, no, dear Mrs. Gaythorne; pray do not say that," Mrs. Carr expostulated.

"I must say it if I think it."

Janet failed to see this necessity; but to Mrs. Gaythorne it was paramount.

"Mary is the most beautiful name in the world," continued Mrs. Carr; "I remember learning a poem when I was a girl, which began, 'In Christian world Mary the something wears'; I forget exactly what it was that she wore, but I know it meant that Mary is the most beautiful name in the world except Edith; and I really don't think it sounds at all Popish unless you put the prefix Bloody before it; I don't indeed, dear Mrs. Gaythorne."

Janet was not yet very strong, so she utterly failed to conceal her amusement.

"I don't remember ever to have heard of a child's being christened Bloody Mary," she remarked.

"Excepting the queen of that name," emended Mrs. Gaythorne.

"I don't think that even she was christened anything but Mary. I fancy the other name was an accretion."

"Janet Carr, do not attempt to teach me history. Bloody Mary was her name and Bloody Mary was her nature; from my earliest childhood I have never called her by any other name, and I never shall."

This was conclusive, so Janet wisely dropped the subject.

"If I had had a daughter," remarked Mrs. Carr, "I should have called her Margaret after poor dear Aunt Susan."

"I do not quite see that, Eveline. How could you call her Margaret after a woman who was named Susan?"

"Because poor dear Aunt Susan's name was Susan Margaret, and Margaret is so much the prettier name of the two, and I think it is so much nicer for a girl to have a pretty name than an ugly one, if it is all the same to everybody and the relations equally pleased. I think Margaret is a sweet name in itself, and Madge or Maggie so nice for her own family and intimate friends, and not quite so stiff and stately, being shorter for everyday use."

"If I had been so blessed as to have a daughter," said Mrs. Gaythorne, "I should have called her Maria after my eldest sister."

"But you said that it sounded Popish, Mrs. Gaythorne." Janet could not resist this temptation.

"I said nothing of the kind, Janet Carr. I said that Mary did."

"But they are the same name."

"Janet Carr, you are talking nonsense. You might as well say that Eliza and Elizabeth are the same name."

"So they are."

"They cannot be; because I was christened Eliza after Lady Summerhill, and my youngest sister was christened Elizabeth after Aunt Elizabeth Latimer; and our parents could not possibly have called two children by the same name. Besides, Lady Summerhill and Aunt Elizabeth Latimer were totally different people, in no way resembling each other."

This again was conclusive; so Janet once more wisely turned to a side issue.

"Well, for my part, I don't see that Maria sounds any more Protestant than Mary."

"It does; my second sister was named Maria."

This was the most conclusive of all. Janet felt that to go on arguing in the face of this statement was beating the air; so she desisted.

"And she was named Maria," added Mrs. Gaythorne, by way of further proof of the good sound, Protestant tendencies of the name (as if any further proof were needed!), "after Aunt Maria Latimer, who always lived in the near vicinity of our birthplace."

It was on the tip of Janet's tongue to ask where that was; but she checked herself. It seemed such a proof of historical ignorance not to know Mrs. Gaythorne's birthplace.

"But we are wandering from Janet's point," Mrs. Gaythorne went on. "The question to be now considered is, what are we to call Janet's baby?"

"He will be called Gabriel after his father," said Janet.

She spoke very quietly, but the two who listened realized that the matter was settled, and that further discussion was useless. So Mrs. Gaythorne dropped the subject. She knew her match—and, what is more, she respected her match—when she met it.

The weeks rolled on; and each day led to the discovery of fresh perfections in the baby Gabriel. No one who has not watched the growth of a little child has any idea of the wonderful developments which are new every morning, nor of the absorbing interest which such developments excite in the loving mind of the onlooker. There is no interest more absorbing—few as much so: yet it is the fashion nowadays to scoff at the delights of the baby-world, and to pretend that modern women need wider fields of thought and occupation than the house and the nursery afford. Let the modern women scoff if they will! But let them also remember that if they would have a foretaste of the millennium here and now, they must put away from them for a time all the cares of this world and the deceitfulness of its riches, and must slip aside into that magic fairyland which lies around all of us in our infancy, but of which, alas! we soon lose the key, so that we can go in and out by ourselves no more. And they cannot do this unless a little child shall lead them.

It was a bitterly cold evening, early in the new year.

Mrs. Carr had gone to visit some friends in the neighbourhood of her own home, leaving Janet to the uninterrupted society of her baby: and Janet was happy in the new bliss that had come to her, although sometimes her longing for her husband seemed almost more than she could bear. But she had learnt to possess her soul in patience, and to wait upon the Lord: and therefore—as is the case with all those who have thus learnt to wait—He inclined unto her and heard her calling.

Suddenly the front-door bell rang: and as one servant was upstairs and the other was out, Janet laid her baby down on the drawing-room sofa and went to open the door herself. She thought it could not be anybody but Mrs. Gaythorne or Fabia at this late hour of the day; and she did not want to keep either of them standing out in the cold.

But it was neither the one nor the other.

On the door-step stood a tall man dressed in a light suit of clothes, over which he wore a somewhat flashy green top-coat with a velvet collar: the sort of costume that would be worn by a fifth-rate actor or a member of the swell-mob. Janet was a short woman, and the hall at the Rectory was but poorly lighted; so that she saw the stranger's clothes before she saw his face, which was in the shadow. But as he stepped forward and the dim light from the hall-lamp fell upon him, what was her incredible joy and gladness to recognize in this showily-dressed stranger her husband, Gabriel Carr !

CHAPTER XXIV

THE FIVE DOTS

WITH a cry of delight Janet flung herself into her husband's arms, and the two clung to each other for a few seconds in the inarticulate joy of re-union: then she drew Gabriel into the house, shutting the door behind him, and gazed earnestly into his face.

Her first thought was that they had lied to her when they told her that sin and shame had written their story upon his features. There was not a word of truth in such a statement. He looked older, perhaps; but his face was more spiritual and saintly than ever.

Her next thought was how much better in health he looked than when they parted; he had lost all signs of delicacy, and appeared strong and well and in good condition.

Then all thoughts were swallowed up in the ecstasy of seeing him face to face, and feeling his dear arms round her once more. It was only now that the misery of it was suddenly relaxed that Janet realized all the agony she had undergone since Gabriel's disappearance: it was only in the revulsion back to joy, that she knew how terrible the bygone pain had been. For a time her whole being was merged in the torrent of overwhelming happiness which swept over her soul. Wherever Gabriel had been, he was now at home again: whatever he had done, he was still her husband, bound to her by an indissoluble tie which could never be broken.

For what seemed an eternity of bliss the two married lovers remained locked in each other's arms, murmuring meanwhile passionate and inarticulate expressions of tenderness and endearment. The first to speak was Janet.

"Oh! my love, my love," she whispered, "it is heaven on earth to have you back again!"

"My dearest, think what it must be to me to come back!" Gabriel replied, covering her face and hands and neck with kisses.

"Dear heart, where have you been this long time?" Janet went on, when her husband allowed her once more to speak. "Life has been dark and hard indeed without you!"

Gabriel's eyes filled with tears as he looked into her face and saw the lines that sorrow had engraved there.

"My poor little girl, what a brute you must think I have been!"

Janet started back, and put her hand over his mouth:

"No, no, Gabriel: I have never thought you that. Although God knows it has been hard to bear, He also knows that I have never once doubted you, nor imagined for a moment that you were in any way to blame. My confidence in you is as firm and unshaken as it ever was. See, my beloved, I will prove it to you by never again asking you any questions as to your absence: as long as you tell me that you have been well and happy, I am content."

"My own darling wife!"

"It isn't that I don't wonder where you have been,

and why you didn't come back to me before," continued Janet; "I have done nothing but wonder that all the time. But if for any reason you would rather not tell me, don't. Remember nothing that you say or leave unsaid will ever make any difference in my love to you."

Gabriel's only answer was another passionate embrace: and then Janet said: "Come into the drawing-room, love, and see baby; and I will get you something to eat."

Even Gabriel, well as he thought he knew her, was astonished at her absolute trust and confidence. Was there another woman in England, he wondered, who in such circumstances would not have insisted upon knowing where her husband had been, and what he had been doing, and why he had forsaken her? He had not found so great faith as this in all his life before.

And when she laid their baby in his arms it was just the same. She gave up the child absolutely into his keeping, without asking why he had left her house unto her desolate until that child was born.

"But, my dear love, you *must* hear why I went away and why I could not come back before," he said, after he had kissed and blessed the boy.

"Not unless you wish to tell me," she repeated. "It is enough for me that the dead is alive again and the lost is found."

And once more he marvelled at the perfection of her faith and love.

But after he had had food and drink, and was refreshed and strengthened, he told Janet his story. And she sat at his feet in the firelight, and tasted the full fruition of human bliss.

"After I left you that day in the inn," he began, "I

walked for a time over the moor; then the fog suddenly became so dense that I missed my way altogether, and when I tried to get back again I found that I had completely lost my bearings. Once or twice I found myself at the edge of deep pits or quarries, and was only just saved from falling over: so—after one or two experiences of this kind—I decided that it was unwise to wander about any more in the fog, and that I had better find some sheltered spot and stay there until the mist lifted."

Janet shuddered. " How terrible!" she murmured.

Gabriel continued :

" Then suddenly I found myself close to a shepherd's hut, and thought I would wait there until it was safe to go back to the inn. It was not yet dark, as it was still early in the afternoon, but the wall of white mist was impenetrable. So I entered the hut: and to my horror found that it was already tenanted—and tenanted by an escaped convict from Dartmoor prison. I knew him at once by his dress."

" Oh! Gabriel, whatever did you do ? "

" I did the best I could in the circumstances: I told him at once who I was and that I had lost my way ; and I begged him of his courtesy to allow me to share the hut with him."

" Was he very wicked-looking ? " Janet asked.

" No ; that is the strange part of the story. He was an exact counterpart of myself in appearance — the same age, the same height, the same colouring, the same features. He might have been my twin brother. I have since found out that he was a noted criminal of Italian extraction, by name Cæsar Costello: and that he was serving a five years' sentence for a burglary near

Exeter, rather more than a year of which sentence was yet to run."

"How very strange that he should have been so like you!" exclaimed Janet.

"Those accidental resemblances are always strange, my darling; but perhaps this one may be to some extent accounted for by the fact that both Costello and I have Italian blood in our veins; and in the two cases the same mixed nationalities have produced the same physical type."

"Yes, yes; now I begin to see how it all happened."

Gabriel continued his narrative:

"But the worst part is yet to come. To my further horror I found that the man was raving mad! At least so he appeared to be at the time; but I have since discovered that he feigned madness in order to suit his own purposes, and was really as sane as you or I—and a great deal cleverer!"

"What did he do?"

"He was silent at first, evidently maturing his plans, and seeing how he could make the most of the opportunity thus thrown in his way. And then suddenly he seized a carbine which he had with him—(he had seized it, I presume, from one of the warders in charge of the party, when he knocked him down and escaped)—and held it at my head, saying that he would shoot me if I would not grant a request he was about to make."

"And what was his request?" asked Janet, absorbed in the story.

"That he might tattoo me on the shoulder. It seemed a mad idea at the time—just the thing for a maniac to think of—but I have since seen how ingenious it was."

"So you submitted?"

"There was nothing else to be done. It seemed certainly preferable to be tattooed than to be shot: and it never occurred to me at the time that the man was anything but the dangerous lunatic he pretended to be: so I thought it my wisest plan to humour him."

"Certainly: you were entirely at his mercy, since he was armed and you were not." And Janet shuddered again at the thought of her husband's imminent peril.

"So he unloaded his carbine, took the gunpowder out of the cartridge, and—with the aid of the finest blade in my own pocket-knife, which he borrowed for the occasion—tattooed my shoulder with five small dots in the shape of a cross."

"Did it hurt?" Janet was always very woman.

"Only like five pin-pricks: it was done in a few seconds. He just pricked the skin and rubbed the gunpowder in. Then he laid down his weapon and became most affable, showing me a similar tattoo-mark on his own shoulder, and I—fool that I was!—congratulated myself upon having humoured his insane fancy so successfully. By that time it really was getting dark: and as soon as the darkness came on the man picked a quarrel with me, evidently in accordance with his rapidly-devised plan."

"What did he quarrel about, dearest?"

"I really cannot remember," Gabriel replied: "it was all so sudden. Before I knew where I was he was wrestling with me and we were fighting for dear life. And after that I remember no more, until I came to my right mind—many months afterwards—in the prison infirmary, after a severe attack of concussion of the brain: and found that I had unconsciously taken the place of the escaped convict."

Janet seized her husband's hand and covered it with kisses.

"Then did you tell them who you were, and explain everything?" she asked.

"Of course I did: but nobody believed me. They had found me lying unconscious at the bottom of a stone pit, close to the shepherd's hut with my head severely injured; and I wore the convict's outward appearance, and was dressed in the convict's clothes. Moreover, if further proof were needed of my identity with him, he was distinguished by a tattoo-mark upon his shoulder—five dots in the shape of a cross: and there on my shoulder was the selfsame mark: which, by the time that I was well enough to ask for confirmation as to who I was, had lost every sign of being recently done, and looked as if it had been there for years. How could they doubt that I was he?"

"Oh! Gabriel, they ought to have known better."

Gabriel smiled the old sweet smile that Janet knew so well. "I do not really see that they were to blame. All the evidence was on their side: and naturally they did not pay much heed to the statements of a man who had been off his head for several months. You see, I recovered physically from the effects of my fall, long before I did mentally. Besides my very hands testified against me; for, as you know, I have so roughened and coarsened them by working with the lads in my parish at carpentering and gardening and the rest, and by conducting the gymnasium for the benefit of the boys, that no one could take them for the hands of a gentleman. They looked as if the picking of oakum had been their wonted occupation."

"Then evidently the man escaped in your clothes; because you were supposed to have ridden to Newton

Abbot in a farmer's cart, and to have taken the train to London," said Janet.

"Was I? Then the man who went to Newton Abbot was Costello wearing my clothes. He must have knocked me senseless, and, while I was unconscious, have changed clothes with me. Then apparently he dragged me out of the hut, and threw me over the edge of a stone pit close at hand, not caring whether I was alive or dead. And then he escaped to London."

"It must have been he whom the Gaythornes saw in Paris." And then Janet related to Gabriel the Parisian incident. "Those are his clothes that you are wearing now, I suppose," she added : "the clothes that he wore when he was first taken into custody ? '

Gabriel looked down at himself with disgust :

"Yes; the prison authorities gave them to me this morning when I left off my convict dress. Are they not too terrible for words ? Costello certainly got the best of the bargain in the way of clothes." And he laughed softly.

"And you? — you served out the rest of his sentence ? "

"I served out the rest of his sentence, my dearest, with the additional punishment that his escape entailed : and God was with me all the time."

Thus the year which the locust had eaten was returned to Janet : and her husband came back to her alive and well. Although (or, perhaps, because) she was prepared to forgive everything, there was nothing for her to forgive: for it is the things which we cannot do that we are called upon to do in this life—not the things which we can. How often we notice that sickness is sent to those who lay unnecessary stress upon the advantage of bodily health, and poverty to those who set undue store upon the possession of riches; while such as exaggerate the happiness of human companionship are doomed to a solitary life, and such as crave inordinately for fame and distinction are condemned to ineffective obscurity.

There was great interest felt and expressed, not only in his immediate circle but all over England, in Gabriel Carr's return. His experience was so remarkable that it commanded universal attention. Of course there was sincere regret expressed in high and official quarters over what had happened, and an elaborate apology was sent from the Home Office. But official apologies, however handsome and well-clothed they may be, hardly compensate to an innocent man for the discomforts arising from false imprisonment. The State can do no wrong: and therefore, when it does, it is no easy matter to put matters right again.

But all things worked together for good to Gabriel Carr. The regular hours and plain fare, and the absence of all responsibility in his prison life, had done more for his overwrought nervous system than any so-called "rest cure" could have done: and Gabriel was once more a strong man.

But although he was restored to health and strength, the Rector of Gaythorne did not resign his country living and once more take upon himself the responsibility of a town parish: he gave all his spare time, of which he had plenty, to revival work: and conducted most successful missions all over England, which were crowned with abundant results. For he felt that in this way he accomplished more work and gained a wider spiritual influence than he would ever have done in one parish however large and populous.

So the Lord turned the captivity of Gabriel as the streams in the south, and blessed his latter end more than his beginning. And he accomplished that which he pleased, and prospered in the thing whereto he was sent: for God was with him.

CHAPTER XXV

CÆSAR COSTELLO

IT was about a year after Gabriel's return, and he was conducting a mission in one of the largest seaport towns in the north of England. As usual he set aside a portion of each morning and evening for seeing privately any who might wish to consult him upon spiritual matters, and giving them discreet and ghostly counsel: and great was his amazement late one night when who should be ushered into his sanctum but the quondam convict, Cæsar Costello !

Once again Gabriel was startled by the man's extraordinary resemblance to himself. And yet hardly to himself as he was, but rather to himself as he might have been, had he chosen evil instead of good, and walked in the broad path that leadeth to destruction rather than in the narrow way, the end whereof is everlasting life. There, but for the grace of God, stood Gabriel Carr—Gabriel Carr as he would have been had not the Master called him to be His disciple, and had he not heard the Master's Voice and followed Him whithersoever He went.

And as Gabriel looked closer he saw—with the trained eye of the priest, which is quick to pierce below the surface and read the hidden things of the heart—that Costello was not the same as when he

358

saw him that day in the shepherd's hut upon Dartmoor. Continued sin and vice and dissipation had ploughed fresh furrows and inscribed new lines upon the man's face. But there was something more than that. Out of the mud, wherein the sinner was wallowing, a pierced Hand had made clay and had anointed his eyelids; and whereas he had been blind, now he saw. Saw himself as God saw him, and regarded his sin as God regarded it: and the sight had well-nigh driven him mad.

In broken accents Costello told Gabriel his story. Told how he had been living in Paris upon ill-gotten gains ever since his escape from prison, draining the cup of illicit pleasure, to the dregs: and how he was then on his way to America, there to seek "fresh woods and pastures new," wherein he might pluck the fruits of sin and cultivate the flowers of vice. On his way to the docks he had passed the door of the hall where the Rector of Gaythorne was conducting his mission; and, having learnt from the notices outside the doors who the missioner was, Costello was compelled by curiosity to look in just to see once more the man who had stood in his place and had suffered in his stead.

And then through the mouth of the preacher God spoke to the sinner, and called him out of the darkness of ignorance into the marvellous light of spiritual knowledge. In that light Costello saw the hideousness of his own soul and his own sins, and cried to the mountains to cover him and the earth to swallow him, so that he might escape from the Presence of the living God. And he came to the man, who had been God's instrument in awakening him out of the sleep of sin to the awful consciousness of his own condition, in the hope that he might thereby find balm in Gilead, and a physician to minister to his spirit's sickness.

For long hours Gabriel talked and prayed with the stricken man. On the sinner's behalf he wrestled until the breaking of the day with One Who is ever mighty to save: and because the fervent prayer of a righteous man availeth much, he had power with God and prevailed.

After the men had risen from their knees, Costello's first thought was how he could make reparation for the sins he had committed: and he told Gabriel that he intended as soon as it was day to give himself up to the authorities so that they might send him back to Dartmoor, there to work out the rest of his sentence.

But Gabriel bade him forbear.

"I do not know if what I am going to say to you is according to the laws of man," he said, "but I believe it is according to the law of God; and I tell you not to give yourself up again to the authorities, nor to return to prison."

Costello was amazed: this had seemed the only course open to him. But he was ready now to subjugate his will and submit his judgment to the man who had shown him the way to the foot of the Cross.

"I will do whatever you bid me," he replied.

"Then listen! Now that you have repented of your sins and are ready and willing to give yourself up to justice, I cannot see that the completion of your time in prison can do you any good: and your soul's welfare is what I have most at heart."

Tears filled the criminal's eyes, and he could not speak. He was dumbfoundered by such generosity.

"I daresay I am all wrong according to the laws of England," Gabriel continued, with a smile; "but I believe that I am doing right according to the laws of Heaven. The end of repentance is the beginning of a

new life: and I have yet to be convinced that associa-
tion with other criminals will prove a salutary atmosphere
for that new life of yours in its present early and tender
stage. Besides surely I have paid the full price for
what I claim: I served fourteen months in Dartmoor
for it, and that was no light matter."

"But mayn't you get into trouble yourself by
screening me!" For the first time in his life Costello
put another's interest before his own. "Oughtn't you
to give me up to justice?"

"No; my conscience is quite clear on that score.
What I have heard from you has been told under the
seal of the confessional, and therefore I am bound not
to repeat a word of it. It would be against every
principle of my sacred profession and calling. All I
could do would be to induce a penitent to give himself
up to justice, if I thought that was the right thing to
do: but in this case I do not think so."

Costello broke down and sobbed aloud:

"Sir, your generosity is almost more than I can bear.
When I think of all you have endured for me and how
I have treated you, I feel I am unfit to live!"

Gabriel laid his hand upon the other's shoulder:

"Ah! now we are coming to the point of the whole
matter. If I give you the chance of starting a new life,
you must promise me that you will fulfil your part of
the bargain, and not go back to the old life again. That
would not be playing the game, you know; and if I
treat you well, I shall expect you to treat me well in
return. That is but fair, isn't it? Remember I shall
expect you to meet me half way." And Gabriel smiled
his whimsical smile.

The criminal fell on his knees before the priest, and
seizing his hand, kissed it.

"I will be your servant to my life's end," he cried: "whatever you tell me to do, I will do it."

"This is what I tell you to do: and though I speak of myself, I believe that I also have the Spirit of God. You shall go to America as you had arranged, and in the berth you have already taken: and when you land you shall go straight to a Missionary Training College, the head of which is a friend of mine, to whom I will give you a letter of introduction: and there you shall learn to serve Christ in the mission fields."

"And I swear that I will serve Him, so help me God!"

"You cannot stay, in England, you see," continued Gabriel; "if you do, the police will track you, and send you back to prison. And I cannot help believing that you can serve God better by carrying His Gospel to the far-off isles of the southern seas than by picking oakum in Dartmoor gaol. Besides," he added, with a humorous twinkle in his eye, "we have defrauded the Government of nothing in that line: I have picked your full share of oakum, so the authorities can have nothing to complain of: though I have no doubt they would complain a good deal if they only knew."

"Sir, I will follow your counsel to the end of my life. You shall never regret what you have done for me this night."

Gabriel's face grew serious again :

"I shall not know how you requite my dealings with you; but Christ will know how you requite His. I shall probably never see you again; but His Eye will be with you even unto the end of the world. Upon you—and you alone—will rest the awful responsibility if you neglect so great salvation. And now we must get to business and conclude all the arrangements," he added, changing his tone; "the day is breaking, and there is no time to be lost, as your ship sails for America in a few hours from now, and I do not want you to miss it and to fall once more into the hands of the police; I would rather let you fall into the Hands of God than into the hands of man; and into His Hands I commit you, body, soul and spirit, from this time forth and even for evermore."

With his usual efficiency and rapidity Gabriel gave the future missionary full instructions as to the new life on which he was about to enter, and the way in which he was to set about it; and wrote a letter to the head of the Training College giving such instructions and advice regarding the convict as he thought necessary. And then he put before Costello food and drink, and finally despatched him with a blessing, to serve God according to his day and generation.

THREE years had come and gone since the events recorded in the last chapter.

In a house in Prince's Gardens a man and a woman were sitting over their dessert.

"I can just finish this cigarette, and then I must get back to the House, my sweet," the man said.

The woman rose from her seat at the head of the table and came round to her husband's side, perching herself on the arm of his chair.

"It's a funny thing," she said, with a sigh: "a very funny thing; but you were right, and I was wrong after all."

He laughed. He knew how very remarkable it always seemed to her to find herself in the wrong.

"As how?" he asked, putting his arm round her.

"Oh! about politics and things. I thought you'd smash up the party and ruin the country when you got into the Cabinet; but you've done neither the one nor the other."

Again the man laughed:

"It is amazing how little permanent mischief even the most gifted and indefatigable of politicians are able to accomplish. The mistakes of the greatest statesmen are not nearly so irremediable as they would fain believe. The great forces of Nature and the Permanent Staff pursue the even tenor of their way, regardless of changing

Governments or fluctuating parties; and nothing really makes much difference."

"Nothing really ever does make much difference to anybody," replied the woman; "except dying and getting married."

"But I believed that everything did," said the man, "when I was young and unofficial. In those far-off times there was precious little that I did not believe."

"I used to think you much too high-flown and ideal, you know."

"So I was, when revelling in the unsubstantial pageants of private membership or irresponsible office. But then the Cabinet 'like an angel came, and whipp'd the offending Adam out of me.' In my unofficial and unregenerate days I aimed at the stars."

"And a very good thing too, Paul! It is the people who aim at the stars that succeed in sweeping their own chimneys: and the people who set out to ascend the Jungfrau, that manage to get to the top of Notting Hill. Now stupid, sensible people—like myself and Wrexham, for instance—only aim at the chimneys, and so do nothing better than ring the front-door bell: we set out for Notting Hill, and so get no farther than the Albert Memorial. Which things are an allegory."

"It is quite true—as a distinguished statesman once remarked—that politics is the science of the second-best."

"I suppose, when you come to that, most things in this world are."

The man's arm tightened round her: "Except one," he said: "and the reality of that exceeds the wildest dreams of the maddest idealist."

His wife nestled up to him:

"You are a very successful man, Paul, and have had

a good many cups of happiness put to your lips; the cup of success, and the cup of fame, and the cup of power, and the cup of rank, and, in fact, quite a trayful of them. Which do you like best of all?"

"There is no comparison, my darling," he answered, with a laugh of absolute content: "of all the cups of happiness that have been put to my lips I have found none to compare with the falsely so-called 'weaker vessel'; so, with your permission, I will just put my lips to it again." And he kissed her with all the rapture of a lover.

The Scene changes.

On the lawn in front of an old-fashioned manor-house a man and two women were having tea. A small girl of two years old was trotting about from one to the other, while a baby-boy lay asleep in a perambulator.

"I consider that it is almost time for Lisa to have a thimble of her own," remarked the elder of the women; 'when I was two and a half years of age I could sew, quite neatly: and at three I joined the village Dorcas Meeting."

"By Jove, mother, but you were an extra forward one!" exclaimed the man, who was lying full-length on the grass at his wife's feet, his tea-cup in a position of imminent danger at his elbow. "You can't expect the poor little kiddie to be as clever as her grandmother."

"That, Charles, is what I do expect. The training of a child cannot begin too early. When I was four I read the 'Fairchild Family' aloud to my dear mother: and at five I was conversant with all the information contained in 'Near Home' and 'Far Off.'"

Lisa's mother smiled languidly:

" If you gave her a thimble now, she would probably swallow it: and I have always understood that thimbles are most indigestible."

But the old lady shook her head :

" I never swallowed anything at that age: nor did my sister Maria."

A shout of laughter emanated from the figure on the grass : his sense of humour had ever been elemental.

" Great Scott i mother, you must have been wonderful children. Do you mean to tell me that you and Aunt Maria never had anything to eat or drink ? "

" Charles, do not be ribald. What I mean is, that my sister Maria and I never swallowed anything that was not intended for swallowing : we were too well-trained."

" Well, it strikes me that you swallowed a good deal one way or another if you were dosed with 'Near Home' and 'Far off,' to say nothing of the 'Fairchild Family.' Eh, mother ? "

" Charles, I cannot permit you to be irreverent: it is an atrocious habit for the young, and I beg you will not allow yourself to fall into it."

The man did not reply to his mother, but he looked up into his wife's dark eyes and smiled : and she smiled back, stroking his yellow hair as she did so. As they were both still on the sunny side of thirty, it struck them as distinctly funny to be referred to as " the young." Ten years later they would have accepted as a compliment what they now treated as a joke. But that is the rule of life: the sarcasms of to-day are the compliments of to-morrow, and yesterday's sneers are to-day's plaudits. So we learn as we grow older to be thankful for small mercies.

" As to the volumes you mention," continued the elder lady, quite unconscious of the fact that she was

MICROCOPY RESOLUTION TEST CHART

(ANSI and ISO TEST CHART No. 2)

 1.0

 1.1

 1.25  1.4

APPLIED IMAGE Inc

1653 East Main Street
Rochester, New York   14609   USA
(716) 482 – 0300 – Phone
(716) 288 – 5989 – Fax

affording much amusement to her juniors: " I derived from them immense benefit. In fact all my present knowledge of Thibet I owe to the reading of ' Far Off; or, Asia Described.' "

" So I can believe," murmured her daughter-in-law. But fortunately nobody heard her.

At this moment the youthful Lisa made a gallant attempt to sit down upon her father's tea-cup; and was only saved from doing so by the prompt action of that parent himself. But her grandmother went on undisturbed:

" As soon as she is old enough to understand it, I shall read portions of the ' Fairchild Family ' aloud to Lisa ; as I know no book more fitted to open the eyes of a child to good sound doctrine."

" By Jove, it does that ! " exclaimed her son, who had been himself brought up on the work in question: " and gives you the shivers sometimes into the bargain."

" If you can make her as good a woman as you are," said the younger woman, " I shall be thankful for you to read to her anything that you choose."

" Thank you, Fabia. And if she is as good a daughter to you as you have been a daughter-in-law to me, you will have indeed cause for thankfulness."

Once more the Scene changes.

In a large Church in the East End of London the newly appointed Bishop of Shoreditch was preaching to a vast congregation. He held them spell-bound, for he was one of the most striking preachers of his day: a man who had already risen to high Office in his Church, and who was destined and fitted to rise still higher: a man who had been as a beacon set on a hill to countless struggling Christians; and who, being endowed with wisdom from on high, had succeeded in bringing many to righteousness.

In one of the foremost pews in the Church, two women and a little boy were sitting, drinking in every word of the preacher's discourse, and filled with pride and exultation because of him: for to them he had been respectively the most dutiful of sons, the most devoted of husbands, the most loving of fathers. And now they rejoiced that at last he was entering into the fruits of his labours. At least the two women rejoiced: the boy was as yet too young to understand anything save that all these hundreds of people were listening to his father, and that he ought to be proud indeed of being the son of so great a preacher.

As for the preacher himself, he had gone through much tribulation, but his faith in God had never faltered; and now he saw the end of the Lord: that the Lord is very pitiful and of tender mercy. He forgot his misery, and remembered it only as waters that pass away: for at last the lines had fallen to him in pleasant places, and he had a goodly heritage.

For the third and last time the Scene changes.

Upon the shore of an island in the southern seas three men—one white and two black—were walking up and down engaged in earnest conversation. The white man was a newly-ordained missionary who had but recently come to those parts, but who had already made his mark there by the untiring zeal and un-flagging enthusiasm which he displayed in his Master's service: the blacks were two native priests, whose sacerdotal pride and love of power were up in arms

against the new faith which was gradually sapping their
influence for evil, and supplanting their religion of hate
and cruelty by the worship of the God of Love.

The Bishop of that district had come on a visit to
this particular island in response to an invitation from
the chief of the savage tribe which dwelt there—a man
considerably in advance of his race and people, who
was anxious to learn and to embrace the doctrines of
Christianity. The young Anglican had rowed the
Bishop over from the missionary station, and was now
waiting—his boat securely stranded on the beach—
while the Bishop and the chief held private converse
together in the hut of the latter, some few hundred yards
away.

It was the opportunity of the native priests: and
they took it. They were well aware that the man
before them was one of the most ardent and untiring of
all the hated band of missionaries: and they believed
that if he were once out of the way, his weaker and
less impressive brethren would soon follow; and that
thus their island would once more be left secure in the
fetters of its former heathenism. Of the Bishop they
did not take much account. He was growing old; and
his sphere of work was so wide that he could visit each
particular island but rarely. But this man was in the
prime of life—not much over thirty—and was distinguished by considerable personal beauty: moreover
his labours were confined to this particular corner of his
Master's vineyard; and he was seen frequently in this
island, preaching the Gospel which the native priests
hated, and promulgated the religion which they regarded
with dread.

At first the two natives approached him in a friendly
and commercial spirit, walking up and down the shore

with him arm-in-arm, and endeavouring by means of costly presents to bribe him to go away and trouble them no more. But to their surprise he refused, and would have none of their skins and furs and feathers.

Then they became angry and threatened him: told him that unless he would give his word as a white man—that word which could never be broken—that he would not visit their island again, nor attempt further to convert its chief to Christianity, they would kill him then and there. And still he smiled his serene smile, and bade them hear in their own tongue some of the wonderful works of God.

And then, as they looked steadfastly on him, they saw his face as it had been the face of an angel: and the devils that were in them were filled with that hatred which the sons of darkness ever feel towards the children of light: so the two savages fell upon the European and slew him then and there, and then fled into the dense forest to hide themselves, until the wrath of their chieftain (on finding that his people had murdered one of his beloved missionaries) should be overpast.

When the visitation of the Bishop was ended and he returned to his boat, he found the young missionary lying dead upon the shore, pierced through with many spears: for the life which was twice redeemed—first by the Master Himself and then by the Master's servant—had been freely and willingly given up to God.

THE END

Printed by Cowan & Co., Limited, Perth.

NEW AND FORTHCOMING
6s. NOVELS.

The Far Horizon .	. Lucas Malet
The Gambler .	. Katherine Cecil Thurston
Queen of the Rushes	. Allen Raine
Made in his Image	. Guy Thorne
A Girl of Spirit .	. Charles Garvice
The Way of the Spirit .	
Captain John Lister	.
The Pride of Life	.
The Magic Island .	.
The Spanish Dowry	.
The Artful Miss Dill	. Frankfort Moore
The House of Riddles	. Dorothea Gerard
A Man of No Family	. C. C. & E. M. Mott
The Wood End .	. J. E. Buckrose
The Only World .	. G. B. Burgin
Thalassa . .	. Mrs. Baillie-Reynolds
Mrs. Grundy's Crucifix	Vincent Brown

LONDON: HUTCHINSON & CO.

Classic Novels

WITH FULL-PAGE ILLUSTRATIONS BY
GEORGE CRUIKSHANK, &c.
In F'cap. 8vo.   1s. 6d. net, cloth.   2s. 6d. net, leather.

By Tobias Smollett

The Adventures of Roderick Random
IN ONE VOLUME

The Expedition of Humphry Clinker
IN ONE VOLUME

The Adventures of Peregrine Pickle
IN TWO VOLUMES

Sir Launcelot Greaves; and The Adventures of an Atom
IN ONE VOLUME

The Adventures of Ferdinand, Count Fathom   IN ONE VOLUME

By Henry Fielding

The History of Tom Jones, a Foundling
IN TWO VOLUMES

The Adventures of Joseph Andrews
IN ONE VOLUME

The History of Amelia
IN TWO VOLUMES

Mr. Jonathan Wild; and A Journey from This World to the Next
IN ONE VOLUME

By Laurence Sterne

Tristram Shandy; and a Sentimental Journey through France and Italy
IN ONE VOLUME

CLASSIC NOVELS

SOME PRESS OPINIONS.

"The Publishers deserve the thanks of a new generation of readers for placing within reach some of the best examples of Georgian fiction in so attractive a form as this series has. The print is excellent, the illustrations are faithfully reproduced, and the format is not to be surpassed even by more expensive editions. This series ought to have a warm welcome wherever the English tongue is spoken."—*Pall Mall Gazette.*

"The volume before us runs to over five hundred well-printed pages. The type is clear, the binding excellent, and, though trained to expect remarkably good productions at inexpensive prices, the public will marvel how such altogether admirable volumes can be placed in their hands so cheaply. The new series is sure to be a great success. It is more than value for the money."—*Observer.*

"Here we have Smollett's famous novel, ' Roderick Random,' without expurgations or emendations, as the first instalment of a new series, the ' Classic Novels.' It is beautifully printed in old-fashioned type on good paper, and contains all the original full-page illustrations by George Cruikshank."—*Lloyd's Weekly Newspaper.*

"The volumes are beautifully printed on excellent paper, and I expect they will meet with that demand from the public which they deserve."—*To-Day.*

"Better value for the money has, perhaps, never been given."—*Newcastle Chronicle.*

"A splendid book for the money; well bound and well printed."—*Academy.*

"A handy edition, similar in shape to the ' dear dumpy twelves' of a bygone time. They are very well printed and neatly bound."—*Manchester Guardian.*

HUTCHINSON'S POPULAR CLASSICS.

Antoinette Sterling and other Celebrities

By M. STERLING MacKINLAY, M.A.

In demy 8vo, cloth gilt and gilt top, with 16 illustrations, and interesting facsimiles in the text, 16s. net

Mr. MacKinlay, who is the son of the late Madame Antoinette Sterling, devotes a good share of his book to his reminiscences of his mother, and it will, undoubtedly, please a large number of her admirers to have this record of her life ; but Mr. MacKinlay, who is so well known in the Musical world, has many personal recollections and many anecdotes to tell of other celebrities, not only in the Musical world, but also in the world of Literature and Art. One of the most interesting portions of the book deals with Manuel Garcia, who, notwithstanding his great age, kindly assisted the author with these chapters. A portion of an interesting music manuscript, written by him at the age of 95, will be reproduced in the book, as well as the painting of him at the age of 100, by J. S. Sargeant. The Author has met so many celebrated men and women of whom he has something to say, that it is impossible to give anything like an adequate list of them ; but they include some of the great artists, actors, singers, writers, and scientists of the present day. The book is written in a light and popular style, and will be of especial interest to library readers.

The Real Louis the XVth

By Lieut.-Colonel ANDREW C. P. HAGGARD, D.S.O.

Author of " Sidelights on the Court of France," " Louis XIV. in Court and Camp," " The Regent of the Roués," etc.

In 2 vols., demy 8vo, cloth gilt and gilt top, with 32 page illustrations and a photogravure frontispiece, 24s. net.

In his last book, " The Regent of the Roués," Colonel Haggard successfully dealt with the period of the infancy of Louis the XVth and the Regency of the Duke of Orleans. In his present volumes the whole of the subsequent Life and Reign of Louis XVth are treated of in the popular and instructive manner which have made the earlier volumes of the Author's Memoirs of Old France so attractive. " The Regent of the Roués " has already gone into a second edition, and the great scope which the Court of Louis the XVth affords has enabled Colonel Haggard to produce two volumes of most exceptional interest, which are certain to be widely read.

By the Waters of Carthage

By NORMA LORIMER

Author of " By the Waters of Sicily," etc.

In demy 8vo, cloth gilt, gilt top, with 32 page illustrations and a frontispiece in colours from an original drawing by MR. BANTON FLETCHER. 12s. net

Miss Norma Lorimer's " By the Waters of Carthage " is in the same vein as the author's " By the Waters of Sicily," of which several thousand copies were sold in this country and America, and it is sure of an enthusiastic welcome. It is even better illustrated, and it deals with a most interesting country. Like the former volume, " By the Waters of Carthage " is told in a series of letters, written by the Doris who won all hearts as the heroine of " By the Waters of Sicily." She is spending her spring in rambling about Tunis, that most perfect type of the Oriental city and the ruins of Carthage, one of the most historical sites in history. The book is full of the romance of Arab life and the romance of the fall of Carthage. But the reader who imagines that he has only found a singularly elegant and illuminating book of travel will be mistaken. It has a love story and a little tragedy running through it, the tragedy of a beautiful English woman married to an Arab, and struggling too late with the horror of being the white chattel of a coloured man, and finding their minds separated by the great gulf which stretches between the children of Europe and the children of Asia or Africa.

There is no reason why this book should not obsess the reading public like the well-known novel of Tunisia published last year, " The Garden of Allah." For the problems of the marriage of a Christian with a Mahometan are even more an integral portion of Miss Lorimer's African romance than the problems of Roman Catholicism were of Mr. Hichens's book.

The Standard Operas

THEIR PLOTS, THEIR MUSIC, AND THEIR COMPOSERS
By GEORGE P. UPTON

Author of " Standard Oratorios," etc.

In small crown 8vo, cloth gilt and gilt top, 3s. 6d. net

This work has been prepared for the general public rather than for musicians : technicalities have been avoided as far as possible, the aim being to give lovers of opera a clear understanding of the works they are likely to hear, and thus heighten their enjoyment. There is a brief but comprehensive sketch of each of the operas contained in the modern repertory, with a notice of the composer, the story of the opera, and the character of the music, its prominent scenes and numbers, and interesting historical information.

Five Fair Sisters

AN ITALIAN EPISODE AT THE COURT OF LOUIS XIV.

By H. NOEL WILLIAMS

Author of "Madame Recamier and her Friends," "Madame de Pompadour,"
"Madame de Montespan," "Madame du Barry,"
"Queens of the French Stage," etc.

In demy 8vo, cloth gilt and gilt top

With 16 illustrations and a photogravure plate, 16s. net

Under the title of "Five Fair Sisters," Mr. Noel Williams tells the story of the lives of Laure, Olympe, Marie, Hortense and Marianne Mancini, the celebrated nieces of Cardinal Mazarin. Brought from Rome to France as children, all five made brilliant marriages, and, with the exception of the eldest sister, who died at a comparatively early age, all had the most romantic careers. The charming romance of Louis XIV. and Marie Mancini, which, but for the determined opposition of Mazarin, would undoubtedly have ended in Marie becoming Queen of France, is related at length, and will be found of the greatest possible interest. Scarcely less interest attaches to the careers of the clever and unscrupulous Olympe (Comtesse de Soissons), "a woman formed for great crimes, whose true place would have been in the Palace of the Cæsars or the Vatican of the Borgias"; of Marianne (Duchess de Bouillon), who, with Olympe, was implicated in the famous Poison Trials in 1680; and of the lovely Hortense (Duchesse de Mazarin), who fled from her jealous and bigoted husband to England, where she became one of the reigning beauties of Charles II.'s Court.

Mr. Noel Williams's many readers will find in this volume the same thoroughness of research and careful criticism, combined with lightness of treatment, which distinguishes all his work.

The Tree of Life

By ERNEST CRAWLEY, M.A.

Author of "The Mystic Rose."

In demy 8vo, cloth gilt, 12s. net

"Thoughtful and suggestive. The book is always well considered, and it carries lightly a large weight of learning in the modern literature of its subject. It will be read with interest and advantage."—*Scotsman.*

"The reader will find much that is instructive and suggestive. It is a valuable contribution to the modern efforts to found the evidences of religion on a more permanent and rational basis."—*Manchester Courier.*

Memoirs of Malakoff

Edited by R. M. JOHNSTON

Author of "The Napoleonic Empire in Southern Italy," "The
Roman Theocracy and the Republic, 1846-1849," etc.

*In 2 volumes, demy 8vo, cloth gilt and gilt top, with photogravure
frontispiece, 24s. net*

"Malakoff" was the name assumed by Mr. W. E. Johnston during
his residence in Paris, where he acted as correspondent for a leading
American journal. The book is largely made up of Mr. Johnston's
letters to his paper, and it covers the whole period of the Second
Empire, interesting accounts being given of what happened, politically
and socially, during this period. They are written in an intimate
manner, for Mr. Johnston was mixed up, directly or indirectly, in
most of the doings of the time, which, of course, included the Civil
War of 1860, the Siege of Paris, and the Commune. He also has
a good deal to say on the Panama Canal Scheme. In order that
the volumes may be easily read, Mr. Johnston's son, Mr. R. M.
Johnston, has edited his father's correspondence, and added the
necessary connecting links to make the narrative complete.

Robert Owen

By FRANK PODMORE

Author of "Modern Spiritualism," "Studies in Psychical Research," etc.

*In 2 vols., demy 8vo, cloth gilt and gilt top, 24s. net
With numerous illustrations*

The present book constitutes the first serious attempt to recount in
its entirety the life-history of Robert Owen, the great Socialist. The
interest in all that concerns him increases daily, as is evidenced by the
largely enhanced value of all literature on the subject of the birth of
the Socialist and Co-operative movement, and the need has long been
felt for an adequate biography of the Reformer. Mr. Podmore, who
was one of the founders of the Fabian Society, has had access to and
has made full use of a recently discovered collection of unpublished
letters—some 3,000 in number—written by or to Owen.

A Deathless Story

or, "THE BIRKENHEAD" AND ITS HEROES

By A. C. ADDISON and W. H. MATTHEWS

In demy 8vo, cloth gilt, with 64 illustrations on art paper and other illustrations in the text, 6s. net, and with gilt top specially bound, 10s. 6d. net

A few years since, Mr. Addison wrote the "Story of the Birkenhead," which was successfully published. The issue of this book had the effect of bringing to the author a large amount of fresh information from many people who were acquainted with the circumstances of the wreck, and also further interesting particulars from some of the survivors. A great many new pictures were also forthcoming to illustrate the work, and it has been decided to publish this revised and enlarged, and practically re-written edition of the book, which will really give the last word on an event which can only be described as the finest example of discipline, courage, and self-sacrifice to be found in naval history. The book has been warmly commended by Lord Wolseley, who hopes "that it may reach the barrack-rooms of every regiment in the King's Army." It marshalls all the documents bearing on the subject, including the narratives of survivors, and every reliable source of information has been tapped to make the book absolutely an accurate presentation of the whole circumstances of the *Birkenhead's* last voyage.

Legends of the Madonna

As Represented in the Fine Arts

By Mrs. JAMESON

With nearly 200 Illustrations, including 29 full-pages, printed on art paper, and with indexes and appendix

In cloth gilt, 2s. 6d. net. In leather, 4s. 6d. net

Mrs. Jameson says: "Through all the most beautiful and precious productions of human genius which the Middle Ages and the renaissance have bequeathed to us we trace . . . one prevailing idea; it is that of an impersonation in the feminine character of beneficence, purity and power, standing between an offended Deity and poor suffering humanity, and clothed in the visible form of Mary, the mother of our Lord."

Printed by BoD"in Norderstedt, Germany